To Tina – A gift from Ann Glendinning, my dear friend and yours. Enjoy!
Carole

SNIPPETS
(bits and pieces of love and life)
by CAROLE

by

Carole Christie Moore Adams

This book is a work of non-fiction. Names and places have been changed to protect the privacy of all individuals. The events and situations are true.

© 2004 by Carole Christie Moore Adams. All rights reserved.

No part of this book may be reproduced, stored in a retrieval system, or transmitted by any means, electronic, mechanical, photocopying, recording, or otherwise, without written permission from the author.

First published by AuthorHouse 09/27/04

ISBN: 1-4184-9500-X (e-book)
ISBN: 1-4184-4462-6 (Paperback)
ISBN: 1-4184-4463-4 (Dust Jacket)

Library of Congress Control Number: 2004090612

Printed in the United States of America
Bloomington, Indiana

This book is printed on acid free paper.

ACKNOWLEGMENTS

My heartfelt appreciation to **Linda Palmer**, a published author, for *making* me write this book. My sincere thanks to her, **Judy Tathwell Hahn, Sylvia Mary Black**, and my husband, **John**, for proofreading the drafts and giving encouragement throughout the entire process.
And, my thanks to our new friends, **Cecil and Greta Ivey,** for their encouragement and efforts toward having it published.

Dedicated to
my husband and best friend,

John Benjamin Adams, Jr.

and to the memory of
my extraordinary and long-time friend,

Sylvia Mary Black

CONTENTS

SNIPPET 000 - A Big Disclaimer.. 1
SNIPPET 001 - It's Me.. 2
SNIPPET 002 - John.. 4
SNIPPET 003 - The Worst Never.. 6
SNIPPET 004 - Predestined... 7
SNIPPET 005 - Test Reader / Editor... 9
SNIPPET 006 - Writing.. 11
SNIPPET 007 - Therapy... 13
SNIPPET 008 - Wake-up Call.. 16
SNIPPET 009 - PD Diagnosis.. 17
SNIPPET 010 - Family Physician... 19
SNIPPET 011 - PD Problems... 21
SNIPPET 012 - Advisory Notes... 25
SNIPPET 013 - Henny's Book.. 26
SNIPPET 014 - Perfect Family... 28
SNIPPET 015 - Oh No, It's Touching.. 30
SNIPPET 016 - Afraid.. 32
SNIPPET 017 - Running Away.. 34
SNIPPET 018 - A Single Stitch.. 36
SNIPPET 019 - Skates.. 38
SNIPPET 020 - Dixie.. 40
SNIPPET 021 - Scratchy Wool.. 42
SNIPPET 022 - Rain... 44
SNIPPET 023 - Gravy.. 46
SNIPPET 024 - Sleepwalking.. 48
SNIPPET 025 - Hash.. 49
SNIPPET 026 - Periwinkle Soup.. 51
SNIPPET 027 - Five-dollar Bill.. 53
SNIPPET 028 - Psychic.. 55
SNIPPET 029 - Kidnapping... 57
SNIPPET 030 - Childhood Lost... 59
SNIPPET 031 - Long Hair... 62
SNIPPET 032 - Trampled.. 64
SNIPPET 033 - Hurricanes.. 66
SNIPPET 034 - Pillows.. 69

SNIPPET 035 - Graduation Dress.. 71
SNIPPET 036 - Is This the Best? 73
SNIPPET 037 - Left-handed Awhile 75
SNIPPET 038 - Ants in His Pants 77
SNIPPET 039 - Mema.. 78
SNIPPET 040 - Carded.. 80
SNIPPET 041 - Bassoons.. 82
SNIPPET 042 - Pencil Points 85
SNIPPET 043 - Acting 87
SNIPPET 044 - Music Clefs.. 90
SNIPPET 045 - Two Rays of Sunshine 93
SNIPPET 046 - Blue Lips 97
SNIPPET 047 - My Stetson Hat 98
SNIPPET 048 - Smashed Thumb 99
SNIPPET 049 - Two Parakeets 102
SNIPPET 050 - Beauty Contest 103
SNIPPET 051 - Just Different... 105
SNIPPET 052 - First Kiss... 106
SNIPPET 053 - Middle C.. 108
SNIPPET 054 - Her First Husband 110
SNIPPET 055 - Put Me Down 112
SNIPPET 056 - The Other "Carole"... 114
SNIPPET 057 - Benches 115
SNIPPET 058 - Special Languages 118
SNIPPET 059 - Dear John.. 120
SNIPPET 060 - The Blouse 123
SNIPPET 061 - Playmates 125
SNIPPET 062 - Committed 127
SNIPPET 063 - Wayne or Bus.. 129
SNIPPET 064 - Lizzybeth... 132
SNIPPET 065 - What Should We Do? 133
SNIPPET 066 - Wedding Preparations 135
SNIPPET 067 - Wedding Dress 138
SNIPPET 068 - Wedding and Reception 140
SNIPPET 069 - Newlyweds.. 144
SNIPPET 070 - Bicycles 147
SNIPPET 071 - Imposed Never's 150
SNIPPET 072 - Together at Last 151

SNIPPET 073 - Incentive Photo 152
SNIPPET 074 - Poorlyweds Diet 153
SNIPPET 075 - Haircuts 155
SNIPPET 076 - Tired 157
SNIPPET 077 - Cars 160
SNIPPET 078 - Your, My, Our 163
SNIPPET 079 - Second Mom 164
SNIPPET 080 - The Toothbrush 166
SNIPPET 081 - Slave Quarters 167
SNIPPET 082 - He Comes First 170
SNIPPET 083 - John's Youth 172
SNIPPET 084 - Oyster Roasts 174
SNIPPET 085 - Explosions 176
SNIPPET 086 - You're Going 178
SNIPPET 087 - Drafty Apartment 180
SNIPPET 088 - Three-inch Neighbors 183
SNIPPET 089 - Socks 186
SNIPPET 090 - One Down, One to Go 188
SNIPPET 091 - Twenty-four Hours to Leave GA 189
SNIPPET 092 - The Witch 191
SNIPPET 093 - So Young, So Bald 193
SNIPPET 094 - Weird Schedule 195
SNIPPET 095 - Efficiency Expert 197
SNIPPET 096 - Four Stitches 198
SNIPPET 097 - 3:00 A.M. Car Wreck 200
SNIPPET 098 - Fixed 201
SNIPPET 099 - Bigger Than 203
SNIPPET 100 - Hair Coloring 205
SNIPPET 101 - I Quit 207
SNIPPET 102 - PhD Dissertation 209
SNIPPET 103 - Our Families Meet 211
SNIPPET 104 - Thanksgiving 213
SNIPPET 105 - Find a Job 214
SNIPPET 106 - Rocking Chairs 217
SNIPPET 107 - Philly and Back 219
SNIPPET 108 - Little Old Ladies 220
SNIPPET 109 - Dumb! 225
SNIPPET 110 - The Teddy Bear 227

SNIPPET 111 - Charcoal Portrait	228
SNIPPET 112 - First Camping Trip	230
SNIPPET 113 - El Cortijo	232
SNIPPET 114 - Blackberries and Jam	235
SNIPPET 115 - Concrete Work	237
SNIPPET 116 - Curious Rabbits	239
SNIPPET 117 - Our Backyard Critters	240
SNIPPET 118 - Swings	244
SNIPPET 119 - George's Fruitcakes	247
SNIPPET 120 - Safety Shoes	248
SNIPPET 121 - Social Security Number	250
SNIPPET 122 - Dancing	251
SNIPPET 123 - Perfume	253
SNIPPET 124 - Our Korats	255
SNIPPET 125 - Furry Painters	263
SNIPPET 126 - Sidney Gets a Bath	264
SNIPPET 127 - Vortex Generator	267
SNIPPET 128 - Nurses	268
SNIPPET 129 - Are You OK?	270
SNIPPET 130 - Psychiatric Ward	272
SNIPPET 131 - Assignments	275
SNIPPET 132 - Taller	278
SNIPPET 133 - Help, Shirley Is Ill	279
SNIPPET 134 - Just You and Me	281
SNIPPET 135 - Patty's Sister	284
SNIPPET 136 - Love Is—	286
SNIPPET 137 - Pianos and Organs	288
SNIPPET 138 - It's in the Genes	290
SNIPPET 139 - Chairs	293
SNIPPET 140 - Timothy	295
SNIPPET 141 - Clothes	297
SNIPPET 142 - Artwork	300
SNIPPET 143 - The Cast	304
SNIPPET 144 - Brace/Cast Advantages	306
SNIPPET 145 - Broken Bones	308
SNIPPET 146 - Her Girls	309
SNIPPET 147 - Projects	312
SNIPPET 148 - Retired Too Soon	315

SNIPPET 149 - Adams Research.. 317
SNIPPET 150 - Doesn't Everyone?... 319
SNIPPET 151 - Volunteer Extraordinaire... 321
SNIPPET 152 - Balloons 322
SNIPPET 153 - Pathetic but Laughing.. 324
SNIPPET 154 - Lawn Mowing 326
SNIPPET 155 - Chaperones 327
SNIPPET 156 - Then, There's Bob... 330
SNIPPET 157 - Eyes... 336
SNIPPET 158 - Housekeeper.. 337
SNIPPET 159 - Magnetic 339
SNIPPET 160 - The Honeymooners 341
SNIPPET 161 - Spared Again... 343
SNIPPET 162 - Trucks.. 344
SNIPPET 163 - Moving In.. 348
SNIPPET 164 - Colonoscopy.. 350
SNIPPET 165 - Wheelchairs 352
SNIPPET 166 - Procrastination.. 354
SNIPPET 167 - Oh, That Judy... 358
SNIPPET 168 - Housework 361
SNIPPET 169 - Frostbite.. 363
SNIPPET 170 - Exercise... 364
SNIPPET 171 - Bobsey Twins 366
SNIPPET 172 - I Wonder 368
SNIPPET 173 - Nicknames... 369
SNIPPET 174 - Yours Is Better 373
SNIPPET 175 - Recipes.. 374
SNIPPET 176 - Birthdays... 376
SNIPPET 177 - Ice Cream.. 378
SNIPPET 178 - Chocoholic 380
SNIPPET 179 - The Cradle 381
SNIPPET 180 - Injection-site Locator.. 382
SNIPPET 181 - Favorite Getaway.. 384
SNIPPET 182 - Songs and Sayings 386
SNIPPET 183 - Rickety-Tickety-Tin 390
SNIPPET 184 - Sun Signs... 391
SNIPPET 185 - Anyway.. 392
SNIPPET 186 - Glad I Didn't Know 393

SNIPPET 187 - Three Gold Rings *396*
SNIPPET 188 - The End *397*

SNIPPET 000 - A Big Disclaimer

The names of many people and some organizations and places have been changed to protect the innocent and the guilty because everything herein is revealed from my viewpoint. We survived the incidents and main events; we have the gray hairs or lack thereof (hair, that is) and the wrinkles and bruises from stress, heartaches, headaches, accidents, diseases, working, dancing, playing, and laughing to prove it. Call this book a memoir or a novel; just don't call me an author—I hate to write.

SNIPPET 001 - It's Me

I don't know why but I have always said, when I call someone on the phone, "It's 'Me'." Interestingly, no one ever responds: "Who?"

Maybe my voice is distinctive, but I doubt it. I sound exactly like my mother did and my three sisters do when talking on the phone; people always get confused as to which of us they are talking to if we haven't told them. People I worked with knew. Even my nephews and nieces know, and I sound just like their mothers. I guess no one else calls herself, or himself, "Me."

"Me" is Carole.

I'm five feet four inches in height, but used to be five feet six inches before osteoporosis set in. I'm very short-waisted; the two inches disappeared somewhere between my neck and waist so that my ribs sit on my hips now. Good thing I have a small ribcage, otherwise, I wouldn't have a waist anymore.

I weigh about 125 pounds but a bit more when I've been eating too much ice cream; I'd rather weigh between 110 and 115 pounds because I feel much better lugging less weight around. (One of these days I plan to rectify that.) I have to buy, because I don't sew anymore, bigger clothes now because fat requires more room than muscle. John remarked the other day that my skin still fits like a glove, although stretched a bit and worn from use. I have the usual age wrinkles; nevertheless, occasionally people will whine to me: "But, *you* don't have any wrinkles." Boy, have I got them fooled! I simply smile a lot and keep my face animated as I talk and listen; when people look at me, they just can't see the wrinkles for all the movement.

I'm still sort of attractive; never was beautiful, although my husband thinks I am.

My best asset was my *legs*. I really liked my legs and enjoyed wearing short shorts or mini-skirts. I don't do that anymore unless I'm wearing opaque or nude-colored support stockings (or knee-high boots) because I badly damaged my right shin snow-sledding Christmas week 2000.

I was "Miss DeLand" in 1958. My college roommate, Marcia, entered me in the pageant as a joke; I went along with it because I

SNIPPETS (bits and pieces of love and life) by CAROLE

thought it was funny. No one—especially me—expected me to win. I found out later that John (who was unknown to me then, but is now my husband) was quite disappointed because his date was second runner-up. I guess he got over his disappointment. And over Karoline!

I didn't used to have a bust, but menopause has given me some now that it doesn't matter anymore. If life is a deck of cards, there must be more jokers in the deck than you usually see.

I have almost-shoulder-length hair that's brown with gray that started showing up when I was twenty-eight, a round face with black eyebrows, sort-of-long black eyelashes and brown eyes. I look better with a tan but don't have one now; health officials are opposed to suntans these days. I wear eye make-up, no powder (unless my face needs it to cover those wretched blemishes I still get), and add lipstick only for special occasions.

Now that I've told you something about me, I'll tell you some bits and pieces about love and life from my viewpoint, some funny, some sad, some entertaining, some interesting, some just ordinary, but hopefully none boring.

SNIPPET 002 - John

It was the first day of calculus class at Stetson University, in late August 1958. He grinned a big lopsided smile at me and sat down in the front row in the desk directly across the aisle to my right. *Haven't seen him before; guess being an English major has me taking all the wrong courses; glad I decided to add some math.*

I rarely sat in the front row, but I had arrived on time for a change. I usually dashed into class late and was forced to sit in a less-desirable desk toward the back of the room, next to one of the radiators. But since I was early, and the front row desks were available, I had grabbed one, thinking that, perhaps, if I sat close to the professor, I wouldn't fall asleep for a change. It didn't help though; I was always too busy for adequate sleep, so I nodded off shortly after the lecture began.

The ringing of the end-of-class bell woke me. Then I felt this tapping on my arm. I looked up, still in a daze.

A distant-sounding, male voice was saying something like: "I'm heading over to my fraternity house for coffee hour from 10:00 to 11:00 A.M.; I always go because we play records and can dance." Then it became clearly focused. "Want to go with me?"

I groggily mumbled a reply. "Thanks, I need some coffee."

I'm glad I went with him to the Delta Sigma Phi house. Maybe it was his smile and the fact that my stomach started doing flip-flops, but I'm still not sure why I did; he was the epitome of all my *never*'s.

Never date anyone who is not: at least six feet in height, handsome, tanned, and has dark eyes with long lashes and dark hair. My dad was six feet two inches tall, rather handsome, tanned, and had brown eyes and blackish-brown hair, though his mustache, when he had one, was auburn-red. I preferred to date guys who were in height six feet four inches to six feet six and a half inches (two meters; Vilmar was exactly that tall), and my favorite thing to do, to each one the day after our date, was to walk head-on into him and chuckle, "Sorry, I didn't see you!" *He* was five feet nine inches tall, light skin with a little tan and some freckles, yellowish-green-rimmed-with-turquoise, doe-like eyes, a bit too small for his face, with short lashes, and blonde (so I thought, because I didn't realize it was multi-shaded red-brown and just sun-bleached) hair. He was not handsome, but he had nice teeth, nice smile, nice muscular physique, and was *so cute*!

Never marry someone younger than myself. My mom did that; she was three years older than my dad. *He* was a sophomore, just eighteen, nineteen in another week or so, and I was a second semester junior, twenty-one plus a few months which means a lot when you're young.

Never marry someone named John; as a child, I knew a man named John that I despised because he gave slobbery kisses to all the little girls. Oh no, I hope I didn't hear that right; he told me his name was *John*!

And there were more *never*'s to come.

SNIPPET 003 - The Worst Never

This morning, June 12, 2002, at the usual 5:55 A.M. on work days, we hugged and kissed good-bye. John shuffled out the door and down the walk to drive to work. I called to him, as I always do, "Have fun and play hard. See ya later, Luv."

It's very difficult watching him (I often get teary-eyed; hopefully he doesn't notice), but he smiled at me as he left.

During the 1980's, he never smiled.

I thought he was upset or distressed with me, so I had asked what was wrong.

"Nothing."

Did he want a divorce?

"Why in the world would I ever want that?"

Was he angry with me?

"No."

Unhappy?

"No."

Did he still love me?

"Always have, always will!"

Lies, lies, lies! We'd had this same conversation so many times.

I would look at his face; his expression was the forever-sad look with a frown; he must be lying! He shuffled around in a daze and hadn't smiled at me in years. Why was I making him so miserable? Why won't he, or why can't he, tell me what is wrong?

I had never heard of PD; how could I ever have guessed he was wearing the "mask" of Parkinson's Disease? What a relief to find out that was his problem. And, what a shock!

The picture of John, smiling and saying it to me as I lay in the hospital bed after my first surgery, flashes vividly in my mind. The statement (the unwritten wedding vow that follows "and in sickness and in health") became one of the standing jokes we have. When one of us is ill, the other stands by, sticks out the lower lip and whines,

"But you *promised* me, you would *NEVER* get sick!"

SNIPPET 004 - *Predestined*

I blame my being a somewhat predestinarian on being christened in the Presbyterian faith, although I later was baptized into the Baptist faith. I believe there is a reason and purpose for what happens, although I don't always understand it until much later, if ever. Most things in my life have just happened without my planning it—my education, my jobs, my husband, my friends, my role in life.

I was the second child in my family, born just fourteen months after my older sister, Edith. An "accident" according to my mother who had planned never to have children closer than two years apart.

Unlike the other three daughters, I was born at home, instead of in a hospital, and had a godfather whose surname is now my middle name, Christie. At birth, I was rather big, weighing nine pounds two ounces, my left thumb was black from sucking it in the womb, and my ears stuck straight out instead of lying close to my head. What a sight for a petite mother who was barely five feet two inches tall if she stood as erect as possible. But, she had had another big baby before me; Edith weighed nine pounds fourteen ounces at birth, so that part probably didn't surprise her as much as just having another baby to take care of.

Although I took all the academic preparatory subjects in school, I had no career in mind, nor had I planned to attend college. I graduated with excellent grades but not because I had any lust for learning; our dad demanded "A's," so we made them or else. I started learning to play a musical instrument in the sixth grade because I had buckteeth and the dentist suggested that my teeth could be corrected by playing a trombone. I didn't relish playing a trombone, and when we moved from Fort Pierce to West Palm Beach, we found out that we would have to purchase our own instrument as the new school had no trombones available. We decided to purchase a saxophone instead, and I liked playing it much better even though it wasn't going to help my teeth. During the seventh grade, the music director needed a bassoonist and asked me to switch instruments; I did and found my niche since buckteeth are perfect for obtaining excellent tone quality on the bassoon. I attended college because I was offered a music scholarship by Stetson University the weekend I happened to be there visiting a friend who was a member of the same church as I and who had been in the school band with me.

I started as a Stetson student majoring in music, but broke my back jumping on a trampoline during the first week of classes and had a semester to think about my choice of majors while I lay around in traction. Not being gifted in music, I decided to study English instead, but when I couldn't keep up with all the reading that was required, I switched to mathematics. In calculus class, I met John and since we both were immediately love-smitten, although not realizing it at the time, we eventually married. I fell into jobs teaching junior and senior high school because the school systems just happened to need a teacher with my qualifications while one or both of us attended graduate school. I quickly discovered that I cared about my students too much and since I didn't consider myself to be a good motivator, I gave up that career. When John started his career in chemistry, I decided to be just a wife and mother with no career outside the home. The lack of offspring pushed me into a career in computers because it sounded like fun. Our only children were four Korat cats that we enjoyed immensely.

After retiring for the third time, I'm now writing a book, which I find rather odd to be doing since I hate to write but find myself compelled to do so. I just happened to reconnect with a high school classmate this past spring (2002) and somehow got launched by her into this phase of my life. Actually, in a way, I was prepared in the late 1950's for this phase. Guy Owen, my favorite English professor at Stetson University, kept encouraging me to write even though I thought it was just too difficult. He so inspired me (and most of his other students, I imagine), that I spent many long hours diligently working on my compositions for his classes; he always said he enjoyed reading them. Although a good friend as well as teacher throughout my college years, I never saw him again after I left for grad school. However, I still have two treasured mementos—a copy of his novel, *Season of Fear*, and a copy of his poems, *Cape Fear Country*, both of which he autographed for me, "…good student and good friend with my best wishes."

I wonder where God will lead me next? For someone with no set plan for her life, it has been a wonderful and interesting one, and I wouldn't trade it for the world.

SNIPPET 005 - Test Reader / Editor

I had never heard of a "test reader." Have you ever? Well, currently I am one—at least I thought I was one—but I assumed another job instead, for Linda.

Linda had disappeared from my world, along with all my other classmates, when I graduated from Palm Beach High School in 1955. She reappeared, but not physically, on March 18, 2002 via e-mail, after Wayne, also a classmate from PBHS who found me this year via e-mail, sent her my e-mail address. We sent notes back-and-forth about what we had been and were now doing, like you always do when you haven't been in contact for many days or weeks, or years in this case. I happened to mention that I like to read mystery books.

Meanwhile, when talking on the phone to Wayne, I thought he said he was going to be a test reader for Linda and that she was in the process of writing a mystery novel.

"That sounds like fun, Wayne! Let me know how you like the book," I said aloud, while thinking to myself, *I haven't a clue as to what a test reader is, but it sounds intriguing to be able to read a book before anyone else; wish someone would ask me to do that.* That's exactly how I got into computers in the 1960's; it sounded like fun, from what people said about programming and all; I had no clue about that either.

Then, a few days after that, Linda asked if I would like to be a test reader for her and I replied an enthusiastic yes.

The manuscript arrived and I started doing my "test reading" in the manner I assumed I was supposed to do it.

"Wrong-o!" (Stole that from Linda, but I think a lot of people say it.) According to Linda (but in my words), if you are a *test reader* you do the following:
1. You pretend that you don't know the writer and you read the book manuscript as a person who likes that type of book (mystery in this case).
2. You tell the writer:
    - whether or not you liked the manuscript while and after reading it,

- whether or not you might buy and read the published version, and
- whether or not you would recommend it to friends who were looking for that type of book to read (in this case, to take their minds off their problems).

If I had read her e-mail message more carefully when she asked me if I wanted to do the task, I probably would have done the job correctly, but, like everybody else who reads "what they want to see" and not "what is written," I hadn't; so I didn't. I was pleased to find out that I did more than expected, but I didn't know *what* it was I had done.

So, I e-mailed Linda asking, "What do you call this type of work (*play* in my estimation since I refuse to work; I have always said, 'if it is work, you quit and find some other occupation') that I'm doing? Since I've never done this before, I'm not sure what it is formally labeled."

Apparently I was being an *editor*.

Linda next said (via e-mail, of course; we still haven't seen each other in the real world), "I forgot to explain the difference between a 'creative' editor and an 'acquiring' editor. Both make the writer work harder so the book will be better, like you're doing. But an 'acquiring' editor has the power to buy a manuscript for the company—up to a certain amount of money. For a higher amount, that decision goes to the head of the publishing house. So, both do the same thing for/with an author, but the second one also has the ability to purchase."

Well, that settles it! I am definitely an *editor*, and a *creative* one at that since John has banned me from purchasing anything until I have a place to put it, which I don't.

SNIPPET 006 - *Writing*

Dang! Brain just won't quit.

How can they stand it? Is this how it feels to be a *real* writer?

I've been at this less than a week. Since June 12, 2002, writing about bits and pieces of love and life from my viewpoint has become a compulsion; I'm not sure why I am suddenly compelled to write about it. The other night, after I broke the news of writing to Patty, my youngest sister, she told me that my dad had always wanted to write an autobiography. That was definitely news to me! She was sure he had come back to haunt me and make *me* write one instead. I'll also bet that it was because he knew I hated to write.

My husband suggested that it might be because I wanted to quit talking about all that has happened—a cleansing, so to speak. "Don't Say It—Write It" was the motto inscribed at the top of each sheet of paper in the note pads where I used to work. Maybe somehow that got impressed into my brain.

I don't know!

Maybe it's just to keep from doing housework. Lord knows I find paying or even volunteer jobs to get out of that kind of work. It's not that I'm lazy, I just don't like to do it; didn't like to do housework as a kid either, although I did do it when I had to or for pay.

But why has it become an obsession? Is "creating" that compelling for others, like artists and composers?

I have a hard time falling asleep, and I can't sleep through the night anymore; I wake up with my head reeling; thoughts just tumble around in my mind; words come so fast they get scrambled. Not surprising to me, however; when I was a kid I would say things like "lightly brighted" instead of "brightly lighted." I don't get out of bed to write down the ideas, no desire to, and just too lazy, I guess. I just lie there, tossing and turning and trying to fall asleep again, hoping that I will remember some of the ideas after I finally get up for the day and turn on my computer.

I have a hard time actually writing, too; I'll be writing on one "Snippet" and something will remind me of something else and I'll wish I were writing on another "Snippet," so I'll quit that one and start a new one. The brain has so many wires and interconnections laid away by the time you become an adult, it's a wonder that you can keep track of anything. Mostly, my thoughts trip all over my mind and all over each other; I call it a "scrambled brain"; I inherited it from my dad.

I have a hard time handling the emotions. When I write about sad events, I cry so hard I can't see the computer screen; my eyes get so puffy that John notices it later and tries to comfort me even though I don't need to be comforted anymore by then. When I write about ordinary things, I don't feel much of anything, like when you're writing a term paper for a course in school. I like it best though, when I'm writing about happy events and I'm laughing so hard I can't keep my fingers on the keys. Nobody who reads it will laugh like that; it's usually one of those you-had-to-be-there events.

Perhaps I'll get a recorder and just "talk" my ideas; maybe that's what *real* writers do. Then again, perhaps I won't; might as well listen to the rambling in my head as to listen to the rambling from a tape recorder.

There are colleges and universities, all within driving distance of my home, where I could take a course in creative writing. I could learn how to organize my thoughts better; but the professor would probably make me *write*.

Maybe it was my reading the book *Care for the Caretaker*, by Henny Backus, that got me started. Like Jim Backus, my husband has Parkinson's Disease; I hope my writing this book, about a just-ordinary couple (us) who views the affliction as just another facet of their lives, may help someone else who happens to read it. Then, all the headaches from the tears shed in the process of writing these notes will be worth it; the laughter definitely will.

SNIPPET 007 - *Therapy*

I had been at this task for a whole week and, with tears running down my cheeks, complained to John, "Writing a book is so difficult it's making me depressed. I think I'll just quit."

"Don't do that," he replied. "It's been only a week. Maybe you just need some therapy."

Well, I've certainly had my share of *therapy*!

I've had *mental therapy*. I have fought depression (it runs in my family) since my teens and have been through one-on-one therapy, group therapy, hospital therapy, and medication therapy. What finally worked best for me long-term for this chronic condition is an anti-depressant, which I will need to take for the rest of my life.

I've had *physical therapy*. I have crushed vertebra in my back (twice), cracked two ribs (at the same time), sprained an ankle, broken a bone in my foot, broken a wrist (two places at once), had a brain concussion, "snapped" tendons in my back, herniated several discs, and maybe broken an elbow. Each time I attended therapy to regain usage and help my balance. It was worth all the hours spent because I fully recovered.

I've had *hypnotherapy*. Allergies, which run rampant in my family, keep me from taking pain medications (discovered that during my first surgery); so, when I was scheduled for more surgery, I took classes in hypnosis to teach me how to relax and control pain without medication. That was really beneficial because it also cured my fear of heights. Someone else in the group had that problem and, apparently, if you need the suggestion as well, your brain responds to it even though the suggestion was not directed at you.

But, when all I need is "everyday-living" therapy, I turn to *rock therapy*. For some reason "throwing" stones and "laying" rocks (medium-sized rocks, various-sized river stones and quarry rocks, and very large, flat, quarry stones) and bricks around the yard does me wonders! It's also a great outdoor exercise to help strengthen my bones. I will never be able to figure out how many foot-pounds of work I've done.

I have made a border around the house, terrace, and part of the yard with over three thousand bricks; the border is a "mowing" strip for the lawnmower when the grass is cut. I'm not a brick-layer and I didn't read any books about how to do it correctly; I just decided where I wanted them, pounded in some garden border strips (of two different styles because I had to get them from two hardware stores because the first one ran out; but that's OK) just to keep the bricks from running out into the grass, spread some ground fabric inside the strips, and then hammered the bricks side-by-side on top of the fabric. Inside the brick border, I spread over 120 tons of pebbles on top of some more ground fabric.

Wherever we wanted to walk through the pebbles (reminds me of "tiptoe through the tulips"), I made a path by laying down very large, flat, quarry stones. In case you've never done that, it requires some body contortions; those stones are HEEAAAVY. You have to spread your legs, bend at the knees (in the proper way that safety manuals show and that you must learn if you work for DuPont Company), lift the stone, then shinny bowlegged, with it hanging between your legs, over to where you want the stone, and plop it down on the pebbles. If it's not lying flat like you want it (remember stones are lumpy), you stand it up almost on edge, smooth or dig out some pebbles, and drop it back in place. After you're satisfied with that, you stand on the stone with one foot close to each edge directly opposite the other, then see if you can make it wobble. If it wobbles, you have to step on the edge opposite the edge that needs to be raised and shove more pebbles under it; you repeat the process until the stone no longer wobbles. My hands get contorted just trying to type the description of this whole process. I hope you understand how to do this, in case you ever need this kind of therapy or a large-quarry-stone walkway.

I placed seventeen tons of medium-sized rocks on ground fabric under our large evergreen trees to keep down the weeds, and I had to do it one rock at a time. The rocks were so full of mud when delivered that I had to whack each one with another rock to knock off the dirt before setting them under the trees. I got a bad case of poison ivy doing that job crawling around on my hands and knees under the limbs. I didn't happen to see that kind of weed; because if I had seen the poison ivy, I would have cleaned my skin with Tecnu™, followed by a soapy shower afterwards, to prevent getting the rash.

After John's PD was diagnosed, we decided I should make the walkways out of bricks. After buying an additional thousand bricks, I

SNIPPETS (bits and pieces of love and life) by CAROLE

pulled up all the very-large-flat-quarry-stones, reversing the process described previously. I then smoothed the pebbles with a board that was three feet wide (sort of, actually however wide that's needed to lay four or five bricks end-to-end) and hammered down the bricks with a rubber mallet until they lay flat. The walkway is easier for him now to walk on and for him later, if necessary, to roll on in a wheelchair. We actually did use it recently for a friend in a wheelchair.

Since the edge of our property is steep for the last ten or so feet at the street, I have covered that with large quarry rocks to keep the soil from washing away. John helped me by placing on the slope all of the rocks that were too heavy for me to move. I like hearing him say, "And I hepped," just like the helpful kid in the TV commercial. Occasionally, our nephew Barret also "hepped" me with the bricks and pebbles.

If you decide to do rock therapy, just don't try to do it all in one weekend; I've been doing mine off-and-on for more than twenty years. And, as with any exercise, check with your doctor first, read some good literature on how to do it right, and complain to someone else (not me) if you do it wrong.

The last area that I covered, around some newly planted trees, needs some more pebbles. We didn't buy enough, so the layer of pebbles is simply spread too thin. That area is what we were looking at and where we were standing while I was crying and complaining about my book writing.

John ordered me six tons of washed pebbles (probably washed, by their usual appearance, in very sandy water). I am typing this Friday morning as I await the arrival of the delivery truck.

SNIPPET 008 - Wake-up Call

I found a "love" note (scribbled onto a scrap of paper like I use for grocery lists); it said "Hi- call me…" I saw it sitting on the kitchen counter by the coffee maker when I reached to pour me the remaining coffee. I had managed to grog (as in groggy) my way into the kitchen after sleepily rolling out of bed this morning, June 25, 2002. I was happy to see the note; I missed sharing breakfast and seeing John off to work this morning. But, what I missed the most was my wake-up call.

He had let me go back to sleep after asking me the usual (just lately): "When did you come to bed finally?"

I told you that I haven't been able to sleep well lately since starting to write this "book," so…last night I had tucked him in and kissed him goodnight and returned to start up the computer again and continue my typing. I remember mumbling a reply about something concerning 1:00 or 2:00 A.M., and his saying something about setting the alarm as he placed it on the bed where he had been sleeping beside me; I was asleep again too fast to notice.

He is a "morning" person but I am a "night" person so we quickly established this daily wake-up routine after we got married because we both had to get up and out the door early; he left to attend college classes and I left to teach junior high school students.

He awakens before the alarm clock starts blaring, so he gets up first, turns off the alarm, and starts the coffee brewing in the pot or coffee maker that I set up each night before bedtime. When the coffee is done, he pours himself a two-cup mug full, tops it off with half-and-half until the color is a very-light tan, and drops in two ice cubes to cool it so he can start drinking right away. Then he returns to the bedroom to wake me.

As I lie there snuggled under the covers, I gradually become aware of a strange noise, which wakes me. I open my eyes and this blurry figure comes into focus. There stands John, grinning as best he can while slurping coffee in my ear.

SNIPPET 009 - PD Diagnosis

In December 1990, at the end of her examination during an office-visit check-up, Dr. Diana, a close friend who became our family physician in the mid-1980's, finally concluded: "John, I think you have Parkinson's Disease. But you are so young to have that; most people who get it are much older than you. I want you to see a neurologist. My staff will arrange the appointment and prepare the referral."

John had been seeing her since August 1984 for various problems such as fatigue, aching, tightened muscles in his neck, shoulders, and back, slight tremors in his head and left hand when he was under stress; all the tests that were done had showed nothing.

Then, he saw a neurologist in Wilmington and was treated for "essential tremor" for about six months; the treatment did not help his problem. He went back to Diana. Since she has known and seen us both for so many years, she was now convinced it was Parkinson's Disease even though the one neurologist did not agree; but, unfortunately, we would just have to "wait and see" if his condition progressed.

During a visit to Savannah in July 1991, John discussed his problem with Becky, his sister. She talked to the physicians she was working for at the time and they suggested that John see a neurologist they knew who practiced at the Hospital of the University of PA.

On October 25, 1991, we had an appointment with that specific doctor. After five minutes of observation, Dr. David concluded that John probably had Parkinson's Disease. He mentioned that, for him, the diagnosis was easy to do because daily he sees so many patients with neurological disorders.

He said, "The only sure way of knowing is autopsy." Then laughing, he added, "Most people prefer *not* to undergo such a drastic procedure; most prefer to try medications. If the meds stop your symptoms, then my diagnosis is correct."

Dr. David mentioned that, if the diagnosis were correct, he would suggest some literature for us to read so we could better understand the disease. We just sat and listened as he talked, accepting all we heard rather matter-of-factly like most people who are hearing bad news that they expected but didn't want to hear. He then prescribed PD medications for John to try; it is always trial and error for most neurological diseases and for some people nothing works. We prayed the selected meds would work, and they did!

Our biggest mistake was watching the movie *Awakenings*, which we had rented from the video store on our way home. Not knowing exactly what the movie was about, but having heard that it was really worth seeing, it seemed to be just the distraction we needed to cheer us up that evening after dinner. No one should watch this movie on the very same day he or she or a loved one receives a diagnosis of Parkinson's Disease!

I don't know if you have seen *Awakenings*; but, basically, the movie is about a charming, caring doctor and researcher who experiments on patients who have been rigid and stone-like, unable to speak or move for as many as thirty to fifty years. He administers to them the drug L-dopa, which now is used to treat Parkinson's Disease. They suddenly are "awakened," able to speak and move again ("on-time" as it is called while the drug is effective) until the drug wears off ("off-time"). He has to keep increasing the dosages to lengthen the "on-time" and the side effects of that, unfortunately, turn the patients into over-active people plagued with spasms and constant writhing. Eventually the drug becomes totally ineffective and the patients return to their stone-like states.

We held each other tightly and sobbed uncontrollably while watching the video and then I cried for the next six months.

If this was what is in store for John, then we were doomed; how could we ever manage to survive this fate?

SNIPPET 010 - *Family Physician*

We've known Diana (and her husband Jim, who worked with John) since the late 1960's when she was a chemist in another department at DuPont Company. Being a very caring and empathetic person, she must have decided that she liked people more than chemicals. Since scientists set up experiments, get the results, and make decisions based on those results, that's what she did. She experimented by working in a hospital emergency room and decided that being a doctor was really her bag. She applied to the Jefferson Medical College of the Thomas Jefferson University in Philadelphia. Medical colleges at that time wouldn't accept people in their thirties; but, Diana is very intelligent and was able to convince the administration that age didn't matter and was accepted as a student.

She lived in Philadelphia during the week and came home on weekends. You can't waste time commuting with such a hard curriculum and such long hours studying and working to become a family physician. I know it was hard for Jim and her not being together weekdays (it was for John and me when I was away during grad school and for out-of-town courses during my employment); nevertheless, they were determined to manage somehow so Diana could achieve her ambition.

Sometimes during the summers when Diana was in town on a weekday, I would take a day off from work, and she would come to our house to spend the afternoon with me. We usually ate lunch, read books (fun stuff for me, textbooks for her) and swam. While we were in the pool, playing volleyball instead of swimming laps, we talked a lot. Actually, I talked and she listened. I had heard in a radio interview (radio is a great pastime while you are driving to and from work) that medical schools didn't at that time have courses in nutrition. I was taking classes in macrobiotic cooking and studying all kinds of cook books, so I would preach to her about what I had learned so she wouldn't miss out on that part of her education. She always listened intently. I don't know if she ever uses all that knowledge I imposed on her, but I hope it helped her. I wonder about it, but don't ask; children ask questions; adults don't because they already know everything or are afraid of the answer they might get.

When Diana became a full-fledged family physician, we joined the patients in her practice. We think she's terrific and we're not just biased because she is a friend. She earned the "Family Physician of the Year" award in 2000. We were invited to the black-tie event and got to see the award handed to her during the ceremony. We had written a letter to support her nomination and these are just a few sentences from it:

"She is a friendly, compassionate, perceptive, gifted, empathetic person as well as being an attentive listener and excellent diagnostician. When she is unsure, she researches your condition, contacts other physicians, and gets back to you with her opinion. She gives you information and options and helps you make the right decision for you. If you need a specialist, she finds the best one that she feels you can relate to and coordinates your care. She is concerned about your whole health and tries to treat the root cause, not just the symptoms, of the current ailment."

Diana is a great friend as well. Right after John's PD diagnosis, she invited us to spend that weekend at the beach with her and her husband, Jim, who is also our friend. She knew we would be upset, have many questions, and needed comforting and reassurance to get through this crisis and learn to cope with his condition. We spent the entire time walking the beach and talking or sitting and talking or eating and chatting and laughing together. It was just "what the doctor ordered" and exactly what we needed.

Diana is a few years younger than I and is thinking about retiring. As a friend, I hope she retires soon so she has more time to play; but as a patient, I hope she never does.

SNIPPET 011 - PD Problems

John is taking his Parkinson's Disease, PD, in stride and tries to live as normal a life as possible. He works part-time because he has enjoyed chemistry since he was eight years old.

There are some problems, however.

He no longer enjoys being around people other than friends because of the stress involved; however, he does try to mingle with other passengers when we are on vacation via ship or train. We laugh more on vacation than at any other time; it's simply marvelous having no cares and having people serve you while you eat and hold hands and gaze at each other across the table. We dance a lot too, even if we're the only ones on the floor; dancing works wonders if it is spontaneous and non-repetitive. When he suddenly gets "board," as in "stiff as a board," we sit down to rest, then start again.

He has great difficulty talking on the phone because his arm and hand get distorted as though he had cerebral palsy, enough so that his head presses phone buttons and he sometimes gets disconnected. We bought a phone headset but he can't get it on in time to answer before the caller hangs up or the answer service cuts in. Consequently, he lets me do most of the talking and almost all of the phone answering.

Multi-tasking is out of the question; he can do only one thing at a time; he eats or he talks or he walks or he thinks or he listens or whatever. I frequently forget this and expect him to multi-task like everyone else. Pain is a constant for him and, in hindsight, was one of the first symptoms we noticed in the 1980's. The pain is caused by muscles contracting tightly due to the lack of dopamine for sending proper signals to them; medications help, but not completely.

An early symptom, before being diagnosed with PD, was his inability to keep up with me, so I began dragging him along when we were walking; I used to have trouble keeping up with him. Frequently, when he was the least bit tired, he shuffled around and was unable to communicate with the outside world; he was just like a decrepit old man. He developed a sudden inability to make presentations and, occasionally, to just express his opinions in meetings at work; he would get very tense and his left hand and neck would start shaking. However, he voraciously composed and wrote chemistry using his computer.

Fortunately, he tolerates the PD medications well and has worked out a regimen that allows him sufficient "on-time" to do most things. For a Parkinson patient the time during which the drugs are effective and the person can carry out fairly normal activity is referred to as "on-time," and the time after the drug wears off is referred to as "off-time." He takes four different medications, at different intervals, so he is swallowing pills every two hours during the day and even sooner when he first arises in the morning; he takes vitamins too that his neurologist recommended. He stops taking the PD medications after 8:00 P.M. unless we are going out or entertaining friends at home. The extended time interval, from a few hours to many days, while the patient is not medicated at all is referred to as a drug-holiday. Since the good effect of drugs typically tends to wane with time, John takes a small drug-holiday every night that he can, with the intent of retaining the effectiveness of the drugs for more years, maybe "forever." Long-duration "drug holidays" used to be carried out in a hospital setting to handle problems that might develop while trying to restore some effectiveness of the drugs; but such long "holidays" are now thought to be a bad idea. Even when a patient is not medicated he/she, if not disabled, can do some activities like walking. If the activity can just get started, by sheer will-power or someone assisting, once it has begun, muscle memory takes over and the brain no longer has to control the activity consciously.

Over eighty per cent of the ten-years-post-diagnosis patients have become disabled. Miraculously, John is "eleven-years-post-diagnosis" (as of 2002) and has been able to work part-time, as much as forty hours per week; however, he is usually exhausted at the end of the day. Frequently he will fall asleep while we are watching TV after dinner.

He sleeps a few hours at a time because some body pain wakes him up when he's not medicated. When he's home, he occasionally naps during the day. We had to give away our waterbed, since he had problems turning over and in getting out of it, and replace it with an adjustable air-system bed. We started using satin sheets to allow him to turn over more easily by himself and quickly discovered that satin sheets are really nice for other reasons as well.

SNIPPETS (bits and pieces of love and life) by CAROLE

Liquor, especially black or white Russians, or wine or our favorite champagne, helps him through the evenings, so we try to celebrate every day and always celebrate "garbage day," which is each Wednesday when we collect all the trash together that evening for Thursday pickup. That special day started one Wednesday evening at a restaurant when our server asked what occasion we were celebrating when John ordered champagne before dinner. John smiled and replied, "Garbage day."

I'm a bit frightened of the day when medication no longer helps. We both feel that surgery is risky and out of the question until it is the last resort or until it offers some type of "cure." Statistically, John is a marvel, mostly due to his determination to "just keep moving" as his neurologist prescribed or "dancing" as he himself prefers. John jokes that he will apply for a job as a drummer if he gets too shaky or as a mannequin or beach umbrella if he gets to be a permanent "board." Peggy Lee's song lyrics come to mind: "…if that's all there is, my friends, then let's keep dancing; let's break out the booze and have a ball, if that's all there is…" Maybe we'll just do that.

There are a couple of other problems, which I momentarily forgot.

The PD medications cause John, and some other PD patients, to have vivid dreams and restless legs and/or arms. He also occasionally talks or shouts or cries or shows other emotions while asleep. The times that he has cried in his sleep, he was dreaming about the death of a loved one or a neighbor friend who died at that exact moment. Sometimes I think I should sleep in a separate bed; but after more than forty-one years of sleeping together, I just can't do it. Most people are paralyzed while dreaming, but the medication alters that for John; consequently, if he dreams that he is running away from some one or some thing or that an animal is biting his legs, he kicks in his sleep. All is OK if he is sleeping on his back; but if he is sleeping on his side when this occurs, I get severely kicked in my shins or calves by his toes or heels.

One night he swung his arms out and the side of his right hand hit me on the bridge of my nose. I awoke with a start and a nosebleed and spent the rest of the day trying not to pass out from the pain.

Needless to say, I now stay way over on my side of the bed.

Fortunately his thrashing around hasn't happened recently. Maybe in the future—never, I hope—we'll be forced to consider twin beds. John says that maybe some day he'll quit kicking or just "kick the bucket."

I'm glad our family physician knows us well enough that she realizes that I'm not a battered wife. Besides, John is too kind to ever hit anyone intentionally.

Sometimes he wakes me when he throws off all our bedcovers because he is too hot; without covers, I get cold. Sometimes, like last night, he wakes me because he is too cold and his shivering shakes the bed. I have to put a heating pad on his body and snuggle up with him until he is warm enough to fall asleep again. As John says: "Snuggling is not all that bad to deal with!"

SNIPPET 012 - *Advisory Notes*

So that we don't have to keep describing my dietary restrictions or his problems with PD, John devised, and typed for us, little notes that we hand to people that have a need to know. Restaurant servers like having mine to give to the chefs and all types of service staff seem to appreciate reading John's so they don't have to ask him what is wrong with him. Here is a copy of each one.

Carole's

NO BELL PEPPERS or PIMENTO (black or white pepper O. K)
NO PAPRIKA
NO CORN or food containing CORN or CORN Product, such as Karo or corn syrup, Confectioners' sugar, corn oil, white grain vinegar (cane, fruit, or maple sugars O.K.)
NO MSG

John's

Hi. My name is John and I have a non-contagious illness, Parkinson's Disease (PD).

I take medicines to help control the symptoms which, in my case, are: stiffness, shaking, too much or too little motion, and slowness of starting to speak. My intellect isn't affected.

So—If sometimes I seem a little shaky, slow-moving, or slow to start conversing, you'll understand.

Thanks for your patience and, when needed, your assistance.

SNIPPET 013 - Henny's Book

The afternoon of March 23, 2002, I received a book, *Care for the Caretaker* by Henny Backus, from Linda, and read it that very night. It's hard to imagine how Henny survived those years. I don't think I've been as brave as she was. We, actually mostly I, cried a lot the first year (and occasionally still do) after John was diagnosed with Parkinson's Disease. For me, the worst thing is watching someone you love so dearly deteriorate right before your eyes. It's hard not to be angry and to keep your spirits up, especially when you have dealt with depression yourself all your life.

Henny has to be an extraordinary person to have done all that she did! She and Jim were very fortunate to have found each other; they had to have been best friends.

It was really quite amazing to read about them and see that we were doing almost all the same things. I even cut up John's food for him when we're dining at home so he has one less thing to pay attention to. I do much of the driving these days; it gives him a chance to see and enjoy the scenery for a change.

The first thing John did after his diagnosis was to go buy a new tuxedo; he planned to party as much as he could. We haven't attended many black-tie affairs these last few years because he doesn't mingle well with others anymore; we go only if our friends are going. We even dropped our subscriptions to two of the three Delaware Symphony Orchestra series; we kept only the Pops; most of the time we stay only until intermission because he gets, as he says, "too Parky" and becomes a "board." If he has to sit for very long, the PD takes over and he becomes bradykinetic, which means your muscle motion becomes delayed and your mind wants to move the muscle but the signal doesn't reach it to make it move. It's like pressing the accelerator of your car and not having it in gear, so the motor races but the car goes nowhere.

I asked John where all in the world he wanted to go, omitting the forty-eight-contiguous USA states and eastern Canada where we have already traveled camping.

SNIPPETS (bits and pieces of love and life) by CAROLE

"Alaska, Hawaii, Caribbean, Europe, Antarctica and, maybe, Australia and New Zealand," he replied several days later after he had taken some time to seriously think about it.

So, we started traveling to those parts of the world in 1998. My gift to him is to plan everything in detail down to computer listings of itinerary with time schedules, items to pack, and exactly which clothes we will wear every day and evening. That way we are totally free to have fun and enjoy the scenery without a single concern during the actual trip. He does better on the trips than he ever does at home because his mind doesn't have to process so much data and can give more attention to his muscles. I wrote about a few events that occurred during our previous trips in other "Snippet's."

I am so lucky to have a husband who tries so hard to cope with PD and live his life the best he can anyway. We have met other people with PD or who have a spouse with, or have lost a spouse to, PD; they are very friendly at first, but, when they see how well we are doing, they just disappear; I think the pain of having a loved one who didn't try as hard as John does, or was unable to do so, just drives them away. The diagnosing-and-early-stages neurologist urged us to stay away from support groups because he thought the people would be too upsetting and discouraging; he thought we coped very well on our own. We do read as much as we can and John is always keeping up with the latest PD drugs; when his doctor suggests changes, John is already familiar with the drug. His current neurologist, another Dr. David, actually lets John set up his own dosing schedule after prescribing and suggesting drug dosages; they even e-mail schedules with progress reports and comments to each other.

What an inspiration you are, Henny; I send my love to you with thanks for writing your book!

SNIPPET 014 - *Perfect Family*

I learned in biology a little bit about genetics. Basically you take the genes from the two parents and mix them up randomly to get the genes for the offspring. There are color genes and there are sex genes; that's all I intend to include here to show you the genetic makeup of my family, even if I explain it wrong. Color genes consist of dominant genes (designated by capital letters) and recessive genes (designated by little letters) and come in pairs, dominant/dominant, recessive/recessive, and dominant/recessive.

If you have a male gene pair, "X/Y," and a female gene pair, "X/X," and take randomly one from each parent ("X" or "Y" and "X" or "X"), the offspring can be "X/Y," male, or "X/X," female. My dad always hoped for "X/Y"; he wanted a boy so he could name him "George." He was the thirteenth consecutive generation "George" in his family and he didn't want to be the last. Unfortunately, all he ever got were girls. At one point, even the family cat, dog, and parakeet (well, maybe not He-she; we couldn't be sure and that was why the parakeet had that name) were females.

George (my dad) had dark brown eyes (E/e), brown hair (but red mustache) (H/h), and dark skin (S/s).

Myrtle (my mom) had blue eyes (e/e), blonde (towhead at birth, darker later) hair (h/h), and fair skin (s/s).

Edith (first child) has hazel eyes (e/E), light reddish brown hair (h/H), and light, slightly freckled skin (s/S).

Carole (second child, me) has brown eyes (E/e), brown hair (H/h), and slightly dark skin (s/S).

Sheila (third child) has dark brown eyes (E/e), dark, slightly curly (don't know where that came from, some recessive gene somewhere), brown hair (H/h), and dark skin (S/s).

Patricia, a k a Pat or Patty, (fourth child) has blue eyes (e/e), blonde hair (h/h), and light skin (s/s).

I won't go into all the other characteristics that we girls received from our parents, but they are divided up just like the color genes although randomly placed. Since a new child came along each time (except one) that we moved to a different city, people always wondered if the milkman had something to do with our totally

SNIPPETS (bits and pieces of love and life) by CAROLE

different looks. Unless people really study us side-by-side, they don't recognize us as sisters.

The six of us may not have looked like we belonged together, but genetically color-wise, we had the perfect family.

SNIPPET 015 - Oh No, It's Touching

Oh no, it's touching! I couldn't stand for one food on my plate to touch another; if it did, I had difficulties eating that meal. My mom said that when I first started eating off a plate, if she placed more than one food at a time on my plate, I would shove with my hand everything, except the one food I wanted to eat first, onto the table. And, as long as they didn't get mixed during the shoving, I would put them back onto the plate, one at a time, in the order that I wanted to eat them; otherwise, Mommy had to get fresh servings for me or I would just quit eating. She must have complied because I was a chubby little kid.

Later on I learned to tolerate foods being on the same plate together as long as they didn't touch. The only exception was gravy; that could touch anything that it tasted good on. But that's another Snippet.

I thought I was the only one who ate that way; but, as an adult, I discovered that I wasn't. Whenever I ate with other people at work during lunch, or dinner when we traveled together, I would watch to see who did, and who did not, allow the foods on his, or her, plate to touch and who then did, or did not, eat one food at a time. Interestingly, the more intelligent I thought the person was, the more likely it was that he, or she, ate like I did. Nick, my coworker and eventually manager, ate the same way I did, and when I asked, he said he always had. I wonder if he still does or if he tried to change like I did.

When in my forties and I was trying to grow up, I forced myself to let my foods touch and even tried to eat bites of different foods in random order. Some things I really like mixed up, but if I'm not careful, I find myself returning to my old habit of eating all of one food before I take a bite of another. If you enjoy eating out in restaurants, which I do very much, then you have to tolerate foods touching one another because your food is plated artistically, sometimes in intriguing piles, and foods are frequently combined, or just mixed, to create uniquely delicious flavors. Even then I sometimes catch myself picking out single foods to eat from the arrangement.

SNIPPETS (bits and pieces of love and life) by CAROLE

If you have to eat that way, a macrobiotic diet is almost the perfect one for you. I say *almost*, because some foods are mixed into a single food like soup or sushi and some are combined as in a couscous cake. But, ordinarily you do eat your foods in a particular order: soup first, then grains (like brown rice), then root vegetables, then ground vegetables (as in lying on the ground, not pulverized), then leafy vegetables, and then fruits. Since you are supposed to eat that way, no one thinks you're just being silly.

I try not to do it anymore, but for a long time after I decided that it must be a sign of intelligence, and since I liked to think I was intelligent like the others, I did it. In order to size up a person, I would always inquire: "When you were young, did you allow the different foods on your plate to touch?" If the person said no, I also had to know: "How old were you when you did let them?"

Since meeting my friend Sylvia, who is one of the most intelligent people I know, I've had to discard my theory; she has always allowed her foods to touch and, as a child, she wouldn't eat if her food wasn't mixed up.

SNIPPET 016 - *Afraid*

The first time I ever remember being afraid of anything was when I was about one and a half years old. The family was living in Titusville at the time. If you stood in the front doorway of our house looking outward, then the long, narrow bedroom that Edith and I shared was on the back left side. My bed was a screened-in crib with the screen at the foot pushed out of the frame on the bottom right corner where I had made a "door" for getting out when I didn't want to stay in my bed. Sometimes, when we were supposed to be sleeping, I slipped out to visit Edith in her youth bed that was across from mine. The sides of our beds were against the outside wall with a window in between at the foot.

Irene, an older teenager, and Denny, her younger teenage brother, lived with their family in the house across the street from us. Irene was our regular baby-sitter; we liked her a lot and enjoyed her company. But, we didn't care much for Denny as we thought he was a meanie; actually, he probably just acted like a typical teenage boy who is mischievous.

That Halloween after Irene had gone home and our parents were asleep, Edith and I were sitting near the foot of our beds and we were busy jabbering, trying to stay awake in our dark room. Suddenly we heard a WHHOOOing cry and a white, lumpy form appeared at the window. Our ear-splitting screams caused the figure to hastily disappear and Mommy to rescue us and calm us down. Denny thought it would be funny to put a sheet over his head and play ghost at our window. He must have been reprimanded for his prank because, to my knowledge, he never did anything like that again.

Eleven and ten-year-old kids should be in bed before ten o'clock, especially on "school" nights, but Edith and I weren't that pitch-black night. We were sitting together on the couch alone in our house in Fort Pierce. We had locked the front door (the house had no other door to the outside) and our dad didn't have a key; back then no one carried house keys because no one bothered to lock the doors to their houses. Daddy had worked late, so we were in the living room watching the front door and the two windows, one on each side of the door, waiting for him to appear so we could open the door for him.

Suddenly, there materialized a distorted face, with nose pushed up and eyes stretched down by a hand, pressed against the left window. Deafeningly shrieking, I bolted off the couch and wildly dashed around the house while Edith, having recognized the face as belonging to our next-door neighbor, chased after me.

"It's just our neighbor, so shut up," she hollered at me.

Even though I understood what she was saying, I couldn't stop, and kept running around in a circle through the dining room, kitchen, short hallway, my dad's bedroom, and back into the living room screaming like a maniac. After she finally caught me and helped me calm down, Edith let the neighbor in.

"I am so sorry; please forgive me," he begged. "I didn't realize George wasn't home yet or I never would have pulled that prank. I was really hoping to scare him."

I never quite recovered from the two frights. Into my early twenties whenever I tried to sleep, even during daylight, if I was home alone, I couldn't sleep in the bed in my own room because the head of it was next to the window. I had to sleep against the wall on the top bunk of Sheila and Pat's beds because it was above the window next to the head of it; and still, every little sound woke me.

Until a few years ago if anyone startled me, I jumped and screamed before I even realized what I was doing; it was simply a reflex action. Even after we got married, whenever John approached, if I couldn't see him, he had to make some kind of noise to let me know he was in the vicinity or he would startle me and I would go into my little banshee "song and dance."

SNIPPET 017 - *Running Away*

I really enjoy "running away." I was barely two years old the first time I tried it.

My mother was an RN (Registered Nurse) and worked in a doctor's office several blocks away from the house where we lived. She started work there some months before I was born in 1937 after she, my dad, and older sister had moved to Titusville from Melbourne, where Edith had been born.

My dad was an undertaker (technically, he was an embalmer and funeral director according to his license; I don't remember what was printed on his diploma from Worsham College of Mortuary Science in Chicago), and he worked at Koon's Funeral Home next door to our house.

We had a woman who came on workdays to our home to take care of us children while our parents were gone. I liked Queenie, but I must have been mad at her that summer day for some silly reason, like not being allowed to go watch Daddy embalm bodies. Edith and I liked to do that. We would cross the yard, sneak up to the screen door, peak into the embalming room, and watch him work. Since there was no air-conditioning, the wooden door, as well as the windows, would be open to let the breezes come inside through the screens.

I decided to *run away* and go stay with Mommy. Stomping my foot, I told Queenie so, then ran out of the house.

I got to the corner of the block, but since I was not allowed to cross the street without an adult, I sat down on the curb and just bawled. Within seconds, Queenie appeared, grabbed me by the hand, and marched me straight to mother's office.

Mom was very busy, the waiting room was full and people were even sitting on the porch of the house where the office was, and she definitely didn't have time for these shenanigans! But Mommy, being the saint she was, told Queenie and me that I could stay the rest of the afternoon but I had to sit on the porch with the overflow of patients. That was the perfect solution for *them*. And maybe for *me* too. After sitting for hours among all those sick people and watching some of them get shots, I decided that I would never run away again.

SNIPPETS (bits and pieces of love and life) by CAROLE

But I never stopped liking the idea of "running away." Whenever I had accumulated too much overtime and needed a break from work, I would slip into the office and stare at my boss across his desk. When he became aware that I was standing there and looked up at me, in a soft, slightly-high-pitched-running-up-the-scale voice, I would squeal, "I'm getting tired of this!" and then, in my normal voice, add, "I have to run away and sew (sewing was my favorite hobby); I'll be back Monday." I never go "on vacation" either; I always tell people: "See you in a few weeks, I'm *running away.*"

SNIPPET 018 - *A Single Stitch*

    Although we were only four and three years old, Edith and I were allowed to go short distances from home if we stayed together. That summer Saturday morning we had walked hand-in-hand a block or so, arriving early at the library for the ten o'clock "Story Hour."
    While we were waiting for it to begin, we were supposed to sit in the chairs and behave. I had too much energy to sit still and obey and decided that it would be much more fun to play with the chairs. I discovered that if you put two chairs back-to-back with just enough room for your body between them, you could put one hand on the back of each chair, pick up your feet and swing them back and forth into the air in the space between the chairs. It was super fun! That is, it was fun until the chairs collapsed and I swung, head first, onto the hard dented surface of the green floor. Bam! My chin hit the floor, splitting wide open—and the blood from the wound started dripping onto my pretty white dress as I stood up.
    Edith grabbed my hand and took me straight home to Mommy while I ran alongside her, crying and leaving drops of blood on the sidewalk.
    Mommy soothed my hurt, put a bandage on my chin, and said, "Go on back to Story Hour. I know you don't want to miss the rest of it. We'll fix your chin later."
    So back we went to the library, just the two of us. This time it was easy for me to find the way; I really didn't need Edith; I could just follow the drops of blood. But, Edith, being older and wiser, made me hold her hand anyway.
    After we returned home, I heard Mommy and Daddy discussing my chin and something about the doctor not being available.
    Mommy said, "I'm going to sew up your chin so it will heal better and leave a smaller scar, and Daddy's going to hold you on his lap. If you are really brave and let us do that, Daddy will give you a silver dollar for ice cream when we're done."
    That sounded good to me because I liked ice cream. (Still do.) So, I sat very still and tried not to cry while Mommy took a needle with black silk thread and put a single stitch in my chin. You can still

see where the stitch was but I'm sure that it healed much better like she said it would.

Since I was very brave, I got the silver dollar. Daddy took me to the store to buy ice cream for everyone and I gave him back the change. I didn't want the money; all I wanted was the ice cream.

This incident taught me a couple of lessons:
- As a child:
  1. If you're going to swing between two chairs, make sure someone really heavy is sitting in each chair so they won't tip over or make sure the chairs are nailed down like at the movies.
  2. Keep the change. You can buy more ice cream later.
- As an adult:
  1. If you need to have children do something, bribe them with something they really would like to have.
  2. Pay for the item yourself. You might not be as lucky as my dad; the kid might keep the change.

SNIPPET 019 - Skates

Edith and I got our first pair of roller skates for Christmas when we were three and two and living in Titusville. The skates were made of metal, could be adjusted to your shoe size, and had green leather straps at the ankles and green leather flaps that laced over the toes of your shoes. While we were learning to skate, Mommy let us skate in the house on the wood floor in the dining room so we could hang on to the table's edge while we skated around it. We would skate in one direction until we got dizzy and giggly and then turn around and skate in the opposite direction. I don't remember ever going outdoors to skate until after we moved to Melbourne a year or so later. There and in Miami we skated up and down the sidewalk along the street in front of our house. While we lived at Morrison Field in West Palm Beach, we skated on the concrete floor of an open hangar, that used to house planes, across the street from our apartment building which had housed military officers during World War II.

Starting about the time I was in the sixth grade, we skated at roller rinks on Saturdays. We would rent shoe skates with wooden wheels and skate on a polished wood rink. I especially liked that because there were no bumps or cracks to be careful of so you wouldn't stub your skate and fall. Most of my friends learned to skate backwards and do some dance steps, but I never quite got the hang of it. I did learn to skate with a partner and do a few dance steps as long as I was the one who always skated forward.

During the seventh grade, I made my own skating outfit that consisted of a billowing-sleeved peasant blouse made of a light golden cotton fabric and of panties and matching circular skirt with alternate quarter panels of dusty green and the same light golden cotton fabric. I was very proud of my outfit and because I felt so good and confident wearing it, I know I skated better.

My senior year in high school, the majorette group that I belonged to won first place in a twirling competition in Miami and was invited to twirl onstage at the ice-skating rink that evening and to participate in the open skating afterwards. Ice rinks were unusual for warm climates in the 1950's and it was the first time for most of us in the group to ever see an ice rink and to try ice-skating. We were thrilled. Our only problem was travelling the seventy miles from there to West Palm Beach, changing into our more elaborate twirling outfits, and returning within three hours. Fortunately, my dad, "armed" with many years of skillful ambulance driving, had driven us to Miami; so, while we watched for the state police, he drove about ninety-five miles per hour both ways and got us all home to change and back to the rink within the allotted time. (Daddy had even driven an ambulance at high speed between two parked cars with less than an inch to spare on either side and not left a scratch.)

Ice-skating feels very different from roller-skating and I had to hang on to someone in order to skate without falling down. One of the male ice-skating instructors helped us enjoy our evening. He was the first Albino person I had ever seen; he was physically very fit and quite handsome with his pale, milky-colored skin, snow-white hair, and pinkish-blue eyes; watching him skate was delightful.

I don't own any roller skates now but do have a pair of ice skates collecting dust in the basement. I have ice-skated some during the last forty years when we have gone to the mountains with friends to play in the snow; but I have always held John's hand for confidence and companionship. Right now I'm too busy doing other things to spend time skating, but I'm so glad I spent all those wonderful hours doing it when I was young.

SNIPPET 020 - Dixie

    This is about Dixie, not "the land of" or the highway that runs along the East Coast of Florida, but my best friend in the second grade at Riverside Elementary in Miami about three blocks from my house where we lived on S.W. 11th Avenue just off Flagler Street. Dixie, with her winning smile and matching personality and her longish-curled-platinum-blonde hair, was petite and beautiful just like her mother. I was darker complexioned, average looks with long braids, had ears that still stuck out, although not as much as when I was born thanks to Mom's ribbons, and wasn't popular like she. But, I liked her a lot and she liked me, so the rest didn't matter.
    Our friendship was probably due to our liking to do many of the same things and doing them together. Dixie sat right behind me at school. Her desk was joined to my seat like my desk was joined to the seat in front of me; therefore, it was easy for me to turn around so we could chat face to face. Our desks were near the back of the classroom, away from the teacher's desk, one aisle over from the windows. Both of us were smart enough to be able to finish our work long before everyone else did and then have the rest of the allotted lesson time for doing something different, like chatting. Neither of us wanted to do any more work than was required because we had so much we had to talk about. We usually got scolded for whispering too much to each other. After being shushed, we would console each other, taking turns tickling, by lightly touching, each other's forearm; we could do that without talking, but we had to stifle our giggles or get scolded again.
    I don't know why neither of us was reprimanded for the way we wrote our lesson papers, but we weren't. We students had to use yellow paper ruled with the horizontal lines grouped together in three's, two red ones over a blue; you were supposed to use the entire group when you printed the letters on the paper because the lines were there to help you learn to proportion the letters properly, like the letters you see typed here. Dixie and I ignored that rule. The two of us already could write in script. Edith had taught me while she was learning how to do it. I don't know how Dixie learned to write longhand; I just know she could. Since the teacher made us *print*

instead of *write* like we wanted to, we two rebels printed only on the blue lines and used pencils sharpened to such fine points that you needed a magnifying glass to read our tiny printing. We rarely got less than "100" on our work anyway and the teacher never scolded us about our doing that.

Because I idolized Dixie (like I do my petite friend Sylvia) and she wore beautiful dresses with matching panties (which her mom considered a necessity for Dixie's wearing skirts so short that her panties showed if she even slightly bent over), I had my mom remake my dresses into ones that were pretty, full-skirted, and short like hers with (of course) matching panties or make me new dresses that fit the description. The panties in my case resembled very short bloomers until I was old enough to sew my own clothes and make matching hip-hugger-style panties or bikinis. The two of us liked whirling around and around, getting dizzy in the process, to make our full skirts fly up to our waists; we could do that and not feel self-conscious or have our mothers or other adults reprimand us for being unladylike.

Although we knew each other for only the one school year, I missed her and thought about her a lot thereafter; when school was let out for the summer, she moved away to who-knows-where and I never saw or heard from her again. Even now as an adult I still think about her and the prankish fun we had together. I've told you all that I can remember about her. To Dixie, I'll remain forever grateful for my wanting to wear pretty clothes and especially for being able to wear mini-skirts, or any other length I desire, that can be blown upwards by the wind or by John's whirling me around while we dance. If people look, I don't have to be concerned; it isn't unladylike; my matching panties are allowed to be seen!

SNIPPET 021 - Scratchy Wool

Edith and I each had a scratchy-red-wool, tank-style bathing suit during the time our family lived in Miami in the early 1940's. The suit caused you to itch all over where it touched your skin and then the rest of your body started to itch in sympathy. That is, until the suit got wet; then your body felt just fine. So, if we had to wear them, which we did because they were the only ones we had, then we made sure we got wet as soon as we could. We wore them when we went swimming at Matheson Hammock and we wore them to play in the rain. Wool was supposed to keep you warm so you wouldn't catch cold if you were wet, and I guess it did because I don't remember catching a cold when I got wet in it. I think it was really Daddy's idea because he's the one who insisted that our bathing suits be made of wool.

The family attended the Riverside Baptist Church on 1st Street several blocks toward downtown from our house. On Sundays, we always went to Sunday School followed by church service in the morning and to Training Union followed by church service again in the evening. On Wednesday evenings, we attended Prayer Meeting and for two weeks during the summers, Edith and I went to Vacation Bible School. We two decided that we should get baptized together on Mother's Day when we were age eight and seven; I liked to do everything Edith did and, fortunately, I was ready to do that when she was, so we could. Mommy was really pleased that we chose that particular Sunday.

This paragraph will explain our decision and what took place that Sunday. If you believe that God is the loving, creating spirit that sees and knows all things, is a holy, righteous and just judge willing to forgive by His intervention of grace and mercy through the gift of His son to redeem us through His death, then you declare your faith publicly before others through baptism, showing your death to your old life and being reborn again into a Christian life, and uniting with a church which preaches and teaches God's Word. Baptism in the Baptist faith is the total immersion of the body in water, in the name of the Father, the Son, and the Holy Ghost, denoting that the person baptized thus professes to believe these three to be God, and to devote himself to His service. The use of water represents the washing away of our sins by the cleansing influences of the Holy Spirit and the act of immersion represents the union of the believer with Christ in His death.

If you were getting baptized that usually meant you got to wear long white robes with big sleeves like people wear to sing in the choir or to graduate from school. And that's what we were going to wear, until my dad found out that they had scratchy-white-wool, bathrobe-style robes if you preferred that instead, and we didn't, but he did, so we had to. And, the robe caused you to itch all over where it touched your skin and then the rest of your body started to itch in sympathy. That is, until the robe got wet; then your body felt just fine. But, during the long wait before we walked down the steps into the baptismal pool, we stood around and scratched. We both went together with the minister into the pool above the choir loft at the church front where the wall was painted to look like a river scene; Edith, being older, was baptized first and then I was. Those few minutes, that the robes were wet and not scratchy, didn't make up for all the time that they were dry and scratchy; we couldn't wait to dry off and get dressed again. We were mad that we had to wear them, but Daddy insisted that he didn't want us to catch cold; I think he was just afraid that when the other robes got wet they would get translucent and someone would be able to see through them.

Even today I still can't stand to have wool next to my skin unless it is very soft wool like cashmere, so almost all of my wool clothes are lined.

SNIPPET 022 - Rain

Playing in the warm summer rain in Florida is a special treat for a child and I liked doing it. In Miami, Edith and I would put on our bathing suits at the first sign of rain and stand out on the sidewalk waiting for the drops to start falling. When they did, we would dance around in the rain and try to catch the drops on our outstretched tongues. If there were no rain in sight for a few days, we would use a hose or sprinkler to create our own rain showers.

The most fascinating thing I ever saw as a child in reference to rain occurred one summer during a day-visit with my cousins in Cocoa Beach. There were dark clouds over and rain pouring down on the house next door to the south, but there were white clouds on blue sky directly overhead and sun shining on us and on the house where we were playing in the yard. As an adult I saw a similar occurrence out in the plains when John and I were driving through the mid-west on a camping trip.

While I was attending Stetson University in DeLand, it seemed to rain around 1:00 or 4:00 P.M. every day during the summer, so I always took my plaid fabric raincoat, black umbrella, and galoshes with me to my 12:30 and 3:30 P.M. classes in the science building. All the other students would laugh at me when I showed up for class lugging my rain gear, and I would secretly snicker in return as I put it all on and stepped out of the building into the rain after class was over. They just didn't understand Florida weather.

Neither John nor I had any transportation vehicle while we were in college; we walked everywhere, even on dates unless we were double-dating with a couple who had access to a car. With the weather unpredictable for dates, we frequently got caught out in the rain with no rain gear; neither of us wanted the burden of lugging it around. Sometimes we made it back to shelter, but if we didn't and got soaked instead, then we just strolled around the campus dripping wet. If it was already dark, we sat on one of the empty benches smooching in the downpour, provided that there was no thunder and lightning.

One evening, John and I had attended a party for the few chemistry majors and their dates held in the back yard of the Bear's home. "Bear" was the nickname given to Dr. Connor, the chairman of the chemistry department, because he ate apples like a bear, spitting out only the seeds. On the way walking back to my dorm, we got caught in a sudden downpour two blocks from our destination. We both forgot that we were wearing the cheap, black-felt hats that John had purchased for us to wear to the party and by the time we reached the dorm, the black dye from the water-logged hats had run down our faces and onto our clothes. When we stood at the door under the lights of the porch, we each laughed at how silly the other looked, not thinking that both of us looked that way.

As her gift for our twenty-fifth wedding anniversary, Edith made us a framed counted-cross-stitch picture of the Hummel figurine of a girl and boy together under an umbrella to commemorate our walks in the rain together. It hangs just beneath another framed counted-cross-stitch picture that a friend (and at that time, my coworker) made as a surprise gift for us. That picture consists of the saying—"*Happiness is being married to your best friend*"—with a pair of girl and boy bears to the right of it and the words, embedded in the surrounding stitched border of small red hearts, "*Carole & John*" above and "*Happy 25th!*" below.

SNIPPET 023 - *Gravy*

As a kid one of my favorite toppings for food was gravy; thick or thin didn't matter, but the richer, the better I liked it. They (the researchers, I guess) say it's the fat that enhances the flavor; that's probably why I liked it—I simply like the taste of fat. I would even swipe a stick of butter, when Mommy wasn't looking, and eat that.

My dad liked gravy too, especially with beef or chicken. After the family acquired a pressure cooker, he decided that using it was the best way to make gravy at the same time as you cooked the meat. You didn't have to stand around while it cooked, you could just put all the ingredients in the pot at the same time, let it cook, and afterwards, when you took the lid off, it was ready for consumption. The only problem with his cooking though was that he didn't like to wait for the pressure gauge to reach the proper pressure; so he would turn the burner on high and go do something else in the meantime. Frequently he would get distracted and forget all about the pot on the stove. He was fixing beef with gravy one time and did just that.

It happened one Saturday afternoon in our house in Miami when I was six. What caught the attention of the family members in other parts of the house was the noise, a booming explosion followed by a swooshing sound like that of a geyser shooting off, coming from the kitchen. I had never heard a geyser spouting, but what I heard sounded exactly like what I would have expected. We all heard it and dashed toward the kitchen. When Mommy, Edith, and I arrived on the scene, gravy was still spraying everywhere and running down the walls, dripping off the ceiling and the cabinets, and slipping into all the kitchen and appliance crevices. A slamming screen door indicated that Daddy had sneaked out of the house to avoid a scolding. Mommy salvaged some of the meat for dinner. We cleaned up a lot of the mess, washing all the dishes, pots, pans and utensils including wiping down the entire kitchen as well as the metal kitchen cabinets and appliances. However, it took many weeks for Mommy to find all the different places the gravy was hiding so she could finish the job. You'd think that I would hate gravy after that disaster, but I don't; I still relish the marvelous flavors.

SNIPPETS (bits and pieces of love and life) by CAROLE

Whenever we visited John's parents, his mom always fixed something with gravy because she knew how much I liked it. She also ensured that there were slices of bread or homemade biscuits for sopping it up so you could mind your manners and not lick the plate.

In my own home I don't have to mind my manners and I can lick the gravy off my plate if I want to; having learned the proper way to do it from our cats, I can lick up every last morsel. After our nephews were older and big enough to eat sitting in regular chairs at the table, that was one of the first bits of knowledge I passed on to them at the end of a meal when we had some gravy that was suitable for teaching purposes. Patty was appalled and chastised me when I taught her three sons proper plate-licking techniques while we were dining with them one evening.

I simply remarked, "Well, that's what aunts are for; to teach children things their mothers would never allow them to do. All children should experience the joy of licking every morsel of gravy off their plates and not getting any on their clothes or on the table or floor."

SNIPPET 024 - Sleepwalking

It feels really weird to wake up in some place other than where you fell asleep. Once when I was about three years old, I woke up with my head under the china cabinet in the dining room; I never quite figured out how or why I did that but guessed that I must have been sleepwalking. I never remember doing anything like that on my own again.

In the summers when we, the kids in my immediate family, stayed with our paternal grandparents, other close relatives would sometimes visit, usually staying overnight, and that meant many people had to have someplace to sleep. Pops (the nickname by which my grandfather was known and called by everyone) and Gramma had one daughter and two sons, and, after the three got married, each union produced four children. We cousins consisted of eleven girls and one boy. Our grandparents' small-roomed house had only two bedrooms, one in the front with a double bed for them and one in the back with a double bed for visitors. The screened-in front porch contained two single beds as well as rocking chairs. The adults and some of the smaller children got the back bedroom and the porch for sleeping. All the leftover children got the living room and had to sleep squeezed in, at least six or seven across, on the double bed mattress on the floor, shoved up next to the inside wall.

If you (a kid) had to get up during the night to use the bathroom, you lost your place in the bed, and Gramma would have to rearrange the rest of the kids so you could get back in bed to sleep. Sometimes she would rearrange us into other beds on the porch or back bedroom with the parents. She would simply arouse us just enough to sleepwalk us elsewhere but never arouse us enough to wake us up. We frequently woke up in a different place than where we went to sleep. None of us ever figured out how she managed to work her magic. It still remains a mystery.

SNIPPET 025 - Hash

John and I used to eat hash that you buy in a can whenever we were tent camping. Not only was it convenient, but you could easily add a few vegetables and make a meal using a single pot over the tiny one-burner stove. However, when I was a child, I hated to eat hash.

During the summers when Edith and I spent a couple of months with Pops and Gramma, we ate a lot of homemade hash. I never figured out whether it was because they wanted us to eat all the food that was served up on our plates or whether Gramma just liked to make us eat hash.

I did figure out that they were rather poor. Gramma always bought day-old bread and cookies when we went to the bakery and she always looked for bargains in the grocery store. Nevertheless, they did have fresh whole, raw milk and eggs delivered to the house by a couple and their severely retarded daughter who had six fingers on each hand and six toes on each foot. (I think they must have splurged just to help that family financially and to allow the girl to play on the swing and trapeze that Pops had made and hung from a sturdy limb on a huge tree on the other side of the dirt driveway from the front porch.) If we had ice cream at home, she made it herself using evaporated milk, lemon juice, and sugar and froze it in ice trays in the freezer, taking it out every hour and stirring it to make it have a creamier texture. When we did go out for a treat, it was at the end of our Friday evening drive to collect cow manure for my grandfather's homemade "fertilizer-tea." At the drugstore each of us kids was allowed to have a single-dip ice cream cone which cost five cents; only our grandparents were allowed to have an ice cream soda, if they preferred that, because it cost fifteen cents.

At each meal we tried to eat everything we were served because anything left on a plate or in a dish or in a pan got scraped together and put into the refrigerator at the end of the meal; the next meal was prepared using those leftovers. Gramma would set up the food grinder, attaching it tightly to the edge of the kitchen table, and each of us kids had to take turns cranking the handle while she put the leftovers into the grinder. If there wasn't enough after it was all ground together, more food was cooked and added to the grinder.

Afterwards, the mixture was cooked or reheated in a frying pan, then served as the main, and sometimes only, course. If she didn't make hash, she made soup. Soup wasn't quite as bad; you could at least distinguish what the foods were in the mixture that you were eating because we didn't have to grind them up.

To me, the absolute worst tasting food combination was her liver hash. The liver she bought had a very strong flavor (it definitely wasn't calves liver) and I didn't like the way she cooked it. I guess no one else did either, because whenever we had liver for dinner, there was always plenty of it left to make into hash the next day. It was bad enough served cut up but served ground up with everything else was even worse. We did our best to keep it out of the hash, but I think she always bought extra because she knew we all, including Pops, hated her liver hash. He never ate that kind of hash; she had to fix him something else. And, if I recall correctly, if our behavior or the way we did our chores hadn't been up to her standards, then that's when we had liver hash the most often. Wish I had realized that back then.

SNIPPET 026 - Periwinkle Soup

Some things really make an impression on you and that's what you remember years afterwards. Aunt Dottie's periwinkle soup was another one of those things like Gramma's hash.

Aunt Dottie, my dad's sister, her husband, and their three daughters and one son lived in the ninth house on the left traveling from Patrick Air Force Base north on A1A toward Cocoa Beach. My uncle was in the Air Force and stationed there at that time. The kids were all younger than I, and in the summers when Edith and I, and sometimes Sheila, stayed with our grandparents in Melbourne, we would drive over there to spend the day. I never knew their address. After Pops drove through the north fence of the base, we kids could easily spot their house by counting the houses as the car passed by them and chanting the rhyme:

"One, two, three, four, five, six, seven, eight, nine.
The house with all the clothes on the line."

The first thing we did when we arrived was to change into our bathing suits and head for the beach of the Atlantic Ocean, which was just across the street and over the dunes. We all liked playing in the ocean waves and building sandcastles, using our hands, buckets, and shovels. Before we could return to the house, however, we had a chore we didn't like, not because it wasn't fun, but because we dreaded what happened afterwards. We had to gather periwinkles, with the sieves given to us for that purpose, so my aunt could make soup. If you aren't familiar with periwinkles, they are tiny salt-water snails, with different pastel-colored shells, that come in with the waves and quickly bore into the sand when the waves retreat. We had to work very fast to catch them in our sieves while they were still suspended in the shallow water and collect them in our buckets. If you tried to get them once they started boring into the sand, you had to spend too much time rinsing them in the next wave instead of catching the new ones that were suspended in the water. When we had collected enough, we could leave the beach.

Aunt Dottie would rinse the periwinkles and boil them in water, strain out the shells, and most of the sand that inevitably came out of the shells when they opened during the cooking process. We kids thought the taste of the soup was disgusting; consequently, she would try to disguise it with V8® or tomato juice. Even with that addition, I had a hard time eating it and not gagging. We all had to eat the soup regardless of whether we liked it or wanted to, because "we needed the protein" or some such nonsense.

So, if I come to your beach house for dinner, *never* offer me periwinkle soup.

SNIPPET 027 - Five-dollar Bill

From about the ages of six to thirteen Edith and I stayed many summers in Melbourne with our dad's parents. Our mom's parents, including her stepmother, died years before we were born; we never even saw them except in a photo or two. The summer between my sixth and seventh grades was my last to stay with Pops and Gramma.

Edith was going through a time of rebellion and just simply refused to help around the house. One afternoon Pops called me aside while I was playing in the yard.

"If you will help your grandmother more by doing all of Edith's chores as well, then I would be very grateful. I would rather have some peace and not have them arguing about what isn't getting done. I will pay you five dollars at the end of the summer provided that you do the work cheerfully and not tell anyone about our deal. It will be our little secret," he confided.

"I don't mind," I said, excitedly agreeing to do it. "I end up doing her chores anyway and I would like to earn the money. I promise not to tell."

So for the rest of the summer that was what I did. When I wasn't helping Gramma, I was playing or reading or attending day camp. Best of all, during the weekday mornings for eight weeks, Edith and I took the school bus to summer school day camp. We both learned to swim and make shell jewelry and Edith learned to knit while I took a few tap dancing lessons. I was quite proud of my tap shoes, contrived from a pair of multi-colored, ankle-strap, wedged sandals, on which Gramma had the repairman at the shoe repair shop add dancing taps to the soles at the toes and heels, and showed them off to everyone. All in all it was a wonderful summer.

At the end of our stay, our parents drove up to take us kids back home to West Palm Beach. After we packed and got into the car, my grandfather came over to the window next to where I was sitting behind my dad in the driver's seat and stood beside my grandmother who was at the driver's window, saying good-bye to us.

"Here's the five dollars I promised you for doing Edith's chores," Pops said much too loudly, thrusting the bill into my hand.

Gramma became livid and bellowed at me: "Why you little *snip*! All this time I thought you were helping because you *wanted* to, but you only helped because you were being *paid* to."

"I don't *want* your money!" I cried, throwing the bill back at Pops, it missing him and floating to the ground. "You broke your promise to me after I kept mine." I began sobbing. I knew that my grandmother would never forgive me and I might never forgive either of my grandparents for violating my trust.

After that day I rarely spoke to my grandparents and then only if I had to, and I never stayed at their home again.

SNIPPET 028 - Psychic

My dad had an uncanny sense of knowing what had happened or was happening miles away. He frequently would walk up to total strangers and tell them where they were born, approximately when, what their occupations were, whether or not they were married, where they lived, and other things that he should not have known.

He also was good at diagnosing diseases that people had, even though their doctors were baffled by their symptoms. In one instance, he correctly diagnosed the scarlet fever that he had when he was in the United States Navy, but the navy doctors refused to believe him until after he had infected all his fellow sailors. The entire company was kept quarantined for a few weeks and left in the USA, missing being shipped overseas during World War II. In others, he diagnosed one man as having tularemia and a second as having athlete's foot all over his entire body; after their doctors treated them for those specific diseases, respectively, they finally got well. The second man had been ill for two years. The instances were too numerous to be accidental. He probably acquired much of his knowledge from his experience; his work in civilian life included embalming bodies and helping medical examiners with autopsies and his work in naval life included being a pharmacist's mate; but, even that can't explain his diagnostic ability.

During phone calls to us daughters, Daddy had said things like: "How did you break your foot?" or "Have you had your arm X-rayed yet? It's broken." or "You wanted me to phone. What do you need?"

Remembering faces, numbers, fingerprints, and other odd things like that was another gift that my dad possessed. He was even quite good at predicting whether or not a person was a criminal. Consequently, he found great satisfaction as a volunteer deputy sheriff or policeman in every community where we lived. I believe for his work in West Palm Beach he was actually paid a salary of one dollar per year with a grand total of a little more than thirty dollars. We all were proud of his work. (I think he was also proud of the uniform he got to wear.)

One afternoon when I was a youngster, I happened to be with my dad when he was telling one of his friends about an incident involving a mutual friend of theirs. Although he was miles away, my dad had envisioned the incident precisely at the time it occurred.

"Yeah, Daddy just seems to know these things," I chimed in. "Did you know he's *psycho*?"

"The word is *psychic*! Not psycho," he resoundingly corrected me.

SNIPPET 029 - Kidnapping

"We're going to get your mother and Sheila and bring them home," Daddy said as he ushered Edith and me into the back seat.

I don't know whose car it was. We didn't own a car; we always took a bus or train to travel long distances. But, we drove from Miami to Englewood that day during Christmas vacation in 1946.

Mommy was staying with her twin brother and his family in the house where she and Frank were born in 1909. She had left home, taking Sheila with her, in October to get away from our dad who had taken her to Rochester to have her committed to a psychiatric institution. His scheme had backfired because the doctors said that although our mom was suffering from severe depression, it was our dad who had the more serious mental problems, not her. They, in essence, said to Mommy, "Learn to live with it or get a divorce." When our dad refused any psychiatric help because, as he put it— "There is nothing wrong with me!"—she wasn't sure she could continue to *live with it* for the rest of her life. She opted for the divorce.

After we arrived, Daddy left us in the car parked on the roadside of the deep, wide ditch at the property's edge, walked across the wooden-planked bridge, and went into the house to get Mommy. We watched them argue and tussle as he led her out into the yard and tried to force her into the car. A deputy sheriff was cruising by in his patrol car and stopped when he saw them struggling at the side of the road; the deputy was a relative of Frank's wife and knew that our parents were legally separated. He put our dad under arrest but Daddy argued and resisted and a scuffle ensued. To end it, the deputy hit our dad on the head with a blackjack, lacerating the skin and fracturing and permanently denting his skull above his left eye, then quickly twisted his arms behind him and fastened a pair of handcuffs on his wrists. The twisting of our dad's arms dislocated his left shoulder again; it, previously, had been dislocated several times, requiring surgery at least once, starting when he was fourteen.

Terrified and clinging to each other in the back seat of the car, Edith and I watched the fracas and Daddy's being put into the patrol car and hauled off to jail. When it was over, Mommy took us into the house and tried to comfort us. We loved her very much and couldn't understand why she didn't love us; we had been brainwashed by our dad and his parents into believing she was mentally ill and no longer loved or wanted us. The whole family tried to make us feel welcomed, but we mostly just huddled together until Daddy got out of jail the next morning.

Later that next morning, even though Mommy refused to leave and planned to keep Sheila with her, Daddy tried to grab Sheila to take her with us, but failed.

"Please let them take my presents with them so they can open them Christmas morning," Mommy begged as she tried to put them into the car after Edith and I got in.

Daddy snatched the gifts from everyone and threw them out into the ditch. Then he jumped behind the wheel and stomped on the accelerator as he slammed his door; the car, toppling Mommy to the ground before she could let go of the back door handle, sped off.

We raced down the road hitting potholes and bumps at a tremendous speed. One pothole was so deep that, as Edith fell back to the seat from hitting the top of her head on the roof of the car, a can of motor oil, lying on the ledge at the back windshield, flew forward hitting her in the back of her neck. Suddenly, we heard the siren of a patrol car coming up behind us in the distance; apparently someone had called the sheriff. Daddy drove even faster and made us get down on the floor of the car and stay there for the next two hours until he was sure he had outrun the sheriff and his deputies.

When we got back to Miami, Daddy had to take Edith to the emergency room to have her neck and back examined. The blow to her neck was hard enough to cause her life-long problems from the injury.

A few days later our grandfather partially succeeded where our dad had failed; Pops did manage to kidnap Sheila while she was playing in the yard in front of Uncle Frank's house. Even at two years old, Sheila was already a tomboy who loved to play in the dirt and was covered with mud at the time. Consequently, our dad and our grandparents claimed she was an abused and neglected child and filed a claim in court against our mom. It was just another one of their lies to force our mother to drop her divorce filing.

SNIPPET 030 - *Childhood Lost*

Being a mother is really fun when it's play and not reality; even grandmothers and aunts like to baby-sit because they know that when they are tired, they can give the children back to the parents.

In 1944, while the family lived in Miami, Sheila was born and Edith and I, at ages eight and seven, got to play mother with a real baby instead of a doll. Mommy let us feed her, change her diapers, and take care of her. Whenever our parents weren't home, we even got to baby-sit. They had an arrangement with two elderly women who lived in the apartment building next door and with an elderly brother and sister who lived in the apartment attached to the row of garages for that building. When requested, a pair of them would check on us periodically or come over to our house if we rang the bell that Mommy used to call us in from playing. It was a great arrangement for me because Edith, being older, basically took charge and I did as I chose.

By the time we were eleven and ten, Edith and I were living in Fort Pierce with our dad. Our mom was living in Lakeland, working as an RN during the night shift at the hospital. Sheila was living in Melbourne with our paternal grandparents where the two of us had lived the entire year previous. Edith, although still a child, suddenly had to assume the responsibilities of an adult and mother, shopping with Lucy, our housekeeper-caretaker, writing checks for purchases, and paying all the bills as well as babysitting with me after our keeper went home. At the time, Edith was wearing braces on her teeth; getting her dental work done was a big responsibility in itself because she had to travel alone to Miami for that. She rode her bicycle to the train station to catch the 4:00 A.M. train to Miami for the day. After her early morning appointment with the orthodontist, she spent the rest of the time either working around his office or visiting a former elementary school teacher or going to the movies. She then caught the 5:30 P.M. train back to Fort Pierce and rode her bike back home, arriving around nine o'clock that night.

Although our keeper was just twenty-six years old and had been ill only once in her life with rheumatic fever, she suffered a heart attack and died. Edith then had to assume Lucy's responsibilities as well. Once in a while, an elderly lady stayed with us during the evening. Except for those short breaks, for Edith there was no time to be just a child.

When she was in the second grade, Edith and her classmates did all of the work required for both second and third grades; those who passed the entire year, went on to the fourth grade like she did. From then on, she had to compete with people a year older than she was. We both were slower than most girls in maturing and reaching puberty, so she had a double disadvantage. It's not surprising that we quickly grew apart when we hit our teen-age years; she became resentfully envious of my having all the pleasures of being a child while she had none. And rightfully so!

Years later Edith discovered copies of Mom's letters, written to her lawyer, describing the abuse she had suffered from our dad and stating that she planned to return to live with him anyway so she could be with and take care of *her girls*.

Mommy came home during our year in Fort Pierce; it was a few months earlier than she had planned because Edith had to have an emergency appendectomy. Edith asked Daddy to phone her.

He answered, "I will, but you know she won't come." He was still trying to make us think our mom didn't love us.

But, even though she was just leaving for work when he called, she *did* come, traveling all night by buses, then phoning from the bus station begging the surgeon to wait until she got to the hospital. She arrived at the beginning of the surgery while Edith was on the operating table and stayed by her side for three days.

"Nothing could have ever kept me away!" Mommy told us. Soon after that, she moved home to stay with us, never to leave again.

For Edith, having the family structure back together came too late. Once Daddy took it away, she never regained her childhood; it was gone forever. She became an adult too soon and couldn't go back.

She began babysitting for pay and, by the time she was sixteen, had a job afternoons and Saturdays at a nursery school in West Palm Beach where we were then living. There, she was frequently left in charge of about fifteen children, two to five years old, for several hours at a time. She learned very early in life that she was an excellent caregiver and it's probably one of the reasons she decided to become a nurse.

SNIPPET 031 - Long Hair

Men like long hair, especially on girls of all ages, and they like to touch it and play with it; and, if they even only like to look at it, they are fascinated by it and by the girl whose head it's on. The adage says that "blondes have more fun," but I say the color doesn't matter at all if the hair is long—be it straight or curly or kinky. And, I know that from experience because I always got more attention when my hair was long, no matter what the style; that is, unless you consider my husband who loves me anyway, although he too prefers it long. I vacillated between short and long, straight and curly, braids and ponytails, and combinations of all of them; but if it was long, the other options didn't matter.

Mommy cut Edith's and my hair short with bangs to the middle of the forehead then straight around just below the earlobes in a "Dutch boy" style until we were about five and four. At that point both of us, since we two always did everything alike back then, begged her to let us grow our hair long and wear it, if we chose, in "pigtails" (a k a braids). When our hair was long enough, Mommy chose to braid it into two "pigtails" almost every day, except Sunday, "to keep it neat and out of our eyes." It was fun to wear our hair simply flowing loose after it dried in braids, preferably "French" braids that started with the hair at the top and ran to the bottom of your scalp as hair was added to each strand brought over (or under) from the outside to the middle of the braid until it finally continued away from your head. The unfurled braids gave our hair, we thought, the marvelous kink and look of the naturally curly hair we wished we had instead of the so-fine-it-looked-thin, straight hair bestowed upon us at birth. We like to whirl around so our long hair or braids could fly in the breeze along with our full skirts.

Boys at school especially liked our long hair, and even more so if it was braided and they were jokesters sitting in the desks right behind us. The desks in those days had inkwells; consequently, if the boy was sitting in the desk directly behind yours, he could delicately move your right braid hanging down your back, thread it through the inkwell hole at the front right corner of his desk's writing surface, and then stick a pencil cross-ways through the braid an inch or so above

SNIPPETS (bits and pieces of love and life) by CAROLE

the rubber band tightened around it. Voila! He had you caught; you couldn't get away until he decided to, or the teacher made him, remove the pencil.

By the time I was in the fifth and Edith was in the seventh grade in school in Fort Pierce, we had come to the conclusion that we would be prettier with short, curly hair and asked our neighbor friend to cut our hair and give us home-permanents. We braided it first so we could put rubber bands at both ends and keep the braids once they were cut off. As a matter of fact, I still have mine, but I don't know if Edith has hers. After our braids were cut off, we jokingly tacked them and a sign— HELP! WE'VE BEEN SCALPED! —to the front door frame of our house as a surprise for our dad when he came home from work. After the perms were done and our hair was set, dried, and combed out, we were quite pleased with our newly curled hair and couldn't wait to show it off. We didn't get the reaction of awe over how beautiful we were from Daddy, however. He was furious! He ranted and raved instead and refused to speak to us for a week. To add insult to injury, my boyfriend Matt hated it too, as he liked my hair long; so he wouldn't speak to me either. That's when I knew for certain that all men liked long hair, and you had better ask permission first if you are going to cut it.

I vacillated between long and short hair until I was in my early forties. At that point in my life I finally decided to grow up. It befitted me to dress in a more professional manner for my job since my long hair looked rather strange extending below the bottom of my suit jackets. Patty offered to cut my hair for me to about shoulder length and has been doing that, as needed, ever since. Nevertheless, I will always miss my long hair; I know John does.

SNIPPET 032 - Trampled

Within the same four-square-block-sized campus on "the hill" (not much of one by ordinary standards but gigantic to those of us who had never seen a bigger hill) in West Palm Beach stood three schools, Palm Beach High School on the north side, Central Elementary in the middle, and Central Junior High on the south side. I was a member of the Palm Beach High School band starting in the sixth grade in elementary school, playing a saxophone, and continuing from the seventh grade in junior high school through twelfth grade in high school, playing a bassoon. Because I was in the band, I had to be able to walk over to the band room for classes during fourth and sixth periods each school day. Consequently, I needed to attend the schools on that campus.

No one school bus went directly to that campus from where we lived in the old Morrison Air Force Base barracks that had been turned into apartment buildings; consequently, I had to ride two school buses each way to attend school. At 6:45 A.M., I caught Bus 40, driven by a lady who lived in a building several streets over from us, and rode that until around 7:20 when it dropped me off many miles farther away from school than we actually lived. At 7:30, I caught Bus 26 when it picked up the last batch of us students that had collected at Four Points from buses coming there from all different directions. That bus then dropped off some students at Conniston Junior High and then the rest of us at the high school at 8:10, just in time to dash into school, hopefully, before the 8:15 A.M. starting bell.

Sometimes I walked the more-than-two miles home from school, but all the books I had to lug plus the large case carrying my saxophone or bassoon made the trip difficult and almost prohibitive for me. I was rather small and probably weighed between seventy and eighty pounds the first few years I was in the band. I'm not sure exactly what I weighed at that time, but I only weighed eighty-nine pounds and was four feet ten inches tall when I entered the tenth grade.

One morning during the fall of the seventh grade, Bus 40 dropped us off early at Four Points, and that particular morning I made the mistake of standing in line too close to where Bus 26 stopped for

SNIPPETS (bits and pieces of love and life) by CAROLE

pick-up. When it did arrive, several big burly students knocked me down trying to board the bus first to get the best seats left, and everyone following them stepped all over me. I got up crying, hurting from the bruises all over my body, gathered up all my belongings, boarded the bus last, and went on to school. As I recall no one was disciplined and no one, except my family, even cared.

After I got home late that afternoon near 5:00 P.M., I remember showing the bruises to Mommy and seeing that the shape of the largest one was a footprint on the front of my right thigh. Although the physical bruises healed without a trace, the whole experience was horrifying and I always feel it over again whenever I hear of, or see on TV, someone else being trampled. I hope it *never* happens to you.

SNIPPET 033 - Hurricanes

For many people, hurricanes can be a disaster; but, for children, it can be a party. In Miami, when we lived there in the early 1940's, our yard always flooded during very heavy rains and hurricanes. Edith and I enjoyed watching the commotion of wind and rain, and then going outdoors to play in the accumulated rainwater, usually deeper than six-inches, floating around in homemade washtub-boats or old tire inner tubes for a few hours or until the water soaked into the sandy soil, ran down the sewers, or evaporated.

In late August 1949, just two weeks after Patricia was born, a hurricane was predicted to hit West Palm Beach, where we were then living. The weather bureau predicted it to hit really hard and the eye was supposed to pass over us. Since our family never evacuated but stayed at home during hurricanes, we made all the necessary survival preparations, filling the bathtub with water, buying food that didn't require refrigeration, filling ice chests to hold the contents of the refrigerator if the electricity went out, and gathering up sufficient flashlights.

The building we lived in had four apartments, each one containing a family with children, twelve in all; downstairs, there were four kids in ours, two across the hall, and upstairs, there was one overhead and five across the hall. Edith was the oldest, age thirteen, and Patricia was the youngest. We kids expected the occasion to be one huge party. The electricity went out almost as soon as the hurricane hit, eliminating the use of all electric stoves or other such conveniences, so the families got together to share resources and meals. Using our two-burner kerosene heater as a stove, my dad cooked fried chicken and other foods for us to eat by the light of the gas lamp provided by the family across the hall. Counting the eight adults there were twenty people in all at dinner, so most of us ate sitting around on the floor holding our plates in our laps. A roll-away bed had been set up in the living room to keep the baby on so we kids could take turns playing with or feeding Patricia to allow our mom to do other necessary chores. We didn't party for long; the hurricane worsened.

SNIPPETS (bits and pieces of love and life) by CAROLE

We tried to keep the damage at a minimum by opening windows opposite from the side of the wind direction to equalize the pressure in the building. You could do that because the wind didn't blow the rain in through the open windows on that side. After a couple of windows were broken by flying debris, we all stayed away from the windows, except to open or close the remaining ones, and kept toward the interior of the building. The roofing peeled off the apartment upstairs across the hall, so the older children helped the available adults mop up rainwater that leaked through the ceiling, and wherever we could, we positioned a pot or pan or bowl to catch the drips. When enough water collected, we emptied the containers and repeated the process of "mopping and positioning."

The area where we lived used to be an air base complete with barracks, plane hangars, and other huge buildings with concrete floors where we kids liked to skate. Since we hadn't boarded up the windows, we could still see outside even though we kept some distance away. We watched huge trees being uprooted and blown around and even saw complete thirty- to forty-foot walls, from the old hangar building across the street from us, flying down the street and being dropped a block away when the gust died down. Mostly the wind blew steadily, but even the wind-velocity recorders at the airport were ripped apart when some of the gusts exceeded 170 miles per hour.

My dad was a hurricane warden and went out during the eye, when it was quiet, to survey the damage. There was quite a bit by then and even more damage after the second half of the hurricane passed through. The next day, we discovered that one hangar had completely collapsed on all the new cars that had been stored there for protection from the hurricane. When the men were moving the cars in from the dealerships in town, they had told my dad that he could store our car there too. But Daddy told them: "Nooo, thanks. I'd rather leave it in the yard and take my chances." Our car did get *scratched* by flying tree limbs and had to be repainted, but it didn't get *squashed* like the new ones did. The yard flooded where the car was parked, but the water wasn't quite deep enough to seep in and damage the car's interior.

The trailer park located nearby was totally devastated and the trailers were all thrown over on their sides or tops or completely ripped apart. Daddy had taken us over there to see it; we sadly observed all the destruction. Fortunately, the people had evacuated to stay with friends or in schools and other buildings prepared as shelters; they were all safe, but they lost all their possessions that they hadn't taken with them.

We kids played for a day or two in the ten-or-so-inch-deep rainwater that accumulated in the yard until my dad and Martha, who lived across the hall from us, became so ill that they had to be hospitalized. They both had contracted polio; and, since no one knew what caused polio, we all had to stay indoors quarantined at home. Health officials came out to interview everyone and to investigate everything around us including inspecting all the garbage. We now know that poliomyelitis is a viral infection, but back then they had no real evidence of that. There was quite an outbreak following the hurricane and some people ended up in iron lungs because they became totally paralyzed. Months later, I saw and talked to one girl who was in an iron lung; I felt very sad and so sorry for her because that was the only way she could live.

Daddy had to spend six months in the hospital because he was paralyzed in both legs, and it took two years of out-patient therapy after that for him to regain their use. Martha faired slightly better, staying only a couple of months. Edith and I contracted polio too, but we were injected with massive doses of gamma globulin early enough that we had fevers and some other symptoms but did not have any paralysis like our dad and others did. The shots caused unbearable aching all around the injection sites in your upper buttocks, so we both cried some from that as well as from the severe pain in all our muscles. We both recovered within a couple of weeks, and the only lasting effect was that each of us has a slight tendency to drag our feet which, though imperceptible to others, sometimes causes us to stumble and fall. After we two got well, the whole family visited Daddy frequently, though not in his room. Because of the fear of contagion and because we had the baby with us; we stood and shouted to him from the parking lot while he looked out his third-story room window and shouted back.

SNIPPET 034 - Pillows

Pillows are a great addition to any couch, chair, bed, floor, or swing and I have some scattered in all those places. You just never know when you might need to use one to make yourself more comfortably situated. The pillows that we have around our home sport all kinds of shapes, sizes, and colors; some are singles, some are pairs or quads as far as the coverings or colors are concerned. Some I bought at stores or "benefit" silent auctions and some were gifts. Some pillows were made by me, some by my mother-in-law, Shirley, a few were manufactured, and one was made by Mickey, Shirley's dear friend and next-door neighbor.

The age of the pillows ranges from five to thirty-five years. The covers range in variety too: fake animal fur, quilted fabrics, appliqued or reverse-appliqued fabrics, plain fabrics, needle-point faces with velvet backs, knitted yarn with multi-colored stripes, crocheted string, crocheted yarn, velour upholstery, felt applique and embroidery on linen, and so on.

I even had pillows on my bed when I was a youngster, but one pillow in particular was a bit unusual. I had a slumber party for several friends one Friday night when I was in the seventh grade and we were all sitting on the bed jabbering. One of the girls picked up that particular exquisite, tufted-ivory-colored-velvet pillow and commented on how beautiful it was but that it was rather stiff.

"That's because it's filled with straw," I explained. "Casket pillows are always filled with that so they keep their shape and beauty when the head is lying on it in the casket."

"*Casket* pillow?" she shrieked, throwing it across the room. "Get that horrible thing away from me!"

"What's the matter?" I questioned. "It was an extra sample pillow and it was never used in a casket. I like it and keep it on my bed because it is so beautiful."

She was so upset, I thought she would never speak to me again, but she calmed down after I put the pillow on the top shelf of the bedroom closet where she could no longer see it.

After they all went home the next day, I put the pillow back in its rightful place on my bed. I wish I had taken it with me when I left for college because it got lost somewhere during one of the family's moves to other houses.

SNIPPET 035 - Graduation Dress

It was on the Saturday before my graduation from Central Junior High School, in 1952, that I told my mom: "All the girls are required to wear white dresses and the boys, white shirts and dark pants. None of my dresses is white, so I have to get one." (Very different from today when children wear caps and gowns at every graduation starting with nursery school, we were not allowed to wear those garments until graduation from high school.) I liked being different and really didn't want a white dress like everyone else was going to wear; I wanted a yellow one, but I didn't tell Mom that.

Mom replied, "We can't afford to buy you a dress, but we can afford to buy some fabric so you can make one yourself. Let's go do that." And off we went to the fabric store.

I spotted some bright yellow cotton batiste fabric that was just the color I wanted for a dress; it was inexpensive enough that I hoped we could buy that too. We then found some fabric that I thought would be perfect if I had to have a white dress. It was a sheer white organdy type with tiny white flowers stamped on it, and the perfect part was that it suited my ulterior motive. Mom, who liked to spoil her daughters whenever she could, bought me both fabrics and a pattern that included pieces for both a sheer dress and the slip to wear under it. Mom had said there was some white fabric suitable for the slip at home and that was why we could buy the yellow fabric too. I was ecstatic!

I had to study every afternoon and evening for exams that week, mostly because the only grades acceptable to my dad were straight "A's"; consequently, I couldn't start making my dress until the night before graduation. I had learned how to sew during the sixth grade when Edith was taking home economics in the eighth. I always had to do the same things as Edith, so Mom taught me then because I refused to wait two more years to learn in home economics class. I could sew quite well, having done it for nearly four years, and made the slip while my mom napped in the evening before going to work the night shift at the hospital. After she left I started on the dress.

There was so much work involved in cutting and sewing essentially two dresses, that, even though I worked all night, I still had the hem to do and was in a panic when my mom arrived home from work at 7:30. We had to arrive fifteen minutes before the 9:00 A.M. graduation ceremony so the candidates could line up for the procession. Mom suggested: "Just baste the hem and finish it later; no one will ever notice."

After hastily basting the hem, I showered and put on my new clothes. The slip had a smooth spaghetti strap bodice with a half-circle skirt and a side zipper; the sheer over-dress had puffed sleeves, a plain U-neck bodice, gathered skirt, and a back zipper. I truly liked the effect. I was so excited that having no sleep didn't bother me a bit. Since we were running late, as usual, the family dashed off in such a rush that no one noticed my outfit.

During the ceremony, the graduating students, properly dressed as required, were seated alphabetically in the front rows, and the happy families were seated in the rest of the rows, all together in the school auditorium. Everyone was ready to applaud each student when he or she walked across the stage and received a diploma from the principal. The valedictorian and the salutatorian were kept secret until that particular student's name was announced.

My family was extremely proud, and I was too, when my name was called half way through the alphabet. I was even more thrilled as I walked across the stage to get my diploma. Being named valedictorian wasn't the only thing that made me stand out from the other students; everyone could see that my white dress looked mostly pale yellow. I had purposely made and was wearing, beneath the sheer organdy dress, my bright *yellow* slip.

SNIPPET 036 - Is This the Best?

I always wanted to please Daddy so he would like me. But I never seemed to be able to do it, so when I got married and left home for good, I simply gave up. I could please John instead and he not only already liked me, he loved me.

I had to be *the* best, not *my* best, at everything; I thought my dad required it. I enjoyed singing and took a few lessons from Mr. Howard who was not only the school band and orchestra director, but also the choir director at my church. I was a soprano with a three-octave range who could sing really high notes and, although I didn't have a strong voice, it was a very pretty one. I often sang solos for church pageants and as a member of the church choir. I sang for my dad's friends when I was young; he sometimes stood behind with his arms around me and sang too in his pleasant tenor voice. I often dreamed of singing for a career but I was afraid I wouldn't be good enough and quit singing. Now I can't sing at all. "Use it or lose it" truly applies to a singing voice; I didn't, and so I did.

The need for approval from male authority figures was deeply implanted in my psyche. Even at work, praise and approval meant more to me than money; nevertheless, I definitely wanted proper monetary compensation for my job. The typical conversation after a job appraisal when I received my raise went like this.

Manager, reading the letter to me in private as I sit in his office in the chair across his desk from him: "…and in appreciation for…your salary has been increased to…"

Me: "Oh, thank you very much. (I pause briefly to contemplate what he just said.) Is that a good percent increase?"

Manager: "Don't you know?"

Me: "Well—no. I don't know what I was making before. I'm not that good with arithmetic; real mathematicians, like me, deal only with letters, not numbers. John's terrific at arithmetic so he handles our finances. I never look at my paychecks or stubs. I let him open the envelopes and do something with them. When needed, I just sign my name."

If I was told the increase was quite good, I left happy and grinning and I don't recall not leaving that way. What I appreciated most were the glowing reports at appraisal time, the Vice President Customer Excellence Awards from management, and the ENCORE noteworthy behavior awards from management and fellow co-workers that I received. Yet, I rather enjoyed the looks of disbelief at pay-increase time as well.

The one thing that I did do, that I know pleased Daddy a lot, was make the right and best choice for my life-time partner. John was not only admired and respected by my dad, but he was the only person my dad allowed to tell him what to or not to do.

I wish I could have looked at his eyes whenever Daddy said it, but I always just stared at the floor, and none of my mom's consoling and reassurance ever eased the pain. When I think about it today, July 18, 2002, I'm sure I missed the twinkle in his eyes when he waved my report card of straight "A's" and quizzed me, "Is this the *best* you can do? Can't you do any *better*?"

SNIPPET 037 - Left-handed Awhile

My fifth-grade teacher was ambidextrous and would write on the blackboard or on paper with either hand that she happened to use to pick up the chalk or pen or pencil. I was fascinated by it and wished everyone, or at least I, were ambidextrous.

I used to watch each boy that I dated or double-dated with in high school when he was driving as he usually drove left-handed so he could have his right arm around his girl friend. A lot of the boys had smooch knobs in their cars; the rotatable knob, similar to a doorknob, was attached to the steering wheel and was a big help in negotiating turns while you drove because you didn't have to move your hand from that one place on the steering wheel. I didn't have a smooch knob in the car I drove, so I practiced until I was an expert without one, using only my left hand to make turns. The ability came in handy on a date whenever I had to drive my mom's car because my boyfriend didn't have a car available.

At the Palm Beach High School Band and Orchestra banquet my senior year, I was seated at a table-for-eight with seven other band members who happened to all be left-handed. Because I was sitting in a middle seat, the group coerced me into eating left-handed too. It's amazing how fast you can adapt when you are a hungry teenager and, besides, it was fun eating like the rest of my friends at the table.

All these lessons came in handy when I was in my mid-fifties. I had finished recovering from a bad fall on the ice in January when I took another spill on something slick in June 1994. This time it was on an oil spot on the pavement near our car in a parking lot in front of the restaurant where we had just eaten dinner. I caught myself on the way down with my right hand and heard two cracks; my wrist had broken in two places requiring a cast covering part of my hand and entire forearm. Amazingly, I found it rather easy to drive a car; all my practicing years earlier had made driving left-handed second nature. The only thing I had to add was using my left hand contorted around to shift the gears on the right side of the steering wheel. In fact, it was much easier than driving when I had a cast on my broken left foot.

Bathing and dressing were a bit harder for me, but John was quite helpful with that. He wrapped my cast with plastic wrap and covered that with a small, plastic, garbage bag held tight to my arm with rubber bands; I could then use the shower and bathe left-handed. It's usually better to break your back or ribs than some other bones, because, in most cases, you get to wear a removable brace instead of a cast; then, you simply remove the brace for bathing. Cutting foods, cooking, and eating proved interesting, but I managed to do that OK too. I was most surprised that the bank accepted and cashed my checks even though my handwriting, scrawled left-handed, looked very different. I guess, since we never complained that the checks were bogus, the bank figured everything was fine.

After Dr. Brent removed the cast, he put my wrist in a brace for a few weeks until the bones got stronger. The therapy I used to help strengthen them was using my hands to bang together two rocks at a time and place seventeen tons of those rocks around the driveway and trees in the yard. After moving about ten tons of them, I was able to stop wearing the brace.

SNIPPET 038 - Ants in His Pants

Daddy had a hard time sitting still, usually getting fidgety after a few minutes and having to go do something or to go pester Mommy.

I overheard her many times saying "George, could you please sit still for just one minute. You act like you have ants in your pants."

Sheila told me the other day about an incident that happened when she was six. She didn't like first grade and sometimes would pretend to be sick so she could play hooky and stay home with Mommy. I think our mom realized that Sheila was still a bit traumatized from being kidnapped from her several years earlier, so she would let Sheila get away with it.

On this particular day, Sheila had stayed home from school and was sitting on the couch in the living room. Daddy was working at a funeral home at the time and had gone to work dressed in a suit because he had to lead a graveside service that morning.

Suddenly the door opened and he dashed in unexpectedly, yanking off his coat, tie, and shirt, while yelling loudly, "Myrtle, get the bug spray and help me!"

Mommy came into the room to see what the commotion was.

"The ants are all over me!" he hollered as he hopped around trying to take off his pants. "And I couldn't leave the funeral to do something about it until now."

In Florida, most yards have ant beds, and the only time it really matters is when the ants are the stinging or biting kind. This wasn't the first time he had gotten covered with stinging ants. On a couple of other occasions, I had seen him hop around like a toad, dash into the house, and jump into the shower with his clothes on. But, those times it didn't matter if his clothes got wet because he had been out in the yard in his underwear, standing on an ant bed that he hadn't noticed, talking to a neighbor.

On this occasion he was on his own again. His wife was no help at all; she was laughing so hard she was doubled over and tears were running down her face. And neither was his daughter of any help because she was roaring with laughter at the two of them.

Mom did manage to hoarsely say, "Gee, George, you really *do* have ants in your pants!"

SNIPPET 039 - Mema

The Palm Beach High School band was going to Jacksonville for the football game after all, the band director had said, when we arrived at school that Friday morning; the hurricane that was headed toward Florida had veered out eastward over the Atlantic Ocean instead. Since few students had taken cars to school that day and because we had only one hour before the buses would leave, I had driven about twenty band members to their homes in my car. They had ridden inside the car sitting several-deep on the seats and outside the car sitting in the open trunk and on the hood and fenders. We had hoped to see some police cars so we could get some help, but we saw none; I just drove slowly, and as carefully as possible, and deposited each student home safely.

Only twenty minutes were left to pack my suitcase and be back at the band room if I wanted to catch one of the three buses needed to haul over one hundred band members plus chaperones, instruments, and luggage. I was a bit panic-stricken due to the timing and I needed help. Mom wasn't in the house; but, since the house was unlocked, I figured she was having coffee with one of our neighbors, like she sometimes did. I opened the backdoor, leaned out, and yelled—"Mom-my, Mom-my, Mom-my"—over and over until it started sounding like—"Me-Ma, Me-Ma, Me-Ma." Mom came dashing home to help me.

Everyone got back to the band room on time and the trip was a marvelous success.

After I got to college, the first letter Mom sent me was signed: "Mema." Even though I had three sisters, I always felt she was "me" (my) Ma. And, my sisters each felt she was her Ma. Mom was special that way; she made each one of us feel like her favorite and most precious daughter.

Our nephew Beau said it best—"*She made you feel good...*"—and that's the way we had it printed on the cover of the "thank you" note cards we sent to people for gifts in her memory to the memorial program of the Northwood Baptist Church; those very words appeared also in her obituary. She made everyone, no matter what gender or color or creed, feel good. She was a nurse and the perfect type to be one: loving, caring, nurturing, tenderhearted, helpful, gentle, and quietly strong-willed. She never cursed or said unkind words; she *practiced* instead of *preached* her religious beliefs. I learned a lot by just watching her.

Mema didn't wear makeup; she liked the natural God-given look. Daddy, however, wanted her to wear makeup. When he worked in a funeral home, he put the makeup on bodies when a beautician wasn't hired to do it; so, thinking he was good at it, he occasionally would try to apply makeup on Mom. She didn't care for the look, and when we kids were young, we laughed because she looked funny to us; we thought she was beautiful enough just plain. She occasionally did wear lipstick just to appease him. I must have inherited that "natural look" trait from her because I rarely wear makeup either. I will add eye makeup and sometimes lipstick if John and I are going out.

After I left for college, whenever I was home for a short vacation, Mom and I would chat around the clock when she wasn't working. She never complained about needing sleep but I'm sure she crashed the same as I did after I got back to my dorm at Stetson University. We were very close and even before I came to the same conclusion, she knew that I loved John deeply and would marry him.

I shall never forget her and I'm sure there are many others besides my family that won't forget her either.

SNIPPET 040 - Carded

Timothy and I had joined his brother Ryan and his girlfriend, Candy, that Saturday, while I was home from college, for a summer afternoon visit at the home of an older friend of Ryan's, located along a riverbank somewhere (don't remember the exact location) in Palm Beach County. The five of us had whiled away the hours taking turns lounging in the hammock, chatting together, sipping the friend's homemade ginger beer, and simply marveling at the beautiful surroundings and watching the river laze by. As dark approached we decided it would be fun to go dancing. Since the friend didn't want to join us, we thanked him for the lovely time we had and said good-bye.

We piled into the car, Timothy and I climbing into the back seat and Ryan and Candy into the front, and off we went. The guys had a favorite nightclub in Palm Beach that featured a great combo, so we headed there. On the way we discussed whether or not we could get in. Ryan was the only one over twenty-one, the legal age for drinking; Timothy was seventeen, I was barely twenty, and Candy was fifteen. We decided that since we hadn't planned to drink any alcoholic beverages, we could probably get in to dance if we only ordered "Shirley Temple's" or soft drinks or iced tea.

When we arrived at the club, the music that the combo was playing had a great rhythm for dancing, so we somewhat danced our way in and onto the dance floor, finishing out the piece. At the song's end we glanced around, spotted an empty table, and sat down. A server promptly came to the table, took our order, and disappeared. The next person to appear was a giant bouncer asking to see my driver's license. He was surprised to see the age of twenty printed on it, because he assumed from my youthful appearance that I was about fourteen or fifteen.

"I'm sorry, but you will have to leave; she is under the legal drinking age," he said pointing to me and then to the door.

"We just want to dance and have ordered non-alcoholic drinks," Timothy explained.

"Unfortunately, the law won't even allow us to let you be in the club, much less serve you any kind of drinks," he said as he ushered us out.

SNIPPETS (bits and pieces of love and life) by CAROLE

We laughed on the way home even though we were disappointed that we couldn't stay at the club and dance. It surprised us all that I was the one who got carded; every one else looked old enough including the fifteen-year old, who actually looked twenty-five and never got questioned when she and Ryan went to nightclubs alone.

The last time I got carded was in the Del Rose restaurant in Wilmington when I was thirty-six and John ordered wine for the two of us. I think the waitress was just being kind; but, perhaps, it was because she was probably in her seventies, and everyone looks much younger to people her age. I hugged her, thanked her profusely, and John left her a huge tip.

It's just another one of the "age" curses; when you're young, you desperately wish you looked older, and when you're old, you even more desperately wish you looked younger. I'll just have to petition the legislature to change the minimum age for legal consumption of alcoholic beverages to the age of at least sixty-six so I can get carded again.

SNIPPET 041 - Bassoons

If you don't know what a *bassoon* is, you may look up the word in a dictionary, like **Webster's New World Dictionary of American English;** that particular dictionary has a picture alongside the definition. Or, you may search for it, using "Bassoon God's Studio" as the search argument, on the Internet; I discovered that this particular site has just about everything you would want to know about bassoons. Basically, a bassoon is a double-reed bass woodwind instrument with a range of approximately five octaves starting at the B-flat note below the bass clef staff. It is the musical instrument that is used for the fun parts in musical compositions like *The Sorcerer's Apprentice*, that was in Disney's delightful movie *Fantasia*, which I hope you saw or will see someday.

I had the fortune to become a bassoonist in the seventh grade in the fall of 1949. Since I had buckteeth, from sucking my thumb in the womb and the next three years afterwards, I was the perfect student for Mr. Howard, our music director, to switch from playing the saxophone to the bassoon when the band and orchestra needed another bassoonist. If you are gifted with an overbite, you are more likely to produce excellent tones on a double-reed instrument, and I was, and I did. Besides, he impressed me with the statement, "If you become a good bassoonist, you can get a scholarship for college." I had no intentions of going to college, but he sounded so enthusiastic that I just had to learn to play the bassoon. And besides, the school system would provide a new instrument that cost, including the school discount, around eight hundred dollars, which meant that the bassoon would be a really good one.

I took some extra lessons from Randy, who was a high school senior and an excellent bassoonist, and who, apparently thinking I would never succeed, complained to my mom: "I think Carole ought to quit and not even attempt to play a bassoon. It's as tall as she is, and she can't even reach all the keys because her hands are too small." To which, as I found out from her years later, my mom assertively replied: "*I* am not going to tell her that; if *she* wants to play a bassoon, she has my blessings; and if *you* don't think she should, go talk to Mr. Howard and have him tell her!" I guess Mom squelched *him*, because no one ever mentioned the problem to me. I did grow enough and enjoyed resting my chin on the open top of my bassoon when we had to stand around waiting to go on stage for a concert; you can't do that with other instruments.

I was provided an instrument and was paid to play in the band and orchestra by the university when I did attend college, just like Mr. Howard said I could six years prior. Very sadly, I had to stop playing after finishing college; I couldn't afford to buy my own bassoon. I looked into buying one a few years ago; but for just playing around home for my own amusement, I couldn't justify the cost; to get the tone quality I prefer and want, I'd have to spend about thirty thousand dollars. Buckteeth have spoiled me. And besides, right now, I don't have time to practice and play in a symphony; I'm busy writing this "book." However, I do have a memento, a pair of earrings for pierced ears, fabricated for me by a colleague bassoonist using two of my used bassoon reeds. I bet there's not another pair like it in existence for anyone else to wear when she attends symphony concerts.

Interestingly, two of my sisters, seven and twelve years younger, also learned to play the bassoon and we each played the same school instrument at different times and at different schools because the bassoon went to the band or orchestra where it was needed. They, Sheila and Pat, didn't get music scholarships; neither has buckteeth.

John and I like to browse through the shops at Barefoot Landing in North Myrtle Beach during midday when we camp at the beach near there. It keeps us off the sand and out of the blazing sun during the *wors*t part of the day—bad for your wallet but great for your skin. We always buy the decal-of-your-choice-applied-free T-shirts and other useful, frivolous things. In the "everything-musical" store I discovered an already-printed T-shirt that I had to buy, even though it came only in a blue that I look wretched in. The front of the shirt has a printing of a marvelous, hairy, brown baboon, with deep red forehead, black eyes, blue (like the shirt fabric) cheeks and pink nose and mouth, sitting cross-legged and holding in its left hand a black bassoon leaning across its body from right knee to left shoulder. Dancing around the baboon are eleven half-peeled yellow bananas and split over and below it is a bright red caption: "I SAID I'M A BASSOON PLAYER". I bought all they had and gave one to a sister, one to a coworker for her stepdaughter, and one to the principal bassoonist of the Delaware Symphony Orchestra. When I tried to buy some more the next summer, the store had none in stock, and the clerk didn't think that particular style of T-shirt was being manufactured anymore. That's really too bad. I think every bassoonist should wear one.

Note: If you don't understand the joke behind the T-shirt, bassoon rhymes with baboon. The joke means: I didn't say, "I'm a *baboon*"—I said, "I'm a *bassoon* player."

SNIPPET 042 - Pencil Points

Procrastination sets in every time I sit down to type. Since I'll do *anything* to avoid doing my "hated" writing, I was sitting here, my fingers on the computer keyboard, my eyes looking downward toward my hands, and began studying the purple patch on the back of my right hand, near my thumb. It was just another "bruise," the result of a tiny blood vessel bursting when I bump my hand into something unbeknownst and only become aware of when I feel the stinging in that area and watch the blood spreading under the skin. My mom had the same problem, so I must have inherited it, along with a lot of other traits, from her. Having wasted a few minutes pondering that side of my hand, I flipped my hand over and spotted the pencil-point-sized, round, gray dot about one and a half inches up the inside of my forearm from the bend in my wrist, just to the left of the two slightly bulging tendons, and thought, *I'd rather write about that instead of what I had planned.*

It must have been my junior year in high school because Rick, with whom I had my first real date ever my sophomore year, and who by then was just a friend, was sitting to my left at the front of the band. Since he played first chair first bassoon and I played second chair first bassoon (same as we did the previous year) in the band, we shared the same stand for one set of music because we both played the same musical part. On the music stand, we kept a very-sharp-pointed pencil (I, along with Dixie in second grade, had learned to like my pencil points very sharp) for jotting notes on the music sheets whenever our band director said to note the best way to play a particular section of music. If you are second in command and using the same music stand as the first in command, you get to do all the menial tasks like getting out the next set of music sheets, turning the pages, and putting them away again; I was, so I did. As I was turning one of the pages for the two of us, I knocked the pencil off the stand's ledge and automatically reached out to catch it mid-flight. Well, I did catch it, but not the way I intended; I caught it point first into my forearm at the spot that I previously described. I quickly decided that, the next time, I'd just watch the pencil fall to the floor, then reach over and pick it up from where it lands. I stared at the pencil, stunned, and yanked it out with my left hand; we needed it to write with and that would be difficult with the point covered. The puncture wound didn't even bleed, probably stopped from doing so by the coating of graphite—good thing too; because, if it had bled, I more than likely would have fainted and been unable to play my part during the rest of band practice. Fortunately, class was almost over, so it wasn't long before I could get the wound taken care of.

My dad took me to the emergency room to get the "lead" out. It really isn't lead, like it is commonly referred to; it's graphite. The nurse scrubbed the hole thoroughly with Tide®, which I considered a bit weird because that detergent is usually used on clothes, not skin and wounds, but she said, "I have to use something very strong to remove the lead and kill the germs." She did remove a layer of skin around the area and probably killed everything in the hole, but the graphite didn't budge. The hole closed on its own and simply healed leaving an itty-bitty short line of scar in the middle of a small gray circle.

I hate scars, and whenever I look at the constant-reminder spot, I think of Lady Macbeth's unfulfilled plea—"Out, out, damned spot."

SNIPPET 043 - *Acting*

In a novel or true-life-story book, there is no actor saying the words to help the reader get the proper feeling or nuance as there is in a play or movie. For me, that's not a problem because I read everything as though I were acting out or actually living the part of each character; I doubt that others read books that way. I even reread dialogue until I get it perfect, in my mind. It's a curse—I read everything that way. That's one of the reasons I took up studying mathematics; I couldn't keep up with all the reading I had to do as an English major; math requires *slow* reading with high comprehension, and I definitely could do the *slow* part.

I always pretended to be a great actress or ballerina or singer as a child and enjoyed being on stage or just the center of attention in class when I had the correct answer to a question. I succeeded using my body to dance or to speak if the part was small but failed miserably if I had to memorize more than a few dozen steps or lines.

In high school and college I played bit roles or sang and/or danced in numbers with a group or danced solos that didn't require formal training, of which I had none. It was great fun although, occasionally, a bit damaging to my ego or my physical body.

In the musical *Finian's Rainbow*, my senior year in high school, I danced in a group of four couples. At one point in the dance, the girl had to jump up with the aid of her boy partner's lifting, lock her legs around his waist, lean over backwards while extending her hands over her head and onto the floor in a partial handstand, and then her partner pushed her legs up and over so that she could complete the flip and end up standing on her feet again. All the girls could do it but me; because my arms were, and still are, too weak to support my weight, I crashed onto my head every time; however, I did manage to make it back up again onto my feet. To my surprise, the director (wonderful Mr. Howard) allowed me to stay in the dance group even though I continued to bang my head, every single time, during rehearsals and the actual performances. Not only did I have a constant headache, but also, for a few days during the last week of rehearsals, I walked funny, and somewhat in pain, due to bruises acquired from the oversized, bumpy, sharp buckle on the belt that my partner wore one afternoon. Needless to say, when I discovered the cause, after the damage was done, I made him remove his belt, and, from then on, I checked his waist each time before I danced with him and locked my legs around his waist.

I played the bit role of a young girl in *Christmas in the Marketplace* while in college and was perfectly (as it became quite obvious later) cast. One evening I was late, as usual, leaving the dorm to go to Stover Theatre, which was about a block away across the street behind the women's gym. After walking across the street, I starting running, leaving the sidewalk and cutting across the grass at the corner where the sidewalk went around the gym, and tripped over a buried water sprinkler; I thudded to the ground with a splat, tearing holes in my tights and knees. With my braids and skinned up knees, I really looked the part of a typical kid, but it was painful spending one entire scene on my knees during the remaining rehearsals and the actual performances.

Other roles were fun too. Modern dancing solo and with a group in *The Trojan Women* was terrific because we got to wear beautiful, unusual, short-sheer-filmy costumes. I really got into that role; I even cried when my "city" burned. Being able to braid my long hair got me the modern dancing role of an Indian princess in *Annie Get Your Gun*. Latter that year, I played the one-liner role of a slave girl in *The Menaechmi*.

During my last semester in the summer of 1960, I took a mathematics course and an acting course for which you were required to purchase at least a half share of stock in the Theatre. Owning a half share required you to do twenty (one share, forty) hours of work per week back stage in sets, costumes, and make-up, as well as act in the plays, with a new play ready for public performance at the end of each two-week period. What a fun way to receive credits toward my degree! The profit gained for my half share of stock came to seven cents per hour; the least amount of pay for any job I have ever had outside of volunteer work.

In the middle of that summer, I was offered a lead in *Visit to a Small Planet*, but had to turn it down. The play was to be publicly performed the same weekend that I had to be in the wedding of Roy and Marcia as her Maid of Honor. It's just as well because I have trouble remembering my lines (I remember everyone else's instead)

SNIPPETS (bits and pieces of love and life) by CAROLE

and probably would have ruined the play. Too bad you can't just read your lines instead of memorizing them; I'm really good at reading aloud.

The part of stage acting I enjoyed most was wearing the makeup. The greasepaint made your skin appear flawless, instead of blemished like mine was, the marvelously colored eye shadows combined with dark eyeliner and mascara made your eyes seem much bigger and enchanting, and the dark red lipstick made your lips look luscious; suddenly *plain ol' you* became—*the ravishing beauty*. Every girl, at least once in her life, should have the chance to look and feel like that.

The only Hollywood actor I ever saw "up close and personal" (besides Burt Reynolds who was called "Buddy" when we attended high school together) was Tony Randall. He was in Wilmington starring in a play at The Playhouse Theatre and had walked about five blocks from there to have lunch at a small, cozy, buffet-style vegetarian restaurant (now gone), where I liked to eat when I didn't brown-bag. He was very friendly and talked to Patty, who had joined me for lunch, and me. Patty and I never mentioned that we recognized who he was, and he never mentioned it either; we simply chatted like we were neighbors. I just felt he wanted to be treated that day like an ordinary person, not a star. I could have let him talk forever because I liked listening to his voice, but I knew that he, like we, had come there for the delicious food.

SNIPPET 044 - Music Clefs

First, I'll give you a few facts you need to know about written music. The importance of your having this knowledge will become apparent, hopefully, toward the end of this Snippet. However, if you are already familiar with musical notation, just skip the rest of this paragraph. A music staff consists of a basic set of five horizontal lines on and between which notes are written, with the placement of each note indicating its pitch; partial lines are added above and below as needed to add notes above or below the basic staff. A music clef is a symbol written at the beginning of a music staff to indicate the range of pitch of the notes that follow. There are two major clefs. The treble or G clef shows the position of G above middle C on the second line from the bottom of the staff and indicates the higher pitched portion of musical notes. The bass or F clef shows, basically by its two dots, the position of F below middle C on the fourth line and indicates the lower pitched portion of musical notes. The treble clef looks like a fancy ampersand and the bass clef looks like a backward C followed by a colon. The line between the two staffs in the sketch shows where the note middle C is located in relation to them.

I designed and made all of the twirling outfits that I wore, during high school, for twirling exhibitions and contests and then, during college, for my position as majorette until my senior year and then as "solo twirler" for the Stetson University marching band. One of the reasons I was chosen for the last position was that I twirled two batons at a time and was the only one there who could. Twirling two

SNIPPETS (bits and pieces of love and life) by CAROLE

batons was one of the requirements for being a member of the prestigious majorette corps that marched in front of the Palm Beach High School band. In order to discontinue playing the much-too-heavy-to-suit-me bell lyre in the PBHS marching band, I had learned to twirl one baton the summer before my sophomore year and became a member of the twirling corps that marched behind the band. That had turned out to be a lot of fun that school year and even more the next as captain. To accomplish my next goal, I had learned to twirl two batons and was a majorette my senior year. The dual solo twirlers for PBHS could twirl, or juggle really, three batons although they usually twirled only two. I couldn't master the first requirement of juggling three balls so never attempted twirling three batons.

Stetson's colors were green and white, so, for my college years, I made my mock-turtle-neck-leotard-style outfits using those two colors or gold which was an additional, acceptable color for usage if it were shiny fabric type like lamé or metallic or sequin. Each of my three favorite outfits was based on one of those colors.

The gold leotard was made of gold lamé fabric and trimmed with gold sequins hand-sewn in a random pattern of triangles. The gold (a good color for me) outfit caught the light, shining and glittering with every movement; the look made me feel bright and cheerful.

The green one was made of bright-but-rich-deep-green velvet fabric and trimmed with five-inch white fringe that came around the neck and over the shoulder near the armholes and formed a "W" at the bust-line in front and similarly around the hips but with an upside-down "W" in the front. The fringe on top and on bottom of that outfit emphasized my twenty-three-inch waist, giving the illusion that I had a perfect hourglass figure. The shade of green complemented my natural coloring. The fringe, swaying to-and-fro and outward as I moved and turned and strutted, captured the attention of the audience thus enticing them to watch my twirling—great for my ego!

My third favorite was decorated for pure, lighthearted fun. The pattern of the decoration precipitated the need to give you the information about music clefs. The leotard was made of white corduroy, even though white is not a good color for me to wear, and trimmed with green sequins. The pattern I designed for the sequins was a music staff, beginning with a treble clef covering my left breast (designating the upper or higher pitch), running diagonally down and around my body, and ending with a bass clef on my buttocks (designating the lower). I don't know if anyone ever caught the significance of the design; no one ever mentioned it. But *I* knew, and now *you* know.

SNIPPET 045 - Two Rays of Sunshine

I had landed in Orange Memorial Hospital in Orlando two weeks after shattering a vertebra between my shoulder blades. I didn't know it was crushed until the orthopedic specialist there showed me the X-rays. He had taken a small rubber mallet and gently tapped along my spine until the pain indicated the area damaged.

"It's probably your sixth thoracic vertebra," he diagnosed, "so we'll X-ray that area of your back to see exactly what type of damage has been done and how extensive it is."

The X-ray showed that it was that exact vertebra; and not only was it crushed, but my spinal cord was being pinched in that area by the bone fragments. The pinching was stopping the flow of nerve messages to my lower extremities and that was what was causing the paralysis in my toes and the numbness that was gradually creeping its way up my legs.

At Stetson University where I was a freshman, I had been seen performing, twirling my two batons, by a small group of male gymnasts with a trampoline/trapeze act for the university; they had asked me to join their group. They were willing to help me acquire the necessary skills and I had gone to work out with them in the gymnasium the first day of fall semester classes. After practicing jumps on the trampoline off and on for about an hour, they felt that I was ready to practice grabbing the hands of the hanging trapezist, swinging like a pendulum with him, and dropping back to the trampoline. On the second jump trying to get high enough to reach the trapezist's hands, the landing knocked the breath out of me, so I stopped momentarily, then tried again; that time the pain forced me to quit for the day.

The next day the pain was still bothering me and I found it difficult to carry my books to and from class and to carry my tray in the cafeteria. Many people, mostly guys, helped me do those tasks but, although I appreciated their help and liked the attention, I wanted to be nondependent. I also needed to regain the ability to maintain concentration in my classes and studying. I was getting quite concerned and decided to visit the infirmary to find out what might be the matter.

"It's probably strained muscles, judging from your symptoms. We'll give you heat treatments and muscle relaxants to help you give those muscles a rest. Let people continue to carry things for you," the nurse concluded.

I followed the nurse's instructions daily, with no improvement in my condition. By the middle of the second week, my toes had lost sensation and my legs had begun to feel a bit numb. The nurse asked the infirmary doctor to examine me and I showed him where the majority of the pain was located in my lower back and hips. The developed X-rays of that area showed nothing wrong.

"You will have to see an orthopedic specialist," stated the doctor, "because I am unable to determine what is causing your symptoms."

After that consultation, I phoned my parents. They arranged for me to see a specialist at the hospital where Edith was in training to become a registered nurse and where my mom had trained for her RN years before.

So..., that's how I ended up in Orlando.

Because my spinal cord was pinched, I was admitted to the hospital and immediately put into bed in hip traction, consisting of a canvas harness, around my hips, attached, underneath my body at the bottom of the harness, by a ring to a long cord with a fifteen-pound weight at its end, hanging over a pulley affixed to the frame at the foot of my bed. The traction worked fine as long as you stayed on your back; but I sometimes forgot, or was asleep, and rolled onto my side, and the weight quickly yanked me, sliding down the sheet, to the foot of the bed. Incidentally, that is also how you take the tension off so you can detach the harness from the weight when you need to get out of bed.

I had to wear a shoulder-to-hip body brace whenever I was upright, except for bathing, during the next eighteen months, so I was measured and fitted for a custom-built one. I was so relieved after learning that I didn't have to wear a body cast, that I didn't mind at all having to wear a brace. The brace was expertly made, consisting of leather-covered, form-fitting, aluminum bars with felt added on the side next to your skin, and canvas plate and straps. Four length-wise bars, two in the back and two at the sides, and two cross-wise bars, one under the shoulder blades and one at the hips, were attached to each other. That framework was attached on each side by three adjustable, canvas straps that fit into prong-teeth buckles on the canvas piece covering the lower front of the body. The top of the framework was held in place by straps attached to the bars at the top of the shoulders and encircling the arms. (I hope you made it through the tedious description of my brace because you will need this knowledge when you read about my blue lips.)

Since Edith was in nurses' training at that hospital, she could come visit me for a few minutes between classes and floor duty. She must have mentioned it to her fellow students because many student nurses were soon aware that her sister was a patient. I was lying in bed in traction one afternoon about my fourth day, feeling really sad and in a lot of pain because my muscles hurt from the constant pull of the traction, like you feel after you over-exercise and try to use your muscles that are sooo sore. Suddenly, the door banged open against the wall, and into my room, two smiling, teenage boys burst like two rays of sunshine.

"A couple of student nurses told us there was a lonely girl up on the third floor that needed some cheering up, so we dashed right over," the one pushing the wheelchair said, bubbly grinning. He was fifteen and had his right hand completely bandaged. He raised it to show me and continued, "Surgery to fix my hand."

The sixteen-year old in the wheelchair spoke next. "I was in an accident and hurt my head and arm and leg." It was rather obvious from the bandages on his head and the casts on one arm and one leg.

They stayed and chatted for about an hour and said they had to get back to their rooms but would return each day until one or more of us was dismissed.

The next day, during the time I was allowed up out of traction in bed to get adjusted to walking while wearing a brace, they showed up; and we all went for a walk down the halls. We took walks together (one rode, of course), meandering around the hospital grounds on the sidewalks under and through the shady trees and out in the bright sunshine, every day afterwards; that is, every day until I stayed gone too long one afternoon, missing the heat and massage therapy for my back, and got confined to my room.

They were wonderful companions that I missed, but never saw or heard of again, after I was discharged from the hospital and sent home first. The two of them had teamed up to help one another through their grief and tragic losses. The younger boy had lost most of his hand; the surgeons were able to save only his thumb, little finger, and half of his palm after a firecracker, he was preparing to throw from his hand, exploded prematurely and *blew* away the rest. The older boy had not only been hurt but had lost a close friend. They had been riding together on a motorcycle and he was seated behind his friend, who was killed instantly, when they hit the coupling between two train cars sitting in the middle of the road at night. They hadn't seen the train because the one headlight on the bike shone in between the two cars making it appear that the road ahead was clear.

Yet, in spite of all that, those "two rays of sunshine" had taken the time to cheer up a sad, lonely teenage girl who had just a broken back.

SNIPPET 046 - Blue Lips

The one marvelous, redeeming, inherent feature of a body brace is that it gives the wearer instant perfect posture. Whenever I was wearing it at Stetson University that entire year of 1956, I felt like the brace made me look *fat*, but apparently others didn't notice it under my clothing. At least, no one seemed to be aware of the fact that I never bent at the waist but always lowered my haunches to pick up items that I sometimes dropped onto the ground. Other students would simply comment on how straight my back was and how well I carried myself. Rapping on the side bar of my brace, I would reply, "Oh, it's extremely easy when you are wearing a full-body brace."

However, because I did feel fat wearing it, every morning I would tighten it around my waist and abdomen as much as I thought was snug, but comfortable, in order to make it as close to my body as possible. One morning, at the end of my nine o'clock class, I wasn't feeling well and asked one of my fellow students to walk with me to the infirmary; I was afraid I might faint on the way.

The nurse took one look at me and said, "Your lips are ghastly blue! You aren't getting sufficient oxygen."

She marched me straight into the examination room and, after making me take off my dress, she reached over and quickly unfastened my brace. The sudden rush of air into my lungs was exhilarating!

Apparently, each morning I had been fastening the canvas front a little tighter with the pronged-held, adjustable straps until, on that day, I could scarcely breathe, much less, deeply. The nurse dismissed me after I promised to be more careful and not so vain in the future.

I was, and I felt fine thereafter.

SNIPPET 047 - My Stetson Hat

As part of the required uniform, everyone who played an instrument in the Stetson University marching band wore a hat made by the John B. Stetson Company hat manufacturer. Although majorettes weren't required to wear them, I decided to buy one of those elegant hats anyway to wear on special occasions since the purchase price—$6.18—was far below cost. To keep the wind from blowing it off your head, you were advised to buy your hat to fit quite snugly; for me, the size was 6 7/8. The color of my felt hat is "fawn" (what the company called it at that time). The interior of the hat's dome is lined with a bright red satin fabric embossed with the Stetson emblem in brown and protected by a plastic covering sewn over it. The interior leather band is embossed with a similar emblem and the words, "Royal DeLuxe Stetson"—all in gold. A narrow flattened, round, grosgrain ribbon adorns the exterior at the inside edge of the brim. Even the wrap-around side of the burnt-umber-colored hatbox is decorated in an endless, pen-and-ink-style design, a scene of cowboys rounding up and branding cattle, printed in dark brown; each cowboy is wearing the exact style of hat that is stored inside. Three times, evenly spaced, around the brown side of the oval hatbox lid is the word "Stetson" printed in burnt-umber.

A few years ago, I added a red feather, tucked under the ribbon, to give my hat a little color. I like to wear it in the winter with my camel overcoat and to special events that call for western attire.

I wonder what my 1955 "Stetson" is worth today in 2002; it looks brand new and is in perfect condition. The hatbox looks almost new too; it is slightly aged and the cellophane inside has turned brown, crumbled, and fallen beneath the cardboard that holds the hat in place. But, I would never sell or give it away—too many wonderful memories would vanish with it.

SNIPPET 048 - Smashed Thumb

A smashed thumb can be a horrible, painful thing. For me it turned out to be a gift; nevertheless, when it happened, it hurt too much to think about anything else.

I was the last one to hop out of our sorority sister's car; several of us had gone to town to buy things. Marcia, my roommate and good friend, had jokingly entered me in the "Miss DeLand Pageant" and I needed to buy lipstick and nail polish. I was hurrying and, frankly, not paying any attention to what I was doing; consequently, I quickly slammed the car door and tried to scurry off. I traveled only an arm's length because my left thumb was stuck in the car door. I screamed in pain, snatched open the door, and stared at my swelling thumb, bleeding profusely internally under the nail. One of the other sorority sisters dashed into a nearby drugstore and got me a cup of ice with water in which to immerse my smashed thumb until I could get back to the Stetson University infirmary to have it taken care of. I remember my thumb getting so numb that you could bang it on something and never feel a thing. The nurse, and then the doctor, tried boring holes in my thumb nail with huge needles and a scalpel to try to let out some of the blood and reduce the pressure, but all that did was to leave several holes in the nail. I left the infirmary quite distressed because the beauty pageant was only several days away, and my talent, unfortunately, was twirling two batons.

On the day of the pageant I went to see the infirmary doctor and asked him to give me a shot of novocaine or something in my thumb so I wouldn't be in such pain. "I have to be able to twirl two batons for my talent in the 'Miss DeLand' contest tonight," I explained.

"That is precisely why I won't do it for you," he said. "If I do, you won't be able to twirl at all because you won't be able to feel any baton with your left hand. Just ignore the pain and twirl your best. You'll be all right and do just fine."

"Hmmm, I hadn't really thought of it like that, but you are absolutely right. Thank you for the advice." I got up from the wood, consultation chair. "Oh, and thanks for your confidence in me." I left and went to practice for the last time before I had to get dressed for the contest.

The individual interviews of the fifteen or so competitors by the group of men and women judges were held in the late afternoon. We were instructed to wear our "Sunday best" attire, and, from the looks of them, the judges were too. Just outside the interview room, we gathered for the introduction of judges and contestants. As our names were called out from the official pageant list, I noticed that most of the other contestants were also Stetson students with three of us having similar sounding first names—Karylin, Karoline, and Carole (me).

My interview came toward the last of them. At the end of it, one of the judges asked me what had happened to my hand and whether or not I planned to continue in the contest since my thumb might impair my twirling performance, during the talent competition, causing me to receive a lower total score. I explained how I had smashed my thumb and assured them that the doctor said I would be fine and that I was anxious to perform that evening anyway.

During the talent portion, I simply ignored my thumb and twirled as if nothing were wrong. My two-baton routine turned out to be the best that I had ever twirled up to that point; I was so proud of my accomplishment, I could neither stop smiling nor feeling grateful to the doctor for refusing my request. I had designed and made all the beautiful dresses that I wore during the pageant and that added even more to my confidence and helped me throughout the bathing suit and evening gown competitions.

The greatest surprise of all came when the winner was proclaimed. The master-of-ceremonies announced, "The second runner-up is Carol"…and I thought he was finished…"line."

Oh, I think he said "Karoline." traipsed, then focused, in my brain. Karoline walked forward during the applause to stand beside the MC. *He did say "Karoline."*

"The first runner-up is Carol" …and again I thought he was finished…"lyn."

Oh my, he said "Karylin." That's not me. And Karylin walked forward, like Karoline had done. I was stunned—and left standing all alone, shaking!

"And the new 'Miss DeLand 1958' is *Carole*."

I couldn't believe what I had just heard and kept repeating aloud, "It can't be true! It can't be true!" Marcia was just as shocked as I

SNIPPETS (bits and pieces of love and life) by CAROLE

was. The photo in the newspaper the next morning showed the happiness I felt.

One prize was "The New American Girl Bracelet Watch" by Bulova®, a beautiful white gold one with a small diamond chip within the V-shaped decorations on each side of the watch face, packaged in a decorative, blue-plastic storage case. I still wear that watch whenever John and I go out for dinner or formal occasions; the bracelet has gotten a few scratches but the watch still works and keeps great time.

What started as a joke ended shockingly different than anyone expected, and probably all because of a smashed thumb which gave me the confidence I needed against all the odds.

SNIPPET 049 - Two Parakeets

Winning something is a wonderful experience no matter how great or small the prize.

Pat, that's what I called her before she grew up and told me I had to call her Patty, had entered a contest at a West Palm Beach pet store.

I had entered a beauty contest—actually, Marcia had entered me, as a joke. But I won, shocking everyone including Marcia and me. I remember, after being left standing alone and hearing my name announced, shaking my head, and babbling aloud over and over, "It can't be true." The prizes I received were a blue overnight case complete with mirror and satin lining, a Bulova® bracelet-watch, a portable radio, an honorary membership in the DeLand Chamber of Commerce, a trophy, and, of course, a ribbon to wear with the coveted title "Miss DeLand" printed in gold letters.

None of my family was aware of the contest; I hadn't bothered to tell them because it was a lark, and I was in it just for fun. As soon as I got back to the dorm after the pageant ended, I phoned home collect, naturally, as all students did that had no money to feed the pay phone in the only booth on the third floor. Mom answered but had to leave for work on the night shift at the hospital, so I had to make the call brief and quickly explain what had happened that evening. She couldn't believe it was true either but was very happy for me and told me she had *always* thought I was *beautiful*. Moms tell that to all their daughters if they love them, but I liked hearing it anyway, because "it makes you feel special."

Sheila, who was soon-to-be-fourteen and, therefore, a teenager who understood the thrill and impact of winning a city title which meant being a contestant for the state title heading toward "Miss America," thought it was the greatest thing that could ever happen. But, reality sets in very quickly when you talk to your much younger, eight-and-a-half-year-old sister who, you think, is as excited for you as you are and everyone else in the family is, having just been relayed the news and handed the phone.

"Wow," Pat exclaimed in my ear, "we both won something today. I won two parakeets and a cage!"

SNIPPET 050 - Beauty Contest

As "Miss DeLand," I participated in the "Miss Florida Pageant" that was held in Sarasota in July 1958. What an interesting experience that was! I had *no idea* what it was really all about until I got there. I knew that I would be judged for beauty in bathing suit and in evening gown, for talent, and for speaking ability in interviews with judges, but was clueless about the rest of the routine. Others seemed well prepared and rehearsed on everything. I should have simply enjoyed it as a lark but thought I should take it seriously; afterwards, I realized my mistake because I was much too tense and trying too hard to really be at my best during the pageant.

Mom was clueless too, but she learned a lot by listening and tried to tell me just to enjoy myself. From the conversations she overheard early in the week, she surmised that my roommate, who was both beautiful and a talented ballerina, was going to be crowned "Miss Florida" at the end. I did try to loosen up a bit and just watch the events unfold; but it was just too difficult—I wanted to win.

In order to be judged equally in the bathing suit competition, we were all issued the same style white suits; however, in reality, the bathing suit made you less than equal if the suit style or color was not flattering to your body type or skin tone. Nevertheless, the group photos taken of us wearing our matching swim suits turned out especially nice and made wonderful mementos.

Travelling in special-driver-designated, city buses, we were bused all over Sarasota to attend different outdoor events, to visit beautiful gardens, and to dine in nice restaurants, accompanied, most of the time, by photographers from various newspaper organizations. That part was really fun for the contestants and even for our mothers or chaperones when they were invited to go with us. When they weren't at our sides, they were usually spending time chatting together or watching us rehearse. Those were the times when Mema found out what was happening behind the scenes. I was so glad she was there that week at the pageant with me; she was always wonderful to have around and I needed her comments not only for giving me encouragement, but for helping me cope with the reality of such an intense competition.

It was especially interesting to watch the interplay of the other girls vying to outdo each other to win the title of "Miss Congeniality." My mom and I guessed that "Miss Sarasota" would win that title and weren't surprised when she did. Having the advantage of being in her home town, when she was behaving, like most of the others, a bit overly friendly, it didn't hit you that way at all; she just appeared enthusiastic about sharing all the wonderful charm of her city with you. As I recall, in her talent act, which was first-rate, she wore a black sequin gown and sang *That Old Black Magic* accompanied by her own backup band.

The talent show was not up to the caliber of today's pageants and it played a smaller part in proportion to your physical beauty. I did OK twirling my two batons but I didn't sparkle like I did in the contest in DeLand; I was trying too hard not to make a mistake in my routine or drop a baton, and didn't, but I didn't feel great about my performance. The whole week seemed unreal and I felt somewhat out of place. Since I didn't really know what the contest entailed or how to make myself fit in better, I just allowed myself to be herded around with the group rather than be treated as an individual. I was really grateful to have had the experience anyway. However, if I had been given the opportunity to do it over again, I would have researched and prepared myself better and then just enjoyed every moment, not caring whether I won or lost, but just doing my best.

Each contestant received a white gold "Miss America" style, Bulova® watch to wear during and after the contest. I still have my watch, although it has a different glass crystal and band now, keeping it for everyday wear or sometimes for special occasions, alternating it with the one, still completely intact and more ornate, that I received as "Miss DeLand."

Luckily for most other contestants, we were judged *head-to-toe*. Some of the girls with the prettiest faces and upper bodies had so-so legs and the ugliest feet. I wish we had been judged from *toe-to-head*. — I had nice-looking feet and pretty legs.

SNIPPET 051 - Just Different

On our second date John asked me to go steady which, according to that era's standards, means you don't dare date anyone else.

My answer was a very firm: "No. I just broke off an engagement and want to date other guys." He had decided that I was the one he would marry (we had never even kissed), so I was afraid that my statement would end our relationship.

Never underestimate a determined person.

After that night we saw each other just as *friends*—friends who ate breakfast, lunch, and dinner together, studied together, attended classes together, went to coffee hours and danced together, and, on Sundays, also attended church together. We dated other people and we even dated each other. Whenever John took me back to the dorm after one of our friendly excursions, he would casually walk me up the steps and across the porch, playfully shove me through the doorway, then slam the screen door and hold it closed between us—all while we continued chatting. This routine continued to be repeated for over a year and a half.

I once asked a sorority sister, Janice, who knew him from Savannah High School, "Is there something the matter with John? He never, ever kisses me good-bye."

"There's nothing wrong," she casually assured me. "Savannah boys are just *different*."

I'll say!

SNIPPET 052 - First Kiss

One evening as I waited in the dorm parlor for John to pick me up for dinner in The Commons, I glanced out the window and my heart flipped, as usual, when I spotted him walking from his fraternity house, where he lived, toward Chaudoin Hall, where I lived. (The Commons was what everyone called the building where the cafeteria was located, even after it was the Student Union Building, built after I started at Stetson.) We both had to eat there. Each scholarship student was required to buy a meal ticket for three meals per day per semester; if you had to be at Stetson on scholarship that meant you were too poor to eat anywhere else, and we both were, so we couldn't. Since I was on time for a change, I decided to surprise him by walking out to meet him on the sidewalk across the street; besides I couldn't wait to be near him. Why wait in the parlor!

I had gotten across the street as he approached cutting across the vacant lot on the corner. When John saw me standing on the sidewalk, he switched from walking to running toward me, whisked me off my feet, threw me fireman-style over his shoulder, and continued running down the sidewalk.

We both giggled as I tried to say, half-teasing-half-singsong, between the jostles, "Jooohnn, put me down!" I really didn't want him to put me down and stop holding me, but I could hardly breathe bouncing on my stomach against his shoulder like that.

He loved being physical with me in play. He would nudge me off sidewalks so I had to walk on the grass; he would pick me up so I could touch the ceiling in a room; he used me as a weight for bench presses and overhead presses; he would whirl me around so fast while we were dancing that my feet would fly through the air. (I felt so sorry for the people my feet unintentionally hit, most of them right in the stomach; if you were one of them, I apologize again.) What fun we had! — And still do; the playfulness has slowed down, due to John's PD, but never stopped.

After being *just friends* for a year and a half, one night when he returned me to my dorm, instead of shoving me through the doorway, he put his arms around me and kissed me for the very first time. The kiss was sensually spectacular, and I *loved* it! It was the kiss I had been practicing for since Terry and I, third- and second-graders, first kissed and liked it so much that we practiced every afternoon after school and on weekends for the whole school year until he, like Dixie, moved away.

I asked John yesterday, July 14, 2002, where he learned how to kiss.

"From Deb. You remember her. We dated off and on all through high school; since we lived so close to each other and both liked each other, we became very good friends. We even studied together sometimes."

Yes, I do remember Deb; we visited with her, her husband, Mark, and their two young daughters at her parents' house across the street when they were back visiting and we were visiting John's parents sometime after we got married. Thank you, Deb! (or Debra, if you prefer to be called that now.) I still love his kisses and my heart still flips when he comes into view.

But, that first kiss *we* shared was "the kiss that launched a marriage!"

SNIPPET 053 - Middle C

Marcia, my roommate for most of several years while we were both at Stetson University, was a Liberal Arts student majoring in elementary education. I used to tease her about reading "kiddie-lit" (that's what I called her text books) while I had to struggle reading real literature by the great authors; I was majoring in English and it took me much longer to read and comprehend one assignment than it took her.

The only time I was of any help to her was when she was studying "music for teachers." Since all elementary school teachers back then had to teach everything, including music appreciation and class singing, she had to take a course in that too. But, Marcia is tone-deaf, and the thought, of taking the course and passing the part of the exam where you had to sing while leading a group of fellow students, panicked her.

"What am I going to do?" she asked me quite distressed.

"No problem!" I reassured her, feeling quite smug. I had taken a voice lesson each week while I was a "two-week" music major in the fall of 1955 and a few others while I was in high school. "Just choose a song in the key of C that has the first note you sing being middle C and I'll teach you how to sing it."

It's a good thing we started the task early in the semester because it took about three months for her to find a song and to learn to sing middle C.

Each evening, after we both got back to our room, we would begin her lesson with Marcia playing the note on her pitch pipe, more for my benefit than hers, since she didn't comprehend the tone anyway. She had purchased the pipe because she was required to— "you need it, not only for the class, but also for your entire teaching career"—according to the professor. After the note sounded, she would try to match the tone with her voice and I would correct her pitch up or down until it matched perfectly. After a few times doing it with the pitch pipe, I made her do it a few more times, but without the pipe.

Eventually, during the day or evening whenever I could, I would, at random times, point to Marcia and command, "Sing middle C." She would sing the note and we would check her pitch against the tone from her pitch pipe. Near exam week, she could actually sing it anytime, anywhere, and without the pitch pipe.

After conquering that, she practiced hard and learned to sing the one song. If she could just pass the exam, she was home free; she had found out that where she planned to teach back home, the school had music teachers that rotated through the different classes, and she wouldn't have to teach music at all. We practiced the entire scenario right up to the hour before the exam: Marcia would play the tone on her pitch pipe, for the benefit of the professor and her fellow classmates, and then sing the song from her rote memory while leading the class.

At the end of the semester when grades were posted, Marcia was thrilled with her well-earned "A." I was really proud of her. After she and Roy got married and later adopted their first child, a girl, they named her Christie because they liked that name. I like to think she's my namesake and, because my *middle* initial is "C" for Christie, I hope that name reminds Marcia of *middle C*.

SNIPPET 054 - Her First Husband

My parents got married in a simple ceremony after church one Sunday, August 13, 1933. A friend took a single black and white photo of them, dressed in their finest outfits, holding hands, sitting on a bench, to commemorate the occasion. You can tell by looking at the photo that my dad, George, was tall, dark, rather handsome, and weighed about 135 pounds, and that my mom, Myrtle, was petite, fair, attractive, and weighed about 110 pounds.

George, who turned twenty-one on May 14, was an ambulance driver for the only funeral home in Melbourne. He met Myrtle, who would be twenty-four on August 23, a couple of months earlier at the hospital where she worked as a nurse. He fell in love immediately and asked her to marry him. Her reply was a resounding: "No." (Does this scenario sound familiar?)

Nevertheless, they kept dating within this short time span and George kept asking the same question and getting the same answer. Since he wanted to get married *now*, he took the next drastic step. At the end of their last date as singles, after Myrtle went inside the hospital dormitory where she and the other unmarried nurses lived, he sat on the front stoop and yelled at the top of his lungs—"Myrtle, if you don't come out right now and agree to marry me, I'm going to sit here and holler until you do!"—and he kept on hollering. Threats from the hospital administration to fire her, and to expel her and her belongings from the dorm, in order to get rid of George, convinced her that she had better marry him.

As the years went by, Mom maintained her size fairly well and still looked like the woman in the photo, just older. Daddy, however, gained about seventy to eighty pounds and didn't look at all like the man in the photo, unless you carefully studied the photo and compared it and him side by side.

Since I hadn't seen it in a long time, I had forgotten about the wedding picture until one afternoon during one of my visits home from college in 1959. As I was walking through the living room, I spotted it sitting atop the clutter on the back of the upright piano that my dad had bought recently at a garage sale. (No one in the family even knew how to play a piano; but that didn't matter; it was cheap

SNIPPETS (bits and pieces of love and life) by CAROLE

and sounded OK.) I picked up the frame to hold it closer and was gazing at the photo when my dad walked into the room.

"That's my favorite picture of us," he reminisced. "I have a lot of fun with it too. Visitors always admire the couple in it and say to me: 'You know, George, I recognize Myrtle; but who is that man sitting beside her?'"

I started smiling as I watched him, his eyes twinkling and his face smirking, as he continued to speak.

"I always say, 'Oh, him? — That's her *first* husband.'"

SNIPPET 055 - *Put Me Down*

When I was small, I used to tease my mom that I could pick her up if I wanted to.

She always said, "Don't you dare, you could hurt yourself!"

So I didn't; I just teased. About the time I was entering tenth grade, I thought I was getting almost big enough; I was four feet ten inches tall, weighed eighty-nine pounds, and had begun growing fast.

At school I ate as many as five sandwiches for lunch, two or three if I bought them on Fridays at one of the three soda shops across the street from the campus of Palm Beach High and lower-grade schools or four or five on the days that I brought them from home. I liked homemade sandwiches better because those had lots of filling. You purchased your lunch that day at the soda shop that sold the particular kind you wanted or that sold the better version of it. A sandwich, mostly bread with thin pieces of some type of food between the slices, cost ten cents, and a chilidog cost fifteen cents. I either bought three sandwiches or two chilidogs so I could also buy a drink, either watered-down orange juice for ten cents or a "destroyer" for fifteen cents.

Whenever I could afford it, I bought the "destroyer" because I liked it best. If you aren't familiar with that drink, it is made using one squirt of each syrup, like cherry, vanilla, cola, root-beer, etc., with an extra squirt of chocolate, from all the soda fountain pumps leading up from the under-counter containers, plus carbonated water. I don't think you can buy them any more because I don't know where you would find a soda shop with a real fountain for making drinks. Even if I did, I couldn't drink a "destroyer" anyway because most of the syrups now contain corn products, to which I have become allergic. Too bad I can't eat that quantity of food anymore either because I would like to; my brain has never quite adjusted to eating less; I just have to quit before my appestat finally signals "halt."

After a few months I weighed about 105 pounds and had grown several inches in height. One afternoon I was talking to my mom about what had happened at school, like I did every day, when I suddenly decided to tease her.

"You know, I could pick you up if I wanted to."

She replied, as she always did, "Don't you dare, you could hurt yourself!"

But I did pick her up, and I didn't get hurt. She weighed about 120 pounds but was about the same height; she was surprised (probably shocked), and so was I, that I could grab her right around her hips, lift her straight up off the floor, and walk several steps with her.

She just hollered, and kept hollering, "Put me down!"

"OK," I delightedly chuckled as I set her back down.

It's interesting that about six years later I was hollering almost the same thing to John as I bounced along on his shoulder, being carried fireman-style, as he ran down the sidewalk.

SNIPPET 056 - *The Other "Carole"*

It's rare to find someone whose first and last name are pronounced the same as your own, but it usually doesn't cause problems unless you happen to live in the same dormitory in college. That is precisely what happened to me. The fact that we spelled our names differently didn't help because everyone spelled our names the same. As soon as she moved in, I apparently disappeared for all practical purposes. She not only got my messages when I was out, but then she sometimes neglected to tell me that she had gotten them. I got a bit livid about it when it came to my "friend" John even though I tried to hold my temper. He was a sophomore and I was for a while a junior and then a senior the first year that we started dating; the other Karyl was a freshman. Since protocol (totally outdated in my opinion) stated that sophomore men dated freshmen, maybe sophomore, women, but definitely not junior or senior women, I sometimes missed my dates with John because the girls working at the desk behind the reception window (where residents signed out and in) would call *her*, not me.

One evening when John came to get me for dinner, the girl at the desk told him I had signed out and was gone. He left and went to dinner without me while I waited upstairs in my room for him to arrive and have me paged on the loud speaker in the hallway. After about an hour, with closing time for the cafeteria approaching, I went on to dinner alone and arrived just as he was leaving the building. We were both distressed at each other until we discovered what had happened. Thereafter, when John came to get me, he either met me where I waited for him in the parlor or made sure that the receptionist used the correct speaker to page the *upperclassman Carole* on the third floor north wing and not the *freshman Karyl* on the first floor south wing.

SNIPPET 057 - Benches

We became quite fond of benches after our first kiss when John and I were dating at Stetson University. Neither of us had a car or much spending money; most dates were simply walks around the campus after sitting and drinking coffee or other beverage in the Hat Rack coffee shop in the Student Union Building. There were benches scattered throughout the campus and some in the Forest of Arden where there was an outdoor stage for events like concerts and commencement exercises. But the one bench that was protected from the elements, mostly rain in Florida, was underneath the outdoor, concrete stairs leading from the ground locker level to the main floor of the men's gymnasium, and that bench became our favorite.

If you wanted to sit on that particular bench, or stand on it, if you didn't want to be easily seen, you had to claim it early in the evening right after dinner, which we frequently did if we didn't have to do research in the library. It was a wonderful place to sit and talk or just smooch (kiss, if you aren't familiar with that word). The fact that other university people who happened to walk by could see you made you feel very safe there, even after dark. (Actually, the entire campus was quite safe.) We considered it to be *our* bench, and if some other couple got there first, we felt dejected and vowed to get there earlier the next time.

It was rare that others got to use our bench when we wanted it, but we tried to leave it by eight twenty during the week so another couple at least got a chance to grab it for a while. Women had a curfew for being in their dorms, but men had none. The standard curfew during the week was 8:30 P.M. for freshman women and 10:30 P.M. for all others, with later-but-still-unequal curfews applying for both groups on weekends; all women were allowed out again at six o'clock the following morning. Even though I had the later curfew, I tried to allow other non-freshmen women equal opportunity during the week, but freshmen had less than ten minutes to sit on the bench with their boyfriends.

For our home in Hockessin, I decided that I wanted two benches forming the shape "| __" in one corner of our courtyard to go along with the three planters and a small bridge over the faux water. It was part of my overall design. The courtyard tends to get too much rainwater run-off from the roof whenever it rains, so John had poured a concrete flooring with a drain in the center to carry the water away from the house. We didn't want to have rain-gutters installed because we felt that gutters would spoil the ambience of the house. I designed a small stream to meander from the corner of the courtyard at the house, diagonally through the center and over to near the corner by the front gate, ending at the covered walkway to the front doors.

The stream is bordered with large river-smoothed stones and filled in with small to medium slices of greenish-turquoise rock to give the appearance of water. John built a four-foot-long, arched, wood-plank bridge to cover the drain and span the stream. Next to the house the concrete is covered with reddish-brown lava rocks up to the stream, and the other side is covered with washed pebbles like all the rest of the pebbles used around the yard. The benches and planters are made of landscaping timbers (four-by-five each), stacked and vertically or horizontally positioned. John had to build the planters in place because, when finished, each would be too heavy to budge or, even worse, to move in from somewhere else. The planters contain evergreen bushes and one small tree, all of which are self-sufficient and growing despite my "brown thumb."

Those benches in the courtyard are where we like to sit and drink coffee early in the morning on spring weekends and, while waiting for gas-fired, hot-air balloons to appear overhead, we reminisce about "our bench" under the stairs of the men's gym.

One Saturday, we were wandering around the quarry in Avondale looking for stone for John to use to cover the fireplace in the basement room that he planned to transform into an entertainment room, complete with bar, where we could entertain friends before or after dinner. I discovered a huge slab of somewhat-rounded-rectangular-but-arrowhead-shaped stone that appeared smooth enough on the topside to form a rough table surface.

"John. I must have a table made from that stone slab. Please make me one for the back terrace," I declared as soon as my brain had a vivid picture of my new table sitting on one of the stone-aggregate concrete slabs forming the terrace within the back "L" of our house.

"You're kidding," he said looking at me dumbfounded.

"No, I'm really serious. It would be perfect as it will never wear out and it will always be available for use."

After looking at it more closely, he agreed.

We bought the 450-pound-stone slab, carried it home in our maroon Chevy Suburban®, and then John, by sliding it from the maroon-carpeted floor, out the back doorway, and down landscaping timbers, unloaded the slab onto the terrace. He built four support legs out of three concrete blocks each, stacked and cemented together, and then plastered with light-tannish-yellow stucco. Three men friends came over to help hoist the slab into place on the oddly-positioned legs and hold it steady while John inserted wedges to keep it level. He also made four individual bench-like seats using two concrete blocks each, finished to match the table legs, and covering each with a wooden top that fits over the stack.

We like looking at and using our unusual stone-concrete-plaster-wood dining set; we can see it from the dining room, kitchen, and master bedroom. People tend to forget about the construction of the set and try to pick up the heavy, cumbersome seats to move them to a slightly different location. They get foolish looks on their faces when the unattached wooden tops lift off in their hands.

SNIPPET 058 - *Special Languages*

There is something wonderful about "baby-talk." Babies don't need to have us talk to them that way; they understand plain old everyday language just as well, but we use it because we love them. And we use it with adults we love dearly because we become playful, little children when we're around them.

There is something wonderful about "pure-fun-dialect" too. That's the kind that is similar (you know, exactly the same, but different) to "baby-talk."

When John and I were dating at Stetson, the couple that we were most fond of was Marcia and Roy. They are married to each other now too, and when they got married, I was the Maid of Honor. We double-dated and ate together whenever we could. We usually met by the radiator near the backdoor of the parlor in the dorm where Marcia and I shared a room and, although we had a specific time to meet, usually one of us (me, most of the time) arrived late. When the last one joined the group, we always spouted off the same conversation, usually with the last person arriving starting it; we never left for dinner without doing our little routine. The conversation went like this:

"Jee-chet?"
"No. Di-ju?"
"No. Squeet."
"Naa. Da-wa-na."
"Yeh-ya-do."
"K. Squeet."

Then giggling together, we would dash out the door and head to The Commons where the cafeteria was.

Here are the words in the conversation again with their translation:

Jee-chet?   = Did you eat yet?
No. Di-ju?   = No. Did you?
No. Squeet.   = No. Let's go eat.
Naa. Da-wa-na = Naa (harsh "a" as in action, meaning no). Don't want to.

SNIPPETS (bits and pieces of love and life) by CAROLE

Yeh-ya-do.   = Yes, you do.
K. Squeet.   = OK. Let's go eat.

Early on, but after we both knew we did, John and I used "touch-language" when we wanted to say "I love you" but not out loud; we would tap three times on the other person's hand or arm.

We now have friends Karl and Chris, who are also married to each other, with whom we share a language that is sort of a combination of "baby-talk" and "meowing-cat-language" which we sometimes use talking to each other, and all of us talk to cats that way. We have had four cats in the past and they currently have eight or nine; I lose count. We even purr occasionally when we're happy.

Sometimes John and I will do something silly when we phone Karl and Chris. Each of us will say every other word in the sentences at the beginning of our conversation. It's fun and it always make us laugh and them wonder what's going on when it catches them off guard.

We also cheerfully say, "Squeeze me" instead of "Excuse me" to friends who are in the way, touching them to get them to move aside, so we can walk past. The statement really comes in handy when train-traveling on the American Orient Express for a week at a time and having to walk through very narrow corridors. (Passing other passengers in a train corridor is an interesting challenge; it is much easier to do if both persons involved turn their bodies toward the center of the corridor, and the one next to the window backs up so that his/her buttocks extends into the space provided by the window sill; that way the two of you get several more inches of space for navigating.)

I'm sure there are other unique languages that people use that I forgot to mention, and I hope you use them. These special ways of talking bring people closer together. So, in my opinion, if you never talk in some unique way to your spouse and special friends (at least in private conversations), you're just *too old and stodgy* to have any.

SNIPPET 059 - *Dear John*

Jonathan's reply letter stated: "I knew what kind of letter it was when I saw 'Dear John.'"

How could I have made such a terrible faux pas? That was the kind of letter it was, but I didn't mean to call him "John" instead of "Jonathan," which I and everyone else called him. I guess I was so wrapped up in *John* that I made a Freudian slip. I wrote him an apology, but how could I ever make up for the mistake; I certainly never intended to hurt him any more than what I was already doing.

Jonathan had spent the previous weekend, "Parents Weekend," at Stetson University that February of 1960, staying in one of the men's dorms and visiting with me so he could meet my parents. Mom knew that the "Dear John" was imminent; a month later she told me that when she and I had chatted together alone that weekend, I had talked only about John, like I always did—never Jonathan.

I met Jonathan the previous summer in Tallahassee during the National Intercollegiate Band conference for music-director-selected-university-musicians only. During our break that first morning, he sat down across from me at the table, where I was sitting with two other musicians in the coffee shop, and introduced himself to the group. He played trumpet in the Clemson Band and was one of the major players in the band at the conference. I had seen him on stage during the rehearsal; I was just an alternate bassoonist so had been sitting with the other alternates in the audience seats of the music hall just watching and listening. Alternate musicians had to be familiar with the conducting and music in case we were asked to play in the public concert at the conclusion of the conference.

I don't remember the exact conversation around the table, but for some reason ages came up as a topic, and Jonathan looked directly at me and asked, "How old are you?"

"Twenty-two."

"Show me your driver's license," he immediately commanded. "I don't believe you."

I dug the license out of the wallet in my purse and handed it to him. He stared at it—disbelieving, but undoubtedly having to believe it because the license was valid.

"How old are you?" I asked him in return.

He promptly blurted out, "I'm twenty-four."—and no amount of needling by me, or by the others, could coax him into revealing his license.

We quickly exchanged brief personal facts, which you do if you want to date and have only a couple of days before you both have to return home or to summer classes. I liked him immediately, probably because he had a persona very much like John's—a little taller, but very similar muscular physique, sandy blonde crew-cut hair, gorgeous smile, a winning warmth to his personality, and, like John, he was a southern gentleman born and raised in Georgia. I thought I might like him more than John. He too liked to dance, not only ballroom which I soon discovered he did quite well, but also adagio. He did the adagio with younger girls while helping his mother during dance classes that she instructed in her own dance studio. He also liked music as much as I. And, the very best thing for me—Jonathan was *older*!

When we parted, we promised to keep in touch and did. During Thanksgiving break, he invited me to visit at his home to meet his family. When I arrived, his mom told me that I had just missed his birthday celebration the day before.

"Oh, I'm so sorry I missed it," I said, wishing I had been there earlier. "Which one was this?" I added quizzically.

He refused to answer the question and gave his mom a look telling her to ignore the question. That evening when Jonathan and I were sitting out on the porch, he finally broke down from my all-day-persistent badgering.

"Twenty," he sighed in reluctance.

I immediately laughed hysterically but didn't dare tell him why even though he kept insisting that I tell him. The "why" was he just blew the biggest reason for my liking him better than I liked John. He wasn't older than I at all and even was two months *younger* than John!

The Monday after Parents Weekend, Jonathan was still at Stetson as he had planned to leave that afternoon, instead of the previous day when my parents left, so we could spend Sunday evening by ourselves. We were eating lunch in the cafeteria, when suddenly we were startled by John's presence. He had plopped himself down in the chair opposite Jonathan and the two began to glare at each other in a face-off.

Oh dear, let me out of here was all I could think of as I hastily introduced the two so they would know the name of the dead one if it came to that. Mercifully it didn't; they were very cordial to each other through their clenched teeth. But I knew, right then and there, I had to decide between the two. For my mom, it was a "no-brainer." For me, it was more difficult; but as soon as John looked directly at me with those soulful eyes full of pain, it instantly became a "no-brainer" for me too. I said nothing to either about my decision, but I had to write the letter to Jonathan after he left town.

When I met John's parents during Easter vacation, Shirley, his mom, asked me what happened during Parents Weekend. He had told them not to come to Stetson because he was coming home instead. And he stood over her every wakened moment, fuming and not speaking at all, while she sewed several shirts and Bermuda shorts that he insisted she make for him. He totally refused to discuss what he was mad about. As I related all the events of those three days, we both laughed heartily together; she finally understood: — John had known that *Jonathan* would be spending the weekend with *me*.

SNIPPET 060 - The Blouse

We were just saying goodbye outside my dorm one evening after dinner when John started shuffling around and nervously asked me, "What is your waist size?"

Not thinking anything about it and proud that my waist was small, I quickly answered, "It's twenty-three inches."

Then he hesitantly added, "Can I ask you another question?"

"Sure."

"How big are your hips?"

Well, now, aren't we getting just a bit personal here? I was thinking huffishly as I asked John, "Why do you want to know that?"

"Ooohh, just curious."

"Well, if you must know, it's about thirty-eight to thirty-nine inches," I replied, then added, "And, do you need to know my bust size too?" I hoped he wouldn't ask for that measurement also; it was barely thirty-two.

"No, that's all," he replied grinning sheepishly.

The conversation ended and I turned away, dashed into the dorm to go study for a test, and promptly forgot all about it.

A week or so later, on Monday afternoon, John brought me a package. Since I had never met any of his family, it was a total surprise that the package was a gift from his mom. I quickly opened it and pulled out a pair of brown plaid Bermuda shorts (commonly referred to as "bermudas").

"That's why I needed your measurements," he said pointing to the bermudas. "Oh, and there should be a matching blouse in the package too. Shirley (everyone, now including John, called his mother by her first name) made you one to match my shirt. I had only asked her to make us matching bermudas, but she thought it would be nice to have tops as well, so we could have complete outfits. We can wear them Saturday." (Stetson had strict dress codes and for the majority of the time a girl's outfit had to include a skirt; the codes were more relaxed on Saturdays.)

"Wow, this is terrific! Please tell her 'Thank you' for me. I must run up to my room to try them on. See ya later for dinner."

I dashed up to my room on the third floor and tried on the outfit. The bermudas fit perfectly, but the blouse was *huge* and much too long-waisted. Since many boys tend to choose girl friends that look like their mothers and sisters (especially if they are fond of them), Shirley probably assumed that John did. She must have extrapolated from the measurements she was given, mistakenly figuring that I was large-busted like all the women in his family and tall like his sister who was my same age.

I was really glad I knew how to sew and could alter clothes. Using the sewing machine provided in the dorm, I remade the blouse to fit, but never mentioned to John anything about having to do that.

Saturday, we wore the outfits with similar socks and shoes. I thought we looked adorable and wished Shirley could have seen us. We didn't discuss it, but John appeared to be just as excited and proud of our matching outfits as I was. We both enjoyed looking like twins.

Several weeks later, John's dad drove down to DeLand to take the two of us back home with him for Easter weekend so we could visit and I could meet the rest of the family.

After the car was parked in the driveway and John had opened the car door for me, I got out and starting walking up the sidewalk toward their house while he and his dad got the luggage.

Shirley must have heard the car drive up, because the front screen door swung open and she stepped out onto the porch. When she spotted *me*, her mouth dropped slightly open and she simply stood there—statue-like—staring. After a few seconds, she shook her head to regain her composure and stammered, "I am *so* sorry for staring. You don't look *at all* like I expected!"

"Yeah," I laughed, "I could tell from the *blouse*."

SNIPPET 061 - *Playmates*

I had never heard of *Playboy* magazine until I found out about it after I said the *wrong* thing to some of John's fraternity brothers.

I always thought that men should be able to enjoy looking at beautiful women; I enjoyed looking at beautiful people, both male and female, myself. After John and I got married, I gave him a subscription to *Playboy* during grad school, thinking he would like having this enjoyable diversion from his studies. As it turned out, he was too busy to take the time, except that he did glance at the pictures that I briefly thrust in front of him on his open textbook as I read the magazine myself.

When I worked with men or traveled with them on business trips, I always made them, especially Evan, aware of beautiful women within sight so they wouldn't miss seeing them. On one trip when I was traveling with Evan, the alarm sounded every time he went through the metal detector. The security guard made him take all the metal objects, but not his wallet, out of his pockets and try again; the alarm still sounded.

"Do you have a Playboy Club card in your wallet?" the attendant asked. "Those cards are made of metal, you know."

"Oh, yes I do," Evan replied awkwardly. After he removed that from his wallet, he passed through the detector without a sound. I was glad that I always pointed out beautiful women to him because, although I had guessed, I now knew for certain that he liked it.

But, lest I forget, back to how I found out about the existence of *Playboy*.

John and I were wearing our matching Bermuda outfits all day that Saturday after they arrived in the mail. We had gone to the cafeteria to eat breakfast and were in the serving line right behind several of John's fraternity brothers. The guys, surprised mostly, I think, at John, commented to us about our matching outfits. John mentioned that his mom had made them and I chimed in immediately afterwards with my comment, with the only thought in my mind being that we were like childhood friends who, not only played together, but also dressed alike or similarly.

"We're playmates!" I said loudly and proudly to the group.

"We are *not* playmates!" John, his face flushing from embarrassment, emphatically corrected me.

He looked around at the others within hearing range and stated boldly and clearly to them, "We are *not playmates*. I don't think she has *any idea* what she just said."

Then, breathing deeply to calm himself, he muttered to me through his gritted teeth, "I'll explain it to you later when we get to a table and sit down."

"OK," I replied timidly, not understanding at all what I had said that was bad enough to deserve such a reprimand.

I completely understood after he told me about *Playboy* and what "playmate" means to an adult. I apologized.

"I'm very sorry, John. I won't say that to anyone else because you are absolutely right; we are not playmates." (— *Yet.*)

SNIPPET 062 - Committed

A three-day trip to New Orleans to see John was my graduation present from John and my parents for finally obtaining my Bachelor of Arts in English in June and then my Bachelor of Science in mathematics in August of 1960. John met me at the airport and took me by city bus to a small hotel in town to check-in. For the next three nights and days, we followed the same schedule.

After eating dinner at a small diner, John and I wandered the streets in town window-shopping or the streets down in the French quarter listening to music. Our favorite street corner was where Pete Fountain and his band played. Too poor to be patrons of the nightclub, we would stroll by very slowly and when the music got too soft to be heard well, turnabout and stroll back. The bars with music along the streets were quite risqué, with pretty, scantily clad girls swinging out through the doorways on decorated swings and bouncers everywhere trying to entice you to come inside. Being rather prudish, I didn't even *look* inside, and I don't remember John looking either. (I now wish I had looked.) But the music was fabulous, so we did enjoy that; many people did, overflowing the bars and spilling into the streets. We definitely were not alone out on the sidewalks all night.

Around 5:00 A.M. we ate breakfast at another diner, and then John dropped me back at the hotel. I got to sleep, but he didn't because he had to work all week. He would hurry home, by way of a long trolley car and bus ride to the fraternity house where he lived for the summer at Tulane University, shower and shave, dress, and dash off to work. He had another long commute—first by bus, then trolley, then bus, then ferry, then taxi before he got to the laboratory where he worked in Gretna. He reversed the commute to get back home. While I was visiting, he would take the trolley to town instead and pick me up at the hotel to repeat our scheduled routine.

My last night in New Orleans, during our evening walk, we happened to pass by a jewelry shop, which like the other stores was open late, and decided to stop in and browse around. We ended up buying two beaded-edge wedding bands, a white gold one for me at the cost of nine dollars and a yellow gold one for John at the cost of twenty dollars plus eighty-nine cents tax on the total. John kept mine with him and I kept his with me.

I flew home the next day. If I had stayed any longer, John might have collapsed from exhaustion. He had had no sleep during my entire stay and had probably functioned only on sheer adrenaline and caffeine. He phoned me that night to make sure I had arrived home safely.

Shortly into our conversation, I casually mentioned to him: "I don't know why we have these wedding bands in our possession; you have never even asked me to *marry* you."

"Well, will you?" John quizzed.

"Of course!" I enthusiastically answered.

The conversation continued as though nothing important had been said. After we hung up, I glanced down at the jeweled Alpha Xi Delta and Delta Sigma Phi fraternity pins linked together, that I had worn over my heart since April, and pondered silently—*I think we just committed ourselves to a lifetime together.*

SNIPPET 063 - *Wayne or Bus*

In the fall of 1960 DeGraff Hall became the first-ever coed dormitory at Florida State University; V-shaped, it housed graduate students with men in the right wing, women in the left wing, and had common areas for sitting, studying, and playing games in the apex. The day I moved in, I ran into Wayne in the sitting room. We both had attended and graduated from Palm Beach High School, attended different universities, and were now starting graduate studies, he in clinical psychology and I in mathematics. After not having any contact during the intervening five years, it was thrilling for each of us to see someone we already knew, even though we didn't know each other well. We had only seen each other around West Palm Beach but had friends in common there.

Although Wayne has cerebral palsy, he became an accomplished gymnast during college and was on the varsity gymnastics team at FSU starting in 1958. I remember the first time I saw him in the gym later in the week that fall semester. Dressed all in white, he appeared handsome, fit, and competent as he demonstrated his gymnastic skills for me. He continued on the team through 1962 with specialties in still rings and high bar and won the 1962 "South Florida" still rings championship. One of his coaches, Jack, wrote an article about Wayne that appeared in *Boy's Life* in 1969.

We quickly became good friends and soon thereafter, he and John became friends with great respect for each other. On the few weekends that I stayed in Tallahassee, Wayne and I would go out to study in the park nearby or to eat pizza together.

During the first week of classes, I was missing John so much that I decided to bus from Tallahassee to DeLand to see him, now a senior at Stetson University. Anticipating my desire to do so, I had prearranged to stay, any weekend that I wanted to visit during that school year, in the Chaudoin Hall dormitory where I had lived at Stetson. (Many students were kind enough to allow others to stay in their rooms while they were away for the weekend.) I mentioned my plans to Wayne and discovered that he too was traveling by bus that weekend, going to West Palm Beach to bring a car back to FSU;

having each other's company for part of the time would make the trip more fun, so we arranged to bus together as far as Jacksonville.

We left Friday evening, seated side-by-side on the bus and chatting non-stop until it got dark and Wayne fell fast asleep with his head on my shoulder. I was too excited to sleep, anxious to be with John. In Jacksonville we parted on separate buses to our final destinations.

I arrived in DeLand at the bus station early Saturday morning to be greeted by the lopsided-grinning-love-of-my-life. We spent as much time as possible together following our usual routine of the previous college year since I had to follow all the rules of a senior student while staying in the dorm. Sunday evening after church, John put me on the bus to return to FSU.

Except for the one weekend that John traveled to visit me and slept in Wayne's room in DeGraff, I traveled to visit him. In the beginning, neither of us imagined that for ten weeks and weekends out of the next several months I would follow the same regimen.

- Thursday: attend classes, check with Wayne to see if he was driving home for the weekend, in which case, hitch ride with him by car to DeLand, otherwise, arrange travel by bus, then, regardless, decide on clothes to take, pack suitcase, and *try* to study.
- Friday: attend classes, catch bus to Jacksonville and then bus to DeLand or study that day and ride with Wayne direct to DeLand on Saturday.
- Saturday: skip classes at FSU, visit with John, and sleep in Chaudoin overnight.
- Sunday: visit with John and together attend worship service at St. Barnabas Church, occasionally chat with Father Leroy in his office about love and marriage, study or while away the afternoon, attend church dinner, catch bus at 9:00 P.M. to Jacksonville and there catch bus to Tallahassee.
- Monday: arrive at DeGraff Hall at 7:30 A.M., shower, attend classes 8:00 A.M. to 5:00 P.M., unpack suitcase, then collapse into bed for some desperately needed sleep.
- Tuesday: attend classes, study and try to catch up on homework and on "missed" classes.

SNIPPETS (bits and pieces of love and life) by CAROLE

- Wednesday: attend classes, study and try again to catch up on homework, and decide whether to visit John over the weekend. Because I just *had* to see John, my big question for the weekend really was: "Will it be *Wayne* or *bus*?"

SNIPPET 064 - Lizzybeth

Her name is Elizabeth and I moved into her room in the dormitory several weeks after I started grad school at FSU. We had some classes together and she and I had become somewhat friends. She lived alone in the two-person room next to mine and had consented to my becoming her roommate after I explained the considerable problem I was having with my current roommate who constantly annoyed me with her weird shenanigans, deliberately keeping me from concentrating on my studies.

As I got to know Elizabeth better that one semester we shared a room, my admiration grew and I lovingly began calling her "Lizzybeth." When we met, I was twenty-three years old and she just twenty, but she too had completed college and was starting graduate studies in mathematics. Not only was she extremely intelligent, but she was attractive, physically fit, and talented as well. She played both piano and organ, sang, composed music, wrote songs and poetry, and, I think, even did some artwork.

She lived a varied, full, well-ordered life and was a great inspiration to me although I could never keep up. She awoke every morning at six o'clock and stretched and did simple exercises in bed before getting up. She attended classes during the day and studied in the evening until her bedtime at ten o'clock. I didn't see her much on weekends because I was usually away visiting John; but I do know that she never studied or worked on Sundays. For Lizzybeth, Sunday was a day of worship and rest or play; she attended church, sang in the choir, played the organ, read books, and played tennis, among other things that day.

After she graduated, she became a math professor at Stetson University. I like to think I had some influence on her decision to teach there. We have shared Christmas letters for decades and visited each other's home once or twice. I read and reread her letters, always full of family news and of the fascinating adventures she had during her vacation travels all over the world.

SNIPPET 065 - What Should We Do?

I was planning to spend a couple of quiet days visiting John in DeLand before heading home for the rest of the Christmas holidays. Wayne had dropped me off Sunday afternoon on his way home to West Palm Beach.

John was busy studying for exams that he had to take on Monday and Tuesday, leaving little time for us to chat.

"I received this, stating that I have been awarded a fellowship for graduate work in chemistry at the University of North Carolina next fall," John said, showing me the letter.

"Well, I don't see any reason for me to continue at FSU if we're going to get married next summer. Graduate students are allowed to transfer only twelve credits and I'm taking more course-credits than that now. I might as well look for a job and move to DeLand so I can live closer to you until then. It would certainly cut out all this traveling," I said aloud as well as thinking of all the possibilities in my head.

Monday morning while John was busy taking an exam, I was busy seeking a job teaching full-time or as a substitute in the public school system. By lunchtime, I had a full-time job teaching science to seventh and eighth graders, starting as soon as I could finish the semester at Florida State University. The regular science teacher had not shown up for classes that morning, and the officials, investigating his absence, discovered that he secretly had moved out of the city to parts unknown, taking his family and the entire contents of their home—the teacher had simply "flown the coop," leaving the door open for me. The principal was desperate to find another teacher to replace him; he was overjoyed to hire me and was willing to use substitutes until I could start. I was thrilled! And couldn't wait to tell John. This job would also count toward one semester of my required three years of teaching to repay my education loan from the state. During my last three years as an undergraduate, I had taken advantage of the loans of two hundred dollars per semester available to college students who planned to pursue a career in teaching in the Florida public schools.

"I have a job! Now what should we do?" I excitedly relayed to John when we met after his morning exam.

"Guess we'd better find you a place to live. I'll check with some of my fraternity brothers and see if anyone knows of housing close by the university." And off he went.

He wasn't gone long before he returned with bad news and good news. A fraternity brother and his wife were separating and wanted to get out of the lease of their duplex apartment just a block from campus. They had talked to the owner and the duplex was mine if I wanted to take over the lease.

"This is wonderful; I have a place to live. Now what should we do?" I asked, totally oblivious to his being under the pressures of exam week.

Appearing quite overwhelmed and kind of shaking his head, he answered, "I'll have to think about this later. I have to go take another exam."

After that exam we sat down in the Hat Rack coffee shop to discuss our options.

John thought deeply for a few minutes and then asked, "Do you remember my mentioning Uncle Charles and Aunt Lib?"

"I remember their names. Isn't Charles your dad's brother and aren't they the doctors who live in Atlanta?"

"Right," he continued. "He's a surgeon in town and she's the head resident at Emory University Hospital. They got married while they were in medical school and had three children, a boy and a girl who were twins and then a single boy, before they finished getting their MD's. The small apartment that they lived in usually had diapers hanging from lines strung all over across the apartment from wall to wall. Well, they managed somehow, and if they can do it, so can we. — *Let's get married.*"

SNIPPET 066 - Wedding Preparations

The following days, since Christmas vacation had begun for most students and faculty members, were extremely hectic; the itemized list below will give you an idea. (Back then, the rule was that no university student having parent(s) or guardian(s) could get married, regardless of age, without written permission from the parent(s) or guardian(s) as well as permission from the dean(s). If you disregarded this rule, marriage meant your automatic expulsion from the university.)

1. Phone John's parents to express our desire to be married and to have them mail written permission, for our marriage, to the dean of the university. (Shirley and John Daddy were both at home.)
2. Phone my parents for the same reason. (Luckily, we caught Mema and Daddy just before they left for Englewood to attend the funeral of her Uncle Stanley, a favorite great uncle of us girls.)
3. Locate Stetson's Dean of Men to get permission to get married and tell him that a letter from John's parents should arrive within a few days. (We found him strolling on campus from the library back to his office. He knew us both and wished us well.)
4. Locate, via phone, FSU's Dean of Women to get permission to get married and tell her a letter from my parents should arrive within a few days. (She just happened to be in her office although she had not planned to be there then.)
5. Rent the duplex. (The owners were a retired school principal and his wife and since we had no furnishings, they offered to provide everything we needed for everyday living except food and clothing, and they did. They treated us wonderfully.)
6. Get blood tests and marriage license. (The tests proved to be the easy part. The officials issued the license, but they didn't give it to us, simply saying that we could pick it up on Friday due to the mandatory-three-day-waiting period for marriage licenses. No amount of pleading on our part—we *have* to take it with us; we're leaving town *today*; we don't need to and *promise not to use* the license for *at least three* days—convinced them to deviate

from the rule. They would not—could not—do that. However, if we paid the postage and prepared the envelope, they would mail it to us. So, we addressed the envelope to me at my parents' home and, because of the holiday mail rush, added the extra postage necessary for special delivery. We hoped that they would remember to post it Friday and that it would get to me promptly. To our relief, it arrived at my parents' home after dinner on Saturday, Christmas Eve, in the very last delivery service by postal messenger that day, after which there would be no mail deliveries whatever until the following Tuesday morning. If it hadn't arrived, there would have been no wedding on Monday.)

7. Bus home. (John went to Savannah. I went to West Palm Beach. For the next two days, my big suitcase roamed around Florida, having been put on the wrong bus by a bus line worker; it eventually was rescued and delivered to the house.)
8. Both arrange to see doctors on Friday for physicals and advice. (John's doctor suggested to him that a small bottle of rum might be helpful. Thankfully, Mom arrived back home in time to go with "nervous" me. My doctor gave me no advice—just a stretching.)
9. Phone my hometown church to see if there is any time slot available within a week for a wedding. (There was exactly one on Monday morning at ten o'clock, complete with pastor and organist. The church was already decorated for Christmas that Sunday, so decorations were taken care of as well. One of the church members was a photographer and available, so we hired him for photos, black and white only as color was too costly.)
10. Phone florist for wedding bouquet, corsages, and boutonnieres for Monday morning and have them delivered to the church.
11. Phone restaurants and caterers to arrange some type of wedding reception. (Unfortunately, most restaurants were closed on Monday, it being a holiday. I discovered that a wedding-cake-and-punch reception at the church would cost the same as a buffet luncheon at a restaurant in Lake Worth that would be open that day; consequently, I reserved the Cub Room of Wolfie's Restaurant for lunch at noon for about, I guessed and hoped, thirty people.

SNIPPETS (bits and pieces of love and life) by CAROLE

12. Phone people to invite them to the wedding. Phone Edith, living in Illinois, to see if she can come on such short notice.
13. Find a maid of honor. (I had wanted it to be Marcia, but she had to be with her husband, Roy, who would be best man for my previous fiancé whose wedding, surprisingly, was also scheduled for exactly the same day. I chose Sheila because she had a green dress that would be perfect in color for the season.)
14. Shop with Mom to find her a dress and one for Pat. (While we were shopping, Mom insisted on buying me a gorgeous negligee set with mid-calf-length gown and robe; I still wear it for John's and my private celebrations.)
15. Make my wedding dress.
16. Celebrate Christmas.

SNIPPET 067 - Wedding Dress

Christmas Eve is a bit late to start making a wedding dress that you have to wear the day after Christmas. Fortunately, I had bought the pattern and fabric during the summer but hadn't planned to make the dress until the next summer when John and I originally thought we might get married. The weather cooperated, with daytime temperatures in the low seventies, so a summer style dress didn't seem too out of place during the early winter in Florida.

The dress fabric was white organdy with about fifteen inches of embroidery along one edge beginning with a row of scallops (each having three protrusions), followed in order by a row of decorated-flattened-curled-U's, a row of daisy-type-flowers-on-leafy-vines, two rows of leaves, then randomly-scattered-leaves; the rest of the fabric was plain to the opposite edge. The embroidered edge could be used as the ready-made hem for a skirt, and I planned to use it that way. The lining fabric was white taffeta. Both fabrics were washable. Since the finished garment was to consist of two layered garments, but give the illusion that it was a single two-tier-skirted, floor-length dress, the combined skirts, the upper one extending slightly over the top edge of the skirt beneath, had to look like one. To accomplish the illusion, I hand-stitched a lined, gathered length of the organdy to the fabric of my large-hoop petticoat, around the bottom portion at the height of the fabric's width, to form the base of the dress and the lower scalloped-edged tier of the garment's skirt. Over the top part of the base, came the top tier of the skirt and bodice of the garment, together in the form of a street-length dress. That dress had a lined, gathered, scalloped-edged skirt and a simple, lined, oval-necked bodice with unlined puffed sleeves made of the plain part of the organdy. To give the outfit a finishing touch, I decided to add hand-stitched, unlined, elbow-length, V-pointed-open-handed gloves, also made of the plain organdy.

John and his fraternity brother, Nick, arrived on Sunday, Christmas Day, and came by the house for a brief visit while I was sewing on the dress. It's a good thing I was fitting it on Mom (she was wearing it instead of me) because the groom is not supposed to see you in your wedding dress before the ceremony. However, I

SNIPPETS (bits and pieces of love and life) by CAROLE

don't think it would have mattered anyway, because we weren't doing anything according to Hoyle.

By midnight, the complete outfit was sewn and pressed, ready for the awaited ceremony. Being my usual scattered self, I totally forgot about needing a veil, but Edith had the foresight to bring me the one she had purchased to wear for her now-cancelled wedding. The veil was perfect, flowing from a crown of pearls and just covering my slightly-below-waist-length hair; it gave me something "borrowed" to wear and added just enough jewels to make up for my lack of jewelry; I had packed none to wear during my visit home for the holidays. The something "old" was the hoop and my white, medium-height-heeled pumps and the "blue" was a satin and lace garter to wear around my left thigh.

I delighted in wearing my layered garment, especially the street-length-dress portion, including crinolines underneath, that I wore to the wedding reception and to several other important events during the next few years. Twenty years later, even though I was barely able to breathe for the duration, I determinedly squeezed into it and wore it for the first couple of hours during our anniversary celebration for fifty people in our home in Delaware.

With the main preparations done, the family decided to get some needed sleep and bedded down around 1:00 A.M. Just as I was falling asleep, I sat upright from a jolt of remembrance and leaped out of bed—I had forgotten to polish my nails! My nails had to look perfect in the photo, to be taken after the ceremony, showing our left hands with matching rings sitting on my lap with my white Bible and flowers on top of them. After my waking her, Sheila helped me apply the nail polish and afterwards, she covered me up in bed so that my hands were folded over my chest on top of the covers to allow my nails to dry without sheet-fabric imprints. Finally, it was OK to fall asleep.

SNIPPET 068 - *Wedding and Reception*

"Daddy, *please* get up and get dressed," I begged from outside the door to my parents' bedroom. "We're already a half-hour late for the wedding and everyone else is dressed and waiting to go to the church."

I just hoped that John loved me enough to wait and wouldn't think I had stood him up at the altar. But he knew my dad was notorious for always arriving late, so I need not have been concerned. When we finally got to the church, he and Nick, the best man, were sitting, patiently waiting, in the basement meeting hall of the First Baptist Church. He greeted us with his marvelous grin and a look of immense relief.

There having been no time for a rehearsal, Dr. Warren, our pastor, simply gathered the wedding party around the speaker's stand and instructed each of us on what to do during the actual ceremony in the church auditorium upstairs.

"I'm concerned, most of all, that there was no time for me to do pre-marital counseling with you before I perform this wedding," Dr. Warren said to John and me.

"Oh, don't worry about that," I assured him. "We received considerable counseling from Father LeRoy during the weekends when I visited John at Stetson this fall."

John agreed that we had been properly prepared.

With that reassurance, the pastor dismissed his concern, and he and the four of us participants signed all the necessary documents. Immediately afterwards, Dr. Warren led John and Nick upstairs so the three could take their places at the front of the church to begin the ceremony.

As soon as they left the room, I donned my veil, looking into mirror of the cosmetic case being held by Pat, with the rest of the family giving me verbal instructions on how to place it properly. I wasn't concerned in the least that John's having seen me in my wedding dress before the start of the ceremony would bring *bad* luck. I had arrived wearing it, but he had not seen the entire outfit, complete with veil and the white Holy Bible covered with an orchid surrounded by carnations with other white flowers and satin ribbons trailing off

SNIPPETS (bits and pieces of love and life) by CAROLE

the top edge of its leather cover forming the bridal bouquet. More so, the rain showers off and on that day would cancel the possibility of bad luck. Rain on your wedding day brings *good* luck, and we definitely were having plenty of that!

The church auditorium was beautifully decorated with an abundance of luxuriant, red and white poinsettias, perfectly complementing the green, white and black colors worn by the wedding party.

The organist played all the traditional wedding music; I hadn't had time to make special selections except for the one song that a friend of the family sang gloriously just before the march down the aisle. That song was *Whither Thou Goest* (based on verses from the *Bible* book "Ruth"), dedicated from me to John.

Toward the end of the ceremony as Sheila lifted the veil away from my face, placing it behind my head, I noticed a tear trickling down her cheek and I was so touched that a couple of tears flowed from my eyes too. Then Dr. Warren told John, "You may kiss the bride." The pastor had instructed me to wait for John to kiss me, but I was so excited that I couldn't wait and kissed him first.

As we hurriedly marched back up the aisle, it was obvious to everyone that we were both deliriously happy to be husband and wife.

After being congratulated by the thirty or so attendees, we had photos taken for our white-leather, keepsake album, "Our Wedding." The photo of our hands was taken as planned and is still one of our favorites. Our hands were sitting on my lap, so my dress could form the background; John's hand was on the bottom, then my hand crossways, then my white *Holy Bible* and the attached bouquet covering the back of my hand. The photographer carefully arranged the bouquet's trailing flowers to cover the tips of John's partially-healed, damaged fingers. John had caught his hand in an autoclave in the chemistry lab just two weeks prior, tearing off the entire nail on his ring finger and splitting the nail of his middle finger to the bone.

Interestingly, all the other women in my family wore dresses with fitted bodices and mid-calf-length, gathered skirts: Mom's pale pink chiffon dress had unlined, long sleeves; Edith's medium blue taffeta dress had short sleeves; Sheila's emerald green chiffon dress had spaghetti straps; Pat's dress had a white chiffon skirt and a deep blue satin bodice with cap sleeves and bow at the waist. Mema's favorite photo of "her girls" was taken when we four posed together in a diamond shape on the steps of the pulpit platform at the front of the church.

The only sad part of the wedding day was that John's parents were missing. They both started to work at new jobs that very same morning so couldn't leave Savannah to be with us. Even more sad was that they now had missed the weddings of both children; Becky had eloped and married several years earlier. A few years later, Shirley told me that John Daddy did manage to slip away from work long enough to sit in a pew in their church during the time our actual ceremony was taking place; he had to be with us at least in spirit.

Before we left for the reception at Wolfie's Restaurant in Lake Worth, I removed the bottom layer of my garment as planned and added a slip of ruffled netting underneath the skirt of the remaining street-length dress, making it much easier for me to maneuver during the luncheon.

Happily, everyone who attended the wedding came to the reception as well. We were extremely happy with my choice to use Wolfie's. The luncheon buffet had a marvelous array of soups, pastries, fruits, salads, pastas, and meats. The chef even prepared us a gorgeously decorated two-layer wedding cake with a bride-and-groom figurine inside a gathered-net-covered-wire heart on top. The fabric has long since deteriorated but we still use the figurine and have it displayed in our dining room china cabinet. It was great fun to cut the cake and feed each other a bite; we have a photo of that and one of us licking our fingers afterwards. The smiling staff presented to us a bow-adorned box filled with pastries and fruit for our honeymoon. "This is for you—just in case you don't want to go out to eat," one of them said with a twinkle.

Before leaving, I tossed my bouquet backward over my head to the anxiously waiting maidens. Sheila, giggling delightedly, caught it, distressing Mema a bit because Sheila was only sixteen. Then John nervously removed the garter from my leg and tossed it into the air towards the guys; my garter missed them, landing instead in someone's soup and splattering it on everyone nearby. Perhaps we had a bit of *bad* luck after all. Being afraid to wait to find out whose soup and who the unlucky ones were, we dashed from the room, through the main dining area, and out the front door of the restaurant.

SNIPPETS *(bits and pieces of love and life)* by CAROLE

I mentioned something to Sheila, months later, about how touched I was that she would cry toward the end of the wedding, guessing that she too had been overwhelmed by the joyful beauty of the setting and ceremony.

"Oh no—it wasn't *that* at all!" she corrected me. "I was feeling sorry for *John*, marrying you and having to join our family. I liked him too much."

SNIPPET 069 - Newlyweds

"Here are the keys to my car; just have it back by tomorrow night," said Melvin, a friend of my family.

We thanked him profusely, shocked by the generous offer. Not only could we drive ourselves to the reception but we could actually go away somewhere for an overnight honeymoon! We hadn't planned on doing that because we had no car and very little money, just $125 total between us, and that had to cover all our living expenses for the two months before I would get my first paycheck as a teacher.

When we arrived at my family's home to pack and leave on our unexpected honeymoon, we discovered that Edith and Pat had dashed home too. As we left the house with our luggage, we noticed "Just Married" written on the back windshield and side windows of Melvin's car.

"You have to let the whole world know you just got married," they both insisted as they helped stash everything into the trunk and hugged us good-bye.

We washed the signs off at the first service station we passed; not because we didn't want people to know—our happy faces and my orchid corsage made "just married" obvious—but because we were afraid the white shoe polish might do some damage.

We decided a honeymoon at the beach in Fort Lauderdale would be wonderful and headed there. When we reached the city, we drove over to Highway A1A and started driving north looking for a nice motel. We eventually spotted the newly built Space Satellite Motel and it looked like it was now open for business. While I waited in the car, John went in to see about getting a room for the night and returned within a few minutes.

"A room costs twenty-five dollars," he began. "But I told the clerk I couldn't afford that much. After glancing around me toward the car, the clerk asked me what I could afford. I told him ten, so he rented us the room for ten dollars. Isn't that terrific?" he continued, smiling his big, beautiful grin.

SNIPPETS (bits and pieces of love and life) by CAROLE

As we walked through the lobby, the clerk called out to me, "Beautiful orchid corsage!" Then I overheard his saying softly to himself, "Hmmm, just married, I bet."

I quietly smiled; the white corsage, contrasting vividly with the red, sleeveless, sheath dress I was wearing, was quite obvious to anyone glancing my way. I'm sure I blushed!

We settled into a large, nicely decorated, room. It quickly became apparent that we were the first occupants as the water ran rusty the first few minutes out of the tap before it became perfectly clear.

John had brought a bathing suit and went to take a swim in the pool while I took a bath. I suddenly wished that I had brought nicer clothes. But, I had not planned to get married over the holidays and had only packed old clothes to hang around the house in, except for the red dress I was wearing which I had brought to wear to church on Christmas Day. I was so grateful to have a beautiful negligee set to be wearing when John returned from his swim.

However, before I could even get the bath water run, there was a knock on the door. I opened it and saw, standing before me, a dripping-wet, shivering man with chattering teeth, saying he hadn't taken a key and could he please come back in because it was cloudy and drizzly, the pool water was cold, and he was freezing… — Well, of course, he could!

The rest of the afternoon has been bleeped out because discussing it is one of the *never*'s. All I'll ever say about it is what I later mentioned to Mema: "You never told me my elbows would get sore."

We ate a delicious dinner, stylishly late, in the romantic dining room that had a "star-lit," dark ceiling. We were the only patrons at the time so we had the violinist all to ourselves, serenading us while we dined. He was hired to entertain the guests and play their requests during the dinner hours. John requested *Hard Hearted Hannah (The Vamp of Savannah)*, but the violinist didn't know that song.

The following day at lunch, John, reaching over to hold my hand, spilled a full glass of milk on me, soaking most of the front of my blouse and slacks. The helpful staff kept my lunch warm in the kitchen while I was gone to the room to change clothes. We finished lunch without any other catastrophes. We still hold hands across the table and I have repaid him, too many times, by knocking over full glasses of wine onto his suits; however, he has been unable to go change clothes; it seems to happen only when we are dining, but not over-nighting, away from home. We now try to plan ahead and move glasses on the table out of the way before we hold hands, but sometimes we forget because we're too preoccupied gazing at one another.

Following lunch, we drove back to my parents' home and left the car for my dad to return to Melvin. Then, borrowing my parents' car, Edith drove us on to DeLand. Pat came along to accompany her back to West Palm Beach. After spending the night, sleeping in the living room of our one-bedroom, duplex apartment, the two of them slipped away before we awoke and came out of the bedroom to see them off. They left a note stating that they had not wanted to disturb the newlyweds.

Ten years later while we were celebrating our anniversary, staying at the same motel, in the exact same room (quite by happenstance) and eating dinner in the dining room, the same violinist was still working for the restaurant and serenaded us once again. John requested the same song as before, but the violinist still didn't know it.

John jokingly chided him, "We gave you ten years to learn that song; I can't believe you still don't know how to play *Hard Hearted Hannah*."

SNIPPET 070 - Bicycles

Our wedding gifts to each other were practical ones—twin Schwinn® racers. We could only scrape up enough money to buy one, so we bought John's bicycle first. It was a typical, white, three-speed, boy's model.

One of John's weekly chores was buying "cracked" eggs (much cheaper than those with unblemished shells), then bringing them home in a paper sack held in one hand while using the other to shift gears and to brake his bike. Quite a feat—and he never dropped or broke a single egg. Sitting on a small pillow to cushion me, I could ride on the cross bar between the seat and handlebars and go with him. It was really neat and I felt so safe riding with his arms around me. I liked barking, "arrrf, arf," at all the dogs that chased us, except for the one time that John got nipped on the leg; I was never allowed to bark while biking after that incident. Pay-back came about fifteen years later when, for no apparent reason, a dog dashed out of a side-yard and bit me on the leg while John and I were biking together along a beach road, lined on one side with houses, parallel to the ocean in Delaware.

After we had saved enough money, we bought my bike, the twin of John's except for being a girl's model. I could then ride, instead of walk, to my teaching job in DeLand. To make it easier for me so I wouldn't have to change clothes to ride my bike to and from school, Shirley made me a <u>skort</u>, which is a one-piece combination of a wrap-around <u>skirt</u> over sh<u>orts</u> or, in my case, pedal pushers. The skort quickly became my favorite piece of clothing. Being made from a dark gray fabric, it coordinated with many of my blouses I already had and all the new ones Shirley made to go with it; consequently, it got worn almost daily. I quickly discovered that if I hand washed it early in the evening, it would drip-dry enough to iron it the next morning before school.

I had only one accident, a rather freakish one indeed, riding that bike. While I was biking home one afternoon, a wind gust blew sand into my eyes and a single grain embedded itself next to the iris of my right eye. The tiny grain of sand had to be removed by a doctor and for the next week I had to wear a bandage over my eye while it healed. I wish I had thought to wear a black patch and pirate's clothing to complete the look; my students would have enjoyed seeing me in a totally different outfit for a change.

When I was in the fifth grade in Fort Pierce, I had a bicycle to ride back and forth to school. (Edith and I had both learned how to ride, the previous summer in Melbourne, on the bike belonging to the young boy who lived across the street from our paternal grandparents.) One afternoon on my way home from school, I was chasing my boyfriend, Matt, who was riding his bike too, and my left foot slipped off the pedal, catching on the pavement and suddenly toppling my bike. I ended up pinned beneath it, slightly burning the side of my face and all other uncovered skin touching the hot pavement and having deeply abraded my left knee and ankle. A mailman was standing at the front door of the nearest house and hand-delivering mail to the lady who lived there. She saw the accident and alerted the mailman, who immediately dashed over to rescue me. The concerned lady was a stranger to me but kindly offered her help. When she was unable to contact my dad by phone, she drove me to the office of her doctor. He checked me out and, although he could not remove all the multitude of minute fragments of dirt and pavement from my leg, he bandaged me up as best he could. Afterwards, the lady drove me home. I was very grateful to her, and so was my dad when I told him all about what happened. Unable to ride my bike, I had to walk stiff-kneed the eight to ten blocks each way to and from school for the next six weeks while my infected leg healed. I still have the scars on my knee and ankle, although they, except the worst one on my knee, have all but faded from sight.

After our car died during our first year of graduate school in Chapel Hill, our bicycles again became our major mode of transportation for the next two years. John's bike also came in handy for transporting our laundry to the Laundromat when we did that on weekends. His bike definitely got more use and, twice, had to be repaired. The need for the first repair job was caused by someone else, carelessly turning his car directly in front of the bike, compelling John to do a rapid-reflex leap off it, toward the sidewalk at the edge of the road, and to allow the bike to crash into the side of the car. The need for the second one was caused by John, standing up on the bike pedals, pumping his way up the steep hill near the chemistry building;

SNIPPETS (bits and pieces of love and life) by CAROLE

the handlebars, breaking from the upward strain, lifted off in his hands. Fortunately, John received only minor bruises each time.

Our development and the surrounding area in Hockessin are hilly and, after we moved there, I found it difficult to ride my bike fast enough to keep up with John when we rode on the back roads. We gave our twin bikes to Ralph and Patty and bought ourselves a Schwinn® tandem that we still have and occasionally ride. Two tiny, "Snoopy" license plates with our names on them, hanging off the seat-springs, designate which seat is owned by whom. The front seat belongs to John, the driver in control, and the back seat belongs to me, the back-seat driver. I don't bark at dogs while we're riding this bike because John expects me to do my share of the pedaling, which means I can't put my feet up in the air out of the way of attacking dogs (and besides, my barking at dogs while biking became another *never*). We each tell people that we like the tandem because we each can let the other person do all the work while each of us just pretends to pedal and enjoys watching the scenery go by.

We have always had bells on our bikes to warn people that we were riding near them. So, when we got a stationary bike for our exercise room, I bought a bell for it too. I told John, "That bell's for you to ring so you won't run over me when you are riding the bike and I am walking on the treadmill."

SNIPPET 071 - Imposed Never's

To be added to my *never's*, that I already had when John and I got married, came a few imposed *never's* from him to me.

- *Never* cut my hair short because he really likes it long. Broke that commandment in grad school. Because it was so long, I had to wash my hair frequently and, since we couldn't afford a hair dryer for blow-drying, it stayed wet, wound up on my head in the bun I had to wear to make me look older while teaching. As soon as I discovered that my hair was falling out from where my scalp stayed damp most of the time, I had it cut. I did let my hair grow long several more times but ended up having it cut shorter for good when I decided to become an adult around age forty.
- *Never* be late. John is very good about this and I try to be, although I don't always succeed.
- *Never* go into debt. We have had to obtain a mortgage for extremely large purchases like our house and truck, but we try to save money for other large expenses and not buy something until we can afford it.
- *Never* remove your wedding band. Technically, we have ignored that one because there are times when removing it is an absolute necessity, like it is, for example, during surgery. However, when you have to remove that ring, the spouse does it for you.
- *Never* die first. You must wait for the other one to die first; consequently, we both have to, and plan to, live forever.
- *Never* discuss our sex life. So I shan't talk about my wearing balloons or about what I wore under the raincoat when I flashed John in the limousine after I picked him up from work the day he retired, etc.
- *Never* reveal our pet names for each other. That means I can't tell you what the initials P and T and PPP stand for either.

SNIPPET 072 - *Together at Last*

I kept telling myself that we were married and it was OK to spend the weekend with John, but somehow, to me, it felt strangely like we were carrying on an exciting, illicit, love affair. Every weekend I traveled from Tallahassee to DeLand just as I had all the weeks before Christmas but now instead of just spending part of two days with John, I was also spending the night.

I was getting used to being called Mrs. Adams by other people; my students at FSU were calling me that now, daily. That first day back from the holidays, I conveyed the news to them by writing on the blackboard: "Miss Moore will no longer be your instructor; Mrs. Adams will be teaching this class until the end of the semester." I immediately left the classroom, paused out of sight while slowly counting to ten, then walked back in. The students cheered and begged to hear all about the wedding, so I briefly chatted about it. Earlier that day, I had proudly shown my new ring to my fellow graduate students who shared the group office, and they, suspecting it to be only an engagement and not a wedding ring, had commanded me to turn it over so they could see the diamond. Everyone had been surprised by the turn of my hand that, unexpectedly, showed the band to be "stone-less." They all congratulated me heartily.

Since we had no car, my dad offered to drive John up to FSU at the end of the semester, late January 1961, to move me to the apartment in DeLand. Daddy made the round-trip from West Palm Beach in a single day, stopping only long enough to get John on his way to Tallahasee, help pack me and my belongings into the car, deposit John and me at our home, and then head back home to Mema.

It was wonderful to be together at last and live as a daily loving couple instead of weekend lovers.

SNIPPET 073 - Incentive Photo

John Daddy's career, as construction superintendent supervising workmen building roads and airport runways, provided an excellent opportunity for John to spend time outdoors with his dad while earning supplemental money. During his summer vacations throughout high school and college, when he wasn't working at the Wesson Oil Company, John had jobs working for his dad in the Eppy Construction Company. He didn't fit in very well at all with the other construction workers; he was not only diligent but he was young and strong and worked faster and harder than the rest of the crew. Consequently, they didn't appreciate his presence as a worker because they found it difficult to keep up with his pace, but they did seem to like his being there as a friendly-mannered person.

Soon after we were living together in our apartment in DeLand, I noticed an eight-inch-by-ten-inch framed photo of John and a group of other construction workers digging what looked like a ditch. I asked him why he had it prominently displayed.

"I worked for my dad during the summers and that photo is a reminder of all the long hours I spent working in the hot sun. That particular summer I helped dig ditches in downtown Savannah. We had to do all the digging by hand with shovels as that area was too small for large equipment to be brought in to do the work. It's my incentive to get my PhD so I don't spend the rest of my life digging ditches instead of doing the chemistry that I really enjoy and want to do," he proudly replied.

That photo stayed in front of him, on any desk where he studied, until he received his final graduate degree in 1965. I then placed it in an album with other photos as a remembrance; it had served its purpose and was no longer needed as an incentive.

SNIPPET 074 - Poorlyweds Diet

John insists, "We were not poorly wed; we were richly blessed and marvelously wed, just monetarily poor." I whole-heartedly agree with his statement, so I want you to know that the word in the title is merely my derivation of "Poor newlyweds." If he misunderstood the title, then you probably did too.

For the first four and a half years after we got married, we had very little money to live on because either John was attending college or we both were attending graduate school. During the one and a half years that I taught grades seven through twelve in public schools, my salary was less than that of other teachers because the state would issue me only an emergency certificate. Although I had taken education courses, I didn't have a degree in teaching; my Bachelor of Arts was in English and my Bachelor of Science was in mathematics. For the remainder of those years that we were getting educated, I had a teaching assistantship that I supplemented by working at part-time-less-than-minimum-wage jobs. We also had my one-thousand-dollar debt from teaching loans repayable to the State of Florida which, because I had stopped teaching in Florida, I was obligated to pay off rather than work off. (The one semester that I taught in DeLand had reduced the original debt of twelve hundred dollars to one thousand; the debt could have been worked off at the rate of two hundred dollars per semester of teaching.) John had a paying job during the first summer only. Fortunately, he had a fellowship for his graduate studies at UNC, but once he started, that obligated him to be a year-round student until he earned his Doctor of Philosophy degree in organic chemistry. What all of this meant was that we had to live on a very tight budget; neither of us wanted to incur any more debts.

We sat down, discussed it, and figured out a basic diet that we thought would be the least expensive, yet adequate, and this is it:

- Breakfast: well-cooked scrambled eggs, made with "the-less-expensive-cracked" eggs, whole-wheat toast, orange juice, and reconstituted powdered milk
- Lunch: sandwiches made with peanut butter and jelly or jam on whole-wheat bread

- Supper: ground beef, lettuce, peas or green beans or corn, and reconstituted powdered milk. (On the rare occasions when we entertained friends, I made a sauce with ground beef, tomato paste, canned tomatoes, herbs and spices, and served it on vermicelli; everyone liked being invited over for our spaghetti dinner.)

The stress was so severe for me during the 1961-1962 school year, due to my trying to keep up with teaching six diffcrent high school subjects (per day), taking twelve hours (per semester) of courses in the Master of Arts in Teaching Program at Duke University, and averaging less than three hours of sleep per night, that I lost twenty pounds. Since we never told our families about our problems (which we figured were ours alone because we were the ones who decided to get married before finishing our formal education), my dad blamed my weight loss on our diet. He demanded John change our budget to include whole milk instead of powdered milk thinking that would solve the problem. We never told *him* it wouldn't; we just started buying whole milk. And, we never told a*nyone* that I had to take medication prescribed by the doctor to quiet my digestive system enough to be able to swallow and keep down at least some, if not all, of the food I ate.

Having eaten so much peanut butter those four and a half years, we switched to almond butter as soon as we discovered it and we could afford to; that was not long after we moved and both started working in Delaware. I have not eaten peanut butter since and neither had John until several weeks ago when he requested that I buy him some for his nut butter and jelly on rye bread sandwiches for lunch at work. My still not eating peanut butter isn't quite true; since I just can't waste any food, I have been licking the remaining peanut butter off the knife after making his sandwich for lunch. I also lick the jelly spoon.

SNIPPET 075 - Haircuts

Whenever I hear the door of the tall, maid's cabinet (we have no maid, just the cabinet) in the kitchen, banging closed, then hear the twenty-five-foot vacuum-hose being dragged across the tile in the kitchen, the rug at the front door, and the wood in the hallway past the two small-bedroom doors, through the master-bedroom doorway, then hear the two bi-folding-doors of our bedroom closet closing and, lastly, hear the seated foot-stool snapping open as its feet hit the tile bathroom floor, I know the barbershop is being set up and will soon be open for business. John wants a haircut.

I know the sounds well because I have heard them every two, rarely three, weeks for the past thirty-two years (as of 2002) in this house and similar sounds wherever we have lived before. I started cutting his hair when we first got married and were too poor for him to have the luxury of getting it cut by a real barber. But after a while, we got used to having the extra money for other things more fun and, besides, he hated to waste the time it took to travel to the barbershop, sit and wait, get his hair cut, and travel back home. I used to use several different clipper heads ranging from size "00" to size "1 1/2" to taper the sides; but now, being lazier, I consider tapering too much trouble and use only two clipper heads for the entire haircut—"00" for the neck and "1 1/2" for all the rest. Then I finish the job, using scissors to trim around the ears.

The wasting of time is why I've never seen his hair longer than a quarter-inch and only an eighth-inch immediately after a haircut. When John was playing football in high school, he found his longer hair to be a pain in the neck because the sweat, caused by the Savannah humid heat, would collect in the hair under his helmet and trickle, off the wisp of hair just to the right of the middle of his forehead, right into his eye, and it seemed like it took sooo much time to take care of it. So, after he timed all the motions needed for taking care of his hair, he sat down at his desk and calculated, on paper, how much time he really did spend washing, drying, and combing his hair each year. It came to thirty seconds eight to ten times per day for combing and twelve minutes per day for washing and towel drying for a total of approximately 104 hours per year. He didn't even count the time for haircuts since he still had to do that regardless of the length. He definitely had better, more important things to do with that much time, like spending two hours more per week doing experiments in his backyard lab.

Fortunately, John has a gorgeously shaped head and looks terrific with his hair cut really short. No matter where we go, people remember us because of John's *hair*, or the lack thereof. It's a good thing that I'm not vain, because women, in general, prefer the couple be remembered because of her, and how she looks, not him. He caused a lot of excitement among the children on the beach in front of The Anchorage Hotel in Antigua when we were there in 1978 to celebrate my "big 4-0" birthday a year late; they all wanted to touch his stubby hair because they had never seen hair cut that short. Each child in turn would run up to us as we lounged in our chairs at the water's edge, pat the hair on top of John's head quickly several times then run giggling back to join the group of other giggling boys and girls. One little boy was too shy, but we assured him it was OK, so he ran up and did it too. The hotel staff serving the beach asked us if we would like them to shoo the children away, but John, smiling, answered, "No, thanks. They're having too much fun."

After we moved to Wilmington and both of us had paying jobs, I decided we could afford the expense of having John go to a real barber for his haircuts. He did that for about a year, but during that time there was a lot of gossip about barbershops hiring topless and nude barbers because some bars and nightclubs were beginning to advertise topless and almost nude waitresses and dancers. I think he had an ulterior motive in mind, because he casually mentioned, as he headed toward the door that one Saturday to go for his haircut at, I assumed, Joe's Barber Shop: "There's a new barbershop in north Wilmington, so I'm going to start going there because the guys at work said that all the barbers are not only good-looking women, but they're nude as well."

That's when I put my foot down—"No way, José, you will only get that kind of barber at *home*!" He didn't get to the barbershop that day, nor has he since.

SNIPPET 076 - *Tired*

When one of us is very tired and really needs to rest, our favorite thing to say to the other is: "Have you ever been tired? I mean *reeeaally* tired?"

If John says that to me, I jokingly respond "Heavens, no. You know I *never* get tired!"

If I say that to John, he jokingly responds, "You're tired? You're a *Moore*. How could you possibly ever get tired?"

Then one sympathizes and encourages the other to go take a nap or go to bed early for the night, and one often accompanies the other to do that. John doesn't enjoy his naps as much any more; there's no cat to curl up beside him or on his stomach, so I sometimes go lie down with him so he can sleep better. If I take a nap, it's usually right after John leaves for work and, consequently, he can't join me; but that's OK because I usually have no problem sleeping.

My family members are all "night owls" (it's in the genes). I think my dad was manic-depressive because he would stay up for days on end, sleeping only ten minutes here and there when he sat down in an easy chair in the living room or sat in a cushioned seat in church.

Depression runs in my mom's family; one relative even committed suicide. I must have inherited the depression gene from both of my parents because I sure have problems due to that. I remember my mom being tired a lot when I was growing up, but I thought it was because my dad kept her awake and because she worked all night. She was a registered nurse and worked the "eleven to seven" night shift so she could be at home during the day for "her girls."

During the night while mom was working, if my dad got lonesome or hungry, he made us "girls" get out of bed to keep him company and/or fix him something to eat; it didn't matter whether or not we had school later that morning. He also didn't like anyone sleeping on the weekend if he wasn't; he would holler, from wherever he was in the house—"Hit the deck!"—a saying he acquired while serving in the Navy. If we didn't want to be punished with a whipping, we had better "hit the deck," so we always did.

Carole Christie Moore Adams

I remember one Saturday, as a teenager, "hitting the deck" ever so slowly, my body wracked with exhaustion. As I sat at the table to share breakfast with my dad, the tears began streaming down my face, my chest heaved in deep sobs. Mom happened to arrive home from work at that moment and, seeing my condition, stared at my dad and demanded, "George, you *will* let Carole go back to bed. She needs more sleep!" My sobs gradually subsided; I wouldn't have cried for very long anyway, because Daddy would have "given me something to cry for" with his belt. I gratefully "hit the bed."

In the interim of my junior and senior years in high school, I missed most of the summer sleeping all night and then napping all day. I simply could *not* stay awake. After a couple of months of sleepiness, I spent a few days in the hospital having tests done. The tests showed nothing seriously wrong; the doctor prescribed, and the staff served me, several meals of malted eggnogs for slight anemia. I was discharged from the hospital to go home *to rest*. By September I felt fine. Must have *rested* enough!

About ten or so days after I broke my back during my freshman year in college, I spent a couple of weeks in hip-traction in the hospital. The shattered vertebra fragments were pinching my spinal cord, causing paralysis in my toes and numbness to inch it's way up my legs. Since I needed an additional sixteen weeks in traction to allow the cord, hopefully, to work its way loose, my parents rented a hospital bed, complete with the necessary apparatus, so I could spend those weeks at home. The family definitely could not afford the expenses of any more hospitalization. I managed to stay awake the four hours each afternoon that I was allowed to get out of my hip-traction and into my back brace to walk around or to sit in a chair. The rest of the time I slept; I guess I was tired again. By the way, the traction worked and my feet and legs are fine (you probably wanted to know that).

After I returned to college in the spring, the problem of staying awake recurred; you and I would have thought that I'd slept enough the previous several years. The dorm council was kind enough to assign other residents in my dorm to study for exams with me in the council room during the evenings and to help me stay awake. I wish they could have sat with me in classes as well; I couldn't stay awake there either. I am truly grateful to have had the helpers; thanks to

SNIPPETS (bits and pieces of love and life) by CAROLE

them, I was able to make the high grades demanded by my father and to keep myself from being yanked out of school to get a job.

By the time I met John, my hair had grown enough to wear it in a long ponytail and, when I did, he kidded me about looking like a skittish squirrel, "bright-eyed and bushy-tailed." But sometimes then (even now), I just felt *"bleary-eyed and bushed."*

SNIPPET 077 - Cars

A car is a special possession; if you have one, you use it all the time; otherwise, you have to make do with some other mode of transportation. The first one I ever drove was the car used by Palm Beach High School for driver education, and I learned to drive it in 1953 during a two-week-summer-school course. After acing the necessary written exams during the course and officer-escorted driving test at the end, I signed my license and proudly headed home to be my mother's sixteen-year-old, *official driver*.

As long as I would drive my mom anywhere she needed to go, I could have my own use of the car to go back-and-forth to school. That car, the family's second car, was a stick shift, 1939 Plymouth®. My dad drove the main car full-time and didn't want to be a chauffeur for anyone else if he could avoid it. Mom had a driver's license, that she obtained before there was a requirement that the licensee know how to drive, that could be held and renewed, without taking any exams, as long as the license was current and the fees were paid. She always kept it up-to-date because she used her driver's license for identification purposes. In 1949, she took lessons from Lowell, a friend of the family, and managed to drive to the grocery stores a couple of times before she quit. When exams became required for the license, she tried once or twice more, taking driving lessons from a paid instructor, but never again got around to actually driving on her own. She expressed her feelings best: "I'm really not aggressive enough to drive out in the real world with all those maniacs." Mom gladly gave me the job.

When I wasn't chauffeuring, I used the car to get to school or band practice or twirling practice or church choir practice, usually with friends riding along with me. The usual fee, for my use of the car on a weekend to drive a group of friends to the beach, was to have a younger sister in tow so Mom could get some needed rest.

Driving a lot, I learned to maneuver the car very well, so after learning and practicing "speed" shifting (which requires delicately, precise coordination of clutch and gears), I became quite good at drag racing, always winning. No one expected a girl to be good at that, so I either won outright or because the guys were caught off guard; I'll never know which. I like to believe that I was just good enough to win; I could certainly speed-shift faster than anyone else I knew.

My family owned a seven-passenger Packard®; that type of car has two pull-down seats right behind the front bench seat for use when you have more than four or five passengers or for leaving stowed-away so you can have all that extra room for your legs to stretch out in. I had the use of that car once in a while. The first time I ever parallel parked it downtown in a parking space between two parked cars, a policeman walked over and rapped on the driver's side window. Although unable to think of what I might have done wrong, I, nevertheless, sheepishly rolled the window down so he could talk to me.

"Congratulations! Your dad has never parallel parked that car on the first try. I plan to tell him I saw you do it," the policeman said.

"Oh, thanks," I replied. "I didn't see you so I had no idea anyone was watching." *Wow*, I thought to myself, *I didn't do something wrong, I did something right, and was caught in the act*!

The Packard® was left over from when my dad started up a funeral home in West Palm Beach. Funeral directors and policemen frequently are friends or, at least, acquaintances; consequently, my dad knew a lot of the police force before, and after, he became a volunteer policeman.

The only time I got a warning and reprimand for my driving was an unofficial one from my dad after a trip from West Palm Beach to Belle Glade. I had driven a group of church friends to a church revival service forty-three miles away. Since we were running late by the time I picked everyone up, I drove at a decent clip, getting us to the church in less than a half-hour. We missed only fifteen minutes of the singing at the beginning and were able to participate in the main part of the service. I drove much slower on the way back.

"I know you had to be driving too fast," Daddy angrily accused, "because the car burned a quart of oil!"

"I'm sorry," I quickly apologized. "I had no way of knowing how fast I was going because the speedometer is broken." Since he knew that was true, my punishment was only verbal, and rather minor.

The first car John and I possessed after we got married was one that John Daddy gave us as John's graduation gift for earning his

Bachelor of Science degree in chemistry from Stetson University. It was a very interesting car—a Dodge® sedan with a "Meadowbrook" emblem on one side and a "Coronet" on the other. That was our first clue that it had been pieced together from a couple of wrecks; the second was that it had no heater or air-conditioner. But, it ran OK; that is, it did for a while. Having no heater meant the car had no defrost either; so, in freezing, cold weather, the front windshield iced over and you had to hang your head out the side window in order to see where you were going while you were driving it. Six months later the car threw a rod. Fortunately, when the rod broke (or whatever it does when thrown), we were within a hundred feet of our apartment in Chapel Hill and the car coasted the rest of the way to a dead stop in the side yard. It sat there, serving as an extra closet for storing boxes and things, until we had it towed to the junk yard the day before we left for Delaware several years later.

As a bribe to get us to ride the train to West Palm Beach for a visit with the family, my dad promised to give us a 1955 Chevrolet® Coupe to drive back to our apartment in Chapel Hill. It was a bribe we couldn't refuse; we needed transportation to go to Wilmington after John finished grad school that spring and afterwards for him to drive to and from work. That car was definitely another interesting one. The driver's side window frequently got stuck, and one day when John tried to forcibly turn the handle to roll the window down, the handle broke off leaving the window permanently in the "up" position. On another day, wanting to back up the car, he forcibly tried to shift gears (which also was very hard to do) and broke the entire gearshift handle off the steering shaft, leaving the car in "drive." You then could permanently either stand the car still using the brakes or move it in a forward direction using the accelerator. Luckily, the handle broke off in a forward gear position and not in reverse. Needing to use "reverse," occasionally, forced us to spend the money to have the car repaired. That car, like the first one, didn't have air-conditioning or heat; having heat was more important so John did install a heater.

I bet you're thinking, "Boy, is John strong!" Well, he is. Once, in the chemistry lab, he tried to open a corroded, lidded jar containing acid and he simply wrenched the jar in two.

SNIPPET 078 - Your, My, Our

The summer of 1961 was the first chance Shirley and I had to spend any length of time together. She was definitely not the stereotypical mother-in-law; she reminded me of my mom, whom I loved dearly. She referred to me as her *brown-eyed* daughter (as opposed to her *blue-eyed* daughter, Becky), never as her daughter-in-law, and treated me wonderfully.

At the beginning of every visit after I became one of the family, she would quiz me. "Is my son being good to you?"

"Yes—of course, he is."

"Are you being truthful with me?"

"Yes, I am. He *loves* me and treats me very well."

Strangely, she never, even once, asked if I was being good to John.

Shirley had decided to make me a new dress and wanted me to help her, mostly to keep her company, I suspect, because she worked and I watched; we spent the entire day doing that. Some people might whistle while they work, but we talked because we had plenty to talk about.

We both liked to sew, so we chatted about sewing, patterns, fabrics, techniques, what we were going to make next—that sort of thing.

We both liked our husbands and we chatted about them too. She told me about what her husband had been doing and I reciprocated about mine.

Being that my husband was a junior, his name being exactly the same as his father's, it got confusing during our conversations as to which John each of us was referring. Shirley finally said, "I sometimes refer to them as John (her son) and S-R (as in Sr.) or John Daddy (her husband)."

But I didn't take the hint and started referring to *my* John and *your* John to distinguish between my husband and her husband.

After my doing this for a few minutes, she stated, matter-of-factly but lovingly, to me: "You realize that, although he is *your* husband, he is still *my* son and so, for *you*, he is not *my* John, he is *our* John."

SNIPPET 079 - Second Mom

    I loved Shirley almost as much as I loved my own mom; she was my second mom, never a mother-in-law. She loved me and treated me like a daughter, never a daughter-in-law. She was a wonderful person with many close friends who, all together, had spent many years watching their children grow up, playing bridge, making artistically creative things, and doing good deeds.
    Shirley was very intelligent, had graduated from high school at age sixteen, then had met John Senior, married him, and started raising a family by age nineteen. Their first child, Becky, was born in February 1937 and John, their second and last, in September, two and a half years later. Perhaps another reason Shirley and I were so close was that I was just one and a half months younger than her own daughter.
    John and I always liked talking to her and enjoyed reading and rereading her letters, written in such a way that even ordinary events made extraordinary reading. She had a vast vocabulary from avidly reading books and working crossword puzzles almost daily. She was self-educated in social skills and graces and did her best to teach them to me; although I was too much a rebel to learn immediately, I am a much better person for remembering and now using much of that knowledge she bestowed on me.
    To save money for other things in life, she made practically everything herself. She sewed slipcovers, draperies, men's and women's suits, vests, shirts, blouses, slacks, shorts, dresses, evening gowns, and decorated hats to match if the occasion called for one. She also monogrammed or embroidered many of the shirts, scarves, handkerchiefs, pillow covers, tablecloths, napkins, and hand-towels that she made or bought. She made clothes for her grandchildren, friends, and even me before and after I joined her "family" circle.
    Knitting and crocheting were another two of Shirley's artistic talents. Sometimes using a pattern and sometimes her own design, she knitted and/or crocheted woolen scarves, caps, sweaters, dressing table scarves, afghans, throw-pillow covers, and tablecloths. My favorite tablecloths are two string cloths, a small square one and a huge rectangular one, crocheted from string in an intricate design, and

SNIPPETS (bits and pieces of love and life) by CAROLE

a linen cloth with matching napkins, all seven pieces monogrammed, painstakingly and lovingly made just for John and me.

Shirley never wasted anything that was reusable. If it was the appropriate kind of wool, she would cut the fabric into strips, dye it if necessary, and hook it through heavy burlap to make rugs in her own original designs or braid and stitch it into oval or round traditional design "rag" rugs. Wall hangings made from heavy fabric which she appliqued with unique pictures fashioned from fabric scraps or embroidered with her own designs were other examples of her endless creativity. Using thousands of fabric scraps that she cut into various shapes, she made quilts for friends and relatives or for donating to her church for bazaar raffles. What wonderful, loving memories come to mind when we gaze at our king-size quilt containing some scraps left over from clothes she had made for us.

After she joined the same church that Mickey, her next-door neighbor and one of her best long-time friends, belonged to, the two of them added sewing church vestments to the other creative projects they did together. After Shirley died there in Savannah, where she had lived most of her life, her cremated remains were buried just outside the front door of Saint Paul's Episcopal Church in remembrance of her devotion and the volunteer work she did there.

This very gifted lady created so many artistic things that the list is almost endless. Her generosity, kindness, and gentle nature make us all miss her very much.

SNIPPET 080 - The Toothbrush

After many years of use, stoves tend to get a bit grubby in the crevices and seams even though you wipe them off each time you're done cooking. In the home of John's parents, against the inside wall of the kitchen, there sat such a stove.

The kitchen was a small room located at the back left side of the house. Directly across the narrow floor from the stove was the typical old-fashioned porcelain sink, complete with high back and built-in drain board. A single light bulb hung on a cord in the middle of the ceiling to light the kitchen at night. Above the sink there was a window to let in the sunlight and to allow you to look out into the side yard while you prepared food or washed the dishes.

One afternoon while we were visiting and Shirley was still at work in the fabric shop, I decided to give the stove a really thorough cleaning as a token of my appreciation for the delicious meals she had prepared for us. Being that John and I were still in grad school and on a very limited budget, we couldn't buy a gift for anyone, so this project would be my gift to her. I got out the cleaning products and a dishrag and looked for some kind of brush that I could use to scrub the stove crevices. I spotted a small handled brush with somewhat worn-out bristles sitting on the sill between the screen and the raised windowpane and grabbed it.

The brush was perfect for the job!

After a few hours of cleaning, I stood back and admired my work. The stove sparkled and looked almost new. When Shirley got home and saw it, she admired it too; she couldn't believe it was the same stove.

"How in the world did you manage to get it so clean?" she asked me.

I pointed to the brush I had returned to its place on the windowsill, and exclaimed, "Oh, it was easy! I used that small cleaning brush."

With a look of shock she whispered, "Please don't *ever* tell anyone you used it. Before he leaves for work every morning, John Daddy likes to brush his teeth here in the kitchen instead of wasting time going upstairs to the bathroom, and that's his *toothbrush*!"

SNIPPET 081 - Slave Quarters

John preceded me to New Orleans to start his summer job at Wesson Oil Company while I finished teaching in DeLand that June of 1961. He and his coworker-friend, Jeremy, had scoured the city seeking a suitable short-term-rental apartment for us to live in. Most housing in our price range required flashlights in the late afternoon to be able to find your way down tiny alleys that led to dingy or dirty one-room-flats. Late one day, they happened to find a converted slave quarters that, at least, had an immensely tall window, in the main room, that overlooked the sunny patio behind a mansion on Jackson Avenue, a block or so from St. Charles Avenue. The trolley and bus stops were close and would make it fairly easy for John to commute to the end of Jackson to ride the ferry across the Mississippi to Gretna where he worked in a laboratory doing research in cooking oils.

I arrived to find a small apartment, made decent enough to live in by John's thorough scrubbing of the entire quarters. After stepping onto the ceramic-tiled floor of the main room, I slowly gazed around. There was an iron-framed double bed on my left under a large eight-foot tall window covered only on the lower half by a red flowered cafe-styled curtain with a matching ruffle at the top of the upper half. A curious occupant on the second floor of the house across the small patio was peering into the room via the uncovered portion of the window.

The apartment was basically one room with two tiny appendages, one housing a sink, a small refrigerator, a tiny stove, and a few open shelves and the other housing a toilet and a three-foot square tub with shower. The only entrance from the outside was through a pair of tall shutters in front of a huge four-foot-wide wooden door leading in from the patio walkway. The shutters let in any welcomed breeze when the solid door was left standing open into the room. As we were standing outside facing this door when we first arrived, John had pointed out, on our right, the appended bathroom along with its six-foot-tall window overlooking the patio. The curtain on this window was simply another translucent shower curtain like the one opposite that kept water off the floor.

"You have to bathe during the day when daylight reflects off the curtained window or after dark with the light off so as not to be ogled by the passers-by," he had stated matter-of-factly.

"Well," I said, staring at the window and the person across the way, "if we want some privacy, the first improvement I plan to make will be a plain red fabric extension sewn to that ruffle. Then, when we close them, the curtains will cover the entire window. Otherwise, we will have to *live* in the dark as well as *bathe* in the dark."

One chest-of-drawers stood against the left wall at the foot and to the side of the bed. On the back wall was another large window with a fan that covered the lower half and obscured the view of weeds and discarded bathtub just outside. Next to that window and straight ahead was a small dining table with two chairs that sat on an old fireplace hearth (the fireplace was gone); to the right of that was the doorway that led to the kitchen. On the right wall hidden by an old teetering cloth screen was a bathroom sink with a mirror over it. To the right of the front door were two closets back-to-back, one facing the main room and one facing the small hallway that led to the "bathroom." The latter closet was totally unusable as water poured into it from the apartment upstairs whenever they turned on the faucets in their bathroom; the other stayed damp and anything, like shoes, left on its floor for more than a day or two molded.

Until John added support to the underside of the dining table, you had to hold onto your plate and utensils while you ate because the table surface tilted so badly that everything slid off. Even after it was fixed, the table was never quite level. The chairs had badly-worn-needlepoint seats that I covered with red vinyl to match the addition to the curtains. The red color added a cheerful liveliness to the room and a rose glow when the sun shone through the curtained upper window.

We invited Jeremy over for dinner as soon as we got settled and had made the minor improvements. The white, fringed, matelassé bedspread he had given us as a wedding present looked terrific on the iron bed which also served as a couch when we had guests. Jeremy and I got to sit in the two chairs, but John had to sit on a box at the dinner table. We enjoyed being together, laughing much of time as we tried to keep the red-meat-sauced spaghetti on our slightly-tilted plates and out of our laps while we ate. The tossed lettuce salad with

SNIPPETS (bits and pieces of love and life) by CAROLE

For one year he was a Cub Scout, but he got bored with that and never became a Boy Scout; he started scouting girls and learning to dance instead.

His social life mainly consisted of double dating with his best friend Hal or dating and studying with Deb or escorting debutantes to balls. I've seen photos of him and he looked adorable dressed in full-dress attire—swallow-tailed coat, white tie, and white gloves.

He lived in a neighborhood of wonderful people, like Deb, and one or two people that he considered a bit unusual, like Wanda. You can find out more about Wanda by reading the book or seeing the movie, *Midnight in the Garden of Good and Evil*.

He was in ROTC (Reserve Officers' Training Corps) in high school and did some exercising to help himself get stronger and to be a better football player. He also liked to run. After we got married and he was still attending Stetson, I happened to notice a medal in among his clothes, when I was putting away his clean laundry, and asked him what it was for.

He nonchalantly replied, "I got it my freshman year here at Stetson for winning the PT (physical training) Competition in ROTC. You had to do pull-ups, push-ups, sit-ups—that kind of thing—as many as you could do as fast as possible, and then run a mile. After I won, they told me I had set a new record. Surprised *me*; I hadn't even exercised in months."

"Did you get really sore muscles the next day after all that?" I asked.

"Nope, but a lot of the guys did and some of them even threw up right afterwards or before they even finished."

I didn't know John while he was a freshman and had not even been aware that he was on campus. It's amazing what you find out about your spouse just putting away his clothes, as long as you quiz him. If I hadn't asked, I never would have known. I wish he still had the medal, but it got lost somewhere during our moves from DeLand to New Orleans to Chapel Hill to Wilmington to Hockessin.

SNIPPET 084 - Oyster Roasts

John loved his dad and liked spending time with him. On many summer weekends, they would either fish or shrimp together. When John was a youngster, they would fish with rod and reel standing or sitting on a river bank, but when he was older, they would go out into the salt-water marshes near Savannah in a rowing-sized boat equipped with outboard motor. John preferred going out in the boat because then they could shrimp. Shrimp is one of his favorite foods, and they always caught a lot of them, sometimes as many as would entirely fill three thirty-gallon-garbage cans—enough shrimp to almost sink the boat. They used a shrimp net that they dragged through the water. The net was a special one with a wooden board on each end, which caused the net to spread out and catch everything in the vicinity; the catch yielded mostly shrimp, but also fish, bottles, an occasional old boot, and other junk that they sorted out and discarded. Sometimes his dad would buy a bushel of oysters before they left the dock area to return home.

Frequently, especially when the catch was plentiful, after they arrived home, they would invite the neighbors over for a fish and shrimp feast and, perhaps, oyster roast. There was an outdoor, brick grill with chimney in the side yard by the back fence of their house on 48th Street in Savannah. The brickwork contained a large steel plate as well as a metal grill that extended over the grating that held the coals; as the coals burned, the ashes would fall through the grating to the area beneath. You could cook food in pots on the heated plate the way you do on a stove burner or charbroil food on the grill.

John's favorite way to eat shrimp was simply to boil them in a pot over the coals, then peel and eat them as soon as the shrimp were cool enough to handle. His favorite way to eat oysters was a bit more complicated. The traditional way to roast oysters was to spread them directly on the steel plate and place a wet croaker sack on top of them so they would roast under the steaming sack. John's way was to get the fire really hot, and while waiting for the coals to become just right, he would shuck the oysters from their shells. Then he threw the shucked oysters directly onto the coals, and when they had cooked enough to become no longer visible, he would grill hotdogs on the

SNIPPETS (bits and pieces of love and life) by CAROLE

French dressing didn't spill out of our bowls and the buttered-garlic bread we finger-held between bites alongside our spaghetti.

Ants really liked our home and invaded it frequently; after a hard rain, entire colonies usually moved in and covered the walls. Spraying insecticide only deterred them until it dried. We had to keep sugar and peanut butter in bowls of water in the refrigerator in order to keep them from being carried off. The ants liked any kind of food, and any crumb that fell disappeared in minutes, leaving no need to sweep the floor after eating. We asked for repairs of the water leaks and for some method of keeping out the ants, but our requests were ignored. It rained heavily the night before we moved to North Carolina and the ants invaded as usual. Having heavily sprayed all the ants, sticking them tightly to the walls, we headed out and said "good-bye" to our interesting adventure in the "slave quarters."

SNIPPET 082 - *He Comes First*

Mema reminded me, whenever I needed it, "You married John because you love him, and if you ever have to choose between him and the rest of the world, including your family, just remember—he comes first."

The summer of 1961 when we lived in New Orleans, John had a three-month job working as a research chemist for the company where he had worked the previous summer. I soon discovered a job for me was impossible; no one was hiring any more summer employees and no one needed volunteers.

Some afternoons, if we had a little money left over, I would leave our apartment at three o'clock, catch the bus at the corner and ride to the end of Jackson Avenue, ferry across the Mississippi River to Gretna as a foot-passenger, then catch a waiting cab and ride to the laboratory facility. There I would wait at the gate for John to leave work so I could accompany him home on the reverse route. That hour and a half trip back to the apartment and the brief minutes during a hasty breakfast and dinner were the only times available for us to hold hands and just chat during the week and, too frequently *I* felt, there was even less time available for that on weekends.

On a few Saturdays or Sundays, when the weather was suitable, we rode the buses and trolleys out to Lake Pontchartrain or just kept transferring from vehicle to vehicle to enjoy the sights, hold hands, and chat; you could transfer all day to anywhere around New Orleans for ten to twenty-five cents. It suited us just fine; we were used to cheap dates at Stetson and we had known there would be little, if any, money to spend on anything besides education and necessities for at least four years after we got married. Longing so much for John's companionship, I relished those days.

John had a fellowship to study organic chemistry and obtain a PhD at the University of North Carolina starting that fall and we knew there would be required placement exams for all the new graduate students during the week before the start of the fall semester.

"If I'm going to retain my fellowship, I have to do really well on the entrance exams. I intend to spend a lot of time studying," John had told me. And he did; he studied all the chemistry he possibly could whenever he wasn't working, commuting, eating, sleeping, or briefly playing. He simply put the majority of our relationship *on hold*.

In an essentially-one-room-apartment, you are stuck in the same room day after day with no other suitable area to spend time in. I had quit grad school to get married and work, so had nothing I wanted to study intently like John did. I was, and he too, madly in love, but I could only look and not touch because he had to concentrate on his studies. He (and, consequently, we) had no time for other friends and, although he knew people at work, I neither knew nor had anyone else to talk to. I could do little more than be a housekeeper and cook, which was easy to do because there were only a few furnishings and we ate a very limited diet. I tried reading books at the library or at home and I tried walking or sitting outdoors, but I failed miserably in both endeavors. The extreme hardship, of the aloneness when he was at work and the loneliness when he was home, devastated me so much that I ended up sitting, staring into oblivion or uncontrollably crying, for much of the remaining summer.

I would hear Mema's words, loudly in my head—*Just remember: he comes first*—and sit by silently watching him study. His diligent, hard work paid off as it did make a difference when he took the tests in the fall. The Chairman of the Chemistry Department at UNC wrote a letter to the Chairman of the Chemistry Department at Stetson University, stating that "the four placement exams, one each in organic, inorganic, analytical, and physical chemistry, are considered difficult and John's passing them all on the first try, and moreover, scoring the highest grade on two of them, is quite an achievement and speaks well for him and for Stetson's Chemistry Department." (No other person passed all four exams.)

Nevertheless, sometimes, during that long, blue summer, I desperately wished *I* came first. Later, I did come first, many times.

SNIPPET 083 - *John's Youth*

Shirley stated to me one day: "I never could understand why John didn't get into trouble like *normal* boys. I even asked my bridge-buddies if they thought something was wrong with him, and all of them said, 'Heavens, no. You're lucky to have such a wonderful son.'" From that and the other tidbits I gleaned from people, he was simply too busy with the things that, at least to him, were important in life to have the time for frivolous mischief with the other kids.

When he was young, Shirley was never able to go out in the yard and look up at the sky if he was playing outside. He frequently would be reading and swinging in his hammock fifty feet up in the tree tops, and it would make her stomach feel queasy when she saw him; so, she just quit looking any farther up than about thirty feet if he was somewhere around home. After he went off to college, she was able to look at the sky again because he took the hammock down.

Another reason she worried was that John kept white phosphorus in water in the attic and Shirley was afraid she might knock it over and the water would spill out and the result would be a fire which would burn the house down. We removed it forever after grad school, much to her relief.

Once he decided, at age eight, that he wanted to be a chemist for his career, he started saving his money for attending college and graduate school. His goal was to have his PhD in chemistry at age twenty-four and to work for a big chemical company like DuPont Company. To earn money, he worked at odd jobs that included short-term money lending to his mom's friends. Whenever her friends complained to Shirley that he was charging usury fees of up to 25%, she simply told them: "If you want to borrow money from John, that is your business. Pay his fee or don't take the money. I refuse to get involved in my son's finances. You'll just have to discuss the matter with him."

She also refused to clean the floor under his bed because that was his bank where he stashed his money—wadded-up dollar bills simply tossed under the bed.

SNIPPETS (bits and pieces of love and life) by CAROLE

steel grill just above them, then eat the hotdogs. At that point the hot dogs had just a hint of oyster flavor from the incinerated oysters. He always left the traditionally cooked oysters for the guests to eat.

Easter weekend when I first met John's family, I went fishing with John and John Daddy out in the boat while Shirley stayed home to prepare the rest of the food to go with our catch. It was fun to watch the two men fishing and interacting together. I even tried my hand using one of their poles and caught one fish, which was so small that John unhooked and released it back in the water for me. When we got back to the house, I met all their neighbors during the outdoor feast we had, eating at picnic tables set up by the grill.

SNIPPET 085 - *Explosions*

There is mysterious allurement about explosives that catches the attention of everyone, especially little boys. Most people like to watch the spectacular and colorful display of fireworks on holidays, but some just enjoy the loud pops and bangs of the explosions. John enjoys both the lights and the noise and, as a kid, made his own fireworks. His favorite use of explosives though was building and shooting off rockets in his backyard.

He had one mishap when he was twelve that almost caused the loss of his eyesight. It turned out to be a good misfortune, however, because he became extremely safety conscious after that event. He was mixing two chemicals when the mixture suddenly and unexpectedly exploded, thrusting chemical particles and glass fragments everywhere with some embedding themselves into his hands and eyes. An ophthalmologist spent hours tediously picking as many as possible of the fragments out of his eyes; his eyes healed just fine with the occasional few flecks remaining that John removed himself as each worked its way to the surface during the next few years. The glass fragments that could be seen in his hands were easily removed but, as with his eyes, small fragments continued to work their way to the surface at random intervals. He experienced a loud ringing in his ears from the tremendous noise but the ringing gradually dissipated over many years. Because of the immediate concern of the possibility of his losing his eyesight, no one bothered to look in his ears. At least one eardrum had burst from the loudness of the noise, but that was not discovered until a routine ear exam years later showed that one and perhaps both had burst and healed. John felt extremely lucky and very fortunate that there was no debilitating and lasting damage. His whole family felt joy and great relief.

For his tenth-grade Science Fair project, he did an exhibit on explosives including, among other things, various methods of making firecrackers. Apparently, some people were even more impressed than the judges were—John's exhibit got stolen. Bet they got a bigger bang than they expected to get from just stealing!

SNIPPETS (bits and pieces of love and life) by CAROLE

He liked to surprise other people with his nitrogen iodide "exploding" paper. If you made the mixture properly (which John, of course, always did), you obtained a dark crystalline solid that was fairly stable when wet; you then could filter off the wet solid onto filter papers and set them to dry in various places for unwary others to move, pick up, or step on. Once dry, the solid was extremely sensitive and would make a loud pop from the weak chemical explosion that took place when the dried chemical was disturbed by as little as the insignificant disruption of a fly landing on it. The chemistry students at Stetson especially liked to do this for the annual chemistry party held in the backyard of the home of the chemistry professor who was the chairman of the department.

John's advice, which he shares with all his lab helpers at work, about dealing with peroxides is: "If you can run faster than six thousand meters per second, then you can avoid the shock wave from the explosion of the peroxide if you are carelessly working with it."

Along with singer/song writer Johnny Mercer and his daughters, one of whom John had dated, John made it into "Social Whirl," the Savannah newspaper society column; but it wasn't for the type of activity that you'd think. Here's the part written about him:

"The 48-49th Street neighborhood is very fortunate to have the peace and quiet of a chemistry lab in it. John, who has been collecting chemical equipment since he was eight years old, now has one of the most complete labs in Savannah. Dr. Royster, chemist, states that it is one of the most complete labs for an amateur chemist he has ever seen. John has devoted an entire building in the backyard to this lab, and occasionally late at night, crashes and explosions can be distinctly heard, and powerful odors creep out into the night air. John plans to return to Stetson University in September where he is majoring in chemistry."

I would have thought they would have written about his charm and the debutante he escorted to one of the balls—but no—they chose to write about his explosive personality instead.

SNIPPET 086 - *You're Going*

"I don't care what your father says, you will not live in West Palm Beach and teach school while your husband attends graduate school without you. That's what we did and I still regret it. It doesn't matter if you have to scrub floors to earn enough to get by; at least you will be together. So don't pack your bags to come home, you're going with John," Mema directed me over the phone.

Daddy had found me a job through some of his associates and had been trying to convince me to move home while John went on to earn his doctorate at UNC without me. I had been debating whether or not to accept the job offer since I had no job lined up in Chapel Hill. John's fellowship would barely cover the living expenses for one person living in a dorm and certainly not two people living in an apartment. But Mom always knew best, so I turned down the offer to teach in the Palm Beach County school system and moved to Chapel Hill with John. I now had, unfortunately, a one-thousand-dollar debt to repay the state of Florida instead of being able to work it off.

We didn't have many belongings and didn't add to them while we lived in New Orleans that summer, so they still fit easily into the U-Haul®, that we pulled behind our car, and into the small apartment, situated on the outskirts of town, that we rented through a real estate agency when we arrived in Chapel Hill.

After John took the placement exams, we met the Chairman of the Chemistry Department at UNC; he was very kind and a tremendous help to us. First, he talked to the administrators and got us an apartment that we could better afford, in the cheaper student housing area of Victory Village, instead of our current apartment that was not near the campus and cost four times as much. Second, he found me a temporary job working in the chemistry library until I could find a teaching position in the Durham County school system.

The teaching job that I obtained had strings attached because I lacked two weeks of teaching in Florida to receive reciprocity in North Carolina. That meant I had to work at the lower pay scale of an emergency rating and had to participate in the Master of Arts in Teaching program at Duke University, carrying a minimum load of twelve hours of courses that met nights and weekends. The job itself

SNIPPETS (bits and pieces of love and life) by CAROLE

was for teaching a different course for each period of the day for students in grades eight through twelve.

But, we had a place to live, I had a job that would prove to be extremely difficult but that would allow us to manage OK financially, and I got to stay with the person I loved. Thanks Mema. I couldn't have asked for more.

SNIPPET 087 - Drafty Apartment

Our apartment in the University of North Carolina's Victory Village was exactly what we needed in some ways; it was cheap, near campus, and we could rent used furniture for it. But it had its drawbacks too. It was so old that the university would not rent stoves or refrigerators because of the floors being so rickety and their concern that the appliances might fall through; you had to supply your own. There were no beds to rent either; however, you could rent a so-called-couch consisting of a single-sized bed with an extra, rolled-and-tied mattress that served as the back, with each mattress having a covering made of black-and-used-to-be-white-striped ticking. We decided that if we had to buy appliances and a bed, we might as well buy new ones; we bought a refrigerator, a small four-burner electric stove, and a king-size bed. We still have the almost-forty-year-old refrigerator for storing extra nuts, flour, and beverages in the barroom that John built in our basement.

We did rent by-the-month: one so-called-couch, that we covered with a blue blanket, at seventy five cents, two unmatched chest of drawers at fifty cents each, two tables to serve as desks, one of which doubled as the dinner table, at twenty five cents each, and two chairs at ten cents each. If anyone came to dinner they had to bring their own chairs until we saved enough money to buy a card table and four chairs to serve as the dining set. We still have those purchased items too, although they're not in as good condition as the refrigerator.

Each set of two apartments shared six to eight steps (our set had eight) that led to the two front porches that had a dividing wall to separate them from each other. The steps were necessary because the building was elevated off the ground by stilts. Each apartment had one front door but no other entrance/exit way. Each also had venetian blinds on the two large double windows, one in the front living/dining room and one in the back bedroom, but had no doors on the "closets" or on the kitchen "cabinets" which were really just somewhat-built-in-book-shelves. The kitchen and bathroom were adjacent and you walked through the kitchen to get to the bedroom; in our apartment the door to the bathroom was on your right just before the doorway to

SNIPPETS (bits and pieces of love and life) by CAROLE

the bedroom. The apartment next door was just the reverse and so on down the line of six apartments.

The first year we survived without any decorations, but I found the environment so depressing that I insisted that I had to do something to make it more cheerful or I was going to scream, *loudly*. To appease me, John allowed fifty dollars for decorating the entire apartment. I bought curtain rods and fabric and transformed the entire place after John installed the rods. For the living room I made short draperies for the front window out of a light brown linen-look print with multi-colored, medium-sized flowers that went perfectly with the blue walls and couch blanket and the brown wood of the furniture. To enclose the shelves in the kitchen I made curtains of unbleached muslin that coordinated nicely with the front window draperies. For the bedroom window, I made short draperies from a silky white colored fabric printed with tiny pink roses lined with heavier white fabric. Then I made a same-as-the-roses-pink dust ruffle for the bed to set off the beautiful white, fringed, matelassé bedspread that Jeremy had given us. We hung white sheets from brass rings to cover the closets. It now felt more like a home and was much more pleasing to the eye.

My dad bought Mom a new vacuum cleaner, so she gave us the old one to use, saving me from sweeping the wooden floor and stirring up the dust that caused me to have allergy problems. The vacuum cleaner was terrific and really got the floor cleaner, I bet, than it had been in years. Unfortunately, the vacuum cleaner created a worse problem than it solved; after I had used it several times, you could see daylight, coming from under the apartment, shining up between the floor boards that had shrunk apart over the years. The rest of that winter and the next winters were terribly cold and drafty. The temperature difference between the ceiling and the floor was forty Fahrenheit degrees and we had to wear extra clothes and wrap in blankets to sit and study. We had a furnace thermostat but it was useless as far as setting it for our apartment.

The thermostat we had was for the entire building so it regulated the heating for all six apartments, not just ours. The other residents complained so much to us about their apartment being either too hot or too cold that John took action to resolve the conflict. He visited each apartment in the building, obtaining from each resident couple their one vote for a recommended temperature setting. He averaged the settings, wrote that temperature on a piece of tape, set the thermostat, and stuck the thermostat in place with the tape so no one could change it. Nevertheless, the couples still complained about the temperature to the housing office personnel; so frequently, in fact, that they sent a maintenance man to our apartment to set the temperature at seventy degrees Fahrenheit, a setting which they considered to be appropriate for all concerned.

When the maintenance man arrived, he said, "The office has received a lot of complaints and sent me here to set the temperature personally."

John led the man across the front room to the inside wall adjacent to the bathroom. As they stood looking at the taped thermostat, John told him about his voting procedure and showed him what he had done.

"Aaagh, just let them bitch," the man urged as he turned about and left. We never saw him again.

After that when people came to us to complain, John simply showed them the taped thermostat approved by the maintenance man; they left distressed but realized that there was nothing that anyone could do but live with it.

It was definitely an interesting place to live. Our thanks to Mema for the thought and the vacuum cleaner, but next time I hope she gives us a new broom instead.

SNIPPET 088 - Three-inch Neighbors

Stuart and Carol, being several years older than we were, had already been out in the working world but had decided to attend graduate school, Stuart to study dentistry and Carol to study chemistry. They lived in the apartment adjacent to our end apartment in one of the buildings on Daniels Road in Victory Village.

The village was a student housing area that had been hastily constructed after World War II to house the many families with husbands returning to college after serving in the armed forces. There were some single family houses but the majority of the dwellings were wooden buildings on stilts consisting of six apartments, two rooms deep, with each set of two buildings joined by flues to a brick structure that housed the furnace for the apartments on both sides. The walls between the apartments were about three inches thick and not well insulated, so you could hear much of what went on in the apartment next to you.

We soon discovered that we would have to resolve the name problem that developed because whenever one of the husbands called out for "Carole," Carol and I both answered. Since she was the older of us two, the four of us decided she should keep the name Carol and I should be called Christie, which is my middle name. Over the years several of my close friends including my college roommate, Marcia, had preferred to call me Christie, so I was used to that and John quickly adjusted to it also.

We enjoyed visiting them at their apartment. Not only were they fun to be with, but they had real furniture which was comfortable to sit on and rugs on their floor making their place more like a home.

I liked Stuart and Carol's method of fighting, which I discovered when I happened to catch them in the middle of an argument one afternoon. I had approached the front screen door of their apartment and noticed them head to head with arms around each other's shoulders talking softly together.

"Come on in. We were just having a fight," Carol called out as I raised my hand to knock on the door.

"That's a bit unusual way to fight," I said as I entered the front room.

"We always fight like this so no one can shout or swing at the other, and it keeps both people involved thinking more clearly and calmly," she added.

Great idea! We should all be taught and required to fight that way. Wish I had learned from their example instead of just noting it in my mind.

One night about 3:00 A.M., our phone rang and Carol was on the other end asking me, "Christie, are you all right?"

"Of course. Why are you phoning me? I thought you two would be sound asleep at this hour," I answered.

"Well, we awoke when we heard this tap, tap, tapping noise and thought you might be signaling for help."

"Oh, I am *so* sorry," I apologized. "I was cleaning the bathroom and was rapping the brush on the edge of the toilet to shake out the water after I finished cleaning with it. I promise not to clean the house again during the night; I'll do it during the day. But, thank you so much for being concerned and calling me; I really appreciate it since John has already gone to the chemistry building, and I am here all alone."

We always heard a light tapping from their apartment every night too as Stuart rapped his toothbrush on the basin to shake the water from the bristles after brushing his teeth. It's amazing what we learned about each other just from sounds.

Carol and I had an unusual bond besides friendship. She was doing experimental work growing crystals that required strong strands of filament, which were unavailable in the fineness that she needed, to suspend them; since my hair was both long and very fine, I supplied her with strands of my hair to use as filaments for her crystals.

One day I was out on our porch leaning over the banister railing pouring water down onto my bed of morning glories and noticed Carol, slightly leaning against and holding onto their porch railing, gazing wistfully into the distance.

"What'cha thinking about?" I quizzed. "You have a far-away, dreamy look in your eyes."

"Oh, I was just thinking about how I wanted us to have our first child before I turned thirty," she smiled, not revealing her secret.

And they did; it was a girl whom they named Kathryn. Carol was pregnant and looked simply radiant!

SNIPPETS (bits and pieces of love and life) by CAROLE

John and Carol frequently walked over to the chemistry building together and he even began to take the stairs extra slowly, though two at a time, so she could keep up with him and not get too tired in her delicate condition.

The best celebration we had together was when the four of us assembled John's dissertation. We each walked around the room gathering up the pages in sequence and completing the number of copies required for the professors who would quiz John during his oral exam and for permanent documentation of his experimental work in the synthesis of cysteine peptides. Afterwards we feasted together with a dinner that included steak, the first we had ever bought, and champagne.

During our three and a half years of living so close, we became great friends. We have visited each other's homes over the years and each time picked up our friendship as though we had never been apart. One year the week between Christmas and New Year's, we sent them a large photo of champagne, glasses, and an uncut loaf of bread with the caption "A jug of wine, a loaf of bread, but where art thou?" We'll always think of them as being our first champagne buddies and our three-inch (away) neighbors.

SNIPPET 089 - Socks

When I was young, all girls had to learn how to darn socks. Using a small gourd that you slipped inside to hold the sock stretched out, you stitched and wove the patch into place with needle and thread. I darned many socks as a child, teenager, and young adult, even after I got married, until we could afford to use old socks as dust rags or shoe-polishing cloths and simply buy new pairs. But the first year we were married, John and I discovered a totally different use for socks other than wearing them or using them as rags.

Even though I no longer use thread to darn socks, I use thread to color-code them. When I buy several pairs of socks that are identical, I code each pair with a different color of thread stitched in the pattern of a dash (—) on the toe of each sock in the pair making it much faster and easier to find the sock mates after laundering them.

One of the most useful wedding presents we received came from Pat, who was just eleven at the time. "I want you to have this piggy bank so you can use it to save all your pennies, nickels, dimes, and quarters that you get as change. Then you'll have money for a rainy day," she had explained. It was a pink-plastic pig, about a foot long and eight inches high, with a hole in the bottom for a stopper and a slit in the top large enough for silver dollars. We used it, faithfully, but had only pennies, nickels, dimes, and an occasional quarter to drop into the bank, never a half dollar or dollar coin.

The week of our first Christmas together alone, we were in Chapel Hill. John was attending grad school at the University of North Carolina and I was teaching at Southern High School in Durham County and attending grad school at Duke University. We hadn't planned to go anywhere for Christmas since we had so much studying and other work to do. On Christmas Eve we decided to go out to buy a tree and discovered that all the trees were frozen and dead from an ice storm that week. We did, however, purchase a small very-real-looking, artificial tree and some ornaments at half price at the dime store fifteen minutes before closing time. We took it back to the apartment and set it up. We had bought no gifts in order to buy the tree. We were sitting back on our so-called-couch, looking at the decorated tree and the lonely apartment, when we both,

SNIPPETS (bits and pieces of love and life) by CAROLE

simultaneously and suddenly, grabbed each other and started crying. We really missed being with family. We immediately called John's parents and asked if we could come home.

"Please do," Shirley said, "we miss you terribly too."

We hastily packed our bags and prepared to leave. The car had very little gas left in the tank, it was too late to cash a check for money to buy gas, and we had to travel over 350 miles to the house in Savannah. This was definitely a rainy day! We robbed the partially-filled-piggy-bank but had nothing to carry all the change in. John remembered that he had a pair of heavy white socks, grabbed one of them, dumped all the change into it, and we set out to go home. We arrived around ten in the morning, Christmas Day.

Throughout the trip, whenever we stopped to buy gas for the car or cups of coffee for us, to help us stay awake and alert, we carried our fat, heavy sock to the cashier and counted out the change to pay for our purchase. We got some interesting looks and comments, but everyone agreed that we had found the best use ever for a sock.

SNIPPET 090 - One Down, One to Go

It was our first anniversary, Tuesday, December 26, 1961. We had arrived the previous morning to spend Christmas with John's parents. We decided we needed to have champagne to celebrate the big occasion and went to the liquor store to buy a bottle. We had only some change left from our trip, so bought a brand that we could afford—the cheapest. We discovered later that buying the cheapest is not the best idea because it wasn't very good, and cheap champagne can give you a terrible headache. But the whole point was to have some champagne; the rest didn't matter.

No one was in the mood to cook dinner that night. John Daddy had eaten a sandwich and had gone to bed early as usual because he had to work the next day. Shirley, John, and I stood around the stove where we were setting dishes of leftovers from the refrigerator nearby. We couldn't decide how to fix the leftovers or what part we wanted to eat, so we just stood there looking at the food and began picking pieces of turkey off the carcass and eating them with our fingers.

Shirley laughed and said, "Are we planning to eat like cannibals standing around the pot?"

"Looks like it," I answered as I kept nibbling.

John decided for us. "We might as well; but if we are, we should do it in style. I'll open the champagne; you get some glasses."

So, that's what the three of us did—we ate like cannibals and drank champagne. What a marvelous but unusual celebration we had!

But, we needed a toast. We discussed it briefly, mentioning that people wondered if the marriage would last since it was done in such a rush. Well, we had made it through one year, and we figured if you are always only halfway through the marriage, you can never get divorced, so it would last forever or at least until one, or both, of us croaked. John and I, giggling as we raised and clinked our glasses together, exclaimed in unison: "One down, one to go!"

Every year we make our toast, exactly the same only different, but now with our favorite, or at least the best we can afford, champagne. This year on December 26, 2002, the toast will be "Forty-two down, forty-two to go!"

SNIPPET 091 - Twenty-four Hours to Leave GA

We never dreamed it would take one complete day to leave Savannah. We had packed the car and were heading back to Chapel Hill that morning of December 27, 1961.

Shirley had asked, "Couldn't you stay just one more day and not leave until tomorrow?"

"We really need to get home to try to salvage what's left of the few days before classes start again, to get some studying done," we both said, sad to be leaving.

We drove off and got as far as halfway up the south side of the very high-arched Talmadge Bridge heading north across the Savannah River. The car coughed and sputtered, barely making it to the top, then coasted down the other side into South Carolina where John steered it to a halt on the side of the road. John let the car sit a few minutes, then started it up again and drove it a short distance before it came to another halt. The fuel pump had started failing. We didn't dare go back across this bridge so we sat then drove for the next several hours, limping the car back to Savannah the long way around over a flatter bridge. A South Carolina highway patrolman stopped us after he had cruised by us several times to see what was going on and offered to call a tow truck for us when we explained the problem. We thanked him and said we couldn't pay the towing fee, so would simply take our time getting back to Savannah to get the car fixed.

We went to a service garage and had a rebuilt fuel pump installed, since we couldn't afford a new one. Thinking the car was fixed, we started out again and got as far as halfway up the Talmadge Bridge. The car coughed and sputtered, barely making it to the top, then coasted down the other side where it came to a halt again. This time the car was too badly in need of repair to get farther than the first gas station. There we phoned the family for help, and Becky sent her husband in their car to take us and our luggage back to John's parents' home.

By that time, John Daddy had returned home from work. I waited at the house with Shirley while John went with his dad in his truck over to South Carolina, chained our car to it, and towed it back to another service garage where his dad knew a good mechanic. John

Daddy came on home while John waited for our car to be repaired. That mechanic installed a different rebuilt pump after removing the one which had been ruined by being installed backwards by the previous mechanic. By the time he was done, about eighteen hours had passed since we first said good-bye to John's parents.

John then drove our car from the garage to his parents' home and stashed our luggage back into the trunk. Before we left again on our long journey, we decided that we had better take a short nap and eat breakfast.

As we hugged goodbye this time, Shirley admonished us: "I told you that you should stay another day; you might just as well have because you were forced to anyway. We could have spent the extra time enjoying each other's company instead of your spending it with mechanics."

"Next time we'll take your advice." I laughed, knowing she hadn't hexed us.

As we drove away, we wished we had taken her advice this time; we always enjoyed visiting them. We decided the Talmadge Bridge would be a good test for the newly acquired fuel pump, so took that route again, for the third time. The car ran smoothly up and over the bridge; we were finally on our way home. But, instead of the usual half-hour, it had taken us twenty-four hours to leave Georgia.

SNIPPET 092 - The Witch

I could fascinate, teach, and inspire only the self-motivated students who desired to learn; the vast majority were not like that; they only wanted to get, but usually not work for, a passing grade and go on. I did not *give* grades, my students had to *earn* them, but I willingly helped them earn their grades if they wanted help.

I had a young girl with an IQ of seventy in one of my science classes who was not only self-motivated but had parents willing to spend as much time as necessary to help her learn and obtain her high school diploma. Her mom came several afternoons a week to work with her daughter and me. I knew the girl studied many hours at home as well, but I gave her no extra compensation when it came to tests, she would have to compete with everyone else in the real world. I was delighted to turn in the final grade for the course to be recorded in the school office and displayed on her report card; she earned an "A."

I gave ten pop quizzes and usually two or three forty-five-minute tests during each grading period. My students hated pop quizzes and moaned and groaned, every time I gave one, as much as I did when I was a student; but I didn't want them to be procrastinators like I was, so I figured I was doing them a favor. They couldn't warn the students in the next class because I only taught one class of each different subject, and that distressed them even more.

If you're wondering why ten instead of some other number of pop quizzes, that was so I could grade them on a scale of one to ten points each. At the end of the grading period, I could simply take the sum of those ten grades and use that as one forty-five-minute test grade to average with the other test grades for the final grade. Anticipating that my students would wonder too, I also explained my reasoning to them during our first class together. John is really fast with arithmetic and I would call out the one- to ten-point grades to him so he could sum them in his head and tell me the total to record. Since we didn't own a calculator, it simply made life easier for me.

One student, in my math seminar for gifted seniors, assumed that being a lead player on the football team would get him a passing grade regardless of how well he did his work; he earned an "F" the first grading period. His father came to see me and demanded I change the grade, but I explained my policy and refused; he watched his son sit on the bench during spring training that second grading period. Amazingly, that student decided he had to earn his grades and he did—all "A's" after that. To my surprise, I think he even liked me a little bit anyway; he helped his classmates teach me how to dance the "Twist."

Discipline was sometimes a problem. I looked younger than many of the students and, consequently, was not regarded at all as an authority figure; I had to make up for that shortcoming by being very strict. Young people don't like strictness either. Some students attending Southern High School appeared to really like and appreciate me, but most referred to me by their bestowed nickname—which I secretly liked and frequently overheard in their conversations—"The Witch."

I commuted the twenty-or-so miles each way to the school in our car with no air conditioner and no heater. When the weather turned cold, as it does in late fall and winter in North Carolina, I started wearing extra sweaters, a coat (sometimes topped by a raincoat), gloves, and galoshes to help me arrive unfrozen at the school; I left the blanket, that was also wrapped around me, in the car when I got out. While I was walking to the building from the parking lot one bitterly cold morning, I passed by two students talking together. I overheard one boy, as he pointed at my galoshes, tell the other, "She probably even wears those in July."

They probably even thought that I, instead of driving my car, preferred to ride a broom when the weather was really hot.

SNIPPET 093 - So Young, So Bald

In the spring of 1962, the high school principal asked me if my husband and I would join some of the other faculty members as chaperones at the Spring Dance to be held the next week on Saturday evening in the gym at the school. I agreed immediately because John and I like to dance and this would be a chance to dance to live music, something we had not been able to afford to do since we left Stetson University after John graduated.

All the students were told which faculty members were going to be chaperones, so the students in my Senior Math Seminar wanted to know if my husband and I danced. Because most of them were going to the dance, I figured they were probably curious to see how old people did it and whether or not they should bother watching us. I said, "Yes," even though I sensed that would not be the end of their questions and would probably spark even more. This class was my favorite; the students were extremely bright and fun to teach, so I shared a bit of myself as well as my knowledge of mathematics with them.

Since the lowest IQ, for a student in that class of fourteen, was 145, this particular seminar class had been established just for this semester so I could teach them college-level mathematics including rings, fields, integral domains, permutations, combinations and any other fascinating topics that I desired. We had no textbooks per se; I simply wrote out the information needed and handed out copies for each day's class. Whenever I gave them a test, I pre-took it myself making sure that it took me two hours to complete; I then gave it to them to complete within the fifty-five-minute class period; no one failed to complete a test and few made a grade less than "95" on it. The extra work meant that I got almost no sleep because I taught five other math and science subjects, with no two the same, the other five periods during the school day.

The next question I was asked was if we could do the "Twist" since that was a very popular dance then. To their astonishment, I said, "No. That's one of the new dances neither my husband nor I have learned." They insisted that I had to learn and they would teach me. We spent the whole period "twisting" and giggling instead of doing math. By the end of class, I was ready to go home to teach John and did just that.

The day of the dance I gave John his biweekly haircut; he has a beautifully shaped head with a slight widow's peak so he looks quite nice with his hair short. Afterwards, we showered, dressed up in our Sunday best, and went to the dance. As we danced with all the younger couples, I happened to notice that the bright rectangular beams of light, reflecting off the revolving multi-mirrored-surfaced-globe, reflected back off his scalp that showed through the stubby, one-sixteenth- to one-quarter-inch-long hair. The shine was so obvious that I assumed others must have noticed it too since my students were scrutinizing us and our dancing, especially during the "Twist," but no one mentioned anything about it that evening.

Monday in my favorite class, we had a quick discussion about the dance and what a great time everyone had. The students had never seen John before and someone asked his age. "He's twenty-two, two and a half years younger than I," I replied.

One of the boys who had gone to the dance, obviously quite concerned, began waving his hand in the air for instant recognition.

I nodded to him and asked, "Do you have a comment? Or a question?"

"A question," he said, looking puzzled. "If your husband is *so young*, why is he *so bald*?"

SNIPPET 094 - Weird Schedule

"If we want to finish graduate school as quickly as possible, we will have to set up a schedule that is different from the other graduate students. During the day, the lab is much too crowded and also much too hot when the temperature hits between 115 and 120 degrees in the summer," John stated at dinner that summer evening after the first two semesters at UNC.

So with pencil and paper in hand and planning aloud, we wrote down a possible schedule; it actually worked and we followed it for the next two and a half years.

SCHEDULE
6:00 P.M. - 2:00 A.M.: sleep
2:00 - 2:30 A.M.: get dressed, fix and eat breakfast, pack lunches
2:30 - 8:00 A.M.: John works in lab; Carole studies in John's office or does house chores then studies at home (on weekends, both do laundry, Carole irons, John vacuums, both clean apartment)
8:00 A.M. - 4:00 P.M.: take classes and study with time out for short coffee breaks and lunch (on weekends, do shopping and other chores requiring stores to be open)
4:00 - 6:00 P.M.: fix and eat supper; shower and get ready for bed

The hardest part of living with this schedule was getting others used to our weird hours. People, especially my dad, liked to phone us after 8:00 P.M. When we went to bed between 10:00 and 11:30 P.M., Daddy phoned at 3:00 A.M. but when that was a good time to phone, he called around 10:00 P.M.; he didn't like our schedule—it did not fit into his.

Doing laundry between 2:00 and 5:00 A.M. usually got us a police escort. Because our car died the first winter we owned it, we had to walk or ride bicycles everywhere. We lived about a mile from the twenty-four-hour Laundromat so had to carry everything to and fro in bags. John carried the large duffel bag full of clothes, and I carried the supplies and a small bag of the clothes that didn't fit in the duffel. Sometimes he rode his bike and I walked alongside, but most of the time we both walked. The police, cruising the campus and town all night in their cars, would frequently stop to question us as to what we had in the bags.

"Just laundry and supplies. We're headed to the Laundromat," John always answered.

The police never searched us but often slowly followed us to see that we really were going to wash clothes. On our return trip home, they would just nod or wave at us.

We always felt safe—no one else ever bothered us.

SNIPPET 095 - Efficiency Expert

Because we were on an extremely limited budget, John required us to write down in small bound booklets, one for each of us, every expense we incurred. It didn't matter whether it was money spent for just a cup of coffee; the expenditure had to be recorded on paper. At the end of the week, he totaled up the expenses from the two tablets; if we had spent too much, we had to cut back the next week until we were on budget again. Since John is really fast with arithmetic, he kept all the financial records, and still does.

The efficiency even carried over into other parts of our living. Since we had to wash dishes by hand, we tried to use only one pot for cooking and we both ate off the same plate and drank out of the same glass. We did have our own utensils to eat with, however, since we both ate at the same time. We even did that when we visited John's parents. And, to save on laundry for his mom (and because we liked doing it), we both slept in only one of the two single beds in his sister's bedroom that became the guestroom after she got married and left home. Our eating off one plate, drinking out of one glass, and sleeping in one single bed somewhat bothered Shirley; she didn't understand our efficiency habits.

We shared the daily and weekly chores so that we could get them done quickly in order to have as much time as possible for our studies. John had an implied schedule to keep that he had made as a child as to when he was to be a "PhD" with a full-time job.

Even after John had a full-time job, he still insisted that we keep track of every expense by writing it down for weekly perusal. After I got a job too and worked for a couple of years, I decided that I was tired of doing that and refused to keep a record of every nickel and dime that I spent. Although I don't record my rare cash purchases, I do have a record of most of my expenditures because I use checks or credit cards for them. Even now we both try not to waste money, but we do allow ourselves a few luxuries, like trips and evenings out.

SNIPPET 096 - Four Stitches

I was now twenty-five years old, and that fall Monday morning, I was in the chemistry building with John in his office, whiling away the time before going to my first math class of that semester at UNC. I had been looking over my schedule and noticed on my watch that it was 8:45 A.M.; I decided that I had better head over to the math building next door for my nine o'clock class. I kissed John good-bye and dashed out the door and down the hallway which, that day, was sporting a very-shiny-highly-polished-newly-waxed tile floor.

So that you will understand how the accident happened, I should explain that I walk very similar to Mary Poppins, the character in the book *Mary Poppins*. Before Marcia, my Stetson roommate, would even consider letting me walk down the aisle in front of her as the Maid of Honor in her wedding, I had to promise to practice so I could walk the distance like a normal human being. I did all that, but it took a lot of concentration, so I still don't normally walk that way. If you haven't seen the movie, which I always get teased about crying through since I am a very empathetic person and feel all the emotions of every person on the screen, the walk is done like this: you stand in the ballet position, I think it's called first position, where your heels are together and your toes point outward to form a "V," and then you just walk straight forward, keeping your toes pointing outward. For me, it's slightly different because my right foot turns out more than the left anyway, so my "V" tilts slightly to the right instead of straightforward—it's a "lop-sided V." Unfortunately, this "lop-sided V" stance causes you to step on the far outside, instead of on the back, portion of your right heel as your foot proceeds through each step. This puts your body in a precarious position as you dash around corners at a fast clip. You may try the "Mary Poppins" walk, but don't try experimenting with the "around-corners" stuff unless you are holding onto a railing or the hand of a person capable of keeping you upright. OK, if you understand what I just told you, read on.

Since I never allow enough time to get anywhere (I learned from my dad how to be late), I dash everywhere, even around corners, and I had to negotiate one left-turn corner before I exited the building. I was wearing a pair of flats that had leather soles and heels and, combined with my odd walk, only an insufficient small segment of the leather touched the extremely slick floor; my right foot slid from under me, knocking into my left ankle, like a bowling ball hitting a pin, and down I went. Bam! My chin hit the floor, splitting wide open—and the blood from the wound started dripping onto the floor and later onto my dress. Does this sound familiar?

The janitor saw me splat and, knowing I belonged to John, hurried to get him from his office a few yards away. John helped me up onto my feet, and while he held tight to steady me, we walked hand-in-hand to the infirmary.

The doctor injected some novocaine into my chin and sewed it up with four tiny stitches. "I'm not going to bandage it," he said, "because it's better to leave your chin exposed to the air so nothing tugs on the stitches until they are removed." This new split, however, was half an inch closer to my mouth, so now I have two scars.

I missed my class and had to take the professor a note from the doctor as to why I did. I only needed the note to verify the time of the accident; the rest was obvious from the set of eight black whiskers, two for each knot, sticking out of my chin. The professor, Dr. Mack, was sympathetic and showed me the scar on his chin. So I showed him the older scar where my mom had mended my chin when I was young. The bond we shared, concerning our chin mishaps, made our upcoming academic relationship, as student and graduate studies advisor, unique and special.

SNIPPET 097 - 3:00 A.M. Car Wreck

Because of our weird schedule, we were always busy during the wee hours of the morning, and this particular summer Saturday in 1964, we had arrived earlier than usual at the chemistry building. John was working in one of the large labs shared by graduate students and I was studying in his office close by across the hall. I got up from the desk around 3:00 A.M. to stretch, use the restroom, and look in on John. I always said "Hi" to John and asked how he was doing when I took a break. Not bothering to look either way, since no one else was usually around, I stepped out of the office into the hallway and bumped smack-dab into Dean, who was walking fast down the hallway from the near-by entrance to the building off the back parking lot.

"Hi, Dean!" I blurted out.

"Gad, you scared me half to death!" he yelped, startled.

"Sorry, I didn't mean to scare you," I sheepishly said apologetically. "What are you doing here? There's usually no one besides John and me around this early."

"I'm heading out on a fishing trip and stopped in to fill my cooler with ice from the ice machine."

Dean didn't look really wide-awake until I startled him, and, I guess, when he left the building, he was still a bit shaken from being accosted. I heard the engine of his car start up and then a loud crash; he had backed his car right into a pole as he was trying to leave the parking lot.

As John and I both recall, he never came to get ice again while I was anywhere nearby.

SNIPPET 098 - Fixed

    I had been having problems ever since I hit puberty and had gone in for a routine exam, late September 1964, at the Clinic. A cyst was discovered growing on my right ovary and Dr. Donald said it should be removed.

    John wanted a second opinion from Dr. Harvey, his family's physician in Savannah, so we packed immediately and drove to Savannah. Dr. Harvey saw us as soon as we got into town. After examining me, he came to the same conclusion; the cyst was growing rapidly and must be removed. Confident that the diagnosis was correct, we traveled back home.

    On October 8, the surgery was done as an exploratory, in case there were other problems to be taken care of, by Dr. Donald and his assisting resident doctor. They removed the cyst, the encased right ovary which had been destroyed, and as much endometrial tissue as possible. They also did a uterine suspension so that I might be able to bear children.

    My uterus was apparently doubled over and tucked back under itself. At the end of each monthly cycle when the menstrual tissue sloughed off the inside walls of my uterus, some tissue, instead of leaving my body, stayed trapped in the uterus or spilled out of the fallopian tubes into my abdominal cavity where it continued to grow. The other endometrial tissue already growing in my abdomen just sloughed off and stayed internal as it had no way of leaving the body. This excess tissue building up in my uterus and abdomen caused excessive bleeding which, in turn, caused considerable tenderness of my abdomen with severe pain and cramping of the muscles. I finally knew why I was having so many problems with hemorrhaging during my periods and was unable to tolerate the pain like other females seemed to be able to. I frequently just doubled over, almost passing out from the pain, and sometimes was even unable to stand and walk. In college, male classmates had often carried me from class to the infirmary during that time of the month. The nurse usually gave me enough medication to make me sleep for a day or two in the infirmary until the pain subsided enough to allow me to function again.

After my surgery, the nurses had repeatedly given me, mistakenly, a particular medication for pain; my chart was supposed to have specified that I had severe problems with that drug and became suicidal when taking it. I was also under treatment for depression as an outpatient at that hospital and had been going to one-on-one and group therapy all year. On the second night when John came in to visit me, I was trying to jump out of the third-story window in my hospital room. Fortunately he stopped me in time, but he had to stay guarding me until the drug completely wore off and I was under control again. After talking to the staff and my doctor, he got an appropriate pain medication prescribed and given to me.

In order to allow proper healing, I had to take high doses of a hormone medication to keep me from having periods or getting pregnant during the next several months. I have never gained weight so fast in my life—thirty pounds in less than six weeks. It took me almost two years to get back to my proper weight.

After I healed from the surgery, I mentioned to John that I thought I was doing quite well and was pleased with my repair job. I had no more of the horrible pain each month.

He grinned as he kidded me. "So far you have lasted better than any of my other toys; I've only had to get you fixed *once*!"

SNIPPET 099 - *Bigger Than*

Having gained about thirty pounds following my surgery the previous fall, I was much heavier than normal when we traveled to Wilmington for John's job interviews at three different departments that did chemical research at DuPont Company. The first set of interviews was with the Indochemicals Department personnel. By the end of that day, John knew that he wanted that particular job. He liked the people he would be working with and everything fit perfectly as the end result of his childhood plans.

"That's marvelous!" I told him late that afternoon when he returned to the Hotel duPont where we were staying our three days in Wilmington. "But, please, don't make a final decision until you have finished with all your scheduled interviews. I want you to be sure."

We had been invited to join John's potential supervisor and his wife for dinner that evening at the Stone Barn restaurant nearby in Pennsylvania. The supervisor had chosen that restaurant, not only for the delicious food, but also for the opportunity to drive through the countryside of upper Delaware and a bit of Pennsylvania to show us what beautiful surroundings we could live in. After work, he stopped by the hotel and drove us to his home so he could pick up his wife and also introduce us to his family before we went to the restaurant.

I had wanted to look my best during the trip so had gotten my hair done by my favorite hairdresser. The latest styles called for teased hair and she had done mine rather high. I didn't realize how tall it made me look when I wore high-heeled shoes or how heavy when combined with all the extra weight I was carrying on my body.

John and I were holding hands, standing together by the sliding glass doors in their living room, looking out into their beautifully landscaped backyard and admiring the view while the last-minute instructions were given to their young children and to the babysitter who had arrived to stay with them. I had a sudden urge to glance back at the group.

The six-year-old son, Luke, was intently studying the two of us. After a moment, he tapped his mother on her arm and, although trying to whisper, exclaimed: "Their mommy is bigger than their daddy!"

She shushed him, and we promptly left for the restaurant.

As soon as we returned home, I changed my hairstyle and started dieting. I didn't want to look *bigger than* John when he started working for Luke's dad.

SNIPPET 100 - Hair Coloring

While I had the role, modern dancing as an American Indian, in a play at Stetson University, I tried using a black rinse on my hair for that authentic look; the coloring didn't take very well, but at least for several days my hair appeared slightly darker.

The next time I tried going "black," I had a beautician color my hair. I had started getting my hair done once a week just for the pleasure of it, earning the money by taking care of baby Alicia three hours each day for a dollar a day so her parents could attend classes that school year of 1964-1965, our last year at UNC. Since we had been married only a few years, I was worried that John might be upset upon seeing my hair when I got back to the apartment. I shouldn't have given it a second thought; men aren't that observant. I walked in and cheerfully said, as I turned around so he could it from all sides, "How do you like my hair?"

He studied it carefully, then asked, "Did you get a permanent?"

I arrived at the conclusion that black hair washed me out and made me look hideous after observing my self in the mirror the next several weeks (not looking constantly though, just whenever I was making up my eyes or combing my hair).

When we moved away from Chapel Hill, the beautician who, for that last year we lived there, weekly shampooed and set, sometimes cut and "permed", and once colored my hair, gave me a gorgeous gold mesh belt.

"It's a good-bye present," she said, "for being willing to be my first customer after I got my license. You even complimented me on my work and gave me suggestions and encouragement. It really helped me gain the confidence I needed in my job."

Both of us, blinking rapidly to keep back the tears, shared a big hug.

You just never know when or how you might help someone; it had never crossed my mind that I made any difference; when the shop owner asked, I answered, "I don't mind trying a new beautician; someone has to be her first customer and it might as well be me." Although my waist is too big now to wear the belt, I'll never get rid of it because it reminds me of her, and I hope I can wear it again someday. I wish I could recall her name this instant; I know it's somewhere in my scattered brain.

I didn't try coloring my hair again for almost thirty years, but Patty, who now cuts my hair, suggested that some coloring would give my hair more body and make it easier to style. My Aunt Dottie and the actress Anne Margaret, both had marvelous shades of red hair that I admired, and since I'm an "Autumn" color-wise, I decided red was the answer. Since John and I both like the gray in my hair (I earned every bit of it), I now have Brenda, the cosmetologist who owns World of Hair, low-light my hair with a flaming, copper red color (as opposed to highlight with blonde) every four to six months. Her mom, Carol, who owned the shop before she died, did it first and then repeatedly for many years. Since I like to wear my hair either parted in the middle or with no part, just brushing the hair on top over to the right side, Brenda omits the narrow sections where the middle part would be and around the edge of my face when she foils my hair. I like Brenda and liked Carol, and I like the way my hair looks when it's done; so even though it takes me forty-five minutes to drive the fourteen-plus miles one-way to the shop, I wouldn't think of going to anyone closer to home.

SNIPPET 101 - I Quit

I sat there alone in the dark crying. I had bought a pack of cigarettes to see if smoking would help. Cigarettes, "cancer-sticks" as my dad called them, was the vice I chose because so many grad students who shared the math teaching assistants' office with me smoked. "It's a great stress reliever," each had said when I asked, "Why do you smoke?" Parliament® was the brand I chose; that's what Bill, an undergraduate classmate that I had dated several years earlier, had smoked and once had said, "These have filters and taste really great with black coffee." I lit the cigarette, the third one ever in my life, inhaled a puff, coughed a little, and felt stupid a lot. The first two were in the office with the other assistants earlier that day when I had tried to smoke them and hide them under the desk each time after I inhaled and coughed. It didn't relieve my stress and John arrived home from the chemistry lab and took it out of my hand anyway.

"Why are you sitting here in the dark and why in the world are you *smoking*?" He turned on the light and saw I was crying as well.

I just repeated what had been going through my mind as I sat there in the dark. I liked mathematics; it was fun making up and proving theorems, and studying all the different mathematical models and creating your own, but I didn't know what I could ever do with it. I had no ambition to teach full-time because I discovered that I was not a motivator; I could fascinate and teach only the students who really wanted to learn; the vast majority of students did not, only wishing to get a passing grade and move on. I had taken enough courses but didn't feel that I was smart enough to create something new enough in the world of mathematics for my thesis. So why even attempt to write a thesis to complete my work for a Master degree? All I would have would be a piece of parchment to display in a frame, and it would cost us both dearly.

John realized that I had had enough and needed help taking the final step of leaving graduate school. He quietly said, "Come on and try to get some sleep. I'll go with you in the morning; I can see that it's too hard for you to do alone."

After finishing the school year teaching at Southern High School, I had decided to try going back to graduate school and studying mathematics at the University of North Carolina. I registered for two math seminars during the summer of 1962 and got a job as cashier for the Morehead Planetarium at the University to pay for the tuition. I worked very hard at both courses, which, fortunately, were taught by terrific professors that made the classes fun to study for and to attend. There were only three separate grades you could make as a graduate student: "F" for Failing, "S" for Satisfactory, "H" for Honors; I made "H" in both. Dr. Neil, Chairman of the Mathematics Department, was impressed enough to offer me a job as one of his part-time secretaries until the department could find money for a teaching assistantship, which I got soon afterwards and kept through 1964. I made mostly "H's" and a few "S's" in the rest of my graduate math courses, so I was no mathematical slouch. I even took a year's worth of German during the first six weeks of our last summer at UNC and passed the reading knowledge exam, translating portions of literature about Hannibal crossing the Alps, to fulfill the language requirement for my degree. John had helped me by speaking only German to me until I passed the exam. But, during the last fall semester, I just fizzled out; the fun was gone as far as a career was concerned. What in the world could I do with a degree in theoretical mathematics?

At seven forty-five the next morning, we walked together over to the math building and into the office of the chairman. John stood beside me holding my hand as I calmly resigned myself to explaining my problem and ending with: "I'm sorry, but I quit."

Dr. Neil said he was sorry too, but my quitting graduate studies meant the teaching assistantship to teach mathematics in the regular undergraduate classes was also ended. Because he knew we needed the financial aid, he offered me a similar position in the Evening College.

I gratefully accepted the offer, and my evening students were a joy to teach.

I hated telling my graduate studies advisor, Dr. Mack, my decision; he had been extremely encouraging and helpful in both my studies and my marriage while I was a student. He had "been there, done that," but he understood and wished me well.

And, by the way, I quit smoking too. Nevertheless, the quarter for the pack wasn't wasted—that money was definitely well spent.

SNIPPET 102 - PhD Dissertation

By early spring 1965 when John had *had enough* with all his studies and original research experiments, he went to his advisor and inquired, "How much more work do I need to do to fulfill the requirements for my PhD?"

"Well, you could have quit six months ago and written your dissertation on the work you had completed up to that point. That was definitely sufficient. But, you hadn't asked, so I just assumed there were more experiments that you wanted to do," Dr. Grant replied.

That evening John immediately started writing his dissertation. If you don't know, a dissertation is a formal and lengthy treatise about the subject of one's original research written in partial fulfillment of the requirements for a doctorate. He completed the draft within a week or so and searched to find someone to type the master copy for the printers.

The cost would be around eight hundred dollars for the typist plus the fees for the final printed copies and binding. We decided to look into purchasing a typewriter and doing that part ourselves. We found that a new IBM Selectric® typewriter, including the additional interchangeable font typing balls that we would need for all the chemical symbols and equations, would cost a little less then hiring a typist and, besides, we would have the typewriter for everyday usage when we finished. So we bought it and still use it today for typing when we aren't using the computer for that purpose.

Since we wanted to get finished as quickly as possible, we typed in shifts for two straight weeks; John typed for twelve hours, then I typed for eight hours. Since John could type faster than I could then, though not now, we decided to let him do the majority of the typing. It was tedious work because we had to exchange the font balls umpteen times per line. During the remaining four hours of the twenty-four, we overlapped our six to seven hours of sleep. We proofread our own work as well as the other's work when we were awake and not typing. We had to use a special kind of paper and type each page perfectly (no corrections allowed) to adhere to the printing requirements for master pages. We dropped off the set of 149 masters at the printer's and, several days later, returned to collect the boxes of individual printed pages to be collated for the binding of each dissertation copy.

Stuart and Carol, our next-door-neighbor friends, helped us to assemble John's work. We plopped the pages in stacks all over the living/dining room area until we covered all the tables, chairs, couch, and most of the floor. Then we walked around the room, each of us dodging the others and the stacks on the floor, merrily gathering up pages in sequence to complete each of the required number of documents. Afterwards, John took the collated copies and had them bound.

A group of his chemistry professors used their copies of the dissertation for reading and studying the material to prepare for quizzing John during his three-hour oral exam pertaining to his original, experimental work in the synthesis of cysteine peptides and to chemistry in general. The group was satisfied with his research and spent the time just quizzing him on his general knowledge during the exam. (John had previously taken a lengthy written exam as well.) The remaining dissertation copies were kept as the official permanent record of his work.

About a month after John's chat with his advisor, he had finished everything, and we headed for Wilmington on April 1, 1965. When he was eight years old, he had planned to be doing that in June 1964, so he was a little behind schedule; but, he had not fitted marriage into his schedule at that point, or all my problems, or he might have allowed himself a little more time.

This evening, July 29, 2002, John retrieved our copy of his dissertation from the shelf of the bookcase on the wall across the room behind me sitting at our iMac®; we both got weepy when we looked through the document again and noticed this page:

**DEDICATED
TO
My Wife**

SNIPPET 103 - Our Families Meet

Most of our family members were going to the June 1961 graduation ceremonies at Stetson University to watch John being awarded his Bachelor of Science. John had met my family and I had met his, but the parents had not met any other family members. Since the ceremonies were held during the day, our families drove to DeLand for the day and met at our duplex apartment near the campus. We walked from there over to the auditorium.

John wore the traditional cap and gown and since the occasion was so special, I wore the street-length portion of my wedding dress. It was a great opportunity for John's parents to see how we looked at the end of our wedding.

George and John Daddy got along just fine, and Myrtle and Shirley bonded immediately because they were both wonderful women who had already gained great admiration for each other from my chatter about them. Interestingly, the dads were about the same size and so were the moms with John's parents slightly bigger. Sheila and Pat came with my parents, but Edith couldn't come and neither could Becky.

After the ceremony, we all gathered in the front yard of our duplex to take photos of the proud group with John in his cap and gown holding his rolled and ribbon-tied degree. Then we had one photo taken of our recently formed family with just John, his parents, me, and, of course, the degree.

That occasion was good practice for June 1965 when we gathered together again to attend the graduation ceremonies at UNC to watch John being awarded his Doctor of Philosophy degree. Since we had already moved to Wilmington, we too would be staying at the motel near Durham, but not too far from Chapel Hill, where we had made reservations for everyone. We had more time to chat together this time because the ceremony was held at night and we all took a two-day vacation.

Again John wore the traditional cap and gown, but this time a hood would be added when he received his degree. I looked different because my hair was short and permed and, instead of my wedding dress, I wore a dress that Shirley had made me while we were visiting her and John Daddy in Savannah during Easter vacation.

This time after the ceremony we all gathered in the parking lot to take flash photos of the proud group with John in his cap, gown, and hood with my helping him hold his unrolled degree.

The two graduations were the only times that both sets of parents were ever together at one time in one place.

It had been a hard road to travel those four and a half years, but we had made it just like Uncle Charles and Aunt Lib had, except that we didn't have three children.

SNIPPET 104 - Thanksgiving

When we moved to Wilmington, it was too far to travel to the homes of our families for the weekend of Thanksgiving, so Jim and Diana, Ralph and his wife, and John and I decided to spend Thanksgiving Day together. We did it for a couple of decades, each couple taking turns to host the dinner at their home. The hosts provided the main course and all the others provided the side dishes and desserts. We all pitched in with a variety of beverages and snacks.

We never were sure who all would be attending as relatives and friends might be visiting or there might be someone at work that needed to be included for the day. It was always a joyous time and it was fun to meet many relatives that we would have never met otherwise. The food was fabulous too, and we shared our favorite recipes afterwards.

Sometimes, John and I would travel to Royston for his relatives' annual Thanksgiving Day "Family Gathering" with all the thirty-plus aunts, uncles, and cousins as well as cats and dogs. We usually took our truck and trailer and our Korat cats and camped in the side yard of the homestead. The relatives all brought their favorite dishes to that feast too. The food array was always a pleasant surprise and of the perfect variety, as if someone had actually planned the menu.

I hope you always get to spend your holidays with people as special as these still are to us. What a marvelous uplifting experience it would be!

SNIPPET 105 - *Find a Job*

After we moved to Wilmington, I found little to do that interested me. I don't enjoy housework; besides, I could have the whole apartment ship-shape by 9:00 A.M. and be free for other pursuits the rest of the day. John frequently came home for lunch, but even with that (along with charting my temperature and all those other things you do), I wasn't getting pregnant so we could start a family. I tried playing bridge with other women in our apartment complex; I made it through five hands and quit because I just couldn't tolerate sitting still that long.

"Maybe I should find a job," I said to John, having thought it often to myself.

I remembered how much fun my friends in grad school at UNC had learning about programming computers and figured that would be much more fun than teaching school. (You can tell that I was getting desperate if I had even considered teaching again.) I started reading the want ads in the local newspaper on a daily basis and found one where Delaware Power & Light (DP&L) wanted an Autocoder programmer with at least two years experience to write programs for their IBM 1401, 8K-memory computer. The requirements listed in the ad kept being lowered every week or so; when it listed "will train," I applied, got the job, and began work mid-December 1965.

I worked there for over a year, but, although I didn't belong to the union since it was geared to the electrical workers and not required in this open shop, I had a problem following the union's rigid work structure. I tended to work outside of, as well as during, the scheduled work hours because I carpooled with John (we owned one car) and arrived an hour early and left late. I also took manuals home to read if I found them interesting. Needless to say, the union got distressed with my actions and wanted me to adhere to the rules. Being somewhat of a maverick, I found that difficult. Fortunately, a friend at work suggested that I set up an interview with Greg, who was a friend of her parents and was a manager in the computer sciences division at DuPont Company.

I saw Greg the next week during my lunch hour.

SNIPPETS (bits and pieces of love and life) by CAROLE

"I would really be happy to hire you, but our policy does not allow us to hire someone who is currently employed in the area," he said shaking his head. Then he added, "*However*, if you are unemployed in the future, please come see me."

"Thank you very much," I replied enthusiastically. "I have a feeling that I will be hitting the streets in a couple of weeks looking for a job."

That night I wrote my two-week notice of resignation from my current job.

On March 6, 1967, I arrived at Greg's office at 7:55 A.M.

"Good morning," I said to Greg as he stepped out from behind his desk. "I have my lunch and could start work this morning if the offer is still open," I continued, holding out my brown bag for him to see.

He asked me to wait by his secretary in the outer office while he made some arrangements. After about an hour and a half, he escorted me to the office of Jake, the vice president of that division, and went in to talk to him while I again sat outside and waited. Through the closed door, I could hear the two shouting at each other with words like "you should have consulted me first" and "don't worry, she will do great" and such. Suddenly, the two men emerged, and the VP stretched out a hand toward me to shake mine as I jumped from my chair to attention.

"Welcome aboard," Jake cheerily said, shaking my hand with firm enthusiasm. "I certainly hope you will like working here."

"I'm *sure* I will," I answered because I really felt that I would.

Women, actually men too, were just getting into that field since it was relatively new, so I worked mostly with men. I really enjoyed being on the "bleeding" (as we called it instead of leading) edge of technology; my group installed, modified, and maintained IBM and other vendors' software. I also got to use my composition and teaching skills in many work assignments, including writing instructions for and training computer operators.

In my eyes it was a wonderful environment for "play" since I refuse to "work." I have *always* said, "if it is work, you quit and find some other occupation." Computer work was all the fun I had hoped it would be, and even after twenty-five years of working for DuPont

Company, I definitely was not ready to retire but needed to because of John's health.

There were times, however, when I needed a break and would go see my supervisor and softly screech in a high-pitched voice, "I'm getting tired of this!" and then take a few days off for my favorite hobby of sewing.

Some people work for money, and so do I, along with all the other reasons; but if you ask me *why* I work, I'll just tell you, chuckling and with a twinkle in my eye,

"It keeps me off the streets and out of trouble!"

SNIPPET 106 - Rocking Chairs

Rocking in a rocking chair does wonders for your psyche. The swaying to and fro of your upper body calms your nerves by making your heart and breathing slow and rhythmical but totally without any effort on your part except for the gentle pushing of your feet against the floor to propel the chair back on its rockers. It can be as soothing as meditating or as rigorous as exercising, as you choose. Children automatically rock to and fro to soothe themselves, and we rock them for the same effect. I think older people like to sit and rock because of the same reasons. When I was growing up, almost every home had one or more rocking chairs. My grandparents had several on their front screened-in porch, and when it was too rainy to swing on the swing outdoors, we sat and rocked while reading books. It was always my favorite kind of chair, and I mentioned that to John after we got married; he decided that some day he would buy one for our home.

When I finally got a job after we moved to Wilmington, I was twenty-eight and worked with people at DP&L who had been in the working world a lot longer than I had. Most women my age, having teenage children, talked about how *old* they were. Thirty was the age at which life was already half over, if not almost entirely over, as far as they were concerned. I hadn't even decided to grow up yet and thirty seemed very young to me. I discussed their concept of age with John so much that he began to tease me about how *old* I was getting. Fortunately, one month before I hit thirty, I had changed jobs; my new coworkers at DuPont Company were five to eight years younger but, like me, were just out of college, so I felt much better being around them even though they considered me to be *rather old*.

John decided that a rocking chair would be the perfect gift for my thirtieth birthday. He found one that he liked but the wood had a cherry finish, so he had the furniture store order one in an oak finish. After several weeks the chair was delivered, but although the label on the bottom of the seat said "oak," it had the same cherry finish as the one in the store. John had the store order one with a walnut finish. The exact same thing happened; although the label on the bottom of the seat said "walnut," it had the same cherry finish as the other two.

It didn't seem to matter what finish you ordered, cherry or oak or walnut, the finish was always the same. He found a different style of rocking chair that was painted black and had fruit and leaves stenciled on it that he also liked the appearance of, so bought that one instead; besides, he thought it rocked smoother and easier and that I would like it better.

"Happy big 3-0," John told me and lightheartedly added in jest, "I figured you needed a *rocking chair* now that you are *so old*!"

We still have the rocking chair in the living room but it clacks now when you rock. Some time ago, John promised me he would re-glue the rockers soon; I wonder when *soon* is.

SNIPPET 107 - Philly and Back

Pat desperately needed a tutor as she was failing chemistry that spring of 1966 when she was a junior in high school. John seemed to be the logical choice as he did some tutoring at Stetson to earn a little spending money, and all the students he had helped thought he was a really good teacher. Easter weekend, Daddy put her on the train to travel from West Palm Beach to Wilmington for a day and a half of concentrated, tutored chemistry. Pat was excited to be traveling to visit us; moreover, because this was her very first train trip, riding, eating, and sleeping on a train became an additional treat.

The train arrived and John and I saw Pat standing at the window of her compartment, waving at us. Knowing that the train would be in the station only briefly, I motioned frantically at her and mouthed, "Get off the train!" She simply looked around as if waiting for something. As the train prepared to pull out of the station, we both started shouting to her, but she just stood there, appearing quite distressed as if she didn't know what to do. The train left, with her still on it, and rapidly disappeared around the bend and out of sight.

We hurried into the station, found the stationmaster, and explained that my sister was still on the train headed to Philadelphia. She was a teenager who had never traveled by train before and was supposed to get off in Wilmington; but, for some reason, she didn't get off during the two-minute stop. We knew she was on the train because we had waved to each other through the window of her train compartment. The trainmaster called ahead and arranged to have her met and escorted to the next train back to Wilmington.

Three hours later, that train arrived; this time, the conductor made sure that Pat and her luggage got off.

Hugging her, we asked, "What happened?"

"The porter said he would come to get me and my suitcase when we got to Wilmington and help me off the train. I was waiting for him when I was waving to you. He forgot about me. I just didn't think the train would leave with me still on it," she explained.

Pat's misadventure cost her three hours of tutoring, but John is such a good teacher that he helped her enough anyway; she earned a "C" in chemistry for the semester.

We were all thrilled with the outcome!

SNIPPET 108 - Little Old Ladies

I entered the "Training Institute" as a trainee at 10:00 A.M. on March 6, 1967, and within six weeks, along with other assignments and classes, had written my first COBOL program, compiled and executed it exactly one time. Since it executed successfully, I was finished with that portion of the training but never did get a chance to complete all the required work and leave the Institute. Since Dave was leaving DuPont Company for a job at Cape Canaveral, I was assigned his job and took over managing the training of forty to sixty employees on three-month cycles for the next year and a half. After that period of time, I was offered a job as supervisor on the administration ladder; but, instead of accepting it, I requested to be offered a job as programmer in computer operating systems (as opposed to being in applications systems) on the technical ladder. Besides, I found a supervisory job to be *work*, and I wanted to *play*, so getting into the heart of the workings of computers seemed to be the best place to do that.

Unbeknownst to me, the new head of the Institute decided to use my COBOL program as a model. One trainee discovered that under certain conditions, my program fails; my program and I became infamous because, after that discovery, every new trainee had to debug "Carole's program" as one of his/her assignments. Apparently, as the new trainees heard about me from those who had been in the Institute a bit longer, the shoes part of my description accurately included my frequently wearing tennis shoes, but the age-when-I-was-a-trainee part changed from my being *older* to *much older* than most trainees ever were. Well, I *was* older by about seven to ten years, being thirty-two by then, and I did have a wide white streak emerging in my hair on the left side near where I part it down the center of my head. And yes, I did wear tennis shoes, instead of my high heels, when I had to dash from my office to the computer room that was in a building about twelve stories and two blocks away. Computer problems had to be resolved in haste because the company businesses needed and depended on the computers to be up and running.

One morning, I was in the computer room, on the side where only authorized personnel could be, behind the input counter attached to

SNIPPETS (bits and pieces of love and life) by CAROLE

the output bins. The input counter was used by programmers to turn in their punched cards to be fed into the computer, and the assigned output bins, open on each end for access from either side of the stack, was where they retrieved their cards and printed listings afterwards. I was wearing a brightly flowered A-line knee-length dress with long sleeves, sheer stockings and, of course, my tennis shoes. I was helping the operators place output into the bins and, therefore, had been bent over much of the time, reaching into the lower bins. When I was completely upright again, I noticed a new face attached to someone, who appeared to be a recent college graduate, standing on the other side of the counter, staring at me.

"Is there a problem?" I asked him.

"Are you the infamous Carole who used to head up the Training Institute?" he asked in return.

I laughed while nodding and saying, "Yes."

"Oh," he quickly apologized, "sorry for staring. I just expected to see a *little old lady* in tennis shoes, and you don't look *old* at all."

Since that incident, I joked about being a "little old lady" and did it even more frequently after I decided to "grow up" at the age of forty. I guess that means that I have been saying it, for over thirty-three years now, even though my mind refuses to believe that I am, at all, anywhere near *old*.

We joined our neighbors, Cliff and Anne, to attend a St. Patrick's Day Dance in the basement of their church on March 19, 1983. We were having a great time partying and chatting with their friends and dancing. In fact, we were having such fun that we started kind of showing off with our dancing, and John was doing elaborate, to-the-floor dips with me. I got careless and, on the next dip, removed my left arm from his shoulder, thereby no longer supporting my weight, so the pressure from his hand broke my two lower right-side ribs. Even though we were directly in front of the band, I heard the two cracks as the sound traveled through my body and into my head. I lost my breath and had to sit out the rest of that dance. Neither of us could believe what had happened (it's the denial syndrome), so we kept trying to dance; but, eventually the pain was too great for me, and I urged John to give other women a chance to dance with him. On Monday, I had to fill out an "Off-the-job Injury" report for DuPont Company where I worked. The report has to not only include how the accident happened, but what can be done to prevent it in the future. For the latter I wrote: "Little old ladies should hold on tight when their husbands dip them to the floor while they are dancing."

Saturday, July 9, 1988, John and I were wandering around on the paths through Longwood Gardens in nearby Pennsylvania and followed them into the woods that are toward the back of the grounds. He was walking a bit faster than I, so I began to run to catch up, looking at him, of course, since we do look at each other a lot, instead of at where my feet would land, and tripped over a leaf-covered, above-ground, tree root near the center of the path. I fell with a thud and heard a bone crack in my left foot. John heard the thud too and turned around, hurried back to where I was lying, and helped me onto my feet. I told him I thought my foot was broken and he offered to carry me, but I refused and hobbled the half of a mile back to our car.

Dr. Diana arranged for us to go through "fast track" at the hospital emergency room, where I was iced down, X-rayed, bandaged up, and given (actually sold, if you think about it), crutches to walk with, and sent home with the suggestion that I call for an appointment to see an orthopedist on Monday. Not only did I do that on Monday, and get a cast on my foot, but I also had to fill out an "Off-the-job Injury" report for DuPont Company when I got to work that day. For the part about what can be done to prevent the accident in the future, I wrote: "Little old ladies shouldn't chase men through the woods at Longwood Gardens."

I got still another chance to report something similar. I was exercising in the basement on one of my compensatory days off. After I finished doing some bent-knee sit-ups with my feet elevated higher than my head on John's slant-board (which I thought was a relic from his one-year-teen-age-self-instructed-body-building era, but which John says is a relic acquired from my dad who acquired it from a policeman he knew), I decided to stretch by lifting my legs upwards into the air and lowering them over my head towards the floor. It quickly became obvious that my muscles are not strong enough for this type of exercise because I heard these two loud, cracking pops as some tendons in my back snapped and my feet crashed to the floor above my head. Fortunately, John had not quite gotten out the door, heading to work, when he heard my screaming voice saying that I was in horrible pain, was seeing white trying to pass out, and that I couldn't get up, much less, walk back upstairs. He, of course, rescued me, took me to Dr. Diana, who sent me home to bed to rest in a fetal position for several days, then start therapy for my back. The next week at work, on the "Off-the-job Injury" report for the part about what can be done to prevent the accident in the future, I wrote: "Little old ladies shouldn't put their legs and feet over their heads when using a slant board while exercising."

The last incident that I will impose on you occurred after we retired; consequently, no report was required. If I had had to complete a report, for "prevention" I would have written: "Little old ladies shouldn't allow their husbands to pet overly-friendly dogs." Dr. Diana's "prevention" stated to me was: "Sled alone!"

We were spending the week celebrating at the Rabbit Hill Inn and on December 27, 2000, the day after our fortieth anniversary, it happened. Thank goodness it didn't happen on the day of our anniversary because I would have just gone ahead and *"champagned"* myself to death. We went out to do our usual three runs on our sled down the owners' very long, snow-covered front lawn. The Inn has sleds and snow-boats sitting on the front porch ready for use by the guests, but we always bring and use one of our own sleds that we bought in Canada. This sled, like our others, has a steering wheel attached to a short middle runner, brakes that dig into the snow, two outside runners, and a seat on which two can ride quite cozily, which we prefer because we think it's much more fun doing things together.

Oscar, the village's big, sandy-colored, over-friendly dog showed up, as usual, wagging his tail and wanting to play. I ignored *Oscar* and commanded John, *"Don't pet* the dog!" Unfortunately, he ignored *me* and petted the dog. The sled run began with Oscar running alongside to the right of us and ended when he jumped in front of us, causing John, not wanting to hit the dog, to swerve left, fly down a short steep slope, and crash the sled into a telephone pole. John's left leg was cut and bruised by the sled. My groin and pelvis area was bruised bouncing against John, and my right leg was badly damaged when it slid under the thick cable, stretched taunt from the pole and into the ground. The cable creased six-inches of the bone and caused an immediate, almost-two-inch-high hematoma above it under the skin on the lower half of my shin. The damage was so severe that, instead of healing properly, the hematoma calcified and left my leg permanently lumpy and discolored; nevertheless, thankfully, my leg is again perfectly useable.

I've said it before, so many times, and I'll probably say it for the last time as I die; as I jumped on the sled behind John and shoved on the tree to start us down the slope, I somewhat shouted to myself, but in his ear—

"*Little old ladies* shouldn't be doing this!"

SNIPPET 109 - Dumb!

We, Sally and I, always said "it" when we discovered that the mistake was a "dumb" one that you shouldn't have made but needed someone else to point out because you kept overlooking the mistake or kept reading what you thought you wrote and not what was actually there.

I first met Sally when she came through the "Training Institute" when I was head of it. Even though she had been doing programming work at a plant site for DuPont Company in Philadelphia, when she transferred to Wilmington, she had been required to attend the Institute just like every new-hire or employee that transferred from some other type of work into information technology. By this point in time, Sally and I were office mates, working together in computer operating systems and, in addition to our regular duties, helping application programmers solve any problems that they had getting their "jobs" executed by the computers via what is called "JCL."

A *job* is a complete task that the computer has to do and *JCL* is a job control language, which is still used by large main frame computers today, that designates what constitutes a complete task, and which, back around 1969, was punched into 80-character cards (and today, is simply recorded on some media). It is a highly structured language, and definitely not straightforward, so it is easy to make simple mistakes like misplacing a comma or quotation mark and like misinterpreting how you code the parameters. The cards tell the computer what to do, where to find the input information needed, like read it on a particular magnetic tape, and where to put the output information, like put it on the printer as a report.

Since JCL was not at all easy, programmers frequently made mistakes, and we occasionally did too even though we were the "experts." What you really needed sometimes was what Dan, one of my later managers, called "another pair of eyes," and that's what we tried to be. The two of us would search for the mistake, and when we found it, we would say "it" together, then tell the person what to do to fix the mistake if that was not obvious to everyone involved. That person who made the mistake might have been one of the two of us, but most often that person was someone else, so we eventually decided to stop doing "it" and say something very *mundane* instead. The "someone else" didn't always take "it" as a joke the way we meant, even though we smiled and were quite willing to be helpful.

If you are going to say "it," you have to do it the way we did; you pitch your voice to match this note, the second E above middle C, on a piano and sort of sing instead of say, "DUUUMMB!"

SNIPPET 110 - The Teddy Bear

I found out that I would need to work a lot of nights and weekends; those were the time slots in which we could get the computers all to ourselves for installing and testing new operating systems, but I had a dilemma. Charlie, my supervisor, was a very understanding boss, happily married with *six* children (earlier, I had thought he had said "three"; somehow I missed hearing the "...of each kind"), so I took my problem to him for some advice.

"John can't sleep if I'm not there in bed with him. What am I going to do when I'm working these weird hours?" I asked.

"That's simple." he quickly replied, "Buy him a *teddy bear*."

"But I can't sleep without him either," I said.

"OK, buy *two* teddy bears."

Problem solved. End of discussion. I decided one would have to do; too expensive to buy two. Since I didn't want John to know I was buying him a teddy bear (he would think it was silly), I asked Bobbie to buy it for me.

I was delighted with the teddy bear she chose! It was about fifteen inches in height with soft, cuddly fur, expressive face and eyes, and a bright red bow around its neck.

Before I left home the first night I had to work, I wrote a little love note, tucked it under the bow, and laid the teddy bear under the bed covers with its head propped up on the pillow as if asleep. I said nothing to John about it.

I got home the next morning after John was already at work. When I crawled into bed, there was the teddy bear on my pillow with a note to *me* tucked under its bow.

We no longer have the bear (one of our cats, Sidney, ripped out its tongue, and later killed it via "death by shredding" during a battle instigated by John), but many, many notes were passed under its bow.

Even to this day, we leave little notes to each other. Most of them, written on Post-It® paper, just say "Hi" and are usually found in odd places such as in between two socks, or in a dish, or under the toothpaste in the medicine cabinet, or on the back of a door, or in a book, or under a pillow—anywhere that you least expect it, but are likely to find it.

SNIPPET 111 - Charcoal Portrait

For Christmas 1959, Jonathan and I exchanged pictures. His to me was a framed studio portrait photograph of himself and mine to him was a framed charcoal portrait of myself.

A few days before Christmas, I happened to be shopping in downtown West Palm Beach. On the walkway of the display-windowed alcove to the entrance doors of one of the stores, was a lady, sitting on a fold-up stool, doing a charcoal portrait of a person who was sitting on a similar stool just to the left of her easel, posing for her. She sketched with such accuracy and just a touch of color that the likeness of the person seemed to live on the cream-colored paper. The hair was done in a jet-black charcoal like the majority of the artwork and, since I had always wanted black instead of brown hair, I was intrigued to see what a portrait of me would look like. The price was about the same as a studio photo, and although the five dollars was all the money I had with me, I *had* to have her do *mine*.

When she finished the portrait she was working on, I sat down and she began to sketch me. She spent almost an hour as I sat there, trying to breathe very shallowly to stay as motionless as humanly possible, and watched her, fascinated. She worked as though she knew it had to be absolutely perfect, then simply signed "Tutcik '59" on the left side angled along the V-neck outline of the top of the sweater I was wearing (that wasn't included in the portrait) when she was done. It was perfect! Moreover, I looked exactly like what I really wished I looked like with black hair. I had it framed in black with a rose pink matting to match the color she had used on the lips, the only true color besides the bit of brown in my eyes and in the slight shading on the right side of my face and neck. I had a terribly hard time sending it to Jonathan; I wanted, desperately, to keep it for myself.

After the "Dear John" letter, I didn't hear from Jonathan again until sometime in the late 1960's when he wrote that he would like to exchange my portrait for his to give to his wife. I had left his portrait at my parents' home when John and I got married, and it simply was lost somewhere in the clutter where no one could find it. I wrote and explained the misplacement, but never heard back from Jonathan. I assumed I would never see my portrait again either. (After my mom died at the end of 1988, the framed photo of Jonathan was discovered in the attic, and I finally was able to mail it back to him.)

Six months passed, from the day of the "misplacement" letter, and one afternoon after we arrived for a visit at the home of John's parents in Savannah, Shirley handed me a thin fifteen-inch-long, paper-wrapped tube from off the hallway entrance table.

"This arrived in the mail a couple of weeks ago," she said, "addressed to you in care of me. I decided not to forward it since I knew you'd be here soon and I could just hand it to you. Besides, I was curious as to what *Jonathan* would be sending you from above the Arctic Circle."

I ripped off the wrapping, as I walked into the dining room, and slid a wound up piece of cream-colored paper onto the table and carefully unrolled it. It was a bit crumpled and hard to keep unwound as it kept trying to re-roll itself, so Shirley and John helped pin the corners down with their hands. I couldn't believe what we were looking at!

"Oh-mi-gosh!" Shirley exclaimed. "It's a charcoal portrait of my brown-eyed daughter. I know a framer that can smooth it out and put the perfect frame on it. But, it was sent to *my* house, so it's *mine* to keep until *I* decide you can have it back."

And that's exactly what happened. The portrait still has double matting with a narrow band of black and a larger band of pale-blue-gray with the same touch of color in the blondish-brown frame. She kept it for over five years hanging in a prominent place where she and John Daddy, and everyone who came visiting, could see it. When she finally decided to give it to us, I hung the portrait on the wall next to John's armoire in our bedroom.

SNIPPET 112 - First Camping Trip

Since we needed to spend money on the house we were building and not on vacation expenses like accommodations and meals, we decided camping would be a great way to do that and still go traveling during vacations. We bought a tent and some other camping gear and installed a cargo cover over the bed of our pickup truck that we had bought for carrying supplies and building materials.

Previously, we had traveled by car to Canada to attend "Expo '67" in Montreal. We had liked Canada but not the crowds at Expo, so we left there to see Quebec City and to drive around the Gaspé Peninsula instead. After we reminisced about how the Canadians had bragged about their campgrounds, the decision of where we might camp became obvious; we both said, "Let's go to Canada."

Because we had only ten days to spend away from home, we took the ferry from Maine to Nova Scotia to shorten our travel time. Having never camped before and because it would be our last chance to sleep in a comfy bed before we started sleeping on the ground, we decided to ease into camping by splurging and booking a room on the ferry for the overnight crossing. Next time we won't waste our money. The food and live music were so terrific that we stayed up all night eating and dancing and never used the room. Well, that's not totally correct; actually we each did use the tub for a bath before dinner. By the time we realized the sun was up, it was too late to sleep in the bed; we had to leave the ferry.

For our first night's camping we found a campground near the Atlantic Ocean. You could put up your tent anywhere on the grounds you liked. We put ours up on a huge flat rock area next to the water where the view was spectacular; in the morning we would be able to see the sun rise just beyond the tent flap, and we wouldn't even have to get up!

You learn a lot during your first camping trip!

1. We learned that it gets cold in Canada at night—during the summer—in August. We were born and raised in Florida and Georgia where it rarely gets cold at night—never during the summer—especially in August. We had packed no blankets and

SNIPPETS (bits and pieces of love and life) by CAROLE

no sweaters. We did have some black plastic, which is handy for a lot of uses, and we huddled together and wrapped ourselves in that. Both of us caught terrible colds; we sniveled and coughed the entire remainder of vacation.

2. We learned that salt spray makes the waterproofing of the tent fabric useless, and the spray collects in water droplets on the top and then seeps through to drip on your bodies—and on your faces—like water torture.
3. We learned that the sunrises are spectacular no matter what you have to endure to see them.
4. We, or rather John, learned that it's not wise to try to eat Eskimo Pies® in the blazing sun. Because, that's when his wife stands there and whines, then cries, like a little child, after the chocolate coating falls off her Eskimo Pie®—and the ice cream melts and runs down her hands—and drips on the front of her clothes—and the remaining third falls off the stick and drops on her shoes—and she has *had* it with camping!
5. We learned that if you arrive at a restaurant around 11:00 P.M., because you arrived on Prince Edward Island that late, and order lobster, you get a lot of extra claws because they only serve lobster on the same day they get it from the fishermen.
6. We learned that the ocean is warm enough for wading and comfortable swimming where the Gulf Stream flows near the top of PEI, or anywhere it flows for that matter.

What we discovered was, that even though we swore at times during the trip that we'd *never* do this again, we just couldn't wait for our next camping trip!

SNIPPET 113 - *El Cortijo*

One night as we were driving home from visiting friends at their home in a small community northwest of Wilmington near Pennsylvania, I said to John, "I could *never* live in Hockessin. It's so far away from everything." — Another *never*.

We lived in an apartment in Wilmington that was convenient to all kinds of shopping and I could take a bus home from work, or even walk if I felt up to the two-and-a-half-mile hike. But John always wanted to live in a house where the nearest neighbor was far enough away that he could turn up the volume on his TV or phonograph or have a party that wouldn't disturb anyone besides us. Consequently, when we had saved enough money, we started looking for such a house or a vacant lot to build on. Eventually our search took us out in the area near Pennsylvania—right where I had said I didn't want to live.

We were out looking at this particular lot for about the fifth time, this time in the pouring rain, since we wanted to see it under different conditions to make sure it was the right one for us. Suddenly, the garage door of the house across the street started opening, noisily.

"Get yourselves over here and out of the rain," commanded the gentleman, yelling at us as he let go of the door to allow it to finish rising.

We did as commanded, dashing across the street, and following him through the garage and into the kitchen of their house.

"I'm Cliff and this is my wife, Anne," he continued cheerfully. "We have watched you every time you've been out here looking at that lot. Just buy it, get your house built, and move out here. We know you'll like living here, so stop fooling around and do it."

"I'll make us all some cocoa, if you can come in and stay awhile," Anne said as soon she could break into his chatter.

"We would like that," I answered, motioning to John to remove his raincoat and muddy shoes like I was doing, having noticed that the carpeting, throughout the rest of the house area within view, was white.

SNIPPETS (bits and pieces of love and life) by CAROLE

During the remaining conversation, John mentioned that the lot was what we wanted, but we weren't sure we had saved enough money to buy it and build a house quite yet.

"You will never save enough," Cliff said. "So, don't even bother to try. Just get as large a mortgage as you can, build it, and do whatever parts of it you can yourselves."

We did just that. It took a year to build the house, and that year was probably the worst ever in our marriage. We had so many problems with the builder that we ended up just short of going to court a couple of times and had to have my dad come up to watch over the workers. For six looong months, Daddy lived in our apartment with us, traveling out to our lot daily to oversee the job and to try to insure that the workmen followed the specifications listed in our contract that they constantly tried to ignore. Our architect eventually refused to deal with the builder although he had told us we were morally obligated to take the lowest bid within the builders he had recommended. We quickly discovered why that bid was the lowest; the builder had no intention of following the architectural specifications.

I shall spare you the rest of the gory details. Needless to say that by the end of the year's time, we were at our limit of our nerves and tempers. If we were to ever get divorced due to outside circumstances, this year was the perfect time. We finally moved in Thanksgiving week 1970, just as soon as the house had passed inspection for occupancy even though it was not finished.

Being from the south, John and I both like the style and openness of Spanish architecture. It's a small house with three bedrooms and two baths, living room, dining room and kitchen, and partial basement, but it suits us nicely. Everywhere the architect had windows, I made them bigger windows or even sliding glass doors to let the light in, not realizing at the time that living in the north, not the south, made the heating of the house in winter rather expensive.

While he was designing it, the architect used some Spanish words in the description, like terrado for the terrace area out the backdoor, atrio for the front hallway, and so on. The rectangular walled-in area at the front of the house between the garage and living room, however, is simply called the garden court. We wanted a masculine name for the house itself and decided on "El Cortijo" (pronounced El'

Kôr-tee´-ho) which means a country house with small farm animals. The surrounding area had deer, rabbits, foxes, squirrels, pheasants, snakes, skunks, groundhogs, and a dairy farm, so that name seemed to fit perfectly. We have the name carved into a sign hanging at the front entrance over the gates to the walkway leading up to the front doors; it was made by an artisan that we discovered in Tennessee when we were camping one spring during the early 1980's. Close by the sign and gates, there is a rust-red, brick-style block with the date "**1970**," that John made, located in the garage wall just two feet above the stone aggregate walkway. The "date-stone" is the same size as the split-blocks used in the outside walls and was laid in place of one split-block when that wall was built.

We began with a five-year plan for completing our work around the house, but that evolved to a ten-year, fifteen-year, and now forty-year plan. We have begun to realize that you are never really finished; that's what keeps it interesting.

SNIPPET 114 - Blackberries and Jam

For the six months that my dad lived with us in our apartment, starting in the springtime of our house building in 1970, he spent his days at the house overseeing the workmen when they bothered to come to work on it. Many days during the late summer, he also would pick blackberries off the thorny vines that grew wild in the weedy yard. Most of the property within the development used to be pastureland and seemed to have good soil conditions for berries to flourish. After returning to our apartment, he would spend the entire evening removing thorns from his fingers and making jam from the blackberries. He would divide the jam into jars and label them with "1/2-inch seeds," "one-inch seeds," and the like or "no seeds." John noticed that one jar labeled "no seeds" did indeed have one seed suspended in the jam and changed the label to "one seed."

Daddy is not a very careful cook (and not exactly safety-conscious either) and tends to put food in pots on burners with the highest heat setting and then leave to do something else, instead of watching the food cook, only to return after the pot has boiled over. The apartment had a gas stove and one morning John started to cook some scrambled eggs for our breakfast and discovered that every single one of the four burners was entirely sealed with blackberry jam and would not light. We had cereal instead, and John banned my dad from using *that* stove or *any* stove we would *ever* have.

After a few years of tending a real garden that contained thornless blackberry vines as well as strawberries, lettuce, tomatoes, and other vegetables, John decided that a pool, instead of a garden in our back yard, would be a better way to enjoy the summers. Therefore, we tore up the enclosed garden and had a pool installed in its place. Around the pool walkway we laid black plastic and five inches of washed pebbles. The following spring, up popped a single blackberry vine through all of the layers. We figured if it wanted to grow that badly, we would let the vine live. It spread out over the years into an area of plants measuring about fifty-by-four feet and provided us with many blackberries.

Our favorite way of eating blackberries is plain or made into blackberries jubilee, like cherries jubilee, over vanilla ice cream, but my dad's favorite was his own homemade jam. During blackberry season when my parents visited us in our home, if my dad wanted to make blackberry jam, he had to make it outdoors using a hotplate that John would set up for him in the back yard. One day he was complaining about his make-shift-stove to Anne, our neighbor across the street, and asked if he could make jam in her kitchen instead of out in our back yard.

Anne quickly asserted, "Absolutely not, George, I know all about the apartment stove and your blackberry jam!"

SNIPPET 115 - Concrete Work

John envisioned having two stone-pier-based lamps near the street, one on each side of the driveway leading to the house, to light the entrance at night. He had never done stone work before but had worked with concrete and had watched the stone masons put the stone facing on our living room fireplace. He thought it would be fun to do and built them on weekends during the summer of the year our house was being built. He had used carbon to blacken the concrete slabs on top for the lamps to sit on, but the rains washed out most of the carbon during the first couple of years, so the slabs are just light gray now. That project was so successful that he decided to do a lot more concrete work in and around the house and yard.

A pebble driveway seemed to be the suitable choice for our Spanish-style house and countryside development. We had it made with crushed stone for the base and washed pebbles on top. However, we didn't take into consideration that the driveway had a rather steep slope for the last thirty or so feet at the bottom next to the road. Consequently, any vehicle (ours, fortunately, since we tried it first) being driven up the driveway caused the pebbles to slide down the slope, scattering everywhere from under the tires; the vehicle could get no farther than ten feet before it came to a complete halt with its tires partially buried.

"No problem," John said as he surveyed the area. "We'll just remove the pebbles and put them back as part of a stone-aggregate-paved driveway. Until then, we'll just park at the bottom instead of up by the house or in the garage."

He immediately bought a 2.5-cubic-foot, cement mixer and began the yearlong project. He had helped his dad build roads and concrete airport runways, so he knew how to do that much, but he had to read up on stone aggregate surfaces and buy some retardant to properly finish the top. Each weekend, weather permitting, we cleared the pebble layer off an area of the driveway and replaced it by building one or two small sections of pavement, pouring the concrete six to eight inches thick and reinforcing some of it with steel rods. John did the mixing, pouring, leveling, and stone aggregate surfacing and I made iced-tea and filled five-gallon cans with stone, shoveling the best pebbles into one can for the top aggregate addition and the rest into cans for using in the mixture with the sand, cement, and water.

Shirley visited us for a week during the time that we were building the sections near the garage door. One afternoon, she had made iced tea for us while we worked. When we finished drinking, one glass had a little tea and a few bits of ice left in the bottom of it, so before she took the glasses back into the house, she leaned out of the garage to pitch the remains onto the weeds. Not thinking about the concrete just being poured and the surface covered with pebbles and spayed with retardant, she stepped with her left foot onto the soft concrete and left her footprint forever in that section of the driveway. John tried unsuccessfully to fix it, but her foot had embedded the retardant too deeply and the next morning more than just the surface washed off. Yet, the footprint did give us an idea; we added our handprints in small triangle patch of concrete at the right-angle corner of the driveway where it turned to head into the garage.

I guess John really enjoys concrete work. Next, he decided to add concrete mowing strips all around the house, driveway, and across the top edge of the stones piled on the bank along the road in front of the house. Then, he built a huge stone planter and stone-aggregate terrace at the back of the house followed by a concrete and stucco building out behind the pool. Our friends keep wondering how long it will be before he has the entire yard covered with concrete.

The cement mixer was a great investment; we certainly have gotten our money's worth, and I think John enjoys playing with this real man's toy. He keeps talking about adding green concrete cacti to the yard; but, so far, I've been able to forestall that project by keeping him busy—away from home—traveling.

SNIPPET 116 - *Curious Rabbits*

Anne, like most of our neighbors and us, has many rabbits living in or close to her yard. There is one in particular that likes to come and sit at her front door like a lost puppy. It visits her every day, and they stare at each other through the screen door. I have seen it there when I have gone to her home to visit. Also, we both have watched that rabbit hopping across the back yard when we have been sitting in her kitchen, looking out the window, while enjoying tea and chatting together.

Our cement mixer attracted two rabbit friends for John. Whenever he was mixing concrete, the noise seemed to squelch the fear of people that rabbits usually have. The two rabbits, each during a different summer, would venture out into the yard and sit within eight feet of the mixer to watch, seemingly mesmerized by the sound of the pebbles banging against the interior of the mixer. They would sit there for hours until John stopped the mixer for the day.

I wonder who's more curious to watch—them or us?

SNIPPET 117 - Our Backyard Critters

Our yard has seen many different types of creatures in the thirty-two years that we have lived here. The first true visitors we had were a flock of thirty-seven ring-necked pheasants that ate the nine bushels of barley seeds that we had put out the fall of 1970 after we moved in Thanksgiving week. We had hopes of cultivating a nice ground cover for the winter since it was a bit late to plant grass that year. A half-circle plot with radius of about ten feet at our back door was all the barley that sprouted and grew. The pheasants lived in the weedy woods between our yard and the houses on the next street behind us. Every morning and evening they would feast their way across the yard, back to front. We enjoyed watching them as they always followed the same ritual.

The female pheasants came out first and began eating and working their way towards the house. After about five minutes, when the males decided that none of the females had been maimed or killed, they ventured out of the tall weeds, staying back a safe distance, and began eating their way across the yard too. If one of the males decided to get a little frisky with one of the females, she squawked at him to leave her alone until after mealtime. In the evenings, the flock always returned an hour or so after their supper to have a short snack as dessert. The flock always came and went together. One evening, one of the youngsters, eating greedily as he worked his way to the front of the flock, wasn't paying attention to the rest of the group's activities. The young bird apparently became aware of the lull because it suddenly looked around, discovered it had been left alone, shrieked at the top of its lungs, and ran back into the weeds to find the others. We had a good laugh, watching, because the little pheasant looked so distressed and acted so silly. Eventually all the pheasants departed to better fields and safer weeds because many neighbors acquired dogs that liked to chase and occasionally kill them.

We had a snake living in our garden until the day it made a sudden move while John was hoeing between the vegetables and got itself instantly whacked into pieces before John realized what it was. He apologized to the dead snake because he hadn't meant to kill a non-poisonous one. We rarely saw snakes after that; I guess they were afraid that the same fate would be theirs.

Living close by, there are nine to thirteen deer that also like our yard to eat and play in. The fawns especially like the weeds that grow by the sidewalk that leads past the garage to our front gates. I took several fabulous close-up pictures of them the other day and was distressed to discover later that there was no film in our camera. One evening when Karl, Chris, John, and I were standing in the kitchen looking out the double window above the double sink, we saw two bucks standing on their hind legs, boxing like two kangaroos. None of us had ever witnessed that type of action before and we haven't since.

Several squirrels have tried to take up residence in our courtyard in one of the planters but have always had to move as soon as the first winter winds howled through there. Snow even gets whipped up like topping on a sundae in that area. A few rabbits have survived there and raised families during the summer months. John discovered one family when he was watering the small bushes and a little bunny head popped up through the leaves, wondering why it was suddenly raining while the sun was shining.

We have always had one or two foxes that like to scamper about and play together in the sand pile out back at the edge of our yard where John keeps sand for the concrete work he occasionally does. Late one afternoon John called me into the kitchen to look at the very small fawn he saw just on the other side of a doe. I grabbed the binoculars and when the doe moved, I saw that the small animal was really a *fox*. Perhaps it was hungry and was trying to figure out if it had found dinner; I think it discovered it had not because it soon ran off. Around 4:00 A.M. one morning, we heard the most god-awful, shrill, piercing cries in two different tones coming from the back yard next to the planter at the end of the terrace behind our house. John dashed to the kitchen, with me following close behind, flipped on the outside lights, and we both, standing at the kitchen window, looked around the terrace area. A large cat and a fox were having a screaming match and a claw fight. It eventually ended in a standoff when the cat, hissing at the fox rubbing its face in the grass, dashed through the fence and up onto the concrete terrace to within ten feet of the back door. The incident certainly disturbed us, and we were glad the outcome was OK.

Since we have a small fountain on our terrace during the warm months and many different kinds of birds nesting nearby, Karl and Chris decided that our yard would be a perfect place for a bluebird house. Karl built us one and put it up on a pole at the back border of our lot. We have had as many as six to eight families in it so far. The beauty of having those particular birds is that the fountain is ceramic and has the same blue and pinkish-purple colors, so when the birds are bathing, the whole terrace becomes a marvelously beautiful, painted scene.

Seven crows frequently strut around the grass like they own the backyard. They like to play in the fountain, usually five at a time, pushing each other around to get the best standing position on the large stones situated beneath the flowing water in the copper pan sitting on the terrace. A pair of cardinals, that live in our blue spruce trees, like to sit on the fence and watch the other birds play in the water, but they never come closer than the posts that are twenty feet away. Other birds, that we see drinking or bathing, are wrens, goldfinch, mourning doves, sparrows, chickadees, and jays. Occasionally neighborhood cats squeeze through the vertical bars of the fence to come in for a drink; they never stay long as they just drop by on their way to someplace else.

Skunks and groundhogs sometimes amble through the yard, never staying long. Bats frequently take up residence under the eaves of the roof, but we hose them down to discourage them from living so close; we prefer them to live in the woods. One time a bat came down the chimney into the house and we had to chase it out with a broom and some help from our cats.

There is a dairy farm, behind the houses across the street from us, just over the border in Pennsylvania. The cattle like to knock down areas of the fence separating the farm from our development, stroll over to Delaware, and munch on the grass and vegetables in our neighbors' gardens. The house next door just before ours as you drive down our road has a lush lawn; the owners added about two hundred loads of mushroom soil and planted the yard with grass when they were building their home about the same time we were building ours. Early one morning we heard their daughter Lisa hollering out in their

SNIPPETS (bits and pieces of love and life) by CAROLE

front yard, trying to chase home the thirty-seven heads of cattle that were eating their grass. None of the cattle were in our yard as ours only has mowed weeds. On other days we have had to walk at the far back of neighboring yards, on our way back from a long walk, to avoid a bull or two standing near the road waiting to be rounded up by its owner and taken home to the farm.

All in all, these animals are great fun to watch come and go in our yard and provide us with many hours of pleasure. John simply calls them *"our backyard critters."*

SNIPPET 118 - Swings

There is something about soaring through the air while still being attached firmly to terra firma that I find absolutely exhilarating. I have almost always had, to my knowledge, a swing or trapeze to play with, either in the yard or on the porch or in my house, and when I didn't, I found one somewhere nearby at a park or at a friend's house. If I couldn't find one anywhere, I made do with swinging between chairs or hanging off the arms of two people when I was small enough to do that.

Our house, where we lived in Miami when I was about five to eight years old, had a porch that extended across the front and left side of the house if you stood looking out the front screen door at the middle of the house. The section at the back third of the house was screened in to make a small room. A bench-style swing hung across the porch at the far right end, and if you swung high enough, you could just barely miss the porch railing behind it. You could sit in that swing like you do in a chair or lie down on your back with your legs up and over the back of the seat and swing forward and backwards, or you could lie down on the seat length-wise and swing side-ways, all the while, in any of the positions, staring at the sky-blue, two-inch-wide-raised-edged board ceiling.

After Daddy got out of the armed services, he hung his Navy canvas hammock by its ropes from hooks in the ceiling near the screened room so we could play with it too. Swinging in that was especially fun because you could wrap the hammock around yourself and turn upside down without falling out. Edith and I took turns doing that when we were on speaking terms and playing together.

Terry (third grader) and I (second grader) didn't use either of these types of swing for "kissing" practice; we liked to sit on the old trunk under my parents' bedroom window on the left side porch for that. But, we did like to swing together on the bench-style swing when we just wanted to chat or stare at the ceiling or the yard.

Now, John and I have a multi-colored string hammock that we bought in North Myrtle Beach that we take on camping trips with us. Our favorite campground, where we always stay near there on the beach at the Atlantic Ocean, has a roofed structure over the picnic table on each site; you can hang your hammock from the huge posts and swing and read all day in the shade. We always book the same site which has the same number as the number on the license plate of Donald Duck's car. If we're there, you will also see our windsocks, but usually not us, hanging from the rafters.

At my paternal grandparents' house, there was a see-saw and a sandbox with board seats on two sides that Pops built for all us grandchildren plus a trapeze and a swing he made and hung off one huge limb on the big oak tree. We spent most afternoons, the summers that we stayed there, playing out under the trees when we weren't helping Gramma with chores. During my fourth grade, when we lived with them year-round, we rode the school bus to school. Every afternoon from three to four o'clock we had to wait for the high school students to get out so the bus could take us all back home. I spent the hour on the swings in the playground; you could swing really high in those because the chains holding the swings were fifteen to twenty feet long.

Whenever we went to a fair, I always had to ride the swings because you didn't have to pump with your legs to go high and swing far out into the air. Sometimes we rode the Ferris wheel. Once, while we were still living in Miami, Gramma, Edith, and I got stuck for several hours with our chair, at the very top of a giant Ferris wheel, swinging scarily back and forth in the wind, until they finally got the motor fixed and brought us back down. It frightened me so badly, because I thought we were going to fall out of the chair seat and die, that I didn't ride another wheel for over twenty years. The next time I rode a Ferris wheel was with John at an amusement park next to the Atlantic City boardwalk. Since you could look out over the boardwalk and beach at the ocean in the late afternoon when the sun lighted the water with its setting rays, I had to overcome my fear at least long enough to enjoy the view with him.

In West Palm Beach, when I was in junior high, we had a metal play set in our yard that included a swing and trapeze. I liked to hang by my knees but never did learn how to hang by my heels like Edith's and my friend Mary did.

When we moved into our house, I wanted to put up a swing. John surprised me on my thirty-fifth birthday with a basket swing that he hung in our living room.

"It's for your *second childhood*," he said with mischief in his eyes and a silly little smile, "since I already gave you a rocking chair on your thirtieth for being *over the hill*."

John and I both like to swing in the basket swing and we used to push each other as high as possible. One day that same summer, we were showing off for some friends we had invited over for the evening; John was in the swing with me pushing on the front edge of the basket chair, making it go really high; the bolt broke and John flew backward, swing and all, into the fireplace. He wasn't hurt because I had made cushions for the seat and back of the basket. The bolt, quite obviously defective to the naked eye looking at the pieces, broke where there was a bubble that went all the way through it except for the tiny bit of metal at the outside edge. Being very safety conscious, John had installed the swing with metal plates attached to the joists above with just the bolt extending down through the drywall; however, there was no way to tell that the bolt was defective before it broke. We replaced the bolt and kept using the swing; the second bolt has been in use for about thirty years now with no problem.

I was delighted having my swing in the living room until Bob, a friend and interior designer, banished it, decreeing it to be hung in the barroom in the basement. Now I have to swing down there near the corner away from the left side of the fireplace; but that's OK—that's where the champagne and wine are stored.

SNIPPET 119 - *George's Fruitcakes*

Daddy liked to bake and for the holidays his specialty was fruitcakes. He always had baked them at home; but one year, while Daddy and Mema were visiting us in December, he decided that it was time to make fruitcakes. He couldn't use *our* kitchen because he had been banned from the use of our stove and was allowed only the use of a hotplate out on the stone table on the back terrace.

My parents, George and Myrtle, had both become friends with Cliff and Anne, our neighbors who live across the street from us. George and Cliff were very much alike in nature, and Myrtle and Anne were similar too. My dad had gotten to know them quite well the summer that he was overseeing the building of our house. Thus, Daddy figured he had the perfect solution. He went to see Anne and conned her into letting him bake fruitcakes in *her* kitchen by promising to give her some of the final product.

Surprisingly, she allowed him to use her kitchen. I couldn't believe it. She was actually delighted when the whole project was concluded because the cakes were delicious and the day passed without incident.

Knowing that Anne knew all about the apartment stove and my dad's blackberry jam escapade, I asked her later why she even allowed Daddy *near* her stove.

Anne chuckled and replied, "I really wanted some homemade fruitcake, so I just made sure he didn't ruin anything. I figured that if I 'watched him like a hawk' and kept him from messing up the kitchen while he prepared the batter and I made sure he didn't fill the loaf-pans too full, everything would be OK. He needed to use the *oven*, not the *burners* of my stove."

SNIPPET 120 - Safety Shoes

At DuPont Company in the early 1970's, it was decreed that everyone who worked in the computer rooms had to wear safety shoes. The computer operators had to mount and remove tapes from the tape drives and large data storage disks from the disk units; therefore, the safety committee deemed it best for those people to wear safety shoes with built-in steel toes. The company would buy each employee who needed them one new pair on a periodic basis.

No one in my group was hired as an operator, but since we installed, tested, and maintained the software that controlled the work in the large main frame computers, we operated them as well. We then wrote the instructions and procedures for the regular computer operators and trained them in running and interfacing with the new operating systems. (Most of the time, I did all the writing part.) That meant we had to do all the same types of work as the operators, which in turn inferred that we too had to wear safety shoes.

The safety store was a mobile one that went from site to site, and when it came to our site, we all went out there to get our steel-toed shoes. It worked out great for those who could get fitted, but no matter how hard the salesman tried, with every different style and size the store had in stock or could order, no pair of shoes fit me. In desperation, the salesman gave me a pair of plain, steel, molded-toe-coverings that actually fit properly over my toes, but that had not yet been built into a pair of shoes.

"Here," he said in exasperation, thrusting the steel pieces into my left hand as I reached out to catch them, "go get your own shoes made for these. That's the best I can do."

I took them home. John and I studied the steel toes, then tried to find a pair of shoes that I already had that we might be able to fit them in or over the toes of. There was exactly one pair of shoes that fit the bill. The steel toes fit over the outside on top of the straps across the toes of a pair of soft-brown-leather sandals. John figured he could bore one or two holes in the steel so we could attach them to the sandals. He broke every drill bit that he used, trying to bore one hole, because the steel was so hard. Nevertheless, he did find a way to secure them—good, old-fashioned tape and string. Voila! I now possessed a legitimate pair of safety shoes.

The next morning in my office, I removed the shoes I had worn to work and put on my *safety sandals*. My manager at that time, Charlie, was aware of the problems I was having getting safety shoes that fit, so I thought I would go show him my new safety shoes. Since our area of the building was being renovated, there was no carpeting on the floor, just old, red, asphalt tile. As I walked down the hallway to his office four doors away, everyone could hear the *click-clack, click-clack* of the steel toes kind of flopping up and down as I walked. Charlie heard it too and came out of his office to see what the noise was.

"Hi Charlie," I said smiling and picking up my straightened right leg, lifting my foot about fifteen inches off the floor. "How do you like my new *safety* shoes?"

"Get - those - things - off - your - feet!" he commanded in a normal tone of voice, though emphasizing and stretching out every word. "I don't *ever* want to see those shoes again. And, from now on, just make sure you wear some kind of shoes where your toes are completely covered."

Soon after that incident, the policy was changed to allow us non-operators to wear close-toed shoes instead of steel-toed safety shoes.

Years later when I worked on the project to move the entire data center to a new location, we were required to wear safety shoes during the practice and actual moves. By then, there was one new style available that fit me. I still have the only-worn-twice pair of shoes, if you're interested and need them.

SNIPPET 121 - Social Security Number

During the 1970's, there was a rash of personal-item, household-appliance, and entertainment-equipment thefts from people's houses. In order to deter thieves and to make it quicker and easier to trace owners of items confiscated during arrests, the police advocated having your Social Security Number engraved somewhere on each item of value to you. (You would never do this today because of the new problem of identity theft.) The newscaster, reporting this during the evening local TV news, stated that if you couldn't afford to buy an engraver of your own, you could borrow one for a three-day period from the police at a station convenient to your home.

We discussed the matter and John decided to *buy* an engraver because he wanted to engrave items on an on-going basis and didn't want to have to borrow one each time he bought a new item. He bought one the next day and immediately began engraving his SSN on everything in the house. I said something about his putting mine on there too, but he assured me that it wasn't necessary because we were married, and what was his was also mine.

The next week at work, during my group's safety meeting, one of the topics was a discussion of the home thefts and the avocation of engraving items that might be stolen. I happened to somewhat complain that, because John was using our engraver to put his number on the back of every item that was of value to the two of us, as well as just to him, there was hardly anything left for me to put my SSN on.

Evan, our friend and my coworker, quipped to the rest of the group, all men who knew John fairly well from my chatting about him: "Yeah, probably not even *herself*; I bet he has engraved his social security number on *her* backside as well!"

At dinner that evening I told John, who likes Evan and enjoys his humor, about the safety meeting and what Evan had said.

He laughed. "That's hilarious! Wish I had thought of doing that."

We joked about the notion.

Even if John thinks someone might, all I can think is: "Who would even *want* to steal *me*?"

SNIPPET 122 - Dancing

When John was in the fourth grade, his mom had him take classes in basic ballroom dancing; it was another of the social graces every young Savannahian had to learn. He apparently learned quite well, and it wasn't long before he was in demand as a dancing partner and escort for one of the debutantes to each ball. If you ever danced with him, or even just watched, you quickly noticed that he has his own style of dancing. He is forceful enough to be easy to follow, and he whirls his partner around to show her off with such skill and grace that all the other guys want to dance with her too, making *her* very popular as well. Both qualities are, you might say, a debutante's dream.

John's dancing ability made him popular at college parties too. Frequently, after we started dating, I missed out on taking him with me to dances sponsored by Alpha Xi Delta, the sorority I forever belong to. Not having money to feed one of the dormitory payphones, I had to wait until I saw John to invite him; and when I did finally, he frequently would have to politely refuse because he would be going with another sorority sister who had already phoned him. Usually I would ask Bob because he was fun to be with and was a good dancer too. Neither of us (John and I) would be great, only good, dates for other people because we would get caught eyeing each other during the entire party.

After we were married and both working at DuPont Company, we joined the Country Club and together took ballroom-dancing classes to broaden our repertoire to include the "Samba," "Polka," "Tango," "Rhumba," "Waltz," and other dances. The money was well spent for the *fun* we had but not for the *dances* we supposedly learned. We had danced together so much by then that, even though we practiced the new steps, after a few weeks away from class, we were back to just doing our own "fling" (as I call it). We keep promising ourselves to try again before the next ball or casual dance we attend; each time, we practice the steps, but when we get on the dance floor and start dancing, we're quickly back in the old rut.

The one dance we avoid completely now is the "Twist" because it is too repetitive; John's Parkinson's Disease takes over and he either shakes violently or becomes stiff-as-a-board and can't move. It is probably a gift to be able to only dance our own way, which is definitely not repetitive, so we will just continue to do that.

One Saturday shortly after his PD diagnosis, John disappeared from the house without telling me that he was leaving or where he was going. A while later, I heard the front door being unlocked, knew it would be him, so went out to meet him in the front hallway. He burst in through the doorway, said he had been shopping (obviously at our favorite men's clothiers where we buy his clothes), unzipped the "Wright & Simon Clothiers" suit bag he was holding, and showed me what he bought.

I looked at him quizzically and asked, "Why the new tuxedo?"

"You heard the neurologist tell me, '[that the best thing for me to do was] just keep moving,' but I decided I would rather *dance*!"

SNIPPET 123 - *Perfume*

The aroma, that wafted off her silky, smooth skin as her body swayed and undulated before us, was absolutely heavenly. I had to find out the name of that perfume!

I wasn't the only one captivated by the odor—or the body—of the belly dancer in that Mediterranean restaurant; the rest of the guys I was with were thoroughly enjoying it too. Even though I was a girl (OK, woman), they always referred to and treated me as "one of the guys." We worked together in Wilmington and had been in Dallas all week attending classes at IBM and were eating dinner our last night in Texas, a delightful summer evening in mid-1974.

She was Zarzara (sounds like Barbara) from Philadelphia. Fabulous dancer and gorgeous woman! Men were tucking dollar bills into her clothing as she danced close enough for them to barely touch her. When the guys at my table ran out of their dollars, I handed them some of mine because it was fun to watch them trying to slip the folded bills into her clothing as she began weaving her way more rapidly around the floor.

As we were leaving the restaurant, Zarzara happened to be near the front door; I dashed up to her and begged, "Please tell me the name of the perfume you are wearing." She said something like "Used-to." I had her repeat it several times, but I still couldn't understand the words through the din of chatter and music, so she scribbled the name on a piece of paper and thrust it into my hand. I thanked her profusely, and we left.

Evan and I had the same flight home early the next afternoon. That morning we all met for breakfast and the rest of the guys left. Since he knew my husband and thought John would certainly appreciate it, Evan decided that we should spend the morning shopping for some of *the* perfume. Fortunately, we found some at the Estée Lauder™ counter in an upscale department store, and I bought a small purse-sized bottle.

We flew to Philadelphia, and Evan and I departed at the airport on different shuttles. As the shuttle approached my house, I applied some (actually, a lot) of the perfume. I was curious to see if John would notice anything different about me.

Shirley had been visiting all week, keeping her "baby" company and cooking for him while I gallivanted off to Texas. Since the door was locked and I had left my keys at home, I rang the doorbell. I had expected to see John, but Shirley opened the door, took a deep whiff, and exclaimed, "*Youth-Dew®*, my favorite perfume!"

John likes it, I think probably because his mom always wore it, although he didn't know what brand it was. He buys me the real perfume, not the cologne, and has kept me supplied ever since that time. I always wear it. I bathe with Youth-Dew® soap as well but won't be able to after I use my last bar; the company, to my distress, has stopped manufacturing it.

SNIPPET 124 - Our Korats

I had never heard of Korat cats and neither had John.

That wasn't what I was looking for; I was looking for yellow cats like the ones he had as a teenager. It was to be a surprise Christmas present. I, and every friend that I could con into doing it, had attached notices to the bulletin boards around work, but just those that John wouldn't, by chance, see. I had no luck, but I did get one phone call from a man, that I didn't know personally, who worked as a mechanical engineer in the same building and department that I did.

"I know you're looking for yellow cats, but I have a friend who raises Korat cats and has some kittens that will be old enough for adoption around the holidays, and I know you would just love them if you ever saw them," the gentleman said.

So I took down Angela's name and phone number and on the way home stopped by a bookstore and bought a cat encyclopedia to look up "Korat." In essence, this is what I found out, supplemented by what I learned later from our cats.

Korat Cat, or Si-Sawat as it called in Thailand, is a distinct, ancient breed of cat and is not often seen outside of that country. There are only a few breeders in the USA. Korats are beautiful, medium-sized cats, silver-blue in color, with smooth fur, having whitish-skin-color roots and silvery ends, that feels like pure-fine-fiber-soft silk (so mesmerizing that you never want to stop touching the fur); different from most other breeds, the fur has virtually no undercoat, just the new coat growing in. Their large eyes, that penetrate you with their gaze, are deep blue-gray at birth and transition through amber to brilliant green-gold at maturity. They like to participate in all home activities (as you will discover), and develop strong affectionate bonds with their owners (and most likely vice versa), but they dislike sudden loud noises. In Thailand the males are renowned as fighters, warning their owners of approaching danger by standing stiff-legged, facing the source, and uttering a combination of strange cries and clicking or teeth-chattering-like sounds.

The breed sounded fascinating and loveable, but I was afraid to get a cat of a different kind and color then I had planned, without consulting John; my *big surprise* to him turned out to be just a *little card* saying that he was getting a cat for Christmas.

We went to see Angela and meet the candidates. We didn't get to choose any of them. Instead, one male and one female immediately chose us, so we adopted them both. Since I had planned to call John's cat, "Shadow," since it would be his "shadow," I decided to call the other one, "Friend," because she was to be a friend for Shadow, and so, that is what they were named.

Neither cat kept its name. A few days after we brought them home, John started calling Shadow, "Sidney," because it just seemed to fit, and Friend kept running behind the clothes dryer and getting all dusty, so she became "Dusty." When we got them registered, we discovered it was appropriate, and customary, to give them more than a single name, so the second name became a descriptive one. We registered them as Sidney Biter and Dusty Friend.

For the first week, we kept the cats in the kitchen because it had a vinyl, instead of wooden, floor. At bedtime, John put a five-foot-tall-left-over-piece of Formica®, held in place by chairs, across the doorway of the opened, swinging door that closes off the kitchen from the dining room, so that the air could circulate and keep the room from getting too hot for the cats during the night. After about four nights, Sidney was able to leap over the barrier to freedom and roam the rest of the house leaving Dusty alone for John to find in the morning. That was when and how we discovered that our Korats were great jumpers.

Since the two of them were the best of friends, and so are we, the four of us got along superbly. John made them almost fifty toys of all kinds—from feathers on a string to old-sponge-cloth-butterflies on coat-hanger wires to leather shoes laces—anything he could make fly through the air or drag along the floor. I made, or bought, at least half a dozen catnip toys that they could play with by themselves; lambskin mice with leather ears and tails were their favorites. He built them scaffolds and seats, in almost every room, that they could climb on to keep physically fit. But most of all, John liked to run the cats up and down the walls, or make them leap into the air, chasing after toys he kept just out of their reach. Both cats could leap six to seven feet straight up easily. It didn't take long before there were little cat-paw-prints on every wall and claw-marks on every ledge and windowsill.

SNIPPETS (bits and pieces of love and life) by CAROLE

It definitely got me over my fastidiousness about the appearance of our home. How could I deprive them of all the fun they had playing together!

The house has three window units, side by side in the east wall of the living room, that had, at that time, a single set of draperies covering the entire expanse plus some wall totaling about fifteen feet in width. I happened to notice, one day, that the rod holding the draperies was beginning to sag. I mentioned the problem to John and he said, "It shouldn't sag. I installed a heavy-duty rod that should easily support the weight of those draperies." Several afternoons later I discovered the cause; I was astounded to see Sidney and Dusty chasing each other, clawing their way up the draperies and running across the rod on top. The impact of their running and the extra poundage of the cats, not the weight of the draperies, were the cause of the rod's sagging. Switching to shades with wooden valences to the ceiling and wooden side-covers stopped the cats' shenanigans. They never bothered chasing along any other draperies—just too short of an expanse, I guess.

Neither cat seemed to mind being shut inside a particular room, but they definitely did not like to be shut out of one that John and I were in. One night we had shut them out of our bedroom when we retired. As soon as the cats discovered that they were out and we were in there, one of them leaped repeatedly against the door and both started hollering with one of them sounding as if it were near the kitchen. John got up to shut the cats in the kitchen, but, when he opened the door, no cat was there on the floor. He happened to glance up, and there, staring down at him, was—Sidney—spread-eagle with two feet on the door jam and the other two feet on the top of the door. John reached up, lifted him down, and put him in the kitchen with Dusty who had already preceded them there.

Sidney had another favorite pastime. He loved to play under clothing, especially coats that were lying around on chairs or on the floor after he got hold of them. He would often tunnel down one of the sleeves and get trapped in the wrist opening with only his nose and eyes squished through and his ears pinned back, looking like an eel and hoping for someone to rescue him when he couldn't back out.

Dusty was a bit fastidious about the appearance of their litter box; she liked the litter to be just so and never in the corners of the box.

Whenever we changed or scooped the litter and shook it flat, Dusty would jump into the box as soon as it was back on the floor and then carefully and neatly scrape the litter away from all four corners. John enjoyed teasing her and would shake the litter flat again so she would have to repeat her task. Unfortunately, Dusty died of sudden kidney failure when she was just three years old. The cat, with which we replaced her, just happened to have been born on the very same day of her death, and we are positive that Dusty was reincarnated in that cat. Our new female Korat had all the same habits, liked all the same things, and, in general, was Dusty's exact duplicate in personality, although not in looks. We named her Suzy Squealer.

Soon afterwards, Sidney got very ill; we bought another male that we named Sammy Hider, in hopes that he would help inspire Sidney to get well. Sidney recovered and lived until eight years old. He and Dusty were show-quality cats which, on average, apparently live about seven to ten years. Suzy and Sammy were just pet-quality and lived to age fifteen and sixteen.

The encyclopedia didn't mention that Korats liked to talk, but all of ours carried on conversations with us. We never quite understood their language, but they seemed to understand ours, so we talked to them like you would talk to small children. The book also didn't mention that this breed followed a definite pecking order. Although we fed them at the same time, each one with its own bowl, the female ate first and then the older male and then the younger male unless, on very rare occasions, they were all so hungry that none could wait. When Sidney and Dusty were young, if we didn't get their food ready fast enough to suit them, they would nip us on the ankles, though never breaking the skin, to speed us up.

I don't know if cats are right-handed or left-handed or ambidextrous like people, but each tended to favor one of their front paws when playing with toys. Sidney definitely was left-handed and even liked to eat with his left front paw by scooping up his food off the plate and then licking it off his paw; but if he was in a hurry, he gobbled it down like the others did, straight off the plate and into his mouth.

We had an unwritten rule that the cats usually obeyed. They had to behave and stay off the table and counter tops whenever we had company. The rest of the time we spoiled them rotten. They liked to sit in our laps a lot, even, or should I say especially, during meals. Each female was very good at sneaking a paw toward your plate and if you didn't keep your eye on her constantly, that paw would slowly and gradually get close enough, then quickly grab a morsel when the cat thought you weren't paying attention. I had seen only one person actually feed a cat at the dinner table. When I was a high school senior and dating Pete, we ate once at his home with the whole family. His older half brother, Darin, had a cat that he fed, as well as himself, with his spoon from the food on his plate; his cat even shared his peaches-in-syrup dessert. We didn't go that far; if the cats received food from our plates, we either fed it to them by hand (or they stole it) or put our plates on the floor, after we had finished eating, and allowed them to eat whatever they wanted from the leftovers.

All of our cats traveled with us. The biggest reason that I decided to give John a cat for Christmas was that we had just bought a travel trailer; therefore, if we did have pets, we would rarely have to leave them at home during vacations. One to three, depending on how may were alive at the time, went with us to visit the forty-eight contiguous states and the eastern parts of Canada. The only time that they didn't like traveling was when we drove too far to suit them during a single day. When they had *had* enough, they screamed at us when we came back to the trailer for a break. The rest of the time, while the trailer was in motion, they played together leaping at anything swinging or slept together on the bed under the covers. Sometimes we would find them with only their heads sticking out of the bedcovers and up on the pillows just like tiny people.

Sammy Hider really lived up to his name. The encyclopedia stated that Korats don't like sudden noises. We think the fifteen-month-old daughter kept him distressed with her pot-banging and loud vocals when he still lived in Angela's home because, after we brought the kitten into our home, he would always run off to hide somewhere at the slightest strange or loud noise. It wasn't until he went almost totally deaf, the year before he died, that he stayed around when someone spoke loudly or even when the dish-washer door clicked as I opened it; before then, he would cry out and dash off.

Surprisingly, however, Sammy also became our great protector. During the time that Sheila, her husband, Raphael, their son, Beau, and their Siamese cat, Syben, lived with us, Sammy guarded the door to their room making sure that Syben didn't get out to attack us, which, of course, it never would have, but Sammy didn't know that. The two cats often played footsies with each other under the door. Since all the cats in the house didn't like breeds outside of their own, we had to juggle the time of day that each breed had the run of the rest of the house.

Our Korats didn't have a lot of "street smarts," so we only took them outdoors on leashes. The males liked stepping out, but the females didn't; they preferred staying in. Of all the cats, Sammy tolerated being leashed the best; he really enjoyed being outdoors in the sunshine. If you said in a high-pitched voice, "Sammy, want to go outside?" or just "Outside, outside?" he would leap up onto the clothes dryer by the backdoor and dance around meowing loudly while you put his harness and leash on him. Or, if you went out the backdoor and didn't close it tightly behind you and the wind blew it open, he would wander out onto the terrace and lie there enjoying his sun bath until you brought him back in. Suzy usually made you aware that her friend had gone out because she would sit just inside the door and reprimand Sammy loudly.

Sidney never *wandered* out when the door blew open; if no one came within a minute or two to close it, he *dashed* out on an adventure. One evening when we arrived home from work, we discovered the backdoor open, Sidney gone, and Dusty hollering in the kitchen. We quickly closed the door and waited hopefully for Sidney to return. After dark, we thought we heard a noise outside in the yard, so John opened the door to take a look around. A streak of blurry-silver-gray flew in through the doorway and continued flying around the cabinets and countertops at about-waist-height. When it finally came to a rest on the floor, it was obvious that our cat had returned. He seemed glad to be back indoors again and sat down to greedily eat his supper. From some minor wounds on his face, it was apparent that he had used up a lot of energy fighting some other animal. That was the second fight he had been in since we adopted him.

SNIPPETS (bits and pieces of love and life) by CAROLE

The first fight occurred while we were camping at the beach in Destin. John had forgotten to close the outside access door to the tool compartment located under the bed toward the back left side of our trailer after he did some work outside. Sidney had discovered a small opening, that we were unaware of in the bedroom area, where he could squeeze from under the bed into the compartment and easily hop out the small doorway. That time he stayed gone until 3:00 A.M. while we searched the campgrounds for him, gave up, and tried to get some sleep. We left the access door open, hoping that he would return the same way he left, and just swatted the mosquitoes that also used the opening to come in to bite us. When he finally did return, he had a small notch carved into his left ear and some scratches, but he was purring. He threw his paws over his eyes to keep out the light and promptly went to sleep curled up between the pillows at the head of the bed. John closed off the small opening so the cats could no longer get into the compartment by way of under-the-bed. Sidney never quite figured out what happened to his escape route; he would occasionally try to find it again.

Sidney and Sammy liked to go everywhere with John. Sidney also liked to leap into any container that John was carrying or onto his back or shoulders just for the ride; he even tried to go to work with him by sneaking into his briefcase. Dusty, and then Suzy, liked to be around me, especially when I was fixing meals. Each one wanted to be on the countertop helping in the preparation; I made her sit on a stool just watching but had to show her what I put into every pot or bowl. Any other time, if John was around, she dashed after him. All four of the cats greeted him first; they liked him best because he knew exactly the right way to play. They would make do with me if he wasn't around or if they just wanted a warm lap and hugging or petting, but they never considered me to be as much fun.

All the cats snuggled together to sleep no matter what size the "bed" was; if the space was small, they would just squeeze in and, if necessary, overlap body parts. If they were sleeping in bed with us, all the cats slept closer to John because he is warmer and hairier. The females especially liked to snuggle up by his knees under the covers.

After we purchased a waterbed, it took a few days for the cats to get use to the way the bed wiggled and felt underfoot. In the beginning, they were real skittish and leaped off again as soon as you put them on it; once they got used to it, they preferred it for sleeping and napping because it was always warm and so comfy. Sammy loved to take naps and John could always count on him, and sometimes on the others, for company when napping in the afternoon. Frequently I would find one cat on his chest and one or two beside him, all sound asleep.

Sidney and Dusty were the most mischievous cats. They were twelve-week-old kittens when we adopted them, and while we were at work, they played like unsupervised little children. They even played pranks on each other; one would hide, usually crouched down in the lidless litter box, and spring out to surprise the other when it passed by. Sidney could open the kitchen cabinet doors by standing on his hind legs, placing his front paws on the top of the door and walking backwards. He could also open the bi-folding closet doors by leaping on them to spring them open; he and Dusty would then drag things off the shelves to play with or swing on the hanging clothes. John had to make stained wood pieces to stick through the two handles of adjacent, cabinet doors or hang over two doorknobs of the double-door closets to keep the doors from being opened except by a person. Consequently, before we left the house, we always counted cats to make sure none was locked in a cabinet or closet for the extent of our time away after the first time it happened. All of our cats liked sitting at the sliding glass doors even when the draperies were closed; they would simply sit between the draperies and the glass. Sidney always preferred to have the draperies open over the sliding-doors in the bedroom; if they were closed, he would leap onto the dresser nearby and try to open them with his teeth by grabbing the cord in the same place as we did and tugging on it; he never managed to open them, being the light-weight in the tug-of-war; the draperies always won and didn't budge. Suzy and Sammy never played pranks on us; even though they too were twelve weeks old at adoption; they had Sidney, who was then an older, mature cat, around to make them behave.

For the time being, we are cat-less. Since pets aren't allowed to accompany us on the trips we have planned, we will just have to wait until later to adopt some more cats. They definitely will be *Korats*— if we can locate some.

SNIPPET 125 - Furry Painters

Sidney and Dusty, our first two Korats, were only sixteen-week-old kittens, weighing no more than three to four pounds each, when they had their brief careers as painters. John was painting the dining room ceiling and walls with "lunar" white and thought the cats wouldn't be interested in the paint because they had earlier sniffed it, turned up their noses, and walked away. But curiosity soon brought them back to test the consistency of the paint with a paw or two which they then used to spread some paint around on the vinyl floor and leave footprints on the wood floor leading away from the room. We quickly cleaned their paws, shut the cats in the kitchen, and then sponged the water-base paint off the floor. The rest of the painting went smoothly.

Afterwards, we decided that we would go out that evening because it was Saturday and I was off work that weekend. John put the paint pan and rollers to soak in deep water in a large, tall bucket sitting in the deeper side of the double laundry sink in the kitchen, planning to finish cleaning them later that evening or, maybe, in the morning. We bathed, dressed, and left to enjoy a wonderful dinner at our favorite restaurant nearby.

When we returned home, we discovered that our little furry painters had been busy painting the rest of the floor for us. Somehow, they were able to get the soaking paint rollers out of the bucket and onto the floor and had dragged them out of the kitchen and all over the wood floors of the house, even under the beds. The water-soaked rollers had to be quite heavy for two kittens, even using teamwork, to wield up out of the water, over the counter edge, and around the floor, and seemed an impossible task for one. As we surveyed their handiwork, all we could do was laugh. The proud, wide-open eyes in their two little innocent faces simply gazed at us over the edge of their kitty-cup atop the clothes dryer as they watched us try to remove the paint from the floor.

The unanswerable question will always be: How in the world did they do that?

SNIPPET 126 - *Sidney Gets a Bath*

    Early in our vacation the spring of 1977, we were traveling across Florida, west to east, in our Chevy Suburban® with Airstream™ travel trailer in tow when the left rear tire on the Suburban went flat. Since the trailer had tandem wheels and was attached to the truck by weight-distributing spring bars in addition to the trailer hitch, the Suburban could still travel for a few miles because some of the truck's weight, usually riding on the now-flat tire, was distributed over the other seven tires. We drove the few remaining miles to Fort Pierce and stopped at a large garage to have it repaired. Our young Korat cats, Sidney and Dusty, were traveling in the air-conditioned truck with us because it was too hot in the closed-up trailer to let them stay there. Since it was late afternoon, John was going to put the cats in the trailer to eat and sleep while the tire was being fixed. Thinking the move would be an easy one, he simply put them into an over-sized canvas bag instead of their carrier. Just as he walked by the mechanic taking the tire off, the man started his pneumatic wrench to remove a nut; the sudden loud noise startled the cats, which hate and dread loud noises, and Sidney leaped from the bag and darted away. John was able to restrain Dusty and quickly put her into the trailer. I hopped in immediately afterwards to sooth her and calm her down.

    Several hours after the tire was repaired and put back on the Suburban, Sidney had still not returned. The garage closed for the night, but the manager allowed us to stay in the parking lot to wait, in hopes that our cat would eventually come back after everything was quiet. Not wanting to make any excess noise, I decided not to cook as that required turning on the noisy exhaust fan. Luckily, there was a pizza shop directly across the highway, so John walked over there to buy us a pizza for a late supper. Neither of us ate much as the distress over the missing cat absconded with our appetites. Around ten o'clock, when the whole area had become quiet, we thought we heard distant cat cries and called out, "Sidney," many times, hoping he would hear us and run to the trailer. Dusty heard the cries too and excitedly called out as well. Then all went quiet for a while. This scenario played repeatedly all the rest of the night—no one slept.

SNIPPETS (bits and pieces of love and life) by CAROLE

Early the next morning as the garage was opening for business again, one of the mechanics went out back to start up the compressors that were inside the fenced yard where they kept old containers of grease and oil. As the first engine started, a terrified cat leaped out from behind a barrel, scaring the man who then hollered to us that he had found our cat. John dashed over with the canvas bag, instead of the carrier, to put him in because Sidney was covered with used oil and grease; this time, though, John rolled the top of the bag down and held it tightly until he stepped into the trailer and closed the door.

The only way we knew to clean Sidney was to cover him with Goop® hand cleaner, then bathe him with a mild soap to remove that. Since John was his favorite person (fortunate for me, not so for him), he was selected to do the job. He stripped and climbed into the small, bench-seated shower, taking the canvas bag containing the now-slippery-dirty-black cat with him. I stood in the tiny area of the bathroom floor, and after John handed me the bag, I quickly closed the wavy-plastic, folding shower-door and held it tightly shut. Sidney, not relishing being scrubbed and showered, tried to claw his way out as John held him from behind with one hand and with the other hand "Gooped," soaped, then rinsed him with the hand-held shower as fast as he could. What a racket all the thumping and bumping made! Fortunately, both survived fairly well with Sidney getting the better of and John the brunt of the ordeal. I took the dripping cat, looking really funny soaking wet, wrapped him in a towel, and dried him with a 12-volt-DC hair dryer. He still looked a bit funny when dry because all of his short fur stuck out fluffy, but bristly-looking like that on an angry cat's back, instead of lying flat.

Success—we unknowingly thought. But, the *end* of that problem was just the *beginning* of another.

Sidney recognized Dusty because she still smelled like Dusty; however, Dusty didn't recognize Sidney because he smelled like Neutrogena® soap. If he was in another part of the trailer, out of smelling range, and meowed, she knew he was back and would get all excited, but hissed and spat at this unknown cat when they got near each other. Sidney had no idea what was happening! He repeatedly tried to be friendly with Dusty and consistently got rebuked, causing the two to get into a screaming match until one or both got tired.

After ten days of this battling, Sidney finally regained enough of his natural odor for Dusty to recognize him.

What a happy reunion for all four of us! — And, finally, relief and peace for John and me.

SNIPPET 127 - Vortex Generator

We like to eat by candlelight, so we always have lighted candles on the dining room table when we have company, and we sometimes have them in the kitchen when just the two of us are eating dinner. We say that we do it because it's so *romantic*, but the *real* reason is that we like to show off our vortex generator.

If you don't have a vortex generator, you need to make one. You simply need a two-pound metal coffee can with a translucent plastic lid. Remove the metal top end of the can and the coffee. In the center of the bottom end, cut out a half-dollar-coin-sized hole. Place the plastic lid back onto the open end. Paint the can any color you like; ours is painted gold. To blow out the candle flame, with one hand hold the can such that you line up the hole with the flame while looking at it through the translucent lid, and then with fingers of the other hand, thump the lid. The rush of air, from the inside of the can, out through the hole will instantly extinguish the candle. You may have to practice a little as the hole might be slightly off and you will need to adjust your aim accordingly.

One summer evening while Becky and her family were visiting us, John got out our vortex generator to extinguish the candles at the end of dinner. Our nephew Thomas, who was about seven at the time, wanted to do it too, but he didn't want any instructions. So John, after extinguishing one of the candles, let him try blowing out the second candle. Thomas grabbed the can, swung it near his hip, and thumped the lid. As luck would have it, he extinguished the candle on his first try. He wanted to do it again and wouldn't listen to John trying to explain that the first attempt was sheer luck. We lit the candles again and Thomas spent the entire evening trying to figure out how to blow out the candles.

The rest of us retired to the adjoining living room a few feet away to finish out the evening, chatting and wondering when or if he would ask for help. The only sound we ever heard from Thomas was the thump, thump, thumping of his little fingers on the plastic lid.

SNIPPET 128 - Nurses

September 1977, in fact, on the day after John's birthday on the sixth, I finally had to undergo major surgery to remove the remaining female organs and as much as possible of the endometrial tissue that was debilitating me. It had to be done although I was extremely reluctant to do that because it meant that I would never be able to bear children.

I was working with Joe, the other half of "The Bobsey Twins," in the Mechanical Department at DuPont Company at that time, and he must have mentioned it to his wife, Dottie, who is an RN. When I opened my eyes, after being returned to my hospital bed following the surgery, there stood, not only John, but Dottie, five feet six inches tall, with brown hair, soft, compassionate, brown eyes and tender smile, all dressed in her white nurse's uniform, holding my hand and saying something like: "I came to stay with you to make sure you're OK and so John could go home to get some rest. The first night is always the hardest, but I'll be right here beside you while you sleep. If you want or need anything or just want to talk, let me know."

I didn't have to ask for anything as she anticipated my every need, and in the morning, she disappeared as quietly as she came. She is just like most of the other nurses I know or have known in the past. *Webster's New World Dictionary of American English* says a nurse is "a person trained to take care of the sick, injured, or aged, to assist surgeons, etc.; specif., a registered nurse (RN) or a practical nurse (LPN)". Unfortunately, the definition excludes what I think are the most important attributes. To me, first and foremost, a nurse is a person who is caring, compassionate, tender, helpful, nurturing, encouraging, and cheerful, and who has almost never-ending patience; they help you heal anything, physical or mental or spiritual, that is broken. The training simply teaches them how to use these attributes in a way that is helpful and not harmful to the recipient of their care.

The first nurse I ever encountered was my mom (RN), and it's from her that I learned all the attributes that the dictionary forgot to mention. The second was Aunt Dottie, weighing one pound nine ounces at birth, who was miraculously kept alive by the nurses who cared for her around-the-clock until she could leave the hospital, and who, in turn, became an RN herself. Over the years I have added to my list.

Edith, who is an RN, has loved and taken care of children since she was a teenager and, as an adult, raised a daughter and son of her own while helping her ex-husband, who is blind, train to become a masseur and be independent. She doesn't let others with handicaps wallow in self-pity but helps them learn how to live well anyway; she has a handicap herself, having extremely limited vision since birth and several eye operations. Edith has rescued sick and disabled people, bringing one child into her home for several years, and helped them all with their rehabilitation so they could move on in their lives. She has worked in hospices not only with the patients but with their families as well. Edith and my dad are the only people I ever knew, personally, who have removed eyes from cadavers for the eye bank.

Sheila was an LPN/LVN (Licensed Practical Nurse/Licensed Vocational Nurse) in intensive care, an extremely demanding job, and went back to school for more training to earn her RN license when she was fifty-three so she could be an even better nurse.

Louise, my cousin, at age fifteen, was taken out of school by Aunt Dottie so she could enjoy her last year to live due to having four undersized kidneys and being sick for a year with rheumatic fever when she much younger. At age sixteen, she decided she had to live and return to school because she wanted to be an RN; she also married and raised two daughters and an adopted son before she died not long ago.

There are more nurses who are relatives, friends, and acquaintances than there is room to name and tell you about. All that I have come in contact with during my life are the kind of people no one should ever have to live without.

My dad always wanted me to be a nurse like my mother, or better yet, a doctor. I fear I lack at least one of the attributes of a nurse. This major one is so necessary as an attribute that it is a *given* and understood without mentioning. You must be able to withstand the sight of a tiny drop of blood. — Fainting dead away renders you totally useless.

SNIPPET 129 - Are You OK?

It was a gorgeous, sunny-blue-sky afternoon, but I couldn't see it from where I lay on the floor. I was in the front hallway by the sliding glass doors that serve as windows by the double front doors to our house. My eyes were closed and I was writhing as though in pain. I don't remember at all how I got there. Maybe I collapsed or perhaps threw myself down there. I don't know.

"God, or somebody, please help me!" I had been screaming over and over at the top of my lungs until my throat was so sore that I could hardly speak anymore, much less scream. I had been crying for hours. My world was bleak and closing in on me. Again I just wanted to die; this was the fourth time in my life that the depression had gotten so bad that I had decided to kill myself.

But the phone rang and I crawled into the kitchen to answer it; I don't know why; I didn't want to talk to anyone, but I was simply compelled to answer the phone.

A soft, concerned voice, that I recognized as Patty's, asked, "Are you OK?"

"No," I whispered because my voice was totally shot.

"Don't do anything. Just stay right where you are. I'm going to call John to come home to get you. And, I'll call you right back. Please answer the phone again."

"OK." The second and only other word I could utter.

I hung up the phone, pulled myself up onto a kitchen-counter stool and sat, waiting for the phone to ring again. It rang within two minutes and Patty just kept me on the phone talking to me until John arrived and took me to see Dr. James, who was our marvelous family doctor for many years.

I had had surgery in September 1977 for a total hysterectomy and removal of endometrial tissue plus an appendectomy. I plunged into surgical menopause and deep depression. For six months, I had hormone replacement therapy, but it only made the depression worse, so the surgeon told me to stop it. After that, I had been trying all different kinds of therapy for my depression and I had managed to last through Patty and Ralph's wedding in August 1978, just several days prior to this dreadfully bleak day. Making her wedding dress and making a dress for Brenda had kept me going but now there was nothing to hide the cloud of darkness I felt. I had been through hundreds of hours of talk therapy, one-on-one and group, but all that it ever did for me was to make me feel worse. Most of the other people in the group sessions had real problems that caused physical and emotional damage; I didn't. I always felt there was something wrong with my brain's chemistry and not my life, and all the talking in the world about my life was worthless for relieving my type of depression.

Our doctor recommended a psychiatrist, Dr. Teng, for me to see and said that there were medications available to control depression that was caused by a chemical imbalance in the brain. I had great confidence in Dr. James and his opinion; he was not only very kind but very intelligent as well, always keeping current with the latest happenings in medical practice. I began to feel that there was some hope for me and that my prayers had been answered.

Later, I asked Patty *why* she had phoned when she did that day.

"I just suddenly knew that you needed me and called to see what you wanted," she said. "It seemed urgent that I do it immediately. You keep telling me repeatedly, 'follow your intuition.' So I did."

I spent eighteen days in a hospital psychiatric ward under the excellent supervision of Dr. Teng and a year or so visiting him in his office. Years of trial and error with different medications as they evolved followed that. By the end of 1990, another doctor, Dr. Robin, finally got the depression under control with the right combination of anti-depressant and endocrine drugs. Nevertheless, I still walk a thin line between being all right and being a crying or screaming, depressed maniac.

I definitely was not OK that August 1978, but I am OK now, August 2002.

SNIPPET 130 - Psychiatric Ward

Some people may think that staying in a psychiatric ward is a terrible way to spend eighteen days. But, for some, like me, it is a way to really start living. I was forty-one, when I was admitted on August 29, 1978, and had been depressed frequently over the previous twenty-five years. For the first time ever, I felt that, maybe, I finally could get rid of that dark, bleak and foreboding feeling.

After discussing the use of medications, Dr. Teng felt that staying in the hospital would be the best and easiest for all concerned since I responded to medications like a child rather than like an adult. Besides, it would remove me from the responsibilities of home and job and allow me to concentrate on just recovering. It would also allow John to continue working instead of having to stay home to monitor me and dole out my new medications. Everyone reacts differently, and several drugs would probably have to be tried and dosages altered until the right ones for me were decided upon.

When the nurse in the Psychiatric Ward of St. Francis Hospital checked me in, she went through all the belongings that I had brought for my stay and removed anything that I, or someone else, might use to harm anyone. I hadn't even thought about that and had brought a nail file that she gave to John to take back home. I got settled in my room and met Cyndy who was my roommate for most of my stay. She had stayed here before as well as in other hospitals; she liked this one best and said she thought I would like it here too. I did; everyone was kind and helpful, though firm and strict.

We had a routine that we followed each day. By a specific time in the morning we had to be bathed, dressed, our beds made and rooms tidied up. Everything else had specific time slots: meals, individual and group therapy sessions, exercise, arts and crafts, and visiting hours. The first few days, I mostly stared into space and cried, even in arts and crafts therapy; there, I couldn't concentrate on anything or decide what to make. The first medications made me so drowsy that even during exercises, if I had to sit on the floor to do them, I promptly fell over onto my side or with my head onto my legs, fast asleep.

SNIPPETS (bits and pieces of love and life) by CAROLE

Eventually, after about a week, I was able to start functioning more like a human being. I even completed some crafts, making two matching leather-loop belts, one for John and one for me, and three metal trivets covered in small colored tiles. I created the designs, a different one for each trivet, filling in the spaces between the tiles with grout. We still have the belts, and we still use the trivets, two on the dining room table and one in the kitchen. I like them; they remind me of the "before" and "after" me. I also have two other reminders, two oil paintings hanging in our living room that Raphael painted, which I double-named *The Depression (Before '78)* and *The Elation (After '82)* when I finally got myself fairly normal.

My last week there, I was stable enough to go on field trips with the group of patients who were ready to get back into the real world again. While we were out on the downtown streets or in a restaurant around lunchtime, I ran into some of my coworkers who had gone out to lunch or to run errands. It seemed strangely weird to see them and, even more so, to chat with them; I felt like I was playing hooky and should be working instead. They treated me as though they had, by chance, seen me on vacation.

John visited me every day. My manager, Dan, came several times to keep me posted on the office happenings, so he said. But, I knew that he really came to cheer me up; he was a very kind and thoughtful person, and so was his wife. Sylvia came to visit me too; we had barely met a few weeks before when she became a part of the information management systems group that I worked in. She helped me immensely in getting back to full-time productive work in my job. We became—and still are—great friends.

When I returned to work, some people shunned me for a while as though I had a contagious disease, but others were truly interested in my well-being and in the medications I was taking. People who thought that either they, or some of their loved ones, might be suffering from depression too, seemed to appear out of the woodwork. One coworker asked if I would visit his mom in Pittsburgh; she had stabbed herself but miraculously survived. John and I both went to see her. She and I gave each other support until it was no longer needed. The medications that helped her were totally different from mine.

Carole Christie Moore Adams

I never tried to hide my problem once I got out of the hospital; I talked about it openly whenever anyone asked. You never know when someone else needs to know that there is available help that truly works.

SNIPPET 131 - Assignments

Sometimes you need someone to tell you what to do when you *don't know* what to do and, especially, when you *do know* what you need to do but just haven't gotten around to doing it. That's when I go see Sylvia.

I first met Sylvia when she joined the information management systems group while we were both working for DuPont Company. A few days, a few weeks at most, later, I landed in the hospital for some mental therapy. Sylvia came to visit to cheer me up, and I was so touched that she bothered to do it (because I already liked her and had hoped the reverse was true) that I bonded with her immediately. When I returned to work, she hovered over me, helped me do all my work, prodded me on, and made sure I got the tasks done correctly and, as they—the authoritative they—say in the business world, "on time and within budget." When your brain is having problems, you need someone to help you like that until you can function on your own again.

Her sister, who lives in New York, sent her a you-have-to-read-this book, *Dress for Success*, which she read immediately. Since Sylvia reads extremely fast, and absorbs it fast in my opinion, she came waving the book at me the next day.

"We have to do this!" she said, opening the book and pointing at a section, which I assume she assumed I could read and absorb as fast as she does, which I can't.

So, we did it. The next day we went shopping for suits, blouses, shoes, and briefcases in order that we could change our images at work. And it definitely did change our images. Moreover, I got more respect for what I said and did even though I said and did nothing differently than I had before.

The other people (not Sylvia and I, of course) in our group did their work like most people do (and a bit helter-skelter, we thought) with plans only in their heads and nothing written down in case something happened to them, like "get hit by a truck" as Greg, one of my managers, would say, and someone else had to finish their tasks. In the real world, this is referred to as *job security*, but in the computer world we worked in, Sylvia and I referred to it as *job disaster*.

"We have to do this," Sylvia said to me, shoving a draft under my nose as soon as I arrived at work and sat down in the swivel chair behind my desk.

So, we did it. We immediately went to her office and I sat down on a straight chair beside her and she sat down in her swivel chair that was moved to face her computer. I'm calling it a computer here so you'll know what I'm talking about; it was really just a terminal, with a screen and keyboard, connected by cables to one of our large main frame computers, but it worked, for all intents and purposes, like today's PC without a mouse. She typed, as usual with only one finger, maybe two, but rapidly, and together we devised a sample work plan for everyone to copy and complete for each work project. The work plan showed what tasks needed to be done, where the task components and essentials were located, how each task should be carried out, when each task should be completed and when that task was actually completed. And, with the blessings of our boss, we made the group do it. The work plans were all kept in a common folder, using today's terminology, on a disk attached to the computer and printed copies of them kept in binders in one of our offices. Over the years the form of the basic work plan got modified, but the plans really helped the group accomplish its goals faster, better, and cheaper because we knew what each person was doing and you could help each other. Also you could see how a similar project was done before, so you didn't have to "reinvent the wheel" for a new project. (I still use "work plans" today, but, now that I'm retired, they're just for traveling.)

I like it when Sylvia says, "We have to do this!" because it means we're going to do something else that is worthwhile or just simply fun, like visit a museum or see a play in New York City, or see an opera or a ballet in Wilmington, or go shopping, or read a new book, or whatever! But I like to kid her—

"Is this *another assignment*?"

P.S. My extraordinary and dear friend Sylvia was a marvelous person and I am devastated that I shall never see her again or have her companionship. We became friends in 1978 and she died at age 57 in

SNIPPETS (bits and pieces of love and life) by CAROLE

April 2003 while John and I were away on a trip. I shall miss her tremendously. She did get to read the "Snippet's" she appears in and almost all the others; I gave a copy of hers from the original manuscript to her family. I found out from her sister that she was a member of Mensa, the international organization of people who score in the top two percent of the population on a standardized intelligence test. I wasn't at all surprised.

SNIPPET 132 - Taller

Sylvia and I like to spend the day in New York City, where she grew up, having lunch in some marvelous restaurant that she knows of or we read about, and then shopping for books and videos or seeing a play or visiting a museum. As a present for my sixty-fifth birthday, she sent me a *New Yorker* magazine with a note that, in essence, said: look on the indicated pages and choose a restaurant and a play, then look on your calendar and choose a Wednesday; tell me your choices, then I'll make the arrangements, and we'll take Amtrak to NYC for the day. It was another one of Sylvia's *assignments*. What a fabulous gift! On the day we went, the weather was spectacular and the events extraordinary.

We used to take a vacation day from work and ride the bus chartered by the Delaware Art Museum for day trips on the third Thursday of the month. Sadly, the museum doesn't sponsor those excursions anymore. It was on the first of those excursions with Sylvia that I made a startling discovery.

Sylvia and I had been working together only a few months, and quite well, I might add, even though my head wasn't working well at that time. Most of the time, we worked together sitting down and, since my legs are long and my body short, we looked eye to eye. If there was a problem with one of the information management systems and we needed to go investigate, we walked together fast, chattering away about what we intended to do, but never looking at each other, because we had a goal of getting to the computer room quickly. As a matter of fact, we both habitually walk fast everywhere.

We had gone to NYC to see a play, and, since we had some time to kill before we had to be at the theatre, we decided to window-shop. As we were strolling along, I turned my head toward the window and, quite surprised, I exclaimed, "Good heavens, Sylvia, would you look at that!"

Sylvia is five feet tall and I was five feet six inches (am five feet four inches now) and until that day when I saw our reflection in the window, I never realized I was so much taller.

SNIPPET 133 - Help, Shirley Is Ill

We received a phone call from Becky, John's sister, telling us that their mom, Shirley, was very sick and in the hospital. We called our supervisors at work to tell them that we were taking several days vacation, packed our bags, and flew to Savannah.

After we found out what was going on, we planned our strategy very carefully using my knowledge from the *Dress for Success* books that my friend Sylvia and I had studied. John dressed in a pin-stripe dark gray business suit with white dress shirt and tie, I dressed in a navy suit with white oxford shirt and beige ascot, and high-heeled shoes with matching briefcase, and the two of us headed to the hospital. John introduced us as "Dr. and Mrs. Adams," not mentioning that he was a PhD, not MD, and that we had come to find out what was wrong with his mom. The doctors and nurses were very cooperative, probably due to our kind, but authoritative, manner and dress, plus John's title. They didn't know what illness Shirley had but she was running a high fever and obviously getting worse because she was almost delirious. We were afraid she would die if we left her there. We decided to take her home to see Dr. James and checked her out of the hospital.

We couldn't get a flight out until the next morning but left on the earliest one to Philadelphia. After arriving home, we took her immediately to our family doctor. After examining her, Dr. James said Shirley had a severe case of pneumonia, and he began treatment immediately. We decided that we could best care for Shirley around the clock at home if my mom could come help us for a while, so I called her. Mom was a retired RN.

"Help, Mema, Shirley is very ill with pneumonia. Do you think Daddy could manage without you for several weeks so you can fly up here to help us take care of her?" I asked. "I know you two like each other a lot and would enjoy each other's company."

It was OK with my dad, so she flew up the next day. Mom was an excellent nurse; she just had that knack of being so caring that you had to get well for *her*, if not for yourself. And, Shirley did get well.

It was during the year of 1979 when Veronica was coming once a week to help with housekeeping until I could cope with all the responsibilities of our home plus a full-time job since I hadn't been very long out of the hospital for treatment of my depression. Mema and Shirley were supposed to stay out of the way, like we did, while Veronica was working in the house because Veronica didn't like people underfoot while she was working. But they didn't, and Veronica apparently didn't mind at all and seemed to gravitate toward our moms like everyone else did. They had a wonderful time snacking and chatting together. Even though she had to stay longer to get her work done, Veronica really enjoyed working the weeks that all three of them could be together.

Eventually, Shirley and Mema each left for home, but both of them were grateful that the illness had brought them together and had given them the opportunity to get to know each other better. It was such a joy for John and me to watch our two moms interact; they were both so dear to us and, by the time they left, to each other as well.

SNIPPET 134 - *Just You and Me*

Mema once said to me, "If you ever have to choose between the two of you and the rest of the world, including your family and friends, just remember there's really *no choice*." She meant it sincerely even when our choice would hurt her personally. The worst hurt we, and therefore she, ever had to endure was the disastrous fallout from our dinner party to celebrate the milestone twenty-fifth wedding anniversary.

We had decided to have a catered affair on the actual anniversary day, December 26, 1985, and had made all the arrangements for a sit-down dinner plus elaborate, buffet-style hors d'oeuvres before and desserts after dinner at Bouli Bouli, one of our favorite restaurants in downtown Wilmington.

We made up our list of only twenty-six to twenty-seven guests because the fire code prevented more than thirty people in the room that was available for parties. (We needed two of the thirty places for ourselves and one for our special guest/entertainer or two if he wished to bring someone.) It was really a tough decision as we wanted to invite all our friends and relatives. After phoning our families and learning that it was impossible, financially and time-wise, for them to travel so far for a one-evening party, we decided to invite only local people. Even that was hard because we thought we had so many friends, but we eventually narrowed the list to the required number.

And then the disasters began!

One day before the invitations went out, at work during lunch with several girl friends, the subject of what I had planned to do on "the" anniversary came up. I casually mentioned the party and the one friend who was not on the list said, "I just have to be invited; I want to come." Consequently, I removed a couple from the list and added the names of her and her guest. They became "never-shows" because they were over in New Jersey that day and "simply lost track of the time and the traffic was bad." Another couple, close friends for twenty years up to that point, refused to come because their children, although we had really wanted them to be included, were not invited. They never spoke to us again, and I cried off and on, about losing their friendship, for ten years, every time I thought about them. A third couple had a flat tire on the way, and even after we begged them to come late when they phoned us at the restaurant, they turned around and drove home after changing the tire. Those four places could have been used by four of my family waiting at our home for us to bring the leftovers and continue the celebration there.

A few days before the party, we had seen a notice in the newspaper that the restaurant was filing for bankruptcy and going "out of business." Before we could panic, however, the owners of the restaurant notified us that even though the restaurant would already be closed to the public, since we had prepaid, they would open just that evening for our party only. Moreover, due to limited staffing, we would be confined to the one room and would not be able to expand our guest list and use the rest of the restaurant.

In the interim, my dad had decided to fly up anyway and had arrived at our house, bringing along some other out-of-town family members to join the celebration. Unfortunately, there was no room for them at the party since the limit of guests had been reached, so we had to leave them at home. My sisters assured me "it's all right," although I knew it was *not*, and my mom told us to "please enjoy yourselves; I'll try to console your dad." Well, my dad never forgave John and me. A week later, in a scathing letter, he disowned me. I eventually resigned myself to being disowned and told him, "It's OK, Daddy. You have to do what you have to do." But, I will never get over the pain it caused even though there was a semi-reconciliation about ten years later in the interval between mom's death and his death.

The restaurant staff did a fabulous job, the food was superb, and the guests who came were wonderful to us. Our special guest, Kevin Roth, entertained us marvelously and even sang our favorite song of his—*The Rooster Song*. (We still have the autographed tape album that we received as a memento.)

Unfortunately, the memories of all the wretched things that happened keep us from ever doing that again. Now, to celebrate our anniversary, we dine, sometimes with a few friends and/or relatives but most of the time just alone, in town at a restaurant or away at an inn or a bed and breakfast that also provides evening meals.

The one thing that I still do on anniversaries, and probably always will, is wear my "25th-Anniversary" dress. It is a gorgeous two-piece ivory, knit-lace dress, with long sleeves and a pleated skirt; I have to wear it because it makes me feel so beautiful and, of course, John adores me in it. Fortunately, I had, by chance, found and bought the dress the year before at Finkel's (our favorite women's clothing shop for many years until it closed) and had secretly saved it for that specific occasion.

We still take my mom's advice, and when the rest of the world seems to hurt us, we hug each other and John will say "Remember, it's just you and me, baby."

If John dies before I do, it will be *just me,* and the thought of that is almost intolerable.

SNIPPET 135 - Patty's Sister

I don't know why I have such a problem with remembering people's names, but I do; I remember faces and I recognize people by the sound of their footsteps, but I frequently forget a person's name until the next day or so when it no longer matters. I often wonder from whom, or which side of the family even, I inherited that trait; must ask one of my sisters who remember things better than I do.

I have even forgotten John's name on occasion and, shockingly, he has even forgotten mine; I guess it's because that's not what we call each other. Anyway, so that we don't embarrass ourselves in front of strangers, when one introduces the other to someone the other doesn't know, the one will start the introduction and the other finishes it by saying his/her own name. At least, that way we don't look like *total* idiots even though everyone thinks that if you've been married as long as we have, you have to be a bit stupid to forget your spouse's name and even a bit strange to have been married that long. This little introduction routine just happens to work for us.

We had arrived early, after driving fifteen miles through unusually light traffic to Ralph and Patty's house, for a party where there would be some people that we didn't know because the guests included friends we had in common and some we didn't. I went into the kitchen to chat with Patty while she finished the food preparations. John went down to the basement with Ralph to help bring up the wine from Ralph's homemade wine cellar which stored the wines he bought along with his homemade wines. He is a chemist, like John, and at that time, since they were childless and had spare time, he made his own fabulous grape or strawberry or blackberry or combination-of-fruits wine in the cooler half of the basement.

We had been talking about our middle sister, Sheila, when Patty glanced out the kitchen window, which faced the street in front of their house, and saw their neighbor friends, a rabbi and his wife, approaching the front door. I said that I'd go to let them in. As the doorbell rang, I dashed to the door and flung it open to usher in the guests while introducing myself. I doubled over in laughter as they

SNIPPETS (bits and pieces of love and life) by CAROLE

entered the house, eyeing me cautiously and easing by me. I couldn't believe I had said it! — "Hi. Come on in. I'm Patty's sister Sheila!"

SNIPPET 136 - *Love Is—*

Many people, wherever I worked, came to me for advice of any type. Maybe it was because I didn't impose my advice; I always reminded them that I gave advice freely and expected them to take it or toss it as they chose. Or, maybe it was because of the Lucy-from-*Peanuts* "Advice 5¢" cartoon-postcard-sign tacked on the wall beside my office door.

One afternoon sometime in the late 1980's, a young male coworker dropped into my office for a chat during his break. It soon became apparent that his long-time girl friend was pressuring him to get married. He wasn't sure if he was ready, and that's why he'd come to me for advice. Toward the end of our conversation he said, "I'm not sure what *love is*. Can you tell me?"

I told him that I couldn't give him a definition but would think about it overnight and jot down what it meant to me.

Here is the text from the note I gave him the next day:

SNIPPETS *(bits and pieces of love and life)* by CAROLE

Love Is—

— holding hands and running down the street together.
— your eyes lighting up when you see one another.
— liking one another and being good friends.
— wanting to belong together always.
— being so happy that you can jump up and down together and not feel silly.
— feeling good just being near one another.
— wanting to protect one another from the hurts of the world.
— enjoying doing things or just doing nothing together.
— wanting to share with each other.
— thrilling to each other's touch.
— getting up early just to eat breakfast together.
— trying to understand and tolerate each other's bad habits.
— trying to help each other grow into a better human being.
— comforting and reassuring one another in times of stress.
— being available when the other needs you.
— all the little things you do for one another.
— being whole yet incomplete without the other.
— taking care of each other when illness strikes.
— doing things for the benefit of both.
— saying "I'm sorry" and making up.
— getting wet in the rain and not caring because you're together.
— getting so excited sometimes when you're near one another that you get sick to your stomach.

SNIPPET 137 - *Pianos and Organs*

For some reason people really like to get things that are free. Why is that? Your senses are free but objects never are. Organizations send you stuff in the mail and play on your guilt to get you to send them money in return; I finally learned to just throw it away unless it's something useful which I then keep and just toss the packaging. If we want to contribute money to any organization, we do it without their asking or sending us anything. Yet, sometimes getting something free does trap us, but it's probably because we would have done it anyway—just not as soon.

Becky took lessons and plays the piano quite well. Years ago, to encourage her to play more often, we bought her a small keyboard so she could play anytime, anywhere, she liked.

John too enjoys music, but only learned how to play "sticks," a percussion instrument, in first grade and how to play *Chopsticks* on the piano with Becky. He always thought it would be nice to have a piano of his own even though he hadn't a clue how to play *real* music on it.

One Saturday years ago, while we were shopping, which we very rarely do, we happened to walk by the Wilmington Piano store in the Concord Mall. After we passed it, John quickly turned around to look again at the large object sitting out in the mall walkway in front of the store. It was a Yamaha™ Electone™ organ with three layers of piano-style finger keys, foot keys, volume pedals, and all the levers, dials, and buttons that you could move or press to become your own full orchestra as you played, and it was *on sale*.

John asked a salesman to demonstrate it for him. As the gentleman played and showed him how everything worked, I could tell John was *mesmerized*. When I heard him ask the salesman, "When can you deliver it to my home?" I knew that it was all over. — John was also *hooked*.

"Why in the world are you buying that organ? You know neither of us can play it," I said rather stunned but pleased that he was doing it because he was obviously so happy.

"I'll soon be able to play it," he proudly reassured me. "Didn't you see the *sign*? It comes with six *free* private lessons."

SNIPPETS (bits and pieces of love and life) by CAROLE

As soon as it was delivered, he took the lessons in sequence as rapidly as possible. He still plays the organ frequently, usually late in the evening before he goes to bed, and sometimes for friends, whether or not they are willing to listen. Even our cats liked to be around when he was practicing, especially if they could walk on the keys and help make the music more interesting. He still insists, however, that he doesn't want "a call from Carnegie Hall" until he is finally fully retired.

SNIPPET 138 - It's in the Genes

Beau, the son of Sheila and Raphael, is a lot like his mother and dad. His physical description includes: height - six feet four inches, weight - 180 pounds, hair - dark brown, eyes - dark brown, shoe size - fourteen (big feet run rampant through Sheila's and my side of the family), and handsome. He is kind, gentle, quiet, and talented; but sometimes he acts more like his maternal grandfather, George.

"Little Jorgé" (pronounced Hor-hay), Spanish for George since his dad is Mexican, is what Beau is called when he does things that remind them of George. *They say* (I really like using that authoritative-sounding phrase, and I use it whenever I haven't a clue as to who *they* are) that traits skip a generation and that you tend to be more like your grandparents than your parents. I guess that's why Beau has some of George's not-so-good characteristics in him—much to some relatives' chagrin—things like flat feet and bad ankles; being bullheaded and stubborn and liking things his way; money burning a hole in his pocket and being a poor money manager in general; and accumulating too many things simply because he might need them in the future. But, he also has some of George's good, distinguishing characteristics—things like being tall and nice-looking; having long legs; having a somewhat photographic mind and being good with numbers; and always fighting for the underdog.

About the time Beau was in first grade, Sheila and Raphael decided they should let Beau make his own decisions. They got too distressed having to stand inside a store or out in public, arguing with him about everything because he was just too stubborn and bullheaded to reason with.

Beau also has a peculiar way of laughing sometimes—he raises his head, as if looking at the ceiling, and lets out this short "ha, ha"— but the majority of his laughs are rather quiet. Raphael had sat around with George, while both watched "George Carlin" specials on HBO, and had seen him laugh in exactly the same manner.

Like George, Beau is very good with numbers. He walks around with everybody's phone number in his head. He breezed through two semesters of accounting in high school and, while he was a senior, worked part-time doing accountant work for a discount store. His job was to do everyone's time sheets and payroll, but the job was so boringly easy that he requested to be transferred to a job working on the floor and restocking shelves instead.

George dressed for comfort, wearing only his underwear around the house and yard; Beau dresses for comfort too, but wearing outer clothes as well, fortunately. He often dressed ahead of fashion in San Antonio; when he was in first grade, he wore his long pants rolled up to his high-mid-calf area. Shortly after that, the fashion world came out with boys JAM's featuring pants of exactly that length. Similarly, George had been the first man in West Palm Beach to wear pink shirts and to wear Bermuda suits (suits with Bermuda shorts and knee-length stockings instead of long pants).

Like George, Beau sits in the driver's seat of a car with the seat as far back as possible with the backrest tilted back too. Of course, some of this is due to his being six feet four inches tall with long legs; his grandfather, at the same age, was six feet two inches with long legs.

Beau does not tolerate anything that is unfair or unjust and will do something about the situation. George always seemed to fight for the underdog and helped people get what was due them.

George could never stay away from thrift stores and buying bargains and would never throw anything away because he just might need it sometime. Beau rarely buys anything without shopping around for the best bargain. When he is broke, which is most of the time because he spends money on stuff just to have it, he shops in thrift stores. He has been able to buy some very nice clothes that way. He too has trouble getting rid of anything because he might need it, and he can't pass up junk he will never use either, like old store magazine racks or lighted beer signs or just anything he thinks is "cool." (My dad gave us an old-cool-looking-lighted-beer-sign to hang on the wall of our barroom.)

Sometimes the resemblance between Beau and his grandfather is subtle as when he does something a certain way. When he was still living at home, Beau would often come out of the bathroom after a bath, wearing just a towel wrapped around his waist, stop at the edge of the living room, raise his head to focus through his glasses, and then look at his parents sitting together watching TV. Raphael and

Sheila would turn to look at each other smiling because they both were thinking the same thought—*He's just like George!*

Just the other night, while we were chatting on the phone, Sheila was telling me about Beau's latest escapade, and her simple explanation turned to exclamation when it suddenly dawned on her — "Oh, my god, it's in the genes!"

SNIPPET 139 - Chairs

I never could figure out why people came to visit us when I was a youngster. After you said, "Please come in," you could never follow that with "sit down, and visit a while." You had to interject "Wait just a minute while I clear a place for you." I guess they found my family *interesting* and just ignored the clutter. I only know that we (all of us) did have visitors.

Although my mom was a good housekeeper, it didn't make any difference. My dad ruled the roost and he collected *things*, what the rest of us called *junk*. He was a child during the depression when his family had almost nothing, and that probably caused him to develop a psychological need to have a lot of *things* around him as an adult.

He couldn't resist bargains either and went searching for them. His favorite places were second-hand stores. You could really find bargains there: a necktie for five cents, a shirt for a quarter, a pair of trousers for fifty cents, a jacket (sometimes even a suit) for a dollar or two. If he needed an item of clothing, he wouldn't buy a new one; he would spend the same amount of money to buy a lot of used ones. The same was true for furniture, dishes, pots, books—just about everything, actually.

He saved everything too because you might find a need for it. Mom frequently made the mistake of throwing away something she found buried somewhere in the clutter. My dad had an uncanny sense of knowing and, often on the very next day, would ask her to fetch it for him.

He never wasted anything either. One time he bought some ivory paint on sale and painted all the walls, doors, and woodwork in our house; but there was some left over, so he painted all the wood furniture and the lamps too. Pink shirts became the rage in fashion in the early 1950's, so he bought some dye and dyed his shirts pink before anyone else started wearing pink; but there was some left over, so he dyed his socks and underwear too (paler, fortunately, than the shirts since the dye color dwindles as you use it).

Well, enough of this—you get the gist.

I decided that when I got married and lived in my own house, I would have places for visitors to sit. When you visit us, I can say,

Carole Christie Moore Adams

"Please come in (and lead you to the living room or the dining room or the kitchen). Sit down and visit a while." But, I do believe that traits are passed, from parents to children, in the genes. Therefore, when you are in our house, if the door to any other room is closed, don't bother to go in there to sit—if there is a chair in there, I've probably set something on it.

SNIPPET 140 - Timothy

I'm not sure I told him during our last, brief phone chat, but he paved the way for me to marry someone his same age. Timothy was fairly tall, enough to suit me, had dark, slightly-curly hair, medium complexion, a nice face and physique, a fun-loving, teasing manner, and a slight lisp which I thought was adorable; as a matter of fact, I thought all of him was adorable. I suspect others did too because he was voted *President* of his class and one of the *Most Popular Sophomores*. We both were in the Palm Beach High School Band; he played percussion, and I played bassoon for concerts and was a majorette when marching.

Senior girls do *not* date sophomore boys. I didn't make that rule, so I didn't follow it and, apparently, neither did Timothy. We had a great time dating; both of us liked music, dancing, swimming, beach walking, hammock swinging, and each other. And I decided immediately that younger men were a ton more fun then older men; I should know because, at the time, I was also dating, and soon stopped dating, a college freshman. For Christmas, I made Timothy a red-blue-black-tiny-bit-of-yellow plaid tie and cummerbund set for his tuxedo and he gave me my first piece, ever, of 14K gold jewelry, an anklet with "**CAROLE**" showing and "**TIMOTHY**" touching my skin when I wore it. I still wear it frequently when my ankles show and wore it constantly for many years, even after John and I married; John doesn't mind because he knows the anklet is special to me and, in a sense, to him.

After I went off to college, Timothy and I dated other people and, occasionally, each other when I was home, but we remained distant friends though out of contact. He came to our wedding to party with us and wish us well; I haven't seen him since that day. Later, I heard he had joined the Peace Corps and was working somewhere in South America, maybe Argentina; that was so like him—a hard worker, unselfish and overflowing with tenderness and kindness.

One night sometime in the mid-1980's, my dad called to tell me that Timothy's father had died and that Timothy had come back from Panama to his parents' home in Palm Beach, bringing his family with him, to attend the funeral and take care of business matters. I said to my dad, "Please give him my condolences and a hug if you happen to see him."

And he said, "He came to see your mother and me; talk to him yourself," then hollered aside, "Timothy, I have Carole on the phone."

I was flabbergasted. "Timothy, I'm so sorry about your dad," I said sadly after he said hello. Then, as I sat there holding the phone to my ear with my left hand, I suddenly remembered the anklet and, lifting my right foot into the air and pointing with my right hand to my ankle as though he could see me through the wires all the way from West Palm Beach to Hockessin, I exclaimed, "You will never believe this, but I'm wearing your anklet and I still love you!"

It didn't bother me to say that in front of John; John knows that I love him more than anyone else and that we are together partly because of Timothy.

SNIPPET 141 - Clothes

Men are funny about clothes. Well, at least my husband is—when we're alone together he prefers that I wear only wedding rings and perfume.

For me, it's practical having John choose my clothes because if he doesn't like them, I don't get to wear them. He was choosing clothes for me in autumn hues long before I found out those were my colors; he seems to have inherited some of his mother's artistic sense. We buy most of my up-scale clothes from people who show and sell out of their homes and have been buying from Valerie who is a Carlisle Consultant for "The Carlisle Collection"™ since 1985. The company is located in New York and has an Internet Web site. Even though he dislikes going to stores, John will go with me to her home and chooses everything that I buy when he is with me. Valerie and her assistants give you undivided attention and help you make selections different from, or that coordinate with, other clothes that you have bought on previous visits since they have a record of that and a picture of the garment with fabric sample for comparison, or that coordinate with a garment that you bring with you from home. It is a pleasure to shop that way. Sometimes I decide to go alone or with someone else, like Bobbie or Chris or Cathy or Diana, because John tends to buy me too much. Nevertheless, if he's not along, I buy only what I think he will like.

I used to design and make all my own clothes—the more outrageous the better! I even made clothes for others to earn extra money when I was in grad school or just for the fun of it for my mom, especially after her osteoporosis prevented her from buying clothes that fit. I enjoyed creating things to wear and it was a great hobby. Nevertheless, I just don't take the time to sew now that I can afford to buy clothes; I have other hobbies, like throwing stones or playing with our computer or planning trips and traveling, to occupy my time. Once we have spent all our money traveling though, I'll have to take up sewing again.

Whenever our friend Anne wants to buy clothes, she always asks me to go shopping with her. I like helping her find just the perfect outfit and will only let her buy what makes her look really good. She knew and liked John's mom, and when a garment is not right for her, she appreciates my telling her in Shirley's words: "I wouldn't buy that, my dear, it's not becoming to your type of beauty."

One of the most fun aspects of clothing is something I have enjoyed all my life—dressing alike with someone I love. First it was Edith because our mom made our clothes and it was easier to make two outfits from the same fabric and clothing pattern, though slightly different sizes. We two enjoyed it and thought it was fun to have people ask if we were twins even though we couldn't understand how people could think that because we were of different heights and looked nothing alike. When Sheila became a teenager, she and I sometimes dressed in the same style dresses but in different colors. In high school, if I dated one person long enough, I made us clothes to match, a shirt for him and a dress or jumper for me. Even my college roommate Marcia and I wore knit shirts and shorts alike occasionally because I had two complete outfits of the same style though different colors, and they fit us both.

John started the two of us dressing alike when he asked his mom to make us matching bermudas. For years I made John shirts or formal vests to match my dresses or evening gowns. We still have many matching sweaters, scarves, and vests that either Shirley or Edith knitted or crocheted for us. Even now, if our clothes don't match, they at least coordinate. We actually get kidded about it often.

Always on trips and frequently at home, when the occasion calls for casual wear, we wear matching fabric Hilo Hattie® shirts and dresses or we wear matching color (and frequently style), usually Lands' End® or Norm Thompson®, shirts, slacks, sweaters, and windbreakers. We have various matching "big cat" T-shirts to wear for daytime or bedtime and even matching Tilley Hats® and straw hats to protect us from the sun. We tell people that it makes it easier to find each other if we get separated; you simply look for someone dressed like yourself.

One afternoon during a cruise on the ship, *ms Amsterdam*, we were wearing matching white tiger T-shirts when an Indonesian gentleman stopped to talk to us. He showed us a photo of his daughter hugging his fabulous-looking, full-grown, white tiger. He takes the tiger to schools to teach the children about wild animals and their protection so that other generations will have them to enjoy. On

SNIPPETS (bits and pieces of love and life) by CAROLE

the *Royal Clipper*, currently the largest full-rigged sailing ship in the world, a group of "Brits," as I call the delightful people from Great Britain with whom we became friends, tried to get all the other couples to dress alike the last night out at sea as a surprise for us. Amazingly, all the couples that could did dress alike. It was a great sight at dinner! On the *American Orient Express*, a premier private touring train, if our clothes just coordinate instead of match, the crew even jokingly chastises us.

Dressing alike is not only fun but it provides us with rare opportunities to meet people that we never would have otherwise. We intend to keep doing it as long as possible.

SNIPPET 142 - Artwork

As a child, whenever I was home sick in bed, I liked to draw or just color pictures to keep occupied until I got well. My favorite picture was one I copied and enlarged from a comic book; it featured the three little pigs dancing down a street with one playing a piccolo and one playing a drum. That one I colored with crayons from my box of fifty-two colors; the more different colors to choose from, the better I liked it. Other favorites (which I still have) were colored-pencil portraits that I drew of A. Conan Doyle, Edgar Allen Poe, and Nathaniel Hawthorne that I used with book reports about their books and a colored-pencil drawing of a house sitting among evergreens for my book report on *The Secret of the Old House*.

In junior and senior high schools, I dabbled with oil painting and used the smooth side of scrap particleboard for my small paintings of garden or tree scenes. I sometimes used chalk or crayons to create pictures of multi-colored, odd shapes to fill an entire sheet of construction paper; I considered those works to be *modern* art. In college during a course in art appreciation, we had to do watercolor paintings. Since I'm not that good with original artwork—I can copy better than I can create—and I'm also lazy, I did an underwater scene with sea grasses and bubbles rising to the surface to show where a diver might have been had I bothered to paint one in; I called it *Last Breath*.

Our first summer in Wilmington, since I had no paying job, and we had little furniture and, thus, little housework to keep me occupied, John thought it would be useful to me, and decorative for the walls, if I did some artwork. We went over to Gaylord's, an inexpensive department store about a block from our apartment, and there we found two paint-by-number pictures on black velvet and two unfinished wood frames for them. John finished the frames and I spent the entire summer painting the pictures. I can't stand to have any imperfections in my work and as a child tried very hard never to color outside the lines on the pictures in my coloring books. Therefore, it took me a lot longer than it takes most people to paint pictures because I used tiny brushes with just a few bristles and even toothpick points to paint the small details in the fruit, flowers, plates and mats. The pair of paintings, at different times, have occupied spaces on almost every wall while we were in our apartment and then in our house. Currently, they are hanging on the wall opposite the closets in the short hallway within our bedroom; the colors go well with the other furnishings in there.

Those particular paintings got me looking at and collecting the artwork of others. I decided early on that I am definitely not an artist, I am a collector (remember, it's in the genes). Although I prefer to collect only the artwork of relatives or friends or at least acquaintances, I occasionally will purchase artistic items, like cups, plates, knick-knacks, and statues, from people I don't know. I buy what I like to look at and never seem to tire of any of it; it all has value to me and usually to John, but rarely to anyone else. I like that aspect because then no one else will want it enough to take it away (except for the painting I gave to Jim, but that comes later). My favorite artists are Shirley and Raphael (relatives) and Linda, Alan (Linda's husband), and Chris (friends). Each one has a totally different style that I really like, and I love each one as a person too. You just can't beat that combination! Every time I look at their artwork, all those emotions come welling up inside me. My collection is so vast now that I have given a few pieces away and have some on ninety-nine-year loan to relatives who wanted to borrow pieces to display in their homes.

Shirley was very creative; she designed and made hooked rugs, wall hangings, and quilts for our home. Our cats especially liked her rugs and the partially-hooked-wall-hanging picture of our house and, consequently, pulled out and ate pieces of them. The cats found the rugs easy to unravel, but they had to use chairs or floor-leaps, yanking the wool out mid-air, to unravel parts of the picture. I think they liked the taste of her homemade dyes that she used if the wool scraps didn't have the exact color she wanted for her creations. But then again, maybe they were adding their own artistic flair; two of them were the cats who painted our floor for us. We finally hung the rugs up on the walls out of their reach until the cats died of old age; some, but not all, of the rugs are now back down on the floor for walking on again. I used to worry about walking on her rugs and getting them dirty; Shirley insisted, however, that "dirt just makes them look mellow."

Raphael is an accomplished artist and I discovered his oil paintings when they lived with us for a while. We have been given, and I have bought, quite a few of his works. Since he doesn't sell his work—he does it for fun, not as a job—I have to buy or barter it on the sly from Sheila. When they have needed things, she has also used his artwork for bartering with other people. He also does sculptures in wood and other media and has made very appealing modern-art lamps and furniture for their home. A sculpture he made for us is reminiscent of an oil painting of his that we have in our kitchen.

Linda has traveled several times to Indonesia to study wax-resist painting with the masters and does the most fabulous paintings I have ever seen. She has branched out into other types of artwork using textured or crocheted fabrics that she uses as a bottom layer to create her paintings on. Alan works mostly in wood and metal, some plaster, doing sculptures and furniture for people all over the world. Some of his work, done in collaboration with another artist, was on display and for sale in New York City; Sylvia and I tripped up there to see it—an awesome over-sized bookcase with torch-style-lighting and stepping-rails and an huge ornate dining table. One interesting coffee table he made consists of a late 1800's ornate gate, bronzed with five different gradations of paint, that is suspended within sandblasted ash wood under thick glass. Alan and Linda are an amazing couple—so talented, loving, and marvelous to be around.

My friend Bobbie and I travel to visit Linda in her studio at home to see what new creations she is working on and then stop in to see Alan in his studio; it is absolutely fascinating to see their works in progress. On a few visits, we have eaten lunch in their home; Linda is a marvelous chef who used to have her own restaurant before she started painting full-time. On other visits, the three of us will eat in a restaurant so we can spend more time chatting philosophically together. If John, instead of Bobbie, goes with me, Alan tries to get away from his studio to join us for lunch. I truly wish they lived closer than forty miles away.

Chris has been a friend for many years too and she and Karl now live close enough to see often. My favorite works of hers are her watercolors and her beautiful pen and ink drawings of which some are black-ink drawings with painted-in watercolor and some are colored-ink, crosshatch drawings. Our friend Jim, Diana's husband, and I had

SNIPPETS (bits and pieces of love and life) by CAROLE

our eye on the same painting at one of Chris's art shows; it was solid black on white with the design of a wine carafe filled with wild flowers scratched into the black so the white background showed through as the design. I bought it immediately before he could buy it. He appeared so disappointed when I told him at the show that I had bought it, that I had second thoughts (guilty ones at that) about my purchase. "Some day, I will give the painting to you so you can enjoy it too," I promised Jim. I kept the painting for many years, but every time I looked at it, I thought of it as Jim's painting and finally gave it to him several years ago for his birthday. I often wonder if he thinks of it as being his now or mine still.

I used to design and make my own clothes with matching shirts or vests for John, but not any more, just too lazy and unmotivated. I did make one artistic tan skirt with bright red and green irises appliqued on its front left side; I copied and enlarged the irises from the bottom border of one of Chris's pen-and-ink and watercolor paintings. I still like to wear the skirt but last year had to lengthen the waistband so I could breathe in it. Instead of sewing anymore, I throw stones and pebbles and lay bricks around the yard and design things for John to build, like benches, planters, walls—anything too heavy for me to do.

John has banned me from buying any more artwork. There is no more money for it in our budget according to *him*. Mainly though, *I* think, it is because there is no place left to put more artwork inside our house; that's why some of it is on display in other homes. So, please don't give me any—unless it's for the yard—I have some artwork there, but there is plenty of space for more.

SNIPPET 143 - The Cast

Early Monday morning, July 11, 1988, after breaking a bone halfway to my little toes from my heel near the outside of my foot while chasing John through the woods at Longwood Gardens on Saturday, I sat in the waiting room to be worked into Dr. Brent's schedule. Dr. Diana had had her staff arrange for me to see that particular orthopedist because she thought he was best suited for me and for my foot. After about an hour he was able to see me and a nurse took John and me back to an exam room.

Dr. Brent appeared within a few minutes and I handed him the X-rays, of my foot, which he stuck up on the lighted viewing glass for all to see and for him to study. He showed us where the fracture was and recommended a cast for my foot.

"I'd rather not have a cast," I said, "because it's such a bother and I've done quite well using the crutches and staying off my foot all weekend."

"Well," he replied and smiled as he started bandaging my lower leg and foot, "we don't have to put a cast on it."

"Good, because I really don't want one; it will be very inconvenient taking showers and going to work and..."

He interrupted me, chuckling. "Frequently we don't put casts on little old ladies (How did he know I called myself that?) because it's too difficult for them to manage, but your foot really will heal faster and be stronger if we do, so I think you should have one."

The conversation bantered back and forth with, in essence, my saying no and his saying yes, as he kept on with the wrapping. All of us were chuckling by now.

He concluded my exam and visit with, "OK. Now, slide off the table slowly and put a little pressure on your foot. Good. Now, bend your leg forward slightly at the ankle. That's perfect! The cast will be hard in another two minutes. — See you in six weeks." He smiled and disappeared out the door.

P.S. I was terribly distressed when I read in today's newspaper that he died at age 50 in October 2002. I adored him and enjoyed being his patient for three other orthopedic problems I had. But, he will never

SNIPPETS (bits and pieces of love and life) by CAROLE

know that because I never told him, and he will never get to read the "Snippet's" he appears in; I did give a copy of his from the original manuscript to his family. I don't dare break any more bones.

SNIPPET 144 - Brace/Cast Advantages

If you have never worn a brace or a cast on some part of your body, you are probably unaware of the advantages it can provide you.

My back brace was marvelous for helping me back up off the floor if I happened to be dipped a bit too far by my partner while dancing, causing my feet to slide out from under me so that I ended up lying on my back on the dance floor. I danced a lot during coffee hours at one of the fraternity houses at Stetson University when I was a freshman. The guy, with whom I was dancing, simply grabbed and held, along with the fabric of my dress, the straps of my brace that went over my shoulders and yanked me upright again onto my feet. You're probably thinking that if I hadn't been wearing a brace, I probably wouldn't have landed on the floor due to the rigidity of my body anyway. Well, I have ended up on the floor a few times since, when I wasn't wearing a brace, as a matter of fact, not too long ago.

Having a cast on your foot gives you privileges too. At your job, you get to park in the handicapped parking spaces or, at least, one close by your workplace and get to ride the elevator instead of taking the stairs to the second floor. You also have an excuse to wear slacks and prop your plastered-foot-with-ice-bag-on-it on the conference table during meetings and not get reprimanded or disapprovingly looked down upon for being unladylike. The crutches are handy too; people will open and close doors for you, even if they think women should do it themselves, and will carry things for you. When others are not available for portage, you can carry things in bags fastened to and dangling off the crossbars of the crutches.

If you have your hand or wrist in a cast, you can threaten to whack children with it if they disobey; you get immediate good behavior from them without doing a thing on your part. If you are right-handed and your right hand is in a cast, you can pretend not to be able to cope left-handed (this also works for the reverse case) and proceed to eat with your fingers or not bother to answer the phone. You can get your husband to help bathe and dress you. John was very creative with plastic bags so I could get in the shower and not get my cast wet or get water down inside it whether it was on my hand and arm or on my foot.

SNIPPETS (bits and pieces of love and life) by CAROLE

If I were not so darned independent, I probably could have thought of a lot more advantages; at least, I thought of a few. You're on your own to think of others.

SNIPPET 145 - Broken Bones

When I was eighteen, I broke the first bone (a vertebra between my shoulder blades shattered) and then didn't break any more bones until, when I was almost forty-six, I cracked the lower two right ribs doing a dip while dancing. I had managed to get by for twenty-eight years without breaking anything. Things went downhill from there; I guess when you're on a roll, you're on a roll. Next came a broken bone in my left foot while I was chasing my husband through the woods. You'd have thought I would have learned my lesson when I fell under my bike chasing after my boyfriend in the fifth grade—but *nooo*. Then I decided to go for the *big one* and crushed two vertebrae in my lower back, maybe broke a bone in my left elbow, and got a concussion on the back left side of my head. No sooner had I recovered from that fall, then I fell again, breaking my right wrist in two places.

The good thing is that I now have broken enough bones to draw some conclusions:

- When a bone breaks, you hear the crack in your head because the sound travels through your bone structure. Others around you don't usually hear it; it's just you and you alone. If they do hear the cracking sound, you're in real trouble. Get help immediately.
- The break site hurts unbearably for three weeks while the bone is knitting and then the pain stops as quickly as it began.
- It then takes three more weeks, sometimes a bit longer, for the newly formed bone to solidify.
- Sometimes you need therapy, like rock therapy, to stress the break site to force it to get strong again.
- Total recuperation time depends on how much longer you insist on drinking to kill the pain. (Or it might depend on how much longer your spouse puts up with being your servant.)

SNIPPET 146 - *Her Girls*

I knew she was dying as soon as I glanced at her holding John around the neck as he carried her frail little body up the walkway and into the house. My dad backed through the doorway behind them, yanking her red wheelchair up the sandstone threshold and into the front hallway. He looked at me pathetically with that for-God's-sake-save-her-desperation in his eyes. It was near Thanksgiving 1988.

"She *had* to come," he declared, "I wanted her to stay home and rest because I thought she was too weak to travel, but she insisted. So I figured maybe Diana would know what to do; none of the doctors at home seem to be helping her at all."

"I made an appointment for her to see Dr. Diana tomorrow morning; maybe she can help her get well again," I calmly said, knowing full well that it was much too late. I had just been reading about AIDS patients and how, once intense itching of the skin begins, it's a sign that the all the organs are failing, and death usually occurs within six weeks. She didn't have that disorder, but she had so many others that I assumed that the same symptoms, showing up in her, meant she had about six weeks too. But I didn't want to face losing my precious mother, so I plunged, like everyone else, into denial.

When Mema and I saw Diana, she referred us to the oncologist who had treated my mom before when she was here visiting us, and to a dermatologist to treat her scratched-raw skin. The oncologist said her polycythemia had depleted her ability to create red blood cells and that she should start getting blood transfusions on a regular basis; she refused as she didn't think it fair to others who needed it more. The dermatologist prescribed a soothing skin cream and oral medication to make the constant, intense itching more bearable.

Late one night the first week in December, we received a phone call from Edith; she had just returned from the hospital emergency room in Carlisle for the remainder of her night's stay at a motel.

"Can you come get me? I fell and hurt myself pretty badly when Janet and I dashed across the highway from the motel to the restaurant. We were on our way over there to eat dinner. I won't be able to drive for about a week. She's going to drive her car on up to Cape Cod so someone will be there to meet the moving van. Maybe

John can keep the cat with him in my truck and drive it back to your house, and I can ride with you so we can chat during the trip. Staying with you will also give me some time to visit Mema while I recuperate. Will that be OK?"

"Of course," I replied. "We'll aim to be there around ten in the morning."

She and her housemate were moving, and Edith had not planned to stop by on the way; she needed to get there quickly to start a new job. Guess Mom's prayer to see her was answered unexpectedly in a way she least hoped for. She had been afraid that she wouldn't get to see Edith; she couldn't figure out the travel logistics because her next scheduled stop was to visit Sheila, Raphael, and Beau in San Antonio on December 27.

We had a wonderful visit together, and Mema was thrilled. Since Daddy had gone home for a few days to check their mail and John and I had to work during the day, Edith had all day to spend alone with our mom. Mema was an excellent player in the card games of Rummy, Canasta, and Bridge and Edith in Rummy and Canasta. The two of them would hobble (Edith with her injuries and Mema with her artificial leg or Edith pushing mom in her wheelchair) into the kitchen and sit at the table playing Rummy until they got tired. Mema always won, and it wasn't because Edith let her; they both were fiercely competitive when it came to playing any card game. At bedtime, and even for naps, after they had retired to the guest bedroom, they would talk until one of them fell asleep.

My parents stayed with us until Edith left, but then, upon invitation, moved over to Patty's house (fifteen miles away) so they could spend all day there instead of just travelling back and forth with us to share meals together. Patty was delighted to have the alone-time to spend with our mom, and Mema was delighted too because she could visit longer with her young grandsons Brandon and Barret, as well as with Patty and Ralph.

I got very distressed with my dad; he simply ignored, and refused to do anything to help, my mom. He just sat in Patty's kitchen, staring at the TV on the table by the front window, and complained if he didn't get waited on as much as he wanted to be by his daughters. One evening, I even screamed at him, "Do something! She's your wife; you could at least help us take care of her!" Maybe it was his way of coping, but it just made me angrier and gladder than ever that he had disowned me. I really wanted nothing to do with him and treated him with civility only because he was Mema's husband.

I felt so sorry for her; all the medications were beginning to make Mema so drowsy that she could hardly stay awake, sitting upright in her wheelchair, to chat with any of us; but she gazed at us with loving intensity whenever her eyes were open.

John and I stopped by briefly on December 26 to visit with everyone before we headed out to dine alone to celebrate our twenty-eighth wedding anniversary.

As I was saying good-bye, Mema squeezed my hand as tightly as she could with her frail hand and began to cry softly. "I may never see you again."

"Of course you will," I asserted, "I'll be here in the morning to ride to the airport with you, and I'll stay with you until your plane leaves." I didn't want to leave, but John wanted to celebrate alone—"Just you and me," he had said. Her words came back to haunt me again: *He comes first.* We left.

The next morning at the airport, she and I said almost nothing; we didn't need to. We just held each other's hand tightly until the last hug before they rolled her wheelchair away to take her and my dad to board the plane.

The morning of December 30, Sheila phoned us. Our mom had almost died several times during the flight from Philadelphia to San Antonio, but she tenaciously made it to there. She had enjoyed a short visit before Sheila asked her if she should take her to the hospital and she had replied, "Please." She had died a few hours later while Sheila slipped away from her bedside to use the restroom. Sheila too is a nurse, and she knew, if Mema was going to die, it would happen when she left her alone.

"Mom was so worried about you, Carole. Will you be OK?"

Yes, I'm OK, but I still get weepy whenever I try to talk about her; she wasn't just my mother, she was a great friend and an idolized love in my life.

Mema had *had* to come, but not to be saved; she had to see all "her girls," as she referred to us, and to make sure we were all right, just one more time, before she felt free to leave us forever.

SNIPPET 147 - *Projects*

John and I have always had projects underway; some get finished fairly soon, some never, staying in suspended animation for eternity, but they all get thought about and usually started. Together we probably have more in progress than all our friends and relatives combined could think of. Mine are usually of the sewing or stone, pebble, and brick type and John's are of the woodworking, concrete-working, tool and "toy" tinkering, and "honey-please-do…" type.

The very first items John made for us were two four-sided end tables and a magazine holder that I designed for the living room in our first apartment in Wilmington. The tables are made of nova-ply (we call it glue-board) and concrete. The only tools he had to work with were a coping saw and a screwdriver that we owned. For each table side, it took John one whole day to cut the design out of the middle so as to leave in tact about five inches at the top edge and three to five inches at the side edges; each side edge formed one half of a table leg. My design looks like the top two-thirds of a fleur-de-lis spread into the shape of a hairpin; that's why it took eight days just to do the sawing. Two of those cutout pieces became the ends for the magazine holder. Hand sanding all the edges was quite a chore too. The tabletops are made of concrete poured, atop the board joining the four sides near the top edges, from a carbon-blackened cement mixture and then shoe-polished to look like rough slate. He painted the tables and magazine holder with a flat black paint and I gilded the edges with gold-paste-wax, shoe polish. We still use the three pieces in our living room today although the tables sit alongside instead of in front of the couch.

The next items were a pair of three-by-five-foot desks with four drawers each for file folders. We don't have them now; our nephew Brandon has them. To replace them, John made us computer desk tops with filing cabinets underneath for our office/library room called "the computer room" or "the junk room" depending on how neat it looks at the time.

Our house had an unfinished basement under a portion of it (the rest is on a concrete slab). Part of that area we decided to make into a barroom for entertaining during the hot summer months because the basement stayed about ten degrees cooler than the rest of the house as none of it was air-conditioned for the first few years after we moved in. That part also contained an unfinished fireplace that we decided would look nice with plaster center and stone facing. John spent the evenings and weekends of one whole summer, stoning the wall at the foot of the stairs and the sides of the fireplace, carrying about two thousand large stones to and from the basement, spreading them on the floor, then choosing just the right ones from the bunch. I really like the rough texture and randomness of the stones; no stone had to be cut to fit because each one was chosen because it already fit into its space.

Next came the bar that is twelve feet long and has lighted shelves for storing bottles, utensils, paper products, and other essentials. It is made of nova-ply with the sides and shelves covered with wood-grain-finished and the top covered with slate-finished Formica®. So that people can lean on the cantilevered edge and not tip the bar over, John poured a thousand pounds of stone ballast into the bottom; you couldn't budge it if you had to. He finished the top half of the walls with cement plaster and vertical wood beams and the bottom half with nova-ply with a ledge top covered in the same fashion as the bar. He added same style low shelves for glassware storage along the wall behind the bar. For places to set drinks and food, he made small tables out of four-inch-square, wooden posts with circular pieces of nova-ply on each end with the top ones covered with slate-finished Formica®. Mediterranean-style tile floor, bar stools, and flicker-lighted lamps, along with black captain chairs, with covers of different colors, completed the room. Over the firewood storage area John built a shelf with four-inch, clay pipes stacked on it to serve as a racked storage area for bottles of wine or non-alcoholic beverages; the clay pipes keep the bottles at an even temperature. It continues to be a great place to entertain and dance to music piped in from the living room sound system just above it.

John started a headboard for the guest/sewing room that was to have matching hanging lamps. The headboard is there, although incomplete for these past thirty years; you wouldn't know it was incomplete if you saw it, but it doesn't have the gold grillwork yet which matches the gold grillwork in the furniture and eventually in the lamps, if they ever get made.

We decided not to wait for the table and end benches to be built and placed at the house entrance because we found exactly what we wanted, already made, in a store about five years ago. We're not sure yet what we will do with the materials we bought to make those furnishings with.

After we adopted cats, John made us a couch for the living room. Since cats like to scratch and shred couches, he made us one that was cat-proof; he completely covered it with carpeting except for the ends which he made to match the black tables and magazine rack. It was very comfortable for people to sit on for reading or watching TV, and the cats liked it too because they could sit on it or sleep on it or scratch their claws on it; it was perfect for everyone. That was also the couch I spent several weeks on when I broke my back and got a concussion. It now has retired to the basement of the house where the desks are and sits facing our pool table that we moved over there since we figured that our three nephews could use it more than we did.

I doubt that we will ever finish our projects; but if we do, you'll know it—the celebration noise and commotion will be deafening!

SNIPPET 148 - Retired Too Soon

At DuPont Company where we both worked, we told our managers and coworkers about John's having Parkinson's Disease. As he said in his letter explaining his newly acquired diagnosis to his management, "Who dealt these cards anyway?" Who knows?

Fortunately, my department was downsizing and offering early retirement packages. Employees had to sign up for the package, and a predetermined number of them would be selected, in the order of high to low years of service, to receive it. I really liked my job and didn't want to leave, but one manager heartily encouraged me to retire because, he advised, "You have much more important things to do at home." I very reluctantly took his advice, but I am very glad I did, now.

Many of my coworkers knew how ambivalent I was about retiring, but they also knew my husband personally. Bryce, in particular, encouraged me to retire. I really liked him; he was one of my favorite coworkers and had been one of my trainees when I headed the Training Institute in 1967-1968. Bryce was somewhat of a maverick too, but a bit more so than I. He dressed for only himself and comfortably in short-sleeved shirts and slacks. He never wore a jacket or suit to work and never wore a coat in the winter, no matter how cold it got. He came in late and worked late because those hours suited him. He worked diligently and was always helpful to others. He acted tough and sounded rather crude but had a big heart that he tried to keep people from discovering. His niche was envisioning and programming large systems to handle the huge overnight production workload on our multiple large mainframe computers. He was a joy to work with and made a tremendous contribution to the success of a large project that I headed. I wrote a meritorious letter to our management about Bryce and his work. He got distressed with me because I had "ruined his image"; he didn't want people to know he was that good or that nice. But I knew, and so did a lot of others, but no one had dared to let him know that we knew.

During the last hour of the sign-up period though, I was having second thoughts about retiring and was getting out of my chair to go withdraw my name when Bryce dashed into my office. He locked the door and sat down in a chair opposite my desk.

"I'm not letting you out of here to withdraw, and you're not letting me out of here to sign-up," Bryce stated matter-of-factly. "John needs you to retire, but I can't afford to retire because Joanne and I need the money. If you remove your name from the list, there will be an open slot for me, and I don't dare take it." (Our years of service were almost identical.)

We sat there, staring at each other until the 3:30 P.M. deadline passed. It was then too late for action, and we both knew the right declarations had been made. What a friend!

I retired August 31, 1992. It may have been the right decision; nevertheless, I still spent the next several months crying and staying in bed most of the day; I missed my coworkers and my job.

Later that year, John's department made a similar offer for a few employees. As a surprise tribute to him, according to what one of his coworkers told me at his retirement party, his coworkers got together and convinced everyone else in the building not to sign up so John would be chosen to retire. What a gift! Instead of struggling to keep up full-time, he could, perhaps, still work part-time somewhere, doing the chemistry he loves.

John retired from DuPont Company December 31, 1992.

SNIPPET 149 - Adams Research

John had received a chemistry set as a gift in 1947 and quickly became fascinated by all the things the set allowed him to do. He liked doing experiments and wanted to be able to do bigger and more complicated ones, but that required chemicals that children couldn't buy. In 1949, to overcome that obstacle, after consulting with his uncle who is a lawyer, he founded **Adams Research**, complete with printed letterheads and envelopes. With letters that he typed using his mom's typewriter, he bought, or obtained free samples of, whatever supplies he needed via the US Mail and Postal Service. He also obtained an AEC (Atomic Energy Commission) license via mail for purchasing radioactive source materials such as uranium and thorium compounds.

John Daddy's friend, who worked in a chemical business in Savannah, knew of John's hobby and supplied him with out-dated equipment that was of no use to the company but of great use to a budding chemist. He accumulated so much equipment and chemicals that his dad built him a chemistry lab on the side of their garage out back of the house. John was in business—even if it was just for fun!

He liked trains a lot too and built a village for his Lionel® O-gauge train to run around in, and he also liked to collect pennies, a hobby he could have for a lifetime. Would he eventually stay with trains or with chemistry as an adult? It was a tough decision. He decided he could make a living as a chemist, but probably not as a model railroad engineer. Chemistry won and he eventually sold his train set and penny collection to be able to buy additional chemicals for his lab.

After he retired, John decided to work as a consulting chemist for **Adams Research**, the company he founded when he was ten. He had new letterheads, envelopes, and business cards printed with his newly created logo, red on a white background, consisting of "A_R" with the remainder of an oval stretching from the bottom left of the "A," extending over the top, and ending at the bottom right of the "R." He made his first dollar for the business, working for some friends who owned a chemical company. To celebrate his success, I framed together a brand-new, dollar bill with his old and new letterheads and envelopes and his new business card. Today, September 6, 2002, he is *sixty-three* and his company is *fifty-three* years old. — Amazing!

SNIPPET 150 - Doesn't Everyone?

The spring of 1992, I received a phone call from Beverly who, at that time, was president of the Delaware Symphony Association (DSA). She said that Sandra, who was on the Board of Directors and a great music benefactor, had recommended that she call me. "Can you meet me for lunch?"

"Sure, I'd like to. Thanks. How kind of you to ask," I replied quite curious as to what this was all about. We arranged a time and place that was convenient for both of us to meet since I was still working at the time and she was quite busy, as well, with her volunteer work.

During lunch she said that Sandra had recommended me as a candidate to become a member of the DSA Board of Directors (BOD).

"Oh, I remember Sandra's talking to John about doing something with the symphony while I was chatting with Lenard (Sandra's husband) at your home (during the Symphony Celebrations benefit party, "A Little Night Music" by the concertmaster and his pianist). Sandra sat directly to John's left during the concert and while we were waiting for the violinist to begin playing, she asked John for his business card. Because he didn't have a card with him at the time, he surprised her by writing his name and phone number on a small Post-It® and sticking it to the back of her right hand when she wasn't looking. After the concert, John told me about her request. I walked over to where she was and told her that I wouldn't allow John to do any volunteer work because the stress would be too much for him since he has Parkinson's Disease. Perhaps she figured I could do some work instead. I do plan on doing some volunteer work after I retire, but that won't happen until the end of August, so I probably won't start volunteering before September."

"Well, you'll just have to start early," she said in a matter-of-fact way with a smile.

I started in May and was a BOD member for three years until it became just too much for me to keep up with after I started working again part-time in February 1995. I'm especially glad I became a member of the Board because it gave me the opportunity to get to know and to work with Beverly and with the other dedicated members as well.

One thing that did surprise me came out in another part of our conversation during my luncheon with Beverly.

"Why in the world would anyone consider John or me for membership on the board?" I wondered and asked.

"Out of all the subscribers, you two are the only people who subscribe to every series that the symphony offers," Beverly replied.

I responded, in my naive and sincere disbelief, "Really? — Doesn't everyone?"

SNIPPET 151 - Volunteer Extraordinaire

I met Beverly when she interviewed me to serve on the Board of Directors for the Delaware Symphony Association. She was a fascinating and extraordinary person and a joy to be around and work with. She did everything with an enthusiasm that was catching and you found yourself doing things you would never have done on your own. She was president or past president of several boards, having held other offices as well, a mother of two talented daughters, the wife of a surgeon and chief administrator, and a mentor to many.

Since I had never seen an opera, she insisted that I go to see *The Merry Widow* that was being performed by our local opera company, OperaDelaware. I enjoyed it so much that I have been a subscriber for the past ten years and attend now with my friend Sylvia.

One afternoon, I was at Beverly's home helping her fabricate baked and shellacked baskets for holding bread, rolls, or anything else you wish. I thought I was doing a lot just rolling out the special-recipe dough, cutting the strips, weaving the strips into baskets over the bottom and sides of baking tins, and then baking them. All the while, she was on the phone confirming arrangements for the benefit luncheon that we were making the baskets for, baking a cake from scratch, fabricating baskets, planning another event, and chatting intermittently with me. I have never seen anyone who could multi-task as well as she. No wonder she is elected to head so many organizations.

She and her husband moved away several years ago. We keep in contact via e-mail and sometimes get to visit. But I miss my friend and volunteer extraordinaire.

SNIPPET 152 - Balloons

One Sunday, we decided to sit on one of the benches John had recently made for the courtyard, so we could enjoy the bright, clear, just-after-sunrise morning while drinking our coffee. As we sat listening to the birds chirping, we became aware of people talking nearby. We looked around, through the huge double wrought-iron gates at the end of the walkway leading up to the front door on our left and through the two slits in the wall by the gate, but saw no one. Then we heard a swooshing noise overhead and looked up. Just above us were two people standing in the basket of a gloriously colored, intricately patterned, giant balloon, chatting together as the balloon began to rise with the air currents. The swooshing noise was the burner that heated the air in the balloon to keep it inflated and sailing through the air. We waved and wished them a safe trip and they waved back as they drifted up and away from our house. That was the first of many balloons that sailed low over our house on weekends when the weather was perfect for flights.

There is a middle school (or junior high school, depending on what part of the country you live in) that is located directly southwest from our house about a half-mile as the crow flies. The field surrounding the school is a convenient place, with no trees, for balloonists to fill and launch their balloons, especially if they want to fly into Pennsylvania. That area, just north of us, is quite beautiful with rolling hills covered with pastureland, trees, and huge, marvelously kept estates. There are many small country roads for their teams to follow and retrieve them after they land again in another field.

We remain fascinated by the array of different shapes and colors of the balloons we see and like to watch them, but have never desired to go up in one; neither of us really likes to fly. TV Channel Six in Philadelphia sponsors a tethered balloon that takes fifteen-minute flights above the Philadelphia Zoo. Perhaps some day, we will go up in that one; we've seen the view from it on TV and it is thrilling. It even accommodates wheelchairs and has room for about twenty to thirty people at a time.

SNIPPETS (bits and pieces of love and life) by CAROLE

We both like ordinary balloons and enjoy having them around for special occasions. One year for John's birthday I gave him only a hatpin stuck through his card. Since he will *never* allow me to discuss our intimate life, you'll just have to figure out for yourself how I wore only the multi-colored balloons that I had blown up, and why John was so thrilled with his gift.

We have also been surrounded by helium-filled balloons and when one of those bursts against your bare skin, you get a sudden, tiny shock of cold air stinging you, making you giggle.

SNIPPET 153 - Pathetic but Laughing

On January 7, 1994, while leaving home in the rain for a luncheon date with my friend Bobbie, I slipped suddenly and without warning, my feet sliding straight out front from under me, and fell on the icy walkway at the garage corner of our house, landing flat on my back, face-up, eyes staring at the sky. I lacerated, bruised, and possibly fractured my left elbow sliding down the wall, hit the left side of my head on a large rock on the pebbles next to the garage causing a concussion, and crushed the T12 (twelfth thoracic) and L1 (first lumbar) vertebrae (in my lower back). Since no one else was around, and my nearest neighbor too far away to hear any calls for help, I forced myself to get up and into the house. I quickly undressed, scared myself half to death by looking at my pasty-white face in the mirror, and collapsed into our waterbed.

From there, using the phone on the nightstand by my side of the bed, I phoned Bobbie and then the Delaware Symphony Association office staff to tell them I would not be going anywhere for a while. Next, I called my doctor to see what I should do for my back. Afterwards, I suddenly realized that I needed to use the bathroom and phoned John at his part-time job.

"I'm sorry that I have to ask you to, but please come home from work. I fell and I need to use the bathroom and simply can not get out of our bed," I apologized, then waited for him to come home.

John arrived home to help me. The pain, from trying to move my traumatized body, was so tremendous that we decided it best for me to stay on the living room couch until I could get in and out of the waterbed by myself. He couldn't take me to get X-rays because I couldn't walk, and he couldn't carry me, that far to the car; besides, it was still too icy outside. However, I did get X-rays of my back about six weeks later, which is how I know what broke there. Since I forgot to tell the technician about my elbow, I never got X-rays of that.

Since I don't tolerate and, therefore, can't take pain medications, I drank a lot of booze instead. I don't think I could ever become an alcoholic because after a couple of days, we had to disguise the whiskey with juices so I could get it down. It was only after I had

SNIPPETS (bits and pieces of love and life) by CAROLE

fully recovered that I learned that you should *never* drink alcoholic beverages if you have a concussion.

Several days after my fall and for the umpteenth time that day, I grasped the handle of the round, ornate-brass bell, that Becky had given us for summoning the other when you don't know if he/she is out of normal hearing range, and rang for John to come to help me maneuver to the closer bathroom, about thirty feet from the couch.

Very bad timing! John was extremely "Parky," his term for being bradykinetic (a k a stiff-as-a-board), and I was becoming quite drunk because I had just downed a four-ounce glass of whiskey that I needed to stop the back spasms long enough to be able to get up and move around. He tried to help me anyway. He couldn't move and neither could I because my legs still wouldn't work properly due to my spinal injury, but he held me, in a sort of dancing-style/dragging-style, and we shuffled together along the hallway across the front of the house. The trip usually had been taking about five minutes, but this time we were moving about one to two feet per minute. About a third of the way to the bathroom, we started talking about how pathetically silly we looked and what people would think if they could see us; we both laughed so hard we almost fell down.

Needless to say, with all of our laughing, the trip took almost a half-hour, but with all of that hugging as well, we both felt much, much better than we had in days.

SNIPPET 154 - Lawn Mowing

Earning money baby-sitting didn't suit my schedule when I was a teenager; I needed my evenings for studying; instead, I did laundry, ironing, housework, and lawn mowing for neighbors and friends of my parents who lived nearby or out in the country. If I mowed several acres, I could earn five dollars or earn thirty-five to fifty cents an hour for the other work. I preferred lawn mowing and did that whenever I could even though it was hard work out in the heat of the day.

After all us girls grew up and left home, our mom did the mowing with an electric mower that you walked behind. She had a lot of problems with the mower dying on her in the middle of the yard because she would forget where the cord was and run over it, mowing it in two.

A few years ago, while John was suffering from two herniated discs in his lower back, I mowed our lawn with our riding mower. You can cut about 30,000 square feet of lawn (or grass mixed with short weeds in our yard) in about an hour with our mower and it's not very hard work, but somehow it just isn't as much fun as I remember mowing to be. I was never asked, moreover, even allowed to do it again though, because John got distressed about my scraping the side of the mower on the mowing strip when I drove into a hole beside it at the front of our yard near the street. Keep that in mind if you need to get out of having to do that job. Or you can do what our nephew Brandon did and back the mower into something, smashing the rear. (I'm not going to say what he hit, but I got a clue from a conversation I overheard at his house that it was Ralph's mower that Brandon's friend was driving while helping him mow our yard while we were away on vacation.) Either accident will get you banned from mowing—at least for a while—but be prepared for your spouse to be just a wee bit upset about having to get the mower repaired.

SNIPPET 155 - Chaperones

We know Karl and Chris quite well and have spent some vacations, varying between two and seven days in length, together. We have gone during the winter twice to Washington near the Blue Ridge Mountains and once to Lower Waterford to stay at inns where we could romp and play in the snow. We like to do other things together and do puzzles, read books, play cards, drive and/or walk around the town, sled if there is enough snow, eat gourmet food, and drink champagne and wine. In fact, Karl and John like to kid Chris and me that we two like to w(h)ine a lot.

We've been twice to Ocracoke. The first time, John and I stayed in our travel trailer at the national park campground and they in their favorite rented beach house farther down the island, and we got together either at our place or theirs. Early mornings, they would come to visit us and then, together, we would walk down to the beach to watch the sun rise over the Atlantic Ocean, sometimes sipping Mimosas, sometimes not, but always enthralled by the beauty and by the birds racing along the water's edge. In the afternoons and evenings we would visit them. The second time, we stayed together in the house; the last of our cats had died and we didn't need to vacation in the trailer any more in order to take them with us. That trip was planned during the spring of 1997 to be taken for the entire second week of September.

Some weeks before we were to leave on vacation, Karl and Chris decided to get married on September 6, John's birthday, instead of waiting until the next spring. We said we wouldn't mind staying home because we didn't want to detract from their honeymoon; but they insisted that we come along as planned.

On the wedding day, Chris and I were both nervous. I ruined the nail polish on two fingernails of my right hand trying to pin the colorful flowers in my hair above my left ear; the colors contrasted beautifully with my pale-olive-and-ivory, stripe-and-flower, bottom-of-calf-length dress. During my own wedding, I wasn't nervous, just excited, as the bride; but during this one, I was very nervous and shook slightly and my smile quivered as I walked into the church as the Matron of Honor; I didn't want anything to spoil their day.

Chris was elegantly dressed in a simple floor-length ivory gown with back-bow train, had colorful flowers pinned in her hair like mine, and carried a basket overflowing with glorious wild flowers of all kinds and colors. I don't think the guys were nervous; they didn't look it, and I was too pre-occupied to even think about asking them.

The wedding ceremony was heart-touchingly beautiful, and during it, John sat on the sidelines with the others in church. His part in the wedding was chauffeuring the four of us to and from the church in our ivory-colored Lincoln® Town Car™.

Afterwards, we went to their new-to-them home, that backs up to and overlooks a stream and the side of a steep hill, for the reception that they held for their close friends and relatives, some of whom traveled quite a distance to join in the festivities. A friend had been hired to cater the luncheon with such an enormous quantity and array of delicious food, that afterwards, the four of us had to eat our meals together for the next two days to finish it all. Karl's mom made the superbly-decorated-and-fabulous-tasting, wedding cake, plus a small birthday cake for John, for all to share. At the honored couple's request, the guests sang "Happy Birthday" to John. We will definitely remember what day their anniversary is; Karl and Chris said they specifically chose September 6 so that we would never forget it.

We were all partying and chatting together, but as the rumor got around that John and I were going to Ocracoke with the pair on their honeymoon, everyone in the group started kidding us about the trip and chiding us for not staying home. Karl and Chris, however, assured each in turn that they definitely wanted us to go because the trip was already planned and the matter settled.

The next week we traveled to the island together but in separate cars because, with so much luggage and stuff, we couldn't fit all of it and us into one vehicle. The newlyweds got the large master bedroom with adjoining master bath, and will get it next time too, since Karl is much taller than the other three of us and needs the extra space at the foot of the bed so his feet can hang over the end. We got the smaller bedroom with the household bath that could be closed off for use only from our room whenever we chose. We all shared the rest of the house and porch and the attention from Razzle-Dazzle, the stray cat that visited every day to comfort us so we wouldn't be so lonesome without the cats back home. John and I, just the two of us,

SNIPPETS (bits and pieces of love and life) by CAROLE

took a walk down the dirt roads each day, and even packed up and left for home a couple of days early, so the honeymooners could spend some time alone.

In the 1960's, we had been chaperones for students at high school dances while I was teaching in Durham County and for our church-sponsored boys-baseball-team while we lived in Wilmington. But the most fun we ever had as chaperones was when we chaperoned the newlyweds—on their honeymoon!

SNIPPET 156 - Then, There's Bob

Like the name "Judy" is for girls, "Bob" is for boys, and we know even more than three of them. Bob and his wife, Mary Anne, are our travel agents; both are fun to chat with, and it's easy to stop in to see them since their agency, Hockessin Travel Service, is located on the road that leads to our bank which is also less than two miles from our house. Another Bob, whom everyone calls "Bob" but I call "Robert" because that's what he called himself the first time I talked to him on the phone, is a personal trainer, and he was mine, and our friends Jeff and Lucinda's too, until too many injuries, done elsewhere, caused me to quit going to the gym. There's Bob who was one of my supervisors, Bob who was a coworker, and Bob who was one of John's supervisors at work. There were students named "Bob" who were our friends in school and one Bob I dated off and on during the year and a half I waited for John to get around to kissing me good night. Another Bob and his wife, Suzanne, are longtime friends who built and moved into a house nearby. There are a lot of people named "Bob" who were, or are now, a part of our lives.

And then, there's Bob who is the interior designer that Cathy introduced us to. He is really different and my kind of maverick person. He has a heart of gold, loves to talk you to death, is extremely opinionated, "calls it like he sees it," and does wonders for your spirits as well as for your home or workplace.

We needed a new dishwasher, ours died, and I had phoned to ask Cathy what brand she might recommend, and she said, "You should talk to Bob."

"Give me his phone number and I'll call him," I said thinking maybe I would or maybe I wouldn't since I didn't know him and wasn't sure that I could afford to talk to an interior designer.

"Talk to him now; he's standing here beside me in the kitchen discussing some changes we want done."

I guess she handed him the phone because the conversation continued with a masculine voice instead of hers. Next thing I knew, Bob had an appointment to come look at our dead dishwasher the next afternoon. That's when I discovered that the voice went with a nice-looking man, about five feet ten inches tall, brown hair with grayish side burns, and physically-fit, muscular physique.

Before he came, John and I talked over maybe making some other changes since we had to replace the dishwasher; we might as well ask Bob what he thought and, if we liked his recommendations, go ahead and do them now. He charges by the hour for his advice and, although the expense concerned us, we soon discovered that the money is definitely well spent. Bob works miracles within those hours; he not only changed our house, he made it much more enjoyable to live in, partly with some new things, partly by having us paint the walls with color, and partly by simply rearranging almost everything.

We had always wanted tile flooring in our kitchen and in our dining room, but couldn't afford it when we built our house, and he turned out to be the perfect one to coordinate all that. He knows the best-young-Italian, tile setters who do it the "old" way, with incredible teamwork and with precision and perfection. We watched in awe the four days of the transformation. Bob designed the dining room floor to appear as though it had a bordered carpet in the center under the dining room table and chairs. He had the setters tile the area, setting the tile throughout the two rooms as though the floor was contained in a single room, but having the floor still look great for each individual room if the door between was closed.

After the flooring was finished, he rearranged all the furniture in the dining room so it was more useable and placed the table so that each person sitting there had a view out either the windows or the sliding-glass doors. Then he noticed the window and door treatments and waving his hands demanded, "Well, what do you intend to do with this?"

"I don't intend to do anything with that," I brusquely answered. "John made those wood window treatments for me using my design, and there's some exactly like it in the living room!"

"Oooh," he stammered. He dashed to look at the living room and returned while I just stood there, slightly dumbfounded. "We'll deal with them after you paint the walls. This *white* just won't do. You need *color* to bring out the beauty of the floor and furniture and soften the lighting in here. On the window walls, we can use the same color of deep terra cotta that we will use in the kitchen and that will incorporate the rust and deep brown stain of the window treatments and then use some other color on the other two walls. We'll do the same in the living room."

Oops. — I forgot to tell you about the "rolling snowball." Fortunately, Bob also knows a good carpenter team that does renovations, so we had hired them. The new colors that we chose for the floor (in the kitchen: terra cotta; in the dining room: terra cotta for center of the tile-carpet, terra cotta and ivory for the three-inch-terra-cotta-with-ivory-diamond-shapes-marble-carpet border, and gray-with-a-hint-of-brown for the between-carpet-and-wall border), meant that we had to replace the olive-green Formica® back-splash and counter tops in the kitchen to coordinate.

As long as we had to replace the dishwasher, we figured we might as well replace the other twenty-five-year-old kitchen appliances. But that meant, since they were in the kitchen along the wall toward the backdoor, the clothes washer and drier had to be replaced and coordinated. And as long as we had to do that, we decided to get under-the-counter models and extend the countertop, that was around the laundry sink beside them, over the appliances to the wall, in order to have more work space. Bob told us what brands to buy that were the best at the time and where the best store was to purchase them.

The refrigerator we had was a large one, and the only one we could buy to fit the space between the cabinets was taller, so that required removing the cabinets over that area.

A new microwave with exhaust fan replaced the one on the countertop and also the old range hood. When the new one was installed over the gas range, the old range hood and cabinet over it had to be removed and replaced with a short knickknack shelf. Since the carpenters had to build that, we figured that they might as well also build a small bookcase to house my cookbooks ousted from the cabinet that was removed. The bookcase now stands next to the tall cabinet by the kitchen/hallway door, hidden by the door in its usual position, standing opened into the kitchen.

Bob had suggested that we simply replace all the cabinets with some more modern ones or update the existing ones with new hardware, but I had said "No, because I like my cabinets, and besides, I designed my kitchen, and we chose these particular dark oak ones with ornate handles because they fit our idea of the Spanish-style of our house." After inspecting the cabinets, Bob said that we should keep them, because they were of such good quality that it would be a shame to replace them, and suggested that we simply stain all the new wood to match. Now, no one can even tell that the wooden pieces weren't all put together originally.

I think I now have you back up-to-date. We had to repaint the kitchen and dining room, of course, since the walls now looked shabby and also the kitchen ceiling because we installed new lighting so we could see better and to show off our new floor and countertops, etc. But then that made the rest of the walls and ceilings in the house look shabby. We couldn't get real painters right away when we wanted them, or at the price we were willing to pay, so I took on that task; besides, it kept me from having to do housework (which I hate more than writing), and it gave John some projects too. He had to buy me a safe ladder with platform and work shelf and lots of paint and supplies and build me a scaffold over the open stairs to the basement, and then clean my used brushes, and rollers, and paint pans since I don't like to get "dirty." An added bonus for me was that I lost five pounds doing all that work because you burn extra calories when you get only two to three hours sleep because you have to paint during the night and work at a real job during the day.

If you paint the walls, you have to remove and put back all the window treatments and all the artwork and fill in the holes left by the nails and screws. I had jokingly complained to Bob that I had run out of room for hanging my artwork and had some artwork left over, so he said, "Just stack them all somewhere and I'll hang them back up for you." And when he did, the effect was marvelous and there was room for them all. He introduced us to Floreat® picture hangers that have such sharp, tiny nails that you can rearrange your artwork whenever you like and just dab a little paint with a Q-tips® cotton swab into the hole that's left in the wallboard.

One day, when Bob delivered the three roll-around-chairs, which he thought would be much better for John to use at our new, round, kitchen table (a dropdown extension of the countertop for the cabinet that divides the kitchen area from the laundry area), I asked him, "Could you just take a look at the living room while you're here? I'm really not that happy with where we've placed the furniture."

"Sure. Leave me alone for a half-hour to look and think." Then he disappeared into the living room by way of the dining room where he prepared a surprise for us with a quick rearrangement of our china cabinet to better display the few nice pieces we have bought or inherited.

Bob wasn't in the living room for more than five minutes when his voice rang out, "Hey John, could you come give a hand for a minute?"

I didn't dare go in there because a half-hour wasn't up; however, from the kitchen where I was working, I could hear furniture being moved and the hallway door to the garage opening and closing. When the time was up, I went into the living room to take a look. Bob and John were sitting on the sofa admiring their work. The arrangement was perfect! Everyone, when seated, could see each other while chatting or look out the windows or watch TV or watch a fire in the fireplace or listen to music surrounded by sound.

Suddenly, astonished that our huge, table lamp was gone, I blurted out, "Where's our lamp?"

"It's in the garage. It is too gaudy and 1960ish," Bob said.

"But we like that lamp." I went to the garage and brought it back into the living room, and Bob took it to the garage, and I brought it back, and so on. After the third time, he resigned himself to the fact that the lamp was going to stay and found the perfect place for it. In return, I had to compromise and move my swing from the living room and hang it from the ceiling near the fireplace in the basement barroom.

Bob hates the rug in the front hallway (I won't tell you what he thinks the color looks like) and keeps asking when we're going to replace that ugly thing. And I keep saying, "Never, probably, because we bought it to coordinate with the background of the batik painting on the wall opposite the front doorway, and besides, we like it."

The whole house is now painted in a rainbow of colors chosen to coordinate with our world outside and inside the walls, instead of Spanish white, and everyone including us likes the transformation. They are even wowed by the window treatments that John made five years earlier and which they never noticed before because of the white walls glaring beside them.

SNIPPETS (bits and pieces of love and life) by CAROLE

Bob phoned several months ago to tell us about a 200-CD-changer that was very inexpensive and that he knew we would like because he bought himself one and it is terrific; should he pick up one for us. I said, "Sure!" He arrived the next evening, installed it, showed us how to work it, and left with the music playing, taking a check for the cost of the changer. He didn't charge for his work, so I added some extra to the amount when I wrote the check, but I didn't tell him. The next week, he brought by an album to hold the CD jacket flaps, in the same order as the changer, so I could throw away all those empty holders that take up so much space; I wrote a check to him for that too.

He phoned again on May 20, 2002. Had we seen the TV program about the new surgical treatment for Parkinson's Disease? We hadn't; but that was OK, because he had taped it for us just in case, and he would drop it by on his way to (magically transform, in my opinion) someone's home, and he could pick it up later when he is out this way again. Bob lives over thirty miles from us somewhere in Pennsylvania.

May your dishwasher forever work and never die. That is, unless you can afford to transform your kitchen, possibly your house, and probably—if you hire our now-friend Bob, the interior designer—your life!

SNIPPET 157 - Eyes

I probably always knew but, consciously, had never thought about it. Every time I looked at John, he was looking at me: when we were in college classes, when we studied together in the library, when we ate, when I entered a room, when we were dancing together, when we were dancing with other partners, and when...—actually, it still happens all the time. Even when I awake during the night and roll over on my side to face him, I'll see (and I say this lovingly) his beady little eyes staring back at me.

This matter was brought to my attention by another Carol.

We met Carol and Jonn while we all were sailing on the *Royal Clipper* around the Caribbean. We connected immediately because "Carol and Jonn" sounds exactly like "Carole and John." The four of us saw each other frequently that week and sometimes sat together at meals or at the evening entertainment. She is about a year older than I and had recently lost her husband to Parkinson's Disease. Mutual friends of theirs had introduced her to Jonn.

One afternoon, while our companions were napping back in the cabins, Carol and I lounged side-by-side under the canopy on the top deck, half-heartedly reading books but mostly chatting together. She is a psychologist who likes to study people, and she was intrigued by the loving, playful relationship between my PD-stricken husband and me. It was so different from her relationship with her husband after his PD diagnosis; they had stopped enjoying life together because he simply gave up and died. She admitted that she watched us constantly when we were in sight. Our conversation ended when John appeared at the top of the stairs leading up from the deck below and started toward us. I hopped up to go meet him and faced her to say goodbye.

She looked at him and then at me. "Have you ever noticed?" she asked. "He *never* takes his eyes off of you."

"Nooo...," I said, shaking my head slowly, "I never have."

SNIPPET 158 - Housekeeper

My mind doesn't stay focused very well if I have several things to do; I want to get them all done at once. I was cleaning the kitchen, some day and time in 2001, which you'd think I'd have remembered exactly because of the rarity of this event, but didn't, and decided to vacuum the floor before I mopped it. (I guess I could at least get the date from my calendar, if I could find it, because we were supposed to join friends for dinner that evening, and I would have written that down on my calendar so I wouldn't forget.) Anyway, I got out the long twenty-five-foot vacuum-hose and attachments for cleaning a wood-or-tile-or-whatever-type-solid floor, assembled it, plugged it into the wall outlet, by the kitchen/hallway door, for the built-in vacuum cleaner (that John had installed before the wallboard went up when we were building our house), and began to vacuum from there towards the back door by the clothes washer and drier.

As I got positioned in front of the washer, I noticed a package, sitting on the counter above it, that I needed to finish wrapping to take to the post office to mail that day; I suddenly decided to stop and do that right then and there and, afterwards, continue with the vacuuming. I turned off the switch on the handle of the vacuum hose in my hand and laid the hose down where I was standing. As I was finishing the package wrapping (that I had started earlier that day before I got distracted by something else I saw sitting on the counter beside the package and decided to clean the kitchen instead), I realized that I needed a different pair of scissors in order to cut the paper hanging out too far to be tucked under the end of the box. Without thinking,—which is usual for me when my mind has too much to think about—I turned and started walking toward the door to the hallway to go to another room to get the proper scissors that are stored with gift/package wrapping stuff.

Unfortunately, I forgot that I had left the vacuum hose and other parts underfoot and got tangled up in the hose and splatted myself headlong onto the floor. First, my right leg and knee hit the hard ceramic tile, bruising it so deeply and badly it took months to heal, and then my face, sliding somewhat, hit the rug in the hallway scraping off some skin above my mouth, splitting my lips in several places, and loosening my upper front teeth—enough to require several weeks for my face and jaw to heal and several days to be able to eat real food again instead of the baby food I had to slurp through closed teeth. Lest you think I'm a total dimwit, I do keep icy boo-boo pads in the freezer and immediately plastered my knee, shin, and mouth with them to lessen the damage and bleeding. (I also keep, in my refrigerator, a dark miso, which is a fermented soybean product, to use as a plaster for insect bites and stings as well as a delicious additive for soups.)

I looked atrocious; so I called Cathy to apologize for breaking our dinner engagement that evening with her and Jack, our long-time and dear friends, and ended my part of the conversation, after explaining my accident, by saying. "I'm really sorry we can't go out tonight, but I look too horrible to be out in public, and, besides, I can't open my mouth wide enough to insert food, and it hurts to chew."

Cathy didn't seem to be sympathetic at all, just annoyed; she simply said, "I keep telling you to hire a housekeeper; she wouldn't leave cleaning equipment lying around on your floor."

The four of us get together whenever we can; Jack and John chat at work and Cathy and I chat off and on via phone; we rarely ever communicate via e-mail. She phoned me on Wednesday evening to invite us to join them for dinner. On Sunday, July 21, 2002, we're going to the very place where we were supposed to have gone for dinner that particular night of the day of my accident. Before we hung up, she made one simple, parting request.

"Please, *don't vacuum* before you come."

SNIPPET 159 - Magnetic

There is something in the genetic makeup of little boys that causes dirt to leap onto their bodies and clothing like iron filings jump onto a magnet.

For men, this principle also applies to any grease—especially carbon-particulate-never-to-be-removed-by-detergent-alone grease. Moreover, the dirt and grease get on their good clothes as well as on their old clothes, which they're supposed to, but often neglect to because they didn't think they needed to, wear for dirty jobs like car and lawnmower tinkering and yard work and roof tarring and so forth.

The typical conversation follows. Pick any day, any time, any clothes, any body part, any task, any place, any greasy or dirty object, and complete the sentences.

"*John*, you have grease (or dirt) on your... And there's some on your..."

"Oh? I do?" (looking surprised)

"*Where* did you get it?"

"I don't know." (shrugging shoulders)

"*What* have you been doing?"

"Nothing, I just..." (looking puzzled)

"*And*?"

"And then I...I guess I must have...but I was just..." (trying to explain)

If it's simply grease or dirt, I have him leave the clothes in the laundry sink, then I use Goop® cleaner or pre-wash spray on the affected areas and finish cleaning the clothes in the laundry. If it's paint or tar or asphalt or anything else that might ruin the clothes washer, he gets to do all the cleaning using whatever detergent he likes, the garden hose, and a bucket in the yard.

It appears that chemicals also jump on men—at least, on John.

After I finished the dishes this hot July evening 2002, I walked out to join John where he was sitting by the pool, keeping my sister and her youngest son company. I took one look at John and his brand-new-first-time-worn-light-herb-color polo that he was wearing and stated in my oh-no-not-again-whining-voice, "Hooonnneey, your new shirt has white spots on the front!"

"It does?" he questioned, looking down and stretching out the front of his polo hanging out, not tucked in.

"*How* did that happen? *What* have you been doing?"

"I don't know. I haven't been doing anything other than talking to Patty and Byron while they swim and play in the pool."

"Well, while I was loading the dishwasher," I accused, "I glanced out the window and saw you walking toward the other end of the pool carrying an object that had water or something dribbling out the bottom of it."

"Oooh, *that* —," he recalled grinning, "I was taking the plastic floating duck over to the storage box so I could refill it with chlorine pellets. I guess the bleach dripped on my shirt." Yes, I guess it did!

Tomorrow morning, I'll order him another polo because he absolutely needs it since the color matches the color of the one I am wearing.

But—if he does this *one more time* —…!

Oh, well, how can I stay distressed or get angry? It's not his fault that he is *sooo attractive*!

SNIPPET 160 - The Honeymooners

Our travel agents, Bob and Mary Anne, always do something a little special to make our trips more fun, whether it is to schedule a birthday or anniversary celebration for the two of us or to surprise us with a bottle of champagne in our room upon arrival. On our trip on the *ms Amsterdam*, we had an even bigger surprise, and since we had only had an overnight honeymoon when we got married, this was really special.

One evening on the ship, we received an envelope under our door. In it was an invitation from the captain and the hotel manager to attend the Honeymooners Party to be held the next evening, Friday, May 25, 2001 at 7:30 P.M. in the Explorers Lounge. We both agreed that this was rather strange, thinking we had received the invitation in error. Our second thought was that maybe Bob and Mary Anne were the instigators. Besides, it was a party, so why not attend. Since we eat dinner at the six o'clock seating, we figured we would go to the party after we finished eating. We also assumed that the party would last about forty-five minutes (like the usual dinnertime cocktail events) and that it wouldn't matter when we arrived.

Friday, we ate a leisurely dinner, staying a bit longer for dessert, and left the dining room in time to arrive about 7:45 P.M. We entered the lounge and were hurriedly greeted by the captain and his hostess.

"You're *late*," the captain curtly said, "and you *missed* the ceremony. But," he added pleasantly, "come get your photo taken cutting the cake."

"We're terribly sorry. We waited for our dessert at dinner, not realizing that we needed to be on time," I apologized, for John and me.

Moreover, we were dressed in casual attire with matching Hawaiian dress and shirt since "casual" was the dress code for the ship that evening; everyone else at the party was in more formal attire. There were other honeymooners present as well as some couples who came to renew their wedding vows. The remainder of the festivities, after we arrived, included music played by one of the ship's musical combos and several songs sung by the daughter of one of the couples who had renewed their vows.

As a keepsake for the event, we received an official "Honeymoon Certificate" and a photo of us cutting the wedding cake and the captain standing beside us, holding our certificate. We can now say that we have been on an official and very real honeymoon; the entire trip was one.

After the photo was taken, the hostess smilingly added, "Congratulations on your marriage."

"Actually, we have been married forty years," I sheepishly stated, "but I guess our travel agents thought we should have a real honeymoon. They must have arranged this for us after we mentioned the short, one-night stand that we got to take on our wedding day. We were totally surprised when we received the invitation."

As we left, we promised the captain, hotel manager, and hostess that we would be on time for the next event. Apparently, if the invitation states only a *start* time, that means you must arrive at exactly that time, and if it states a *between* time, you may arrive at or after the starting time but before the ending time. After that party, we had a great time kidding them and being kidded by them for the remainder of our trip.

Since that party, even on subsequent trips, the hostess has forever referred to us as—not John and Carole, but—"the honeymooners."

SNIPPET 161 - Spared Again

September 11, 2001, was tragic in many ways but joyful in one. Our nephew, Thomas, who is a Top Gun helicopter pilot, was stationed at ground zero of the Pentagon until late August. His office and the surrounding ones needed renovating, so he and some of his coworkers were moved to other offices next to that area. He and a coworker were watching the events in New York City unfold on a TV monitor in the coworker's office when the plane hit the Pentagon. Even though he was knocked down and covered with debris, smoke, and fumes from the plane-crash impact and fire and lost all of his office equipment and some personal items, he got out OK.

An e-mail message from his younger brother, David, brought the good news to us shortly after it happened. He and his wife had called Thomas, right after they saw the crash on TV, and had reached him on his cell phone, which just happened to still be in his pocket. They found him badly shaken and trying to hitchhike home to be with his family; driving was out of the question since personnel could not get to vehicles in the parking lot near the crash area. Thomas's wife, quite pregnant with their son, was teaching at an elementary school near their home. Fortunately, the baby waited to come, full-term.

We went to visit them that very weekend. During the few hours that he was home, every sudden noise from their very young daughter startled him. The rest of the time, he was back working overtime at the Pentagon. It made us feel better just to hug him, be with his family, and share our gratitude. Our presence seemed to have helped soothe the family as well.

A few years prior to that event, Thomas had been in a helicopter accident when someone else was piloting. He received only minor injuries in that crash and simply climbed down out of the tree that the helicopter landed in.

There must be some special purpose for Thomas's life. — It was spared again.

SNIPPET 162 - *Trucks*

I didn't like riding in trucks or cars that resembled trucks, so I certainly would *never* buy one.

John figured we needed a pickup truck to carry supplies, when we were building our house, because he wanted to do some stone work and maybe some of the finishing work inside and out.

"But I don't like trucks. And I don't like the way they look," I argued.

"There's beauty in function," he insisted, and that settled it.

The first one we bought was a white Chevy® pickup with dark green interior. While my dad was living with us to oversee the builders, he used the truck daily for transportation. Mostly what he transported was himself and gallons of blackberries that he picked in the back yard when the workers didn't show up. After we moved into the house, we put a shell over the truck bed and used that vehicle when we went tent camping. The truck was also handy for going to dances after a heavy snowfall; John loaded the bed with ballast, which he had made from tubs filled with poured concrete with inlaid handles for easy moving, and put chains on the tires if the roads were icy as well.

When we gave up sleeping in a tent to sleep inside a truck, we bought a maroon Chevy Suburban® with matching interior to replace the pickup and put a mattress on the back floor. I made curtains all around for privacy and screens so we could leave the windows open while we slept. That truck also pulled our first travel trailer after we got tired of not being able to stand up for long stretches of time when it rained during our camping trips.

After we had seen most of the eastern part of the USA and Canada, we wanted to visit many of the National Parks out west. Since the Suburban bogged down to thirty-five MPH on I-95, just going up minor hills when we traveled north or south, we knew it would never make it up mountains with altitudes of twelve thousand or more feet. We had to start looking for a truck with a larger engine and better pulling capacity. What we found to fit the bill was an International®, crew-cab truck that you had to have built to your specifications.

SNIPPETS (bits and pieces of love and life) by CAROLE

Just specifying what you wanted in an International® was a feat in itself. You had to answer a lot of questions like those in this list:

- What engine? What size? Cylinders? Horsepower? Turbocharge?
- Engine block heater? Ether cold-start? Winter screen? Bug screen?
- What transmission? Two- or four-wheel drive? How many gears? Three or four or five or ten? High? Low? Gear ratio? Locking hubs? Transfer case?
- What brakes? Parking brake?
- Batteries? Alternator? Head lights? Tail lights?
- What gauges? Tachometers?
- What type of fuel? Fuel tanks? Fuel capacity? Inter-connected tanks? Locking hand throttle? Fuel filter? Water separator?
- No-spin rear end?
- How many wheels? Dual rear? Tires? What size?
- Front axle load? Rear axle load?
- How long a frame for the bed?
- Springs? Where? What kind? Leaf or coil?
- What load should the rear end handle?
- Bumper? Front and/or back? Heavy-duty or chrome?
- Horn?
- How many doors? Open which way?
- How many seats? What kind?
- Grab bars?
- Glass? Mirrors? Heated? Inside or outside?
- Heat and A/C?
- Glove compartment? In dashboard and/or under seat?
- What kind of paint? Regular? Imron? What color?

We decided to have our "one-of-a-kind" truck painted black so it would look *petite and demure* instead of like the monster it was. John nicknamed it "The Black Heap," but Shirley always referred to it as "The Black Maria." In the winter, however, John called it something different and had black magnetic signs on the doors that said, in large-bold-reflective-white-letters, **"SNOW LIMO."** And indeed it was!

We drove it through the blowing snow to many black-tie affairs and surprised everyone around when we stepped down from the cab in our tuxedo and formal-gown attire. We also have used the truck to pull cars and other trucks out of snowbanks or sand ruts.

Since John would sometimes drop me off at work, we had to have an extra stepping bar added on my side of the truck so that I didn't have to hike up my suit skirts so high (that you could almost see my unmentionables) just to get in and out of the cab. The "sissy bar," as I called it, made the first step only about twenty instead of thirty inches off the ground. For me, grab bars stationed within reach at each door were essential for helping me hoist myself into the cab; other riders seemed to like to use them too.

What I liked most about riding in the International was being up so high; you can see much more than when riding in a car. If you ever rode in a school bus, you know what I mean. That's a great advantage when you are traveling and sightseeing in the mountains. Because our truck was so large, we always kidded that "we can go anywhere we fit."

The huge black truck evoked interesting questions and comments from people everywhere. Children were intrigued and liked to ask, "Do you carry bears in the box?" Women were aghast and wanted it to be elsewhere and "not in my backyard." But men actually *loved* it and spent a lot of time drooling over it. Park rangers always needed to inspect it, but I really think that they were just curious to look all around inside and out. They would inquire as to whether we were carrying seismographic equipment or poaching apparatus for bear, elk, moose, bison, and such. A ranger, in Yellowstone National Park, even drove out to West Yellowstone to verify that we actually did have a travel trailer parked at the campground. After that, we always kept our park entry receipts to show that we really have been allowed to enter as legitimate visitors and campers.

John designed three different hitches before he got one he really liked for towing our travel trailer. The last hitch had leaf springs and hydraulic shocks so that the truck's nineteen-thousand-pound-rated, rear end was easy on the trailer's structure when it was towed.

We now have another Chevy Suburban®, white with tan interior, since we replaced our Airstream™ with a Roadtrek® that I can drive, and no longer need the International for towing. I never had the strength to drive the huge truck longer than fifteen minutes at a time; my legs would start shaking from using the clutch and brakes and I couldn't move the gearshift with one hand. Even John had problems shifting gears when the truck was new; he had to wear a glove on his right hand to protect it after he blooded his knuckles several times on the dashboard when his hand flew off the handle as he tried to forcibly move the gearshift forward into the next gear. As John's Parkinson's Disease progresses, I will need to do more of the driving for our sightseeing and camping.

We "sold" "The Black Maria" this year to our nephew, Thomas, who was, at the time, exactly the same age as John was when we bought the truck near the end of 1981. It seems as though men like the same toys at the same ages. I hope his wife adjusts to the shock and learns to enjoy it as much as I did. I know their kids will.

SNIPPET 163 - Moving In

Most of our friends are younger than we are, and some, like us, don't have children. Jack and Cathy are, and they don't. John and Jack both used to work in Indochemicals Department at DuPont Company, that's how we met them, and now John works for Jack at Chromacol in Kennett Square. Just two months after John retired, I convinced Jack that he had to hire John to keep him happy playing in a lab and out of the house. Everyone knows retired husbands need to be kept out of the house so they won't pester their wives all day by being home and in the way—*of what?* — I wonder.

Cathy is older (slightly) than Jack, and I am older than John (much, much older according to John), so we have that in common. Younger men are a lot more fun; they can actually keep up with you! She and I both taught school, she taught German (Hmmm, why not French? She's French.), and I taught math and science, but she did it about ten times as many years. When she retired from that, she went into horticulture and was terrific at that as well.

How we got to know them goes like this.

In the 1970's, we supported different charities than they did, but they invited us to go with them, and about five other couples, to some of their fundraisers. As we got to know each other better and discovered that we liked so many of the same things, we gradually began to see each other on more occasions.

Jack and Cathy like to dance, and I think they're very good at it. We do too, and I like to think we are. Sometimes we swap and dance with the other's spouse, but most of the time we don't anymore because we've been dancing with our own spouses so many years that it feels strange dancing with someone else's; besides that, we're now more apt to step on their feet.

They like to eat in great restaurants, and so do we. Often, just the four of us eat out; sometimes, several other couples join us, or we join them, as the case may be. Cathy is a fabulous cook and when we eat at their house, she serves authentic French cuisine; she and Jack are both of French ancestry and their names are really Catherine and Jacques. They met through a mutual friend when they both lived in Montreal. Occasionally they come eat at our house; I serve whatever

SNIPPETS (bits and pieces of love and life) by CAROLE

kind of dishes I happen to be dreaming up that week. I guess we are just getting old because, lately, we all prefer eating in restaurants and letting someone else do the work while we sit and chat.

A big group of us used to get together for "Super Bowl" parties and each couple has taken some turns having it at their home. Last year nobody bothered; I think most of us were out of town; and there's some talk about some of us not being around for next year's either. We may not get together for a party, but I'm sure we'll all be watching the game somewhere.

They like to travel (good thing too because Jack has to travel a lot for work) and fly to places, rent a car, and drive to stay in hotels or resorts. We like to travel and get out our camper and drive to places to stay in campgrounds. Since all four of us like to go to the beach to walk or swim or just read in the shade, we took a vacation together and did it their way. I like their way better because you get pampered by not having to cook and clean and make the bed and stuff; I plan vacations just like that for the two of us now—unless John *has* to go camping.

Jack and Cathy play tennis, so they're building a house in New Orleans to be able to spend more time doing that after Jack retires. Some of their relatives already live there. I sure hope the guest room in their new house has a small kitchen, large closets, and a Jacuzzi in its bathroom; because, if we get too lonesome without them here, we're going to pack up and fly down there.

They may think we're just visiting, but we're *moving in*.

SNIPPET 164 - Colonoscopy

On March 14, 2002, I sent a note to Judy, a friend from my high school days, after getting her e-mail address from Wayne, who thought she lived somewhere in Delaware, and immediately received a reply that went something like this:

"This is going to sound a little strange, but a few weeks ago my sister had a colonoscopy at the Endoscopy Center, and she asked me to drive her there. While we were sitting in the waiting room that morning, a woman came into the building with a man who was dressed in brown clothing. I told my sister, who also went to Palm Beach High School, graduating two years ahead of me in the class of 1953, that the woman at the reception counter looked exactly like a girl I went to high school with, whose name was Carole. Was it you? If so, you haven't changed a bit!"

My reply back to Judy was:

"Might have been; I had a colonoscopy at that very place the morning of February 6 and John was with me, but I don't remember what we were wearing. I'm shocked that you would have recognized me as I think I have aged a lot. I was too nervous to notice anyone else. I've had a lot of surgeries and adhesions from them and was concerned that I would have problems. As it turned out the adhesions kept the doctor from seeing anything, so he quit as I had asked him to do if there were any difficulties."

It's amazing that we have lived within ten to twenty miles of each other for so long. We moved here in 1965 and Judy moved her family to Wilmington in 1973; in spite of that, we had never seen each other around town. We quickly rectified that and have been getting together ever since. How wonderful to be reunited with a classmate who was also in the PBHS band; she played a clarinet and I played a bassoon. My older sister was in the same class as Judy's older sister, whom she wrote me about; they didn't have many courses in common so neither knew the other as more than just a classmate.

Because I hate to write, I corresponded with very few people I knew in high school or college after I graduated and, thus, quickly lost track of almost everyone. With e-mail making correspondence so much easier, maybe I'll catch up with more of my classmates.

SNIPPETS (bits and pieces of love and life) by CAROLE

I am so grateful that Dr. Diana sent me for that colonoscopy. You just never know what wonderful things can happen while you are there waiting for the procedure. — A friend from out of your ancient past may get a glimpse of you and a whole new relationship may begin. — Judy, her husband, Clyde, John, and I plan to spend more happy times together.

SNIPPET 165 - Wheelchairs

    Wheelchairs are extremely handy vehicles when you need one to get around in; they can even be fun if someone pushes you because then you have some company as well. My mom had a red (her favorite color, and mine) wheelchair to use when she couldn't use her prosthesis after her leg was amputated, and my dad had a bigger, green one, after mom died, when his legs gave out thirty-five years after he had polio. Both wheelchairs are stored at Patty's house in the basement now. We borrowed the green one to use for several weeks for John when he ruptured a couple of discs in his lower back and then again for me when I damaged my leg so badly sledding.

    Our friend Wayne, who has cerebral palsy, uses one when he has to walk more than a few yards because it's faster that way, and you have to get there fast because that's how society does things these days. A few months ago, Wayne (from PBHS and FSU) sent me an e-mail message and connected me up with Linda, who is making me write this book, and with Judy, who I am making write so I can have someone to be miserable with. Judy and I decided that all-these-having-to-write shenanigans were really Wayne's fault, because if it weren't for him, we all wouldn't be friends again, and Judy and I wouldn't have to write anything. Oh, well, it's OK. — We like him anyway.

    Wayne thought it would be great for the three of us who live on the east coast (Linda's on the west coast) to get together so we could meet each other's spouse and see again, after so many years, the people we had been e-mailing. The reason was that he figured that we probably don't look exactly like our high school yearbook pictures, which you always wish you did, but don't. We e-mailed back and forth, and since two of the three classmates live within six miles of each other and majority rules, Wayne and his wife, Emily, had to come here to meet with Judy, Clyde, John, and me. Since we live in a ranch-style house and Judy and Clyde live in an upper floor condominium, we decided to get together at our house for most of the weekend of June 1, 2002. Wayne and Emily spent two nights in a bed and breakfast nearby because they were headed to Philadelphia to see their daughter and grandson after they left us.

SNIPPETS (bits and pieces of love and life) by CAROLE

Friday evening, we met here and went out to eat at The Back Burner, our favorite restaurant close by, and the next day picked up gourmet food for dinner from their take-out shop, The Back Burner To Go. With such marvelously prepared food available, why cook? We could spend the extra time catching up on the forty-seven years we spent apart.

Saturday was such a beautiful sunny-blue-sky day that we went to Longwood Gardens to visit the conservatory and to have a noontime snack in the cafe. Getting around there requires a great deal more walking than just a few yards, so Wayne rode in his wheelchair, which we took turns pushing, while we wandered through the lush, awesome plant life, marveled at the enormous number of species, and sniffed the vast array of aromas.

When we got home, we decided to sit by the pool, and again Wayne got to ride with John pushing his wheelchair, this time around the side yard over the brick walkway I had laid in the pebbles. John had me lay the bricks last year because he thought we'd probably need them someday for a wheelchair; I'm glad he had thought of it. The rest of us walked through the house, out the backdoor, down the step, and over the terrace and some stones and bricks where a wheelchair couldn't go. We heard the two guys chattering and laughing as we all approached each other.

John was casually joking with Wayne as he had done at Longwood Gardens and lastly said, "Just remember; you're the driver, I'm the motor, so if we hit anything, it's your fault, and you get to pay the ticket!"

SNIPPET 166 - Procrastination

I had to write "Wheelchairs" last evening, so I finally crawled into bed around 01:38 A.M. rather than 10:00 P.M. or so like I'm supposed to. There's a digital clock, with two-inch-tall, red numbers that you can read even in the dark, sitting on the middle shelf of the tall bookcase against the wall, across John's side of the bed from me. I always look at it before I go to sleep because I have to add seven hours to the time to determine when I should get up again. I don't know why I bother; it makes no difference since I ignore the number of hours, but psychologically, and maybe physically, it does matter. Seven hours is about right for me; too much less or too much more than that and I have to drink excessive coffee because I'm too tired or too groggy and have acquired a headache. — Today, it's the latter. — That means I should get up around 8:30 A.M., but normally would get up anyway around 5:30 A.M. to spend a half-hour with John before I send him off to work and then go back to bed. In spite of trying to ease into bed, I unintentionally waked John as I crawled in, and then he knew what time that was because he checks it whenever he awakes, which is frequent during the night now (that's why the clock is there where it is). Consequently, instead of waking me at the usual time with his coffee slurping, he kissed me and whispered that he was going to eat and leave; please go back to sleep and get up later. I glanced up at him and whispered back my usual have-fun-play-hard-see-you-later good-bye, closed my eyes, and drifted back into sleep.

I looked at the clock at 7:28, 8:14, and again at 9:43 A.M.; I repositioned myself every time and went back to sleep; I just didn't want to get up, because if I did, I knew I would have to *write*. At 9:55 A.M., I rolled over one more time, this time onto my right side. I must have had thrown my arms overhead at one point while lying on my back, because my arms were "dead," and I had to wait for the feeling to come back. As I listened to my heart pounding in my chest and in my ear against the pillow, I could also hear my blood rushing around and hear the pillowcase rustling in my ear as my breathing slightly moved my body and, simultaneously, moved my ear on the pillow. The *noise* is what really woke me up. It's strange what you notice when you really don't *want* to do what you *need* to do. At 9:58 A.M., my feet finally "hit the deck," as my dad would say, and I decided I would write about procrastination today; it seemed the right and proper thing to do while I was heavily into it.

I got to this point in my writing when Anne phoned to say she had to go to the doctor again this afternoon about her eyes acting strangely and her head still aching off and on, and that she was back from her trip with her grandson John to attend the wedding of a relative and, whenever it was convenient, could I bring over her mail that we had collected for her in her absence. I had to go see her immediately, so I interrupted my writing since you would never notice if I made *you* wait, because you will still get to read this "in one swell foop," but I could never do that to *Anne*. We needed to chat about how she could best describe her problem so that the doctor would understand it and, besides, I knew she was dying to tell me about the wedding and the inn where it was held.

When I got back from her house, I remembered that I was supposed to have made an ice-cream-run early this morning. I had procrastinated about going and had started writing instead, so now the grocery store would be crowded with all the other people just getting around to it, which meant we all would have to wait longer in the check-out line. Besides, if you're going to be there in the store anyway, you might as well pick up a few more items that are on your list for the real grocery shopping later in the week and maybe get some cookies and other snacks, and so forth. It would take much longer now to do that errand than I had planned, but I went anyway because I didn't want John to come home from work and look in the freezer for some ice cream that he wanted and find none there. Then, when I got home, I had to eat some ice cream myself—just carrying it into the house made me hungry. Now, I'm back writing again after being away for about five hours.

Is procrastination inherited too, along with all our other traits? Or do we just learn it by osmosis? I only know that I have been a procrastinator for as long as I can remember.

As a child I could never get around to changing my bed and cleaning my room on Saturday mornings even though Mommy promised us we could go to the movies when we were done. Edith and I found that it was more fun to have pillow fights and do everything else but. You also have to play with everything that you're supposed to be dusting or picking up and putting away. We would finally get our forty-five-minute chore done around suppertime when the threat of my dad getting home loomed over our heads or, on rare occasions, by matinee-movie-time if it was a movie we just had to see.

When I was a student, I never studied for a test until the night before or did research or wrote a paper until it was almost too late to start it and get it done and turned in on time. I did my homework each evening but always started doing it around nine or ten o'clock when I should have been going to bed. I never started cutting out and sewing a new dress or complete outfit until the night before or the very day I had to wear it.

Even now, I start preparing dinner at the last minute, look in the refrigerator and freezer, and sometimes on shelves of cans and packaged foods, stare at the choices a while and ultimately decide what we going to eat. In my mind I can hear my mom in the other room: *Don't just stand there looking; make up your mind, and close the door.* As a child, it was especially fun to stand, undecided, peering into the refrigerator or into the freezer on a sizzling-hot-Florida-summer day to catch the cold air as it wafted out the door and onto the front of your body or just your face; that's when Mommy would really holler about the door. Then, I grab something for protein, something for vegetables, and something for salad, prepare, cook or throw that together some way that's appetizing, and shout to John. — "Dinner's ready."

Speaking of dinner… While I was working at DuPont Company, whenever several coworkers, our manager Charlie, and I, attending an out-of-town computer convention, headed out to dinner together in the evening, we would wander the streets near our hotel and read the dinner menus in the all restaurant windows. If no one had made a decision about which restaurant we should eat in by the time everyone was tired enough to start complaining, then Charlie would decree, at the next restaurant we came to, that we were "eating in there, period." After a few evenings of doing this, someone would emerge as a non-procrastinator; obviously, it wasn't I.

I haven't gotten around to reading the newspaper this week or finding out why my medical bill wasn't paid for by my health insurance after Medicare was done with it. That last one's going to

SNIPPETS (bits and pieces of love and life) by CAROLE

require a phone call. I've moved that bill around the house for the last two weeks to be in sight to remind me to do that, but instead of getting the task done, I just keep moving the paper so it won't get lost, as though it was a return envelope you needed to keep track of.

I'm getting better, now, with packing for a trip and actually start several days or weeks or months ahead of time since the rest of the world works differently, and if you want to go where, when, and how you want to go, you have to plan ahead.

Interestingly, I rarely ever procrastinated about doing any of the tasks of my paying jobs in computer systems or of my volunteer jobs, probably because those tasks were very interesting and really more like play than work. Nevertheless, when it comes to the rest of my life, I'm still one of the "World's Best" procrastinators.

Oh dear... John just drove up and nothing's been accomplished that he'll be able to see, except for the ice cream in the freezer. Sooo glad I at least did that! It's already past time for dinner too.

SNIPPET 167 - Oh, That Judy

"Judy" seems to be a very popular name or, at least, it was popular when I was young. We have three friends who share that first name. Well, technically, they don't *share* the same first name; each one has her own. Three is a good percentage of our friends who are close in age to John and me (close, relatively speaking, since everyone in that group is now in the second half-century of being alive).

Yesterday, July 2, 2002, Judy sent me a draft, to comment on, of her new writing work, her second piece—she's been an author only a few days now. It really helps to have someone else read your work and make written suggestions. Linda does that for me; and since I "infected" this particular Judy with the contagious "compulsion-to-write-bug," like Linda did to me, I am somewhat obligated to make written comments, even though I hate to write. The other reason that I *have to* write comments is because she sent it to me in an e-mail message and then, of course, you (the proverbial "you" meaning "me" in this case) *have to* reply; it's the kind and proper-etiquette thing to do. I send my "Snippet" drafts as attachments to e-mail messages to Linda knowing that she will *have to* comment, but I don't feel bad about that because Linda *likes* to write; she even *publishes* her work.

I started reading Judy's draft, and when I got near the end, I realized she was writing about my husband. What threw me off, at first, was that she referred to him as a "man" in the first paragraph and, afterwards, never mentioned the man's name. John and I never think of ourselves as "men" and "women" even though we fall into those categories; we simply forget we are old enough to be called that. We also don't respond immediately to "Dr." or "Mr." and/or "Mrs."; if people don't address us as John and/or Carole, we don't quickly realize that they are referring to us. Unfortunately, for Judy, I was so touched by the tribute that I cried and still remain totally unable to critique this work. She'll just have to write something else so I can critique that. I hope she will; she already has a good command of language and should become an eloquent writer even if my comments never help her improve her skills. Sometimes, all you need is a friend to encourage you long enough to keep you going until you reach your goal on your own.

After I got my composure back, I hollered to John, who was in the kitchen snacking, as usual, "Hooonneey, you must come read this tribute Judy wrote and attached to the message she e-mailed to me; it sounds like the *man* she is writing about is *you*."

"Judy?" he hollered back, sounding puzzled.

"You know, the Judy that I conned into writing so someone else could be miserable besides me."

"Oh, that Judy."

P.S. I thought you would enjoy reading Judy's composition; so, with her permission, I included it here. I hope she continues to write.

Judy's - *A New Friend*

Recently, a new friend has come into my life. This is a man who has much to teach us all, and does so without even realizing the enormous impact of his influence. His lessons are taught not by lecture or self-important pontification, not by monopolizing conversations with stories about himself or his accomplishments, nor by attempts to persuade the listener to accept his point of view on any subject. In a very meaningful and refreshing way, he teaches by example. The lessons I'm learning from this individual have nothing to do with his impressive educational credentials or career related success (which topics I have never heard him mention). These are lessons of a very different and infinitely more valuable sort; they are lessons about life itself.

A man of considerable professional stature, my friend has, in the prime of his life, been stricken with a neurological disease that has had life-altering effects up to the present time, and threatens potentially devastating consequences over the long term. He and his wife have had a strong and long lasting marriage, and together they continue to live their lives to the fullest. While one who hasn't experienced their difficulties cannot possibly presume to know what the days and nights are really like for them, one can only imagine. In spite of it all, they move on, bolstered perhaps by their deep love and affection for each other and their strong faith in God. They obviously have made a clear choice between self-pity and celebration of life. They travel because they love to travel and they want to do it all while he has the necessary mobility and is able to enjoy himself. They draw close to one another and hold on to the strong bond between them.

This new friend is the husband of a girlhood friend of mine whom I lost track of years ago as we both went out into the world after high school graduation, each in different directions. When we met again after 47 years I was delighted to reconnect with her, and for the opportunity for our husbands to meet. This man with a twinkle in his eyes, a dry wit, and a great sense of humor has a quiet dignity about him. I know that I can learn a lot from the courageous way he is living his life. He makes no attempt to draw attention to himself, but rather is quick to push the other person's wheelchair, open car doors for others, participate in the care and upkeep of the home he shares with his wife, work as a consultant, and welcome guests into their home. Each of these activities must surely be more difficult for him than it was before he was stricken, but he does it all in a way that shows the observer without a doubt, that he cherishes his life and is determined to focus on the things he CAN do rather than those he cannot.

Thank you, my new friend. You have caused me to take a good look at all of my blessings. You demonstrate for me and surely for many others, that happiness is not a destination, but rather it is a way of traveling.

SNIPPET 168 - Housework

I phoned Karl and Chris this morning and left a message, "Hello, Chris-and-Karl's-answering-machine, it's me. And John too. Will you be able to come over tonight? I need to know if I have to clean the bathroom. Give me a call. Bye." I phoned them earlier too, but the phone was busy, and now there's no answer; they're probably out running errands.

I cleaned both bathrooms, just in case. Also, I picked up all the clutter lying around in the rooms in the rest of the house that we'll use when, and if, they come over. It's a glorious, end-of-June day in 2002: the sun is shining, the sky is a hazy blue-gray, and it's definitely hot enough to go swimming to cool off. I hope they can come. I don't have a clue about what we'll eat or where, after we play volleyball in the pool, or what we'll do for entertainment. Maybe we'll drink wine, curl up under afghans on the sofa and loveseat and watch a video like we usually do, or sit at the dining room table playing a card game or doing a picture puzzle like we do when we vacation together. Anyway, that's not what I want to write about right now.

I'm always shocked, and actually pleased, when visitors say to me, "Your house is always so neat and clean." Neat maybe, clean sort of. It's amazing but true that, if the house is neat and tidy, people just assume that it's also clean. They don't notice dust, but they do notice piles of clutter. For me it was a great revelation because I hate housework. I do it only if I absolutely have to because I'm just too busy ordinarily or, if I'm not, I find something so that I am. I can do any or all of these things—

- work at a paying or volunteer job
- do stonework in the yard
- do some laundry or iron some clothes
- phone someone that I haven't talked to in a while
- play at the computer, e-mailing friends and relatives
- look at a catalog, folding the pages to point to things that I would like to buy, but won't
- read the newspaper, sitting at the kitchen table or standing at the counter over the clothes washer, after I take the wrapper off

- read a book while propped up in bed
- write a book (just discovered that option)

—There's no end to the possibilities when you put your mind to the task.

Shirley taught me, in one of her lovingly-given, early-marriage lessons, that when you don't have the time to thoroughly clean something, you give it a lick, like a cat giving her kitten a quick face bath after it eats, and you promise yourself to give it a real cleaning later. You just tidy up by removing the clutter and clean whatever looks the worst. If it's evening, you keep the lights low and light some candles. You fluff the pillows on the sofas and easy chairs so people can use them to get more comfortable. If it's chilly inside, you place Afghans within reach for quick and easy usage. She impressed upon me that what people really want are comfy places to sit, gracious hosts, interesting chatter, maybe some food and drink, and some smiles and hugs; they come to see *you*, not your house. Consequently, when we want to have company over, I don't wait until we have time to clean the house; I just do what she recommended.

Some day, probably after I *really* retire, my house must get a thorough cleaning; but right now, because there are so many other much-more-important-and-interesting-and-fun things to do in life, the house will get only "a lick and a promise."

SNIPPET 169 - Frostbite

We had finished a fabulous, gourmet lunch, which Judy had prepared, and the four of us had retired to the living room to continue our chat. Judy and Clyde had come to our home for lunch a few weeks prior and now we had gone to theirs. We discussed our mutual love for traveling, and how it is best to spend your savings on traveling than to leave it all to someone else when you're gone. Judy asked us what traveling we planned to do next, and we mentioned that our next trip would be on the American Orient Express to see some of the national parks out west.

After our discussing that further, I said, "We would like to take a trip around half of the world to visit all the other places John wants to see, like Antarctica and the South Pacific, before he can no longer travel or dies from his PD. We plan to blow all our savings on trips." (Since Clyde's brother had been stricken with Parkinson's Disease, the couple was quite aware of the problems involved.) Then, turning my head to look at John, sitting next to me on the sofa, and patting him on the hand, I jokingly added, "Since there will be no money left to buy John a casket when he dies, we'll have to have his body *cremated*. Actually, we both plan to do that with our bodies anyway."

John continued my joke saying, "If I die at sea, they can just slide my body down a plank."

"I'd rather have my body *frozen* so I could be thawed out when a cure is found for all my ailments," remarked Clyde.

This started us into a short cryogenics discussion, and on the ramifications thereof, which Clyde concluded by saying what we all were starting to think to ourselves, "But that might be a *bad* idea after all, because I would have *no clothes*, I would have *no money*, I would have *no job*, I would have *no friends*, and…"

John interrupted him mid-sentence adding, "Yeah, and you would probably have *frostbite*."

SNIPPET 170 - Exercise

I exercise, not because I like to *exercise*, but because I like to *eat*! As a matter of fact, I find exercising very boring and, like housework, do my best to avoid it, but I can't or I'd weigh about five hundred pounds as I gain a pound a day when I don't. This writing obsession is really deadly; it's the perfect excuse to eat ice cream and chocolates for energy and inspiration and to not exercise, and I use it as often as I dare.

We have another finished room (most of the work done by John and a little done by me) in the basement that has elegant wood paneling, acoustical tile ceiling, commercial grade carpet squares, a huge mirror, bookcase-type shelving, and TV and VCR with a John-made-cabinet beneath. This room is filled with exercise equipment that we have collected over the years and artwork that I hung on the walls—all of this to be conducive to exercising and keeping fit. I have used every single piece of equipment at some time or other, but never all of it consistently; I eventually find them boring and quit. Besides, they distract from what I'm watching on TV or video whether it's *Midsomer Murders* or *Magum, P.I.* or *Murder She Wrote* or a "Discovery" or "Travel" or "A&E" or "Poirot" or "Nero Wolfe" program or a ballet or an opera or a movie. I find it simply easier to just use the treadmill; like today when I walked three and a half miles while watching the opera *Nabucco* by Verdi.

I'd walk outside in the sunshine and fresh air, but then I might get sunburned and that's bad for your skin because it gets more leathery than it is already or, even worse, cancerous; or my lungs might get polluted and that's bad for breathing; or I might get overheated and have a heatstroke and that's bad for your health and your brain; or I might trip and fall and break another bone and that's bad for both you and your health insurance because they don't like claims. I guess that's why I exercise, if at all, indoors. I do go walking (completely covered from the sun, of course) with John and/or friends along the seashore or on the roads near home because then I don't have time to worry; I'm too busy looking at the scenery and chatting and, if John is along, holding hands sometimes.

SNIPPETS (bits and pieces of love and life) by CAROLE

I had a personal trainer three times a week for about a year at Gold's Gym fifteen miles from my home. I really enjoyed lifting weights, using the different machines for aerobics, and having him to make me exercise; Robert was great and treated me like I was forty instead of sixty-four. I eventually had to quit because of a long-time torn rotator cuff and other injuries that occurred outside the gym. I miss him; I miss his wife Mary, who is a schoolteacher, and their two young sons, Logan and Trent; all four have beautiful bodies and light blonde hair. I saw and chatted with them frequently at the gym and sometimes exercised alongside of Mary when we worked out at the same time on the elliptical machines. Now, I have to be self-motivated, and, for me, that's extremely hard because I get so lonesome exercising alone, in spite of having my TV screen to watch.

I have to attend a retirement luncheon on July 31, 2002, for a former coworker, the other half of the "Bobsey Twins." I need to lose at least seventeen pounds to get somewhere near the ideal weight for my small bone structure (I had it checked by a nurse) because I want to look good; I haven't seen most of the people, who will be attending, since I retired ten years ago. I once heard, or maybe read, that each time you have sex you burn off 90 calories worth of fat; since I don't like to diet, let's see if that would work. There are 9 calories in a gram of fat, ~454 grams in a pound, and, therefore, ~4086 calories in a pound; that means that there are 17 X ~4086 = ~69,462 calories that I need to burn. At 90 calories each time, that's ~772 times in the next 2 weeks or 55 times a day or 2.3 times per hour provided that I don't sleep, and John doesn't work or sleep. I guess I'll have to find another method; this simply won't work— there's no time left to eat!

SNIPPET 171 - Bobsey Twins

Joe and I were the same height, five feet six inches, then in the mid-1970's, although I've shrunk to five feet four inches now; he weighed about twenty pounds more than I did and had green eyes and reddish-brown hair and I had brown eyes and white-streaked brown hair. Today we're both heavier, probably proportionately so, and his hair has turned gray but mine has turned to reddish-brown with some gray, thanks to low-lighting with flaming, copper red. But the eyes on both of us have remained the same—zealous and bull-doggedly resolute but friendly, and impish when no one else is looking.

Each of us had the best, but completely opposite, way to do things, so we would fight it out until the perfect method emerged. When it came to being a team, we were absolutely terrific, and since we were always seen as a pair, whether walking the halls or solving problems in the computer room, the computer operators nicknamed the pair of us: "The Bobsey Twins."

We first worked together in the group that installed, tested, maintained, and solved problems as they occurred, in the operating systems for the large IBM main frame computers in the Mechanical Department. Later we teamed up in the group that did all that for information management telecommunications in the Infosystems Department, after the computer sections of both departments merged together within DuPont Company.

There were two things—I hope only two—for which he never forgave me. Just remember, Joe, I still like you, anyway!

The first was making him eat dinner at J.W.'s in Chicago during the mid-1980's. We had attended a week-long IBM software class; it was our last night there and, therefore, our last chance to go to one of the best restaurants in the city. Joe wanted to go to Benihana of Tokyo, which is a restaurant with authentic Japanese hibachi cooking where, he said, "You sit at the table where the chef is, and he cuts all the food right in front of you with his amazing utensil acrobatics, and his knives are *so sharp* he'll *cut off your fingers* if he misses."

Well, that did it! Being naive and gullible, I believed every word and I was *not* about to eat in any restaurant where I might *lose my fingers*, so I said "No, absolutely not! Let's go eat at J.W.'s because

SNIPPETS (bits and pieces of love and life) by CAROLE

those are your first two initials and that means the restaurant should serve great food." Because I sounded so demanding, I guess, he backed down—but like a quietly seething bull.

We ate at J.W.'s, and sensing, *loud and clear*, that Joe was a slight bit miffed, I shared a chateaubriand (a favorite of his) for two with him to ease the pain. But it obviously didn't; he never traveled anywhere with me again.

The second thing was that I was only *five* years older and got to retire in 1992, but he had to continue working *ten* more years—without me—before he could retire in 2002.

For several years afterwards on his birthday, July 21st, I took Joe homemade blackberries jubilee (it's like cherries jubilee, only a whole lot better if you like blackberries like he and I do) so we could party in his office. Also, I could celebrate how much older and percentage-wise closer to my age he was getting and could check on my big potted tree-type plant that I forced him to take care of when I retired.

But I digress. Back to the original story at hand.

One day, for work, Joe wore a bright-blue-stitched-cream-color-jeans suit, which I immediately noticed and recorded in my memory. I happened to have a bright-red-stitched-white-color-jeans suit with butterflies embroidered in patterns on it and might have even worn it to work once, prior to that particular day.

The next weekend on Saturday evening, Joe and Dottie, his wife, came to our house to have dinner with John and me. As we were sitting after dinner, the "Bobsey Twins" nickname came up as a topic in our conversation. Either Joe or I (I can't remember which) mentioned the jeans suits and wouldn't it be fun to wear them on the same day. We were both a little concerned that our spouses might be a bit distressed that we even mentioned thinking about our doing that, because we already feared that they were a bit jealous of our getting to spend so much time together at work since our jobs required working odd hours and some weekends, but Dottie and John both thought that it was a great idea and that we should do it Monday.

What a fabulously fun and unforgettable day Monday was! Joe and I paraded around, not only acting like and looking like, but also dressed like, a real pair of "Bobsey Twins."

SNIPPET 172 - I Wonder

My friend Bobbie comes and goes in and out of my life and has ever since we met in 1967. We have shared the same office, made Christmas decorations, traveled together on business trips, shopped together, visited friends together, dined and gone to plays, concerts, and operas together, cried on each other's shoulder, and done all the things close friends do. Bobbie comes from a very close-knit family and spends most of her vacations and spare time with them, so it is not unusual for us to have months pass by without any contact with each other. When we do get together, it's as though we had never been apart, if you discount all the catching up we have to do.

We both share an interest in art and a friendship with the artist Linda, who does magnificent paintings. Bobbie had her do a large wax-resist painting of blue poppies for her home. Something about the dark sky in the painting distresses her; consequently, she gave it to me for safekeeping until she gets another painting to replace it. The painting looks marvelous hanging on the deep terra-cotta-colored wall near the stone fireplace in our living room. I love to gaze at it and think of Bobbie. Maybe someday she will let me buy it from her to add to my collection of "Linda" paintings.

Jason, a mutual friend of ours that I saw at Joe's retirement party, told me that Bobbie recently retired. She and I had each gone to work at different companies after DuPont Company sold off their information technology sections.

I must phone Bobbie. I wonder what's she doing.

SNIPPET 173 - Nicknames

I wonder why we do it because it's weird that we give nicknames to people, places, and things, but, seemingly, we all do it. A nickname can be funny, or affectionate, or derisive, or just a shorter version of a name; I use every kind of nickname, but I tend to nickname *people* only if I *like* them.

The first nickname I remember ever hearing, as a child, was mine; my parents called me "Pugsy" because I have, or had as a child, a pug nose. When I heard them use my nickname or my first name, I knew they loved me and everything was fine (for me); but, when I heard them use my full given name, I knew they were angry and trouble was brewing (for me). No one called me "Pugsy" after I started the first grade; I must have outgrown it, or my nose changed to a ski-jump and the nickname no longer fit. I don't know. These things just happen, I guess.

I sometimes gave myself a nickname to indicate the type of assignment I was given at work. The first one, of the nicknames that I remember, I acquired during the time I was a systems programmer working with large main frame computers. When my boss first assigned me the task of watching the computer console to see what kind of programs were being run and whether the computer was holding up, that is, not crashing, I stated, "'Mother Hover' will do that and report back." Charlie caught the quip, and, thereafter, whenever he wanted the same task done again, he assigned "Mother Hover" to hover. The same was true for my solving computer problems; he would assign "Madam Supersleuth" to the task. Whenever I was giving advice, I called myself "Lucy," like the character Lucy in the *Peanuts* cartoon.

I liked to play with coworkers' names too and said "Ravioli" for Romagnolty and "Ed" for a girl whose initials were "E.D." I called one guy "William The" and John called him "Attila," because his last name was Hunn; unlike the historical figure, William was really very kind and a terrific Scottish dancer. I dubbed another coworker "Sandie" because, when she phoned and said, "It's Andie," I would answer, "Hi, Sandie," to which she always replied, "No, I said, it's Andie." Then I would say, "Right. Hi, Sandie." We made it a game.

Some people I didn't give nicknames because they already had ones that would do. When I answered the phone at work, I only said my last name with nothing else as a greeting; I thought it was cool because Charlie did that. I hope they all didn't mind; no one complained to me—can't ask—don't see them anymore. Except that today, June 30, 2002, I did see Sandie leaving the grocery store while I was parking my car to go grocery shopping; she must live not too far from us. If I can remember, the next time I see her, I should ask.

When a pair of us worked together frequently, the computer operators usually nicknamed the pair. For Sylvia and me, because she is much shorter, it was "Mutt and Jeff." For Joe and me, it was "The Bobsey Twins."

The men in the computer systems group that I worked with and, therefore, sometimes traveled with, had a nickname for me; hopefully, it was only because they considered me as "one of the guys," which they did. Men never seem to need to use the restroom as much as women do; at least, that was the case for my group, so the guys had to wait for me while I ran off to the "sandbox," what I call a restroom. After a few occurrences, they (I bet it was Joe actually, but he won't confess) gave me a nickname. Thereafter, each time as I dashed off to the restroom, one of them would jokingly call out, "Oookaay, 'Bittybladder,' we'll just staaannd here and wait. Hurry up, and don't take too long in the sandbox!"

I'm sure it was Wayne who nicknamed me "PeeMoore" when the two of us were in grad school, but he says, "It was not!" John says, "It was too him!" Wayne's high-school friends called him "Shaky" because he has cerebral palsy; I called him "Wayne" back then because he wasn't a friend yet, just an acquaintance.

Edith, who goes by her middle name, was easy to nickname, especially when I was mad at her. I would taunt her with nicknames like "Winnerbean" or "Winnijean" or "Winnergreen" and, unfortunately, then the kids at school would call her that too. She came to hate her first name and refuses to use it, substituting a "W." instead. It's a shame, because Winogene is really a pretty name, and mom loved it so much; I think she found that name in a storybook.

When I was a teenager, I lovingly nicknamed Sheila, "Butch," because she was smaller than I and seven years younger, until someone told me that it was a horrible thing to do because "butch" referred to a lesbian. I didn't know what a lesbian was then, but I stopped calling her "Butch" anyway because it was "a horrible thing to do"; I went back to just calling her "Sheila" and still do. When she was very young, she called herself "Tee-wah" because she couldn't pronounce her name. She called me "Caw-dee" because she couldn't pronounce "Carole" either.

When I was still living at home, we nicknamed Patricia "Pat," but years later she told me to call her "Patty," so I had to get used to a new nickname; it took me a while—habits are die-hard. When I phone Patty, and Ralph answers, I always ask, "Is 'Madam' around?" I don't know why I started calling her "Madam"; it just happened one day; I guess I suddenly realized that she was an adult, not my baby-sister anymore; at the time, she was forty-seven, married, and had three sons. Instead of "Ralph," I sometimes say "Rrralph, Rrralph" or just "Rrralph" as if barking like a dog. Two of their sons had nicknames bestowed on them by their follow band members; Brandon, who is sixteen, is called "Sasquatch" or "Big Foot" because he wears a size sixteen shoe; Barret, who is fifteen, is called "Little Foot" because his shoe size is littler than Brandon's. I don't think Byron, who is eleven, has a third nickname yet; I guess I'll have to think of one so he won't feel left out. Ralph calls them "B-boy," "Bear-boy," and "By-boy," respectively. Since the boys' first names all start with "B," John and I nicknamed them individually by size as "Big B," "Little B," and "Bitty B," and collectively we refer to them as the "Busy B's" and address mail to the group using that. Their cousin's first name also begins with B, so Brandon and Barret, when they were very young, nicknamed Beau "Giant B," because he was a lot bigger and older at the time. They may out grow him; he's only six feet four inches and wears size fourteen shoes.

I nicknamed my mom "Mema," but I've already told you about that. Until then, we called her "Mommy" like a lot of children do or "Mom."

My dad was "Daddy" for the same reason (children) but we never called him "Dad." He always referred to himself as "George Harry" and introduced himself to people as "George Harry Moore," mostly to distinguish himself from his dad who was "George William Moore." Because it was what they thought they heard, people who didn't know better called him "Mr. Harrimore"; after that, everyone else started calling him "Harrymoore" instead of George or George Harry.

There's a man, whom we know through some friends, that I call "Steve Allen" because, to me, that's whom he looks like, and I've done it for so long that I can't remember his real name. I'll have to ask him the next time we see him.

There was one man we saw at many of the symphony concerts. I guess he could never remember my name was "Carole" because he always called me "Mary," so I told him it was really "Jeffrey." Unfortunately, he believed me. I don't know why I said "Jeffrey"; it just happened to be the first name that popped into my mind. I should have added, "I'm kidding, I'm kidding." — But, I didn't. I have to say that a lot to people, because I've apparently learned how to sound convincing and not crack a smile even though I chuckle afterwards.

There was a neighbor once that John's other neighbor called "Bitty-brain" because she was really "scattered."

John always calls cashews "ka-choos" as if he were sneezing.

See? I told you nicknaming was weird. You'll probably see and hear a lot of nicknames now that you are more aware of them.

John and I have nicknames for each other too, but I can't mention them; he's a very private person, and talking about them is another one of his imposed *never*'s.

SNIPPET 174 - Yours Is Better

As a child you always measure what you have or what you get by comparing it to what others have or get. John and I have outgrown that except when it comes to each other. We share just about everything, so, in that case, neither has anything better or different than the other, but when we don't share, we make we make a game of kidding about it because, in that case, *yours* can be better than *mine*.

This is true for chairs at a table, seats in a car or bus or train or airplane, towels, pillows, suitcases, sections of the newspaper, vehicles we drive, chores we have to do, just about everything in daily living. And, it gets downright silly when it comes to food. When dishing out separate bowls of our favorite fruits, I have to cut each strawberry in half, count the blueberries or blackberries or grapes, anything too small to cut in two, so we each get the same amount; nevertheless, there is still the perception that one bowl is *better* than the other. When dishing out the rest of our foods, I do it according to what each body needs. Lately, I've been trying to learn to apply the same principle to fruits.

We especially have fun when we're dining in a restaurant where the servers know us well enough to understand and tolerate our humor; if our server doesn't, I end up having to explain that I'm only joking and grab my plate as it is almost whisked away to be replaced or swapped with John's. After a new course is served and the plates are set on the table with one in front of each of us, I'll stretch my upper body towards John's plate (regardless of whether our choices were the same or different), crane my neck and face around toward the server, and say in a southern-accent-child-like-voice, "His is better than mine." Occasionally, I'll hesitate, so John can say, "Hers is better than mine." If our gestures indicate, we will each stretch toward the other's plate and, just like we so frequently do at home, say in unison, "Yours is better than mine."

SNIPPET 175 - *Recipes*

Scientists always use recipes for doing or redoing experiments. John even has one for doing laundry in my absence. Daddy never used a recipe, although, when he wanted to make something new, he sometimes phoned me to find out what ingredients were needed. In home economics class in the eighth grade, I learned how to cook with recipes, and, at home, Mom showed me how to make simple dishes without them.

I like to read recipes and still have, even though I have given away a bunch, over a hundred cookbooks of various kinds and dietary styles including vegetarian and macrobiotic. Regardless of having them, when I get ready to cook, I rarely use a recipe; I just use whatever ingredients I have on hand. When I do use a recipe, I usually change it to use organic ingredients and whole grains and, if possible, everything unrefined. If I've used a recipe, the book will have my modifications jotted alongside the ingredients and instructions. Many times I will devise my own recipe and even have a notebook of my original ones.

One summer, when our nephew David was visiting, he asked, "What can I do to impress the girl that I'm dating?" He was sixteen at the time.

"That's easy," I replied. "Bake her a cake or serve her a hot fudge sundae with your own homemade sauce. If you want to bake a cake, the simplest one to make is a cream cheese cake."

David decided to learn how to do both, so I supervised while he made his own cheese cake and hot fudge. When he returned to Savannah, he tested his newly acquired skills; his girlfriend was very impressed, and David and I were happy about his good fortune.

I told my nephews, Brandon, Barret, and Byron, that each one could come over to bake his own birthday cake for his tenth birthday. I let Byron bake his when he was nine because he said, "I don't want to wait until I'm ten. Why can't I make it for this birthday?" — And, why not? — Each one read recipes and chose what kind he wanted to make; then, I bought the ingredients. Together, we would change the recipe to make a different size cake or to modify the ingredients to make it more healthful. Brandon's birthday cake was a three-layer cake with the bottom layers filled with chocolate ice cream, the top layers filled with vanilla ice cream, and the whole cake topped with a melted dark chocolate glaze. Barret's cake was a vanilla cream cheese cake with sour cream topping decorated with green, red, and black seedless grapes. And Byron's was a sour cream pound cake topped with ice cream and strawberries in a fruit puree. Each one had to read and follow the modified recipe and do all the work with some supervision and very little help on my part. The hardest thing for them to learn was to always turn off the hand mixer before they lifted the beaters out of the bowl. You certainly don't want to lose any of the delicious batter to the kitchen countertop, walls, and floor; you want it all in the pans. All their cakes looked great and tasted fantastic. I'm not sure who was prouder of their accomplishments—the boys or I.

SNIPPET 176 - Birthdays

Since I never expected to live until age twenty-one, having anticipated from early childhood that I would die sometime about the age of eighteen, I have, since reaching twenty-one, celebrated each birthday as a true gift of another year of life.

My favorite thing to say, and I always do on that day, is: "It's my birthday, and I can do anything I want to, and I don't have to do nothing if I don't want to!" (Very bad English—but I don't care.)

When I was working at DuPont Company, I refused to work on April 6 and, if it fell during the workweek, I took a vacation day. Moreover, on every birthday that my age was divisible by five, I still took my vacation day but spent most of it in my office partying and inviting all my coworkers in for a visit. I spent many days preparing and freezing the desserts that I would share with them. I usually had about eight to ten different ones like chocolate-Kahlua®-nut-cookie balls, apple-raisin-walnut cheesecake, plain cheesecake, cherry pie, apple pie, honey-almond cake, lemon pound cake, oatmeal-raisin cookies, chocolate-chip cookies, carrot-raisin-pineapple-walnut cake, pecan pie, chocolate-fudge-pecan pie, and other selections that struck my fancy that particular year.

I also have a rule that when a young relative turns ten he or she can come to my house to make his or her very own birthday cake of any kind. I give them cookbooks to read ahead of time in order for them to make a decision and for me to buy the ingredients. If necessary, I will revamp the recipe so that it calls for whole grain flour and other healthful ingredients, showing them how to do the conversions and letting them do all the calculations for making the cake larger or smaller than the recipe indicates. If they don't already know how to break open and separate eggs, I teach them that as well. They always choose an interesting cake to make and we have fun doing it. Each one has been very pleased with making such a delicious cake, with very little help from me, and being able to serve it to family and friends.

On April 6, 2002, I hit the big "6-5" as in Social Security and Medicare. I didn't decide to grow up until I was forty, so how can I be this old? I should be only in my mid-forties now and although my

SNIPPETS (bits and pieces of love and life) by CAROLE

mind is, my body isn't quite. My body is a lot closer to my real age, but I refuse to treat it that way; I make it keep up with my mind even if it hurts. Anyway, we celebrated, with a few friends and relatives, having a marvelous luncheon at our favorite nearby restaurant and, afterwards, gathering back home in the basement barroom and enjoying a port wine tasting. Surprisingly, in 1986, we just happened to see and purchased a 1937 (my birth year) Ramos-Pinto® port and set it aside for one of my birthdays after I retired. Sixty-five seemed right since it marked another rite of passage. A couple of weeks prior to the celebration, we added one bottle each of a five-, ten-, twenty-, and thirty-year port, all Ramos-Pinto®, for the tasting. I hope I'll be just like the port we drank—the *older* it was, the *better* it was!

SNIPPET 177 - Ice Cream

One redeeming curse of Parkinson's Disease is that, with all the constant motion, your body burns a lot of calories. For John, that's a good thing because he *likes ice cream*. His favorite flavor is vanilla, but he will eat others.

John didn't even mind getting his tonsils out when he was a kid because he got to eat lots of *ice cream*. Following his surgery, his mom kept him well supplied for comfort, especially after he told her, "If you eat enough, fast enough, the ice cream 'freezes' your throat and makes it quit hurting."

He always liked to eat ice cream when he studied after school at the desk in his small bedroom, at the top of the stairs, on the second floor of their house. When he desired some, John would holler, "Hey Mooomm, I need some ice cream, on the double!" And, on the double, Shirley would appear at his desk and hand him a large bowl of it. It worked both ways; he did things for her too—on the double!

The cashier, at the grocery store checkout counter, always stares at the items I'm buying. A typical weekly basket-full includes:

- several packages of fish or meat (preferably unadulterated)
- the organic stuff: nuts and seeds, jars of nut butter and jam, whole grain bread, yogurt, milk, cereals, eggs, dark lettuces, vegetables, fruits, juices, crackers, cheeses, brown rice, veggie burgers and coffee
- some paper products, plastic products, and cleaning products
- a few other odds and ends
- the essential three packages of chocolate chip (with extra chips) cookies
- and ice cream (double the quantity if selling at two-for-the-price-of-one or buy-one-get-one-free):
  - 2 half-gallons of Breyers®, vanilla or French vanilla
  - 4 pints of Godiva®, dark chocolate truffle (my favorite)
  - 4 pints of Haagan Daz®, rum raisin (John's favorite)
  - 2 pints of Ben & Jerry's®, coffee Heath® bar crunch
  - 2 3-pack Haagan Daz® bars, vanilla with dark chocolate or chocolate with dark chocolate

- 1 6-pack Klondike® bars, vanilla with dark chocolate
- 1 4-pack Dove® bars, vanilla with dark chocolate

It is not a redeeming curse for *me*. When John eats ice cream, I sit down and also have some (a lot, really, just like he does). But I don't need all those extra calories! So, if I'm trying to avoid eating ice cream because I have gained too many extra pounds, I buy only Klondike® and Dove® bars; those contain corn syrup. I have become allergic to corn and corn products and do not relish suffering the consequences of eating any of that ice cream.

SNIPPET 178 - Chocoholic

I hope you are not a chocoholic like I am. Shortly after I met Sylvia, she introduced me to Godiva®; so, I blame her for my downfall. Once I discovered the taste of really good chocolate, Sylvia and I became partners in crime. We indulge ourselves with a chocolate dessert whenever and wherever we eat out together if it's on the menu; fortunately, it usually is. We have even selected the restaurant according to the dessert menu instead of the lunch or dinner menu. Whenever we visit New York City, we stop by a Godiva® shop to buy truffles to savor during the trip home.

I refuse even to check to see if I'm allergic to chocolate; my mom and dad both were. It didn't matter to him. But it definitely mattered to her, and it certainly would to me! I felt sorry for Mema and used to bake her cakes made with carob instead of chocolate; the cakes tasted really good, but carob is just not the same as rich, dark chocolate. There's even a cake referred to as "Better Than Sex Chocolate Cake," but I have a recipe, that I think is even better, that I use whenever I want only the absolute best.

It's far better that I never see, or have near me, any kind of chocolate, especially *dark* chocolate, my favorite, preferably milk-free. Moreover, I don't like and almost never eat white chocolate. I will tolerate milk chocolate sometimes if dark is unavailable.

Lately, I have been cursed with the "buy one, get one free" sale on Godiva® ice cream at the grocery store. Hopefully, the sale will be off when I go next time or I will gain another ten pounds! My favorite flavor is "Belgian Dark Chocolate," but the new "Chocolate With Chocolate Hearts," milk chocolate ice cream with solid dark chocolate hearts, is beginning to move into first place.

Since I am allergic to corn and corn products, I must check the label of each package because some Godiva® products contain corn syrup. I should be grateful that I have some restrictions or else I would be blimp-sized from all the ice cream.

I discovered, unfortunately, at the Harvest Market health food store nearby, some marvelous dark chocolate truffles with dark chocolate centers that are made with honey. Those truffles are ostensively delicious perfection—and my newest downfall!

SNIPPET 179 - The Cradle

There is a tradition that we always follow whenever drinking wine or champagne. I have no clue as to its origin or to its validity. The tradition is that the woman who gets the last bit of wine or champagne at the bottom of the bottle, "the cradle," poured into her glass, will be the one to get pregnant next. After the first time we heard it mentioned, John or I tried to make sure that I got the last drops from each bottle that we shared. It never seemed to work for me; I didn't become pregnant no matter how hard we tried.

After my total hysterectomy, it was impossible, of course, for me to get pregnant, but that never stopped the tradition for us or for our friends. They always gang up on me, and one or all of them will make a request to whoever is pouring, even if that person has to squeeze out the few remaining drops:

"Give Carole the last drops from the bottle; she *has* to get 'the cradle' because we are all hoping for a miracle!"

SNIPPET 180 - Injection-site Locator

Recently, John has been learning how to give me my biweekly injections, in order that, when we are traveling, he can do it instead of our having to find a medical center and a nurse. On several occasions, he watched Cynthia, one of our family physician's nurses, give me the injection in my upper outer derriere. When he thought he was ready to try giving me the next injection, she gave him a syringe and vial of sterile water so he could practice drawing up the serum and injecting it into an orange at home. Apparently oranges give about the same resistance as a person's tissue and are the perfect thing for practicing your needle thrusts and injecting the fluid.

It seems like chemists need recipes for everything or, at least, tools to do the job perfectly. When we got back home, John measured exactly where the latest injection was using my spine and waist as starting points and the tiny circular Band-Aid®, placed after the completion of the shot, as the ending point. As he worked, he wrote all the details on a large pad of paper. He disappeared, to the garage, I think, and I went about doing some chores. In about an hour, he reappeared beside me, proudly displaying his new invention—a strange-shaped, acrylic plate with a hole and some markings.

"It's an *injection-site locator*! This will make the process really easy," John boasted. "All I have to do is place this marked starting-point on your spine at your waistline, press the plate against your rear, and put three or four dots, using a ball-point pen, just inside the rim of this hole," he continued, pointing to different parts of the device. "Then, I simply remove the locator, swab the area within the dots with alcohol, and insert the syringe needle right there. Isn't that terrific?"

I had to admit that it was, although I thought it required a lot of effort. It seemed to me to be easier to learn where the proper location was on the upper area of the cheek and then look, swab, point, and shoot. But, I'm not a chemist; they do things so differently than the rest of us.

On our next visit to the doctor's office, John whipped out his invention and used it, along with Cynthia's supervision, to give me the injection. I was pleasantly surprised at how expertly he did it. She was pleased too.

"Sooo, what do you think of John's injection-site locator?" I excitedly though hesitantly asked her, wanting but fearing her honest opinion.

"It's really nice," Cynthia replied, rather unimpressed. "But, I'm really not surprised that John made it. Remember, I work for Diana who was a *chemist* before she became a *doctor*."

SNIPPET 181 - Favorite Getaway

One of our favorite getaways is The Rabbit Hill Inn in Lower Waterford, Vermont. Outdoors, we like to walk the paths that start at the spring-fed pond and meander through the acres of fields, streams, and woods, or swing in the swing near the gazebo by the pond or play in the winter snow. Indoors, we sit by the fireplace, eat fabulous food, do Stave™ puzzles, drink and play games in the inn's Snooty Fox Pub, read books, or simply relax and chat with other guests or the marvelous innkeepers and staff. We found it a few years ago when we were switching from camping to staying at bed and breakfast establishments and inns. The first time we stayed there was for two nights during mid-September, 1999. We immediately decided that two nights was totally inadequate, so we scheduled another stay for a week mid-winter. We now try to get there for at least a week each winter and convinced Karl and Chris to join us for a few days last year to celebrate Chris's birthday in February.

We try to arrange to be there the same week as Kirk and Debbie, a fun-loving couple that we met during our second visit. It was terrific to find another couple that enjoys playing in the snow as much as we do and will go sledding with us on the giant lawn in front of the home of Brian and Leslie, the innkeepers. Their home is within a short easy walk, even while pulling a sled, as it is located across the lane that runs alongside the second house of the inn. Kirk and Debbie, as well as the innkeepers, are young enough to be our children, but we enjoy a lot of things in common. The most important thing, probably, is that they have two marvelous cats at home that they spoil as much as we spoiled ours. The innkeepers, Brian and Leslie, also have cats, some at home plus Zeke, their cat that lives at the inn. Maybe that's why we all get along so well together—we are all "cat people."

Meals are a real treat for me. I have a list of food allergies that I send the staff ahead of time. Using that as a guideline, the chefs prepare me fabulous meals that meet all my needs. The office staff prints a special dinner menu (which changes every several days during our stay), with my name even printed at the top, that one of our servers brings me to use. I know I can order anything I want from my

SNIPPETS (bits and pieces of love and life) by CAROLE

menu without ever asking what ingredients have been or will be used or how the food has been prepared. They even make special loaves of bread just for me. For breakfast, the server tells me which foods I can eat from the fruit and pastry buffet and which entrees are OK. At afternoon tea, the chef has an individual plate of snacks prepared for my enjoyment. What more could anyone ask for? To me, that is the ultimate in pampering!

The Inn has an Internet Web site: www.rabbithillinn.com. Karl likes to pronounce the "rabbithillinn" part of the address as though it rhymes with "penicillin" because the Inn "cures your ills." We like the place because it does just that. — The Inn and the people there rejuvenate your body and soul!

SNIPPET 182 - *Songs and Sayings*

A FEW FAVORITE SONGS WE LIKE TO DANCE TO
- "Sweet Caroline"
- "Leroy Brown"
- "Rollin' On the River"
- "Feelings"
- "Time In A Bottle"
- "Anniversary Song" (when the waltz is played especially for us)
- "The Love I Found In You"
- Anything written or just played by the music trio Off Center
- Any Latin rhythm with a good beat for slow rock n' roll dancing
- Anything with a good beat for slow dancing with lots of dips and spinning around

A FEW FAVORITE SONGS JOHN LIKES TO PLAY
- "What Are You Doing the Rest of Your Life"
- "Memory" (from the musical *Cats*)
- "The Shadow of Your Smile"
- "The Straight Life"
- "Once Upon A Time"
- "Sam"
- "Colour My World"
- "Weekend in New England"

A FAVORITE BALLAD JOHN LIKES TO SING
- "The Irish Ballad" (Rickety Tickety Tin)

A FEW FAVORITE SONGS I USED TO SING
  (but don't anymore; I stopped singing years ago)
- "If I Loved You" (from the musical *Carousel*)
- "Old Devil Moon" (from the musical *Finian's Rainbow*)
- "Look to the Rainbow" (from the musical *Finian's Rainbow*)
- "When I'm Not Near the Girl (Boy) I Love" (from the musical *Finian's Rainbow*)
- "That Old Black Magic"
- "Anniversary Song"

SNIPPETS (bits and pieces of love and life) by CAROLE

A FEW FAVORITE SAYINGS

"And that reminds me, dear, of you." (me or John, said in a sing-song manner whenever something does)

"I'm trying, I'm trying." — "Yes, veeerry trying!" (me then John, or vice versa; Marcia then Roy, or vice versa)

"Hafta-go-da-batrum." (meaning "I have to go to the bathroom."; me, said in a rapid, squealing manner); then:
"I thought you did that last week." (John, spoken with disbelief)

"Don't do as I do; do as I say!" (my dad, said in loud commanding manner, if we wanted to do something he was doing, and he didn't want us to, like eat dessert before as well as after dinner)

"Wheeee! We're running away!" (me, every time we go somewhere)

"Look what I bought you." (John or me, whenever the item is obviously *not* for the person being spoken to)

"What's on your agenda for today (evening)?" (John or me, whenever one wants to know if the other's plans fits into one's own, hoping that they do)

"There's beauty in function!" (John, to me whenever he has made or fixed something in a manner that I don't think is aesthetically pleasing, like when he permanently attaches a large piece of foam rubber to a corner he sometimes bumps into)

"It's exactly the same, only different." (John or me, whenever we see or are describing something that is totally different but reminds of something similar)

"I'm kidding, I'm kidding!" (me, whenever I think someone has taken me literally or factually when I'm really joking. I frequently have to say that to people after making a previous comment because, while I was commenting, I sounded too convincing and forgot to crack a smile, even though I chuckled afterwards.)

"I make them up." (me, my reply usually to John and sometimes to others whenever I have expounded on a topic and the person says to me, "Wow! How do you know all these things?" I don't care whether I really did read or hear the facts somewhere or simply made them up, it's just fun to say that. As a matter of fact, John and I have that particular type of conversation a lot.)

"If you can't dish it out, don't take it!" (me, whenever I should have said: "Don't dish it out if you can't take it.")

"Well, of course, I'm *smarter* than you. Just look at who[m] *you* married!" (John or me, said to the other)

"One spouse, two spice." (me, said after I have used the word "spice" instead of "spouses" in a statement. It's a misuse of the word spice for the plural of spouse patterned after the plural of mouse as in "One mouse, two mice." I don't mean you should have two husbands or two wives. It's quite obvious that *one* is enough!)

"Where are the simple joys of Parkyhood?" (John, sung to the same tune as the phrase "Where are the simple joys of maidenhood?" from the song "The Simple Joys of Maidenhood" from the musical *Camelot*, when he's dyskinetic or bradykinetic, which he refers to as being parky, due to his PD)

"It was festination, my love…" (John, sung to the same tune as the phrase "It was fascination, I know" from the song *Fascination*, when he's festinating, trying to walk or dance, due to his Parkinson's Disease)

"Better never than late, but we came anyway." (John or me, when we arrive late)

SNIPPETS (bits and pieces of love and life) by CAROLE

"It's your birthday, and you can do anything you want to, and you don't have to do nothing if you don't want to!" (me, to someone on his/her birthday)

"What he doesn't know, won't hurt me." (me, referring to my dad)

SNIPPET 183 - Rickety-Tickety-Tin

John first heard this song in a Savannah nightclub in 1955 and liked both its quirkiness and the tune so much that he memorized it on the spot and has been singing it ever since. He has always called it "Rickety-Tickety-Tin" but the real title is "The Irish Ballad." I don't remember when he first sang it to me, but I liked it too and for the same reasons. We've yet to find any singer/pianist/musician who knows it, so John ends up singing it to him/her, but the person never quite catches the tune because John sings a bit off-key. The ballad is a comically gruesome song about a girl who whimsically kills her entire family, then casually admits her crime to the police because "*lying* is a sin."

"The Irish Ballad," music and words by Tom Lehrer, can be found on the Internet; just do a search on the title and composer.

Sylvia, as well, likes Tom Lehrer's songs and her favorite is "Poisoning Pigeons in the Park"; she used to live in New York City.

SNIPPET 184 - Sun Signs

It's a good thing that I never read Linda Goodman's *Sun Signs* before we got married; since we are totally incompatible, I would *never* have married John. But, then again, I might have because he is the same sign as my mother whom I loved and adored; she, however, was on the cusp and was somewhat a "Leo."

I'm an "Aries." Some of the characteristics I share with that sign are: instant smile, firm handshake, forceful manner, somewhat idealistic, disarming naivete, innocence, vulnerability, helplessness, temperamental, yells as a reaction to stress, a reddish cast to my hair in sunlight, can't lie worth a darn, always walk as if in a hurry, frank, honest, direct, tough, impulsive in speech, attentive listener, helpful, trustful of others, often a career girl, money is not the prime aspect of a job, prefer flexible schedules, perfectionist, faith in myself, romantic, passionate, loving, happy, prefers the company of men to women, puts her loved one on a pedestal and expects him to live up to it. I also happen to be a "night owl."

John is a "Virgo." Some of the characteristics he shares with that sign are: quiet, methodical, uncomfortable in crowds, serious, always thinking, worries, clear eyes sparkling with intelligence, muscular, more strength than appearance suggests, expresses love as unselfish devotion rather than romantically, unquestionably dependable, sincere, cleverly witty, gentle, truthful, likes punctuality, dedicated to his work, buys things by the case because it's cheaper, habitual, has an apparent blindness to his faults, hates generalizations, criticizes your statements with hair-splitting arguments that drive you wild, is annoyed by vulgarity, stupidity, and carelessness, and likes cats, birds and helpless creatures (which includes me). He also happens to be an "early to bed, early to rise" person.

I am "fire" and he is "earth," so does that make clay pots that are apt to get broken? I really don't know and it's too late to find out. I guess that I'll just be grateful that (using all the clichés) opposites attract and we simply jumped in over our heads assuming that love conquers all.

SNIPPET 185 - *Anyway*

I know he's going to say it. I can hear his voice softly in my head.

When I complain that I've eaten entirely too much and exercised too little and feel fat and lazy, he will say "It's OK. Tomorrow you'll do better and…—"

When I have been too busy to clean the house, he'll start vacuuming to help me out and say, "I didn't marry you to get a housekeeper. Just remember…—"

When I decided I needed a boob job because I wanted to look better, he said, "Absolutely, not! That's just too risky. Besides, you have nice legs and…—"

When I announce for the umpteenth time that I think I'll get a tummy tuck because I can no longer hold in my stomach, he'll just say "Please don' t even think about it because…—"

When I complain that I'm getting old, he'll remind me, "So am I, and I need you to grow old with and…—"

When I have any problem actually, he says something encouraging, and then, he will hug me (or touch my shoulder or squeeze my hand or just smile at me) and add those precious words:

"— I love you anyway."

SNIPPET 186 - Glad I Didn't Know

Sometimes you are better off not knowing things. "Ignorance is bliss" certainly rings true for me. The person who first said it must have truly understood the essence from experience. There are many things in life that I am really glad I didn't know, but here are just ten. Ten seems to be the right number as all lists include the "Top 10"; these may not really be *my* "Top 10," but these came to mind first. You too could probably make a long list.

1. I'm glad I didn't know until I was forty, and that my mom didn't know either before then, that I could have considerable health problems due to my heart murmur, mitral regurgitation, and bradycardia and, accordingly, should have restricted my exercise and slept with my head elevated. I would never have played so hard, learned to twirl a baton, marched in a band, exercised, danced, moved rocks, and slept without a pillow. What a wretched life I would have led, missing all that, and since it didn't kill me by age forty, I continue to ignore it. I did know that I got out of breath easily and got tired faster than others, but just assumed I wasn't as physically fit as they were; I guess I truly wasn't.
2. I'm glad I didn't know that all the various pills I swallowed would counteract each other and not even make me sick because I would have used some other method of suicide when I was nineteen and not be here today.
3. I'm glad I didn't know that staying awake for thirty-six hours straight every weekend for ten weeks wouldn't cure my depression. I accomplished so much during each of those thirty-six-hour stints and, during my last two, made a long dress for the daughter of one of my cousins to wear to the wedding and made Patty's wedding dress too.
4. I'm glad I didn't know that a specific diet wouldn't cure my depression either. I attended cooking classes; read books about nutrition and tried to educate myself and others about eating a more healthful diet; studied macrobiotics, including learning about and trying shiatsu and reflexology, and incorporated that

into our lifestyle; read a book about juice fasts and did a one-week fast; and read books about food allergies and learned how to do the "pulse test" for determining major ones. Best of all, while seeking a cure, I met many wonderful and dedicated people. In my bookcases, I have numerous books on diets, nutrition, vitamins, minerals, herbs, cooking, and healing for reference even if I haven't completely, or even at all, read each of them. It would have been a shame to miss all that because the knowledge is useful every day.

5. I'm glad I didn't know that I shouldn't go wandering off from my hospital room and stay out of traction too long and miss my back heat/massage therapy sessions. Otherwise, I would never have had the joy of walking the hospital grounds with and getting to know two teen-age boys who were helping each other put their lives back together after disastrous injuries and yet took time out to cheer up a lonely teen-age girl who simply had a broken back.

6. I'm glad I didn't know that you shouldn't drink alcohol if you have a brain concussion, because I can't take pills for pain and needed something to quiet the spasms from my crushed spine so I could get to and from the bathroom. However, I am glad I knew how to care for my spine from having broken it before and wrapped myself tightly with an extra-wide-body-shaping-exercise band, that Patty bought for me, to form a brace.

7. I'm glad I didn't know about the total experience of sex, or even what a live man looked like naked, until I was married. I did have extensive book and picture knowledge from reading my mom's nursing textbooks and chatting with her; I'm so glad she, along with our religious beliefs, had encouraged me to wait. It was such a joy to learn with someone who was gentle and kind and who, like me, was discovering and experiencing the thrill of it all for the very first time.

8. I'm glad I didn't know about the "Grafenberg spot," better known as the "G spot," until I was fifty-six. Apparently now, girls learn about that before they leave high school and probably not from class. After I retired, I took some courses for people aged fifty-five and older in the Academy of Lifelong Learning, an extension of the University of Delaware. One course was about human sexuality and our textbook was *Our Sexuality*. If I

SNIPPETS (bits and pieces of love and life) by CAROLE

had known about the "G spot," I would have missed all the fun doing the homework assignment after studying about it that day in class. The assignment was that each woman had to find her "G spot," or have her spouse do it for her, and each man had to find his wife's, and then report back during our next class whether or not we had. That wasn't the only thing I learned from the course; I learned a great deal about life from birth to death. The course even taught me about different sexual orientations and what physically causes each during the development of the fetus, and although I was never biased against people of non-heterosexual orientation, it made me understand those types of people, in general and in my circle of friends, better. That course, along with all the other courses I took, made me realize that I never want to stop studying or learning or trying new things.

9. I'm glad I didn't know how hard it was to write a book before I committed myself to the task. I've had to think about my life and found out how glad I am to live it. I'll probably have to write more than one more book because it's like turning on a faucet and breaking the handle so you can't turn off the flow.

10. I'm glad I didn't know that John and I were totally incompatible (I read that book too late) or that marriage would sometimes be very difficult and heartbreaking. I never would have married him thus missing the sharing of my life with someone who has been my closest friend, lover, and confidant, and who, no matter what, loves me anyway.

SNIPPET 187 - Three Gold Rings

    Do you know of anyone who wears three wedding bands? I do—It's Me—all three at the same time and all three from one husband.

    The first ring is a *white gold* beaded band that John slipped onto my finger during the wedding ceremony in 1960 when he was twenty-one. Since we couldn't afford an engagement ring, he had given me his jeweled fraternity pin instead to attach to my jeweled sorority pin. For the next twenty-one years that one band was all I wore on my left hand.

    The second ring is a *yellow gold* beaded band, to match the first in all but color, that he slipped onto my finger for our twenty-first anniversary when I had been married to him for half of his life.

    The third ring is a *rose gold* beaded band, slightly thicker than the first two to wear in between, that he slipped onto my finger for his birthday in September 2002. He couldn't wait until December for our forty-second anniversary when I will be married to him for two-thirds of his life.

    John's not sure what to do for the ring he needs twenty-one years from now, but I'm sure he'll figure out something by then.

SNIPPET 188 - The End

If I wrote about you and you wish I hadn't, or if I didn't and you wish I had, I am truly sorry. Maybe you'll be in, or left out of, *SNIPPETS II,* or *SNIPPETS, JR.* as John refers to it. But right now, I have to leave. The shuttle driver is taking our suitcases and stuffing them into the trunk; he'll be back, momentarily, to take us to the car, help us into the backseat, shut the door, and drive us to the airport. I told you that we have some more traveling to do before it's too late, so I'm off to show John some of the marvelous, glorious scenery of the world that he just *has* to see.

"WHEEEE! WE'RE RUNNING AWAY!"

ABOUT THE AUTHOR

Born and raised in Florida, Carole Christie Moore Adams graduated from Palm Beach High School in West Palm Beach. She has a Bachelor of Arts degree in English and a Bachelor of Science degree in mathematics from Stetson University, DeLand, Florida, plus graduate study with honors in mathematics. After teaching for several years in upper school and college, she spent twenty-six years playing with large mainframe computers and retired as a computer systems specialist. She has written technical documents and occasionally has taught classes and given speeches pertaining to her software occupation. She lives in Delaware with her husband, John Benjamin Adams, Jr., a retired Ph.D. research chemist who is a published author of patents and technical literature articles.

Printed in the United States
22693LVS00002B/1-36